# THE POOR BOYS OF LONDON.

## OR DRIVEN TO CRIME

# THE
# POOR BOYS OF LONDON
## OR, DRIVEN TO CRIME.

No. 1.]  **A LIFE STORY FOR THE PEOPLE.**  [ONE PENNY.

*"Don't, please," the little outcast pleaded, feebly. "I'm so tired, I can hardly stand."*

## CHAPTER I.
### A NIGHT IN A MALE CASUAL WARD.

IT was midnight in London. The vast city lay hushed in quietude and slumber. The streets were deserted, save for a few straggling wayfarers, and the silence was only broken by the solemn chimes echoing to each other, and floating faintly through the wintry air. It was an awful night; snow falling, and congealing into ice while descending, swept before a keen and bitter wind, that seemed to search into the very marrow of those who were as yet unsheltered; but there were not many of these.

A solitary policeman here and there—a cabman on the look out for a late fare, to finish his day's work—the few general wayfarers—a drunkard reelling home—and perhaps a wretched girl, the more miserable because of a sin unpardonable in the eyes of society: homeless, way-worn, and outcast.

It was a night when any human being with a spark of Christian feeling would not have left a dog without a place of refuge.

Yet, crouched upon a doorstep, a poor boy lay numbed into sleepy stupor, with the lamplight flickering on his face.

He had wandered far before he crept with faltering steps here to find a resting place; for wasted, weary, and faint, pallid with hunger and exhaustion, and sick with long fasting, he could not drag himself another step.

The lad had suffered. That was told with painful force by wasted form, thin cheek, and hollow eye. Had he been kindly cared for, well fed, and warmly clothed, he would have looked a finely grown and not unhandsome fellow of twelve years or so; but poverty had stunted growth and destroyed the beauty of his youth.

It was a sight to bring reflection and cause the heart to ache for this desolate destitute child. A hard, stern fate, that left him helpless in the world, where he dared not beg or steal, and, being very poor, could only starve.

So worn that, in spite of the snow beating down upon his uncovered head, spite of the wind seeking his shivering form through every rent in his thin garments, he went to sleep—to dream of home, a mother and father whom waking he should know nevermore.

A policeman pacing round his beat turned the light of his lantern upon the door, and the light flashing downwards glanced upon the boy.

"Hallo," said the officer, "there's another of them little wagrants, and he's fast asleep, too; or perhaps its only pretence, and he's a shamming, or he may be a burglar's plant."

A plant, indeed, but not in the sense intended by the man in uniform; the lad was an offshoot from a giant tree, whose Upas branches fill the world with crime and misery and all things that are a scourge and blight. A plant which too often yields bitter fruit. A tree whose leaves are paupers and felons, whose trunk is ignorance, and the root poverty.

"Now then, youngster, get up," growled the constable, "you can't lie here. Where do you live?"

The boy was awake—a rough push from the policeman's foot had broken his slumbers.

"Where do you live, eh? Come, wake up. What do you want here? Where do you live?"

The boy, evidently unused to this style of treatment, trembled with terror.

"Nowhere, please sir," he replied, in quavering accents. "I haven't got any home. And I was tired, sir."

"What brought you here?"

Two very tired, ill-shod feet, blistered and sore

with broken chilblains and the cold, the boy might have said.

"I had nowhere to go, sir; and I was tired."

"You said that before. What's your father?"

"Dead," said the boy, beginning to cry.

The policeman spoke very kindly this time.

"Dead, eh? And your mother?"

"I don't know, and she said she wasn't my mother, and she went into the workhouse."

"The workhouse, did she. Which one?"

"Down at Norwich, sir."

"Norwich, eh? And she said she wasn't your mother; that's a queer tale, anyhow, but you can't stay here!" the constable said, after a moment's reflection.

"No, sir."

The poor lad moved away submissively, drying his eyes meanwhile on a well worn cuff.

"Better go to the casual," suggested the policeman.

He was not so rough and unfeeling as his bearing made him seem. He had an arduous duty to perform, and vagrants occasioned him much extra trouble.

But here was a real case apparently. There was nothing of the young uncultivated vagabond in the boy before him—nothing but sorrowful hunger and exhaustion.

"Turn to the right, and keep straight on. It's on the left hand side, just before you come to the work'us. Can you read?"

"Yes, sir."

"Then you'll see it on a white bill, printed with black letters—Casual ward. The old man will see to you. Kick at the door."

"Thank you, sir."

The boy trudged wearily on.

"Can't leave my beat," said the constable to himself, "or I'd see to him. But I've got to keep my heye on Leary Jock and the Bosker. They are up to their games to-night. I thought the boy might be a plant to get me out of the way. It's an old dodge getting a young cove to pretend to be a wagrant, though there's quite enough real 'uns without. I don't know where they all come from."

Keeping his bull's-eye lantern half-shaded with his hand, the policeman went on his beat with his "heye" mentally fixed on Leary Jock and the Bosker.

The boy, a stranger to the metropolis, went down the dingy street, dragging behind him a well-worn broom, with which he had endeavoured to pick up a few coppers by sweeping a deserted crossing, until he reached the building set apart for the casual poor.

At first sight it struck him as being like a temporary slaughter-house or a cowshed; a second glance would have told one that it was much too insecure and wretchedly constructed for either purpose; it could, in fact, have been put together for nothing other than the use made of it—a casual ward—a refuge for homeless human beings.

The boy's heart failed him as he took a survey; twice he approached, intending to kick at the door, but each time recoiled.

The vile, revolting language he heard within frightened and horrified him.

"I can't go in there," he said, shuddering, "I feel afraid : perhaps if I go a little further I shall find a cart or a gateway where a policeman won't disturb me. I'll try to go to sleep. Sleep ! Ah ! me, how tired I am."

He turned away wearily, his teeth chattering, and hot tears falling upon the two emaciated hands that supported his chin. Ten steps he took, then hesitated ; bad as was the place it gave a chance of shelter from the bitter night.

While hesitating thus a small hard ball of soddened snow struck him in the face with cruel force, and a brutal laugh followed the successful aim. The poor boy gave a piteous moan ; an act that another time might have seemed like sport unnerved him utterly.

"Right in his ear. Let him have another, Tike ; oh ! lor, ain't he a guy."

Another laugh, and the boy shrank from the second ball he saw being prepared.

"Don't, please. I'm so tired I can hardly stand," the little outcast pleaded feebly.

The tearful face and faint broken voice touched his young assailants. They were several rough lads, rather older than himself. Vagrants from infancy, hardened, callous, and—Heaven help them—blind, soul blind, with unholy, savage ignorance.

The elder of the gang—Tike—pausing in the act of throwing the second missile, stood irresolute. Moved by the appeal, but not liking to waste the ball, finally he broke it into fragments, which he dropped on the naked foot of a companion.

"Why, jigger it, Chimbley, if he ain't snivelling. What's the matter ?"

"Don't yer see, he's done up," interposed the youngest and the quietest of the lads. "Let him alone. I know what it is to feel like that, when, if a cove was to kick me I couldn't give him a smack in the eye back. Let him alone."

Tike and his comrade, Chimbley, fell back a step, ruled unconsciously by the last speaker.

"That's Alick all over," observed Tike, "allers sticking up for a strange un."

"Well," said Alick, "you was a strange un till I knowed yer ; but when we once got pals I never turned agin yer."

"No ; I don't say yer did," Tike confessed, "not when I prigged anything neither, though you wouldn't have any of what I got for it. I wasn't saying nothing about that."

"Well, then, he's a strange un, and p'raps he's hungry, and he don't seem to know his way about much."

"I know mine," put in Chimbley, "and that's to the casual. No error, I ain't a going to stand here a shivering."

"No more am I," said Tike ; "no mistake. Kick at this 'spectable door. Some gentleman's been and pinched the knocker."

"I ain't a going to kick when I've got no boots," said Chimbley. "You kick."

"What's the use ?" Alick observed. "We must go to the work'us, or we shan't get any grub ; and look here, you had better come along with us. I'll see yer right."

"Thank you ; if you only would," said the little outcast. "But I'm afraid to go in there."

The strange boy crawled close to Alick's side. He felt protected when near to him.

"Afraid ! what of ?"

"They use such awful language."

Alick laughed, and Tike gave quite a yell of delight, while Chimbley danced wildly with his shoeless feet until a sharp stone caused him to cease the performance.

"Oh, carry me out and bury me decently—here's a treat—afraid to hear 'em swear."

"You'll soon get used to that," said Alick, quieting Chimbley with a gesture; "besides, it's quiet by about two—at least they leave off swearing. Better come and have a doss."

"A doss ?"

"A bed. Don't you know ?"

He did not.

"We calls it a doss. It's a mattrass, and a rug over us ; we gets a lump o' toke, too, sometimes, us casuals—come on."

Feeling greater courage now, the boy kept close to Alick, and they went to the workhouse door.

A crowd had collected there—a small noisy throng, numbering about ten persons—more than half of them were women.

Here, again, the language was horrible to hear. It was difficult to look upon the draggled, gin-bloated, foul-tongued crew, and think they claimed kindred sex with the gentle women we have at home.

"Hammer the door in, the old brute. Let me have a go, I'll bring him out !"

This from a girl who could not have seen more than sixteen years of sin and misery ; her training must have begun early. She had been weaned on gin, accompanied her parents to the tavern when she could scarcely toddle, gained infernal precocity by mingling with older companions, and at twelve was well on the downward road.

A legion of fiends let loose from perdition's Bedlam could not have made a more horrible clamour than did this girl and her companions. Occasionally there was a lull ; then an obscene jest and a laugh dreadful to hear.

The door opened at last. The porter stood there.

"Every ward's full, mind. There's nothing but the shed for the men."

"What are we to do?" shrieked the girl.

"Here's a night to be out in. Let us in, you old vagabond."

A wild chorus succeeded her cry.

"You'll find a lodging in the station if you arn't quiet," said the porter, grimly. "We've had enough of you lately."

"Now then, you lads, come in," he continued. "There's room for you, but we can't take any more."

The men wanted no second invitation. Alick hurried up the steps with the strange boy, Tike and Chimbley followed, and the door was shut upon the women.

The sound succeeding this act mingled in peculiar discord with the howling wind. The strange boy standing before the desk in the workhouse-hall felt his blood run cold.

Alick and his companions were evidently used to it. They made graphic remarks in a low tone, and in language that, bad as it was, betrayed the keen quick humour for which our street boy is remarkable.

The boys were attended to first. The men had to wait, shivering with cold, and eyeing hungrily a large basket containing a few hunches of bread. Apparently the demand had been extensive, for the basket was almost empty.

"What is your name?" the clerk asked of our strange boy.

"Gilbert, please, sir."

"Gilbert what?"

"That's all, sir," the boy replied.

"Well," repeated the clerk, lifting his brows in surprise, "where did you come from?"

"Norwich, sir."

The clerk would have questioned further, but the casuals were growing impatient.

"Gilbert, Norwich," he wrote, hastily. "Where did you sleep last night?"

"On a doorstep, sir."

The clerk nodded for him to stand away from the desk, and beckoned Tike. He knew the others, which was obvious by his remark.

"Here again, eh?" he said.

"What is your name?" he said to Tike.

"Bill Wokeling, I am."

"What are you?"

"A thief," replied Tike, looking the clerk full in the face, steadily. "I came out this morning, and haven't seen anything worth pinching, or I shouldn't be here! If I ain't out of luck let me know."

"Take them through," said the clerk. "I know the others."

"In course," said Chimbley, with a flourish of his naked foot, "his mother used to do my washing. His old man's in the workus. You wouldn't think it to look at him."

This cheerful banter left the clerk entirely unruffled, and he went on busily entering the first batch of grown-up casuals.

"I don't know how to do about bread," said the porter; "it's late, and it's nearly all gone."

"I don't want none," said Tike, "I had a tightner this morning; but that little cove looks well nigh famishing. Give him a chunk."

The porter counted the pieces and the claimants. There were two of the latter for every "chunk."

"One bit will do between us," said Chimbley. "Pick out a crusty one. My docter says crust is good for my complaint."

The porter selected two of the largest pieces.

"Share 'em among you, and come on," he said.

"I say," said Chimbley, "you promised to get me a pair of boots, you know you did. I wants 'em bad enough, and no bloomin' mistake."

These words were addressed to the clerk, who replied—

"We'll see about it in the morning."

"You'd better, and, if you don't, I'll take away my washing from your mother, there's no kid about it. And mind as they fits—hobnails and toe-plates, that's the sort. I'm goin' in for mashin' the gals in Rotten Row."

The man laughed as the light-hearted young vagabond danced after the porter; but he stopped his dancing at the bath-room door.

"I say," he said, "none o' that, old man. You knows me and Alick had a bath last night. It's cold, don't I know it—rather."

"I shan't take no bath," said Alick, quietly, "and come out dirtier than I went in; and if my clothes ain't kept clean, I shall be a refractory in the morning. It's a bloomin' shame, putting us clean uns in the bath where the dirty uns have been, and putting our clothes along with theirs. They all gets alike by the morning."

"I've done nothin' but scratch myself through being in the trough where some filthy gentlemen had been," said Tike, with a peculiar strong expression, "and I don't go in no more. I goes in the Thames by the barges when I wants a proper sluice."

Perhaps the boys had complained justly. Perhaps the porter did not wish for too much trouble at this late hour. He let the lads have their own way, and did not enforce the bath.

He ordered them to undress, and providing each with a warm worsted rug, gave them into the care of a pauper, who conducted them into the ward.

It was the building before mentioned. A shed which the demand for casual accommodation had obliged the authorities to convert into a place of shelter.

Gilbert saw his clothes tied up in a bundle and ticketed, then flung into a corner with a heap of other bundles. His heart misgave him.

"I shan't lose my things?" he said, timidly.

"Lose em—no! Here's your ticket."

"No fear of losing them," said Alick, with caustic bitterness, "and they won't lose anything by being there."

"No," added Chimbley; "just sing out your number in the morning and whistle for 'em, they'll come to yer."

Gilbert did not understand what they meant yet.

He still kept close to Alick, munching his dry bread rapidly the while.

"Pick out your own corner," said the pauper in charge of the ward, "but keep together. I'd find you an extra rug, for it's a bitter night, but every one's in use."

"You are a good sort," said Tike, with the addition of another strong adjective. "Joe."

"Hullo!" said Chimbley.

"That's the place for a doss. We shan't get the wind through the cracks there."

He indicated a corner which as yet had but one occupant, who, hearing Tike's voice, raised his head.

Such a head. Eyes that were bleary, cheeks sodden, every trace of reason stamped out, nothing but brutish instinct remaining.

"Hullo," he said, in a voice that suggested the idea of a rasp having recently been down his throat, "what cheer?"

"What, my Boozer, my old Spitalfields, I thought you were in for ten years at the wery least."

"No, Tike, my boy, I got out of that."

Tike, my boy, entered into an animated discussion with the Boozer respecting the merits of various prisons, the fare, regulations, gaolers, and governors.

"The House of Detention's the worst of the whole lot," said Tike, savagely, "that tall gaoler with the mustache, he's a wretch he is. Give me toke and water for the rest o' my life if it ain't like the torture we reads about in the books—takes every bit of pluck out on yer."

He finished by invoking such horrible pains and penalties on the head of the tall gaoler with the moustache that Alick called him to order.

Alick exercised a peculiar authority over his companions, yet he rarely raised his voice or uttered a threat.

That he had some kindliness of nature was evinced by the care he took of Gilbert. His better instincts made him cling to the friendless lad, who, in turn, took an almost affectionate liking to his young protector.

Gilbert recoiled from Tike entirely.

The inherent ruffianism of the young thief made his nature revolt against such companionship. About Chimbley Joe he was rather in doubt. Joe seemed to be an odd mixture of fun and vice—reckless vice that his savage fun made less repulsive.

"This is snug, this is," he said, pulling the rug up to his chin. "Licks Lime'ouse into fits. I went there once, and got a bit of wood for a doss and the ceiling for a blanket."

"Got a bit 'o bacca, Boozer, old son?" he asked, patronising a man old enough to be his father.

"Yes; got a pipe?"

"Make no bloomin' herror. Catch me without. Catch me without a dud. Who'll gi' me a bit o' that gaslight?"

Not obtaining an answer, he addressed himself very emphatically to all in the immediate vicinity of the gas, and having filled his pipe from a screwed-up piece of paper generously produced by Boozer, he paddled across the damp floor to get a light himself.

"I earned sixteen and tenpence in the jug" (prison), he said, coming back, and making himself as comfortable as possible.

This statement excited general interest.

"Yes, I did. I soaped parson over, and he got me put in the work-room."

"What did you do with it?" asked Chimbley.

"Met Ikey Belsea, the sheeny, and tossed him for browns, and he got the whole blessed lot. I got a tanner out on him, though, and went to the gaff; that's when I met you."

"Tain't a bad penn'orth now," volunteered Joe.

"No; that gal, she's a new un, ain't she?"

"Come the week afore last," said Chimbley.

"She wasn't there when I was out, I know; but don't she chuck her trotters about! Make no error."

This allusion to a ballet-girl at the gaff gave rise to a string of remarks such as we would rather the reader would not even imagine.

For quite an hour the shed rang with laughter raised by such sacrilegious stories of human wantonness as would have made even those who are held to be vile shut their ears in disgust.

Gilbert fortunately understood no word of it. His companions did. The Tike equalled any of the rest. Chimbley Joe laughed chiefly, and said little. Alick listened in half moody bitterness; the boy had a soul above the horrible crew surrounding him—untaught, uncultivated as yet, this soul, but it was there.

Now, in the midst of this den of reeking vagabondish scum there were many decent, respectable men, not a few of whom had their sons with them. These were labourers out of work, and men whose trades gave no winter employment.

Honest—guilty of no worse crime than abject destitution, they had no alternative but to herd with the ruffian horde, or expose themselves and children to the miseries of a night in the streets.

They felt the humiliation keenly—felt more keenly than all the risk of contamination their children ran by being forced into such diabolical society.

The care shown by one poor fellow to avert this was a beautiful touch of nature. He had thrown an arm round the head of his boy, and had it cuddled closely to his breast, giving warmth and covering his ears at the same time.

"I paid rates and taxes for five years on and off," said this man to one of his own class men, "and I didn't think to come down to this."

"They ought to find us a better place, or at any rate keep us away from these," said the one addressed. "I should like to know where the rates and taxes go to if this is the best the vestry can afford the poor."

"Perhaps there's a little mismanagement," suggested the first speaker, ironically, "and it's possible that a Government inquiry into the large item set down as ' general expenses ' by the vestry would yield some interesting information. Some of the men in office came down our way to inspect the sewers the other day. Then they went in for a heavy lunch, with wine, at the 'Wessex Arms.' I suppose that will go into the next account of general expenses. And we who have paid the piper, get a dog hole like this to live in."

"The shame is that boys and men are thrown together," said the other, "for some of this horrible filth must sink into them. I wouldn't believe such a thing could be till I saw it. I don't wonder at poor devils preferring the prison to it. A man has a chance of reformation there. This would pollute Satan."

"Hark at those young vagabonds," said the first speaker again.

He spoke of Tike, who was entertaining his listeners with a story of a night spent under the dark arches, where in the stench and darkness men and women herd together like cattle.

"He's not sixteen yet. What will he be in ten years' time?"

"A convict, dragging a chain, that's most likely. But whose fault is it? What turned him to thieving! If this isn't the way to make a vagabond, I should like to know what is."

"This, and the rest we get," said Alick, who being near the speaker overheard the conversation. "Look here. This is a youngster only just come from Norwich; he's a regular innocent, for I heard him whispering his prayers to himself before he went to sleep. What will he be unless something is done for him?"

"Poor lad," said he whose own son's head was on his breast, "it seems a pity for him to be here; he's a pretty little chap."

"I tell you," said Alick, dashing away a fierce tear, "it's not so long ago that I have whispered my prayers even here. I hadn't got hardened then. I wanted to be something good. I ain't done anything wrong yet, but Heaven knows how soon I may."

"Don't talk like that, lad," said the father, kindly, "keep your pecker up and try again. Look at me, I've got three more mouths to feed besides my own and this one here, but I don't give in."

"Don't," exclaimed Alick, as though defying his own despair; "but here's where it's bad: say that I sleep here to-night, I came with clean things and all right, and its just as likely as not that in the morning my clothes will be swarming.* Why don't they give the clean uns a place to themselves. If I had ever such a good chance of getting a crib I couldn't go to it in that state."

"That's true again," said the man, feelingly, "and I have thought of it once or twice since I came here. It's a mere mockery, the bath and striped shirts. It would take something more than them to clean such a lot of dirty beggars as come here."

"Or to keep us from being made dirty by them," said Alick; "and then see what we learn. I'm only a boy, but I could teach you a little."

"Sorry to hear you say so. Knowing too much can't be healthy for you."

"I know that. I never want to come here," said Alick. "I tell you, sir, that many and many a day I've tramped about without so much as a bit of crust to stick my teeth in. I have gone into different shops when I have seen 'A Boy Wanted' in the window, but they wouldn't have me. I have gone down on my knees and cried for them to give me a trial, but it was quite enough for me to say I had no home, no parents, and that I slept in the casual."

"Poor lad."

"It's this," said Alick, huskily. "My mother was as a good woman as ever lived, and she died heart-broke, 'cause of father. He took to drinking, let the home go to smash, and sent my sister Poll out of doors to do the best she could. And Poll's a right un, 'or she'd have gone to the bad long ago; but when I met her last—she's at a workroom a making shirts, and lodges with another girl—she says to me—

"'Alick, never mind what comes to you so that you don't go wrong. It's better to be hungry than eat sinful bread. Mother always said so.'

"And I says to her—'Never you fear, Poll; it's a fight between me and the world. I want to get OUT OF THE GUTTER. The world wants to make a vagabond of me; but,' says I, 'with Heaven's help, I'll go the right way, so as we can go both together to mother's grave, and say, we have bought no shame to you, mother.'"

The lad's voice broke here.

"Keep up," said the man, kindly, "I hope my boy will have the same good pluck."

"I hope the same, sir. It depends on you and his mother. When mine was dying she says to me and Poll—

"'It's lighter for me, 'cause I know you will never come to wrong. I know when the grass is over me you will kneel on it to tell me so. No matter how poor you come, if it's bare-foot and ragged. One day you will come to me with no sin in your hearts.'

"And says we—

"'We will.'

"And she died, and was buried by the parish; and Poll and I hadn't so much as a bed to lay on. Father had turned into a reg'lar public-house moocher, doing a day's work now and then, and never doing any more till he'd spent the money. I ain't speaking ag'in him, don't yer know; but it's the truth."

"There's too many like him," said the man; "a lot too many."

"I don't make another one," said Alick, "you may take my word for that. I only want to get a chance. I know I've got good stuff in me. I don't want to be a vagabond. I want to work my way up right on to the pavement like, and get ahead. Let them give me a chance and see how soon I'll get out of the gutter."

The noise had lulled by this time.

Most of the casuals were asleep. The gas had been turned down, and the semi-darkness that did not entirely veil, left in obscurity and partial silence such sights and sounds as never should have arisen from the oblivion of hell.

## CHAPTER II.

### NIGHT IN A FEMALE CASUAL WARD.

ONE O'CLOCK—one hour after midnight.

The casual wards were closed now.

The late taverns had finished business for the night, the gas-light in the streets flickered dimly, the vast city lay hushed into quietude—not a sound save the dull plash of heavy rain.

One o'clock. Every door closed, no shelter since the temporary refuges for the homeless poor were shut.

Just as the last solemn chime tolled from the solemn bell at Westminster, a woman tottered on to the bridge.

She walked wearily, and led a little girl by the hand.

Young and beautiful yet, in spite of squalid garb and wretched face, this poor creature staggered onward with her burden of love and misery, till the child reeled and fell at her feet.

---

* It must be remembered that the incidents of this story refer to some years ago. Casual wards are much better managed in these days."

"Hopeless," she murmured—"hopeless; yet could I reach there—a shelter for Flo—a place to die in!"

Her fainting footfall ceased, she paused, sank to her knees, and fell forward on her face; fell hopeless, dying, and with only sufficient strength to help the instinct that made her try to keep the child from being crushed by her weight.

"Flo, little Flo, my child; so cold! so very cold! help! oh, help!"

Low as was her voice it brought succour.

A young man had stood on the opposite side of the bridge, listlessly watching the lights quivering from the wharves and bridges upon the river.

He was thinly clad in well cut clothes, now in their last stage of threadbare shabbiness. He was a gentleman—the noble profile gave unmistakable token of that.

"A woman and a child," he said, pityingly, leaping across the road and stooping over them, "out in such a night as this, and I was thinking myself miserable; what in Heaven's name must they be?"

The child was asleep or dead, he could not tell which, it lay so still and pallid; the woman breathed heavily, but did not speak—she could not.

"By heavens," said the stranger, "this is dreadful. A woman literally dying of starvation. Some help must come or she will be dead."

His voice rang out, startling the echoes, and bringing a constable to the spot.

"Hallo!" he said, "what's up?"

"This woman must have help, and quickly. Wake the child, and let her stand, then help me lift her."

The constable obeyed. Some persons seem born to command men, like the stranger, whose voice and manner brought instinctive obedience.

"The little gal's as cold as ice," said the policeman, as he turned the light upon the woman's face; "it ain't a case of drink, is it?"

The angry "No" with which the stranger answered made him sorry he had uttered the suggestion.

"Perhaps we'd better get a stretcher and take her to the station," he said after a pause, during which the stranger had raised the woman's head to his knee, "unless we can get her to walk."

They made an attempt.

"Come," the stranger said, "try if you can move; make an effort for your child's sake; have you far to go?"

"Far!" this with a wan smile; "only to eternity."

"Nay. Where were you going?"

"To the workhouse I wanted refuge for my child. Don't cry so, Flo don't cry."

"Then you have no home?" the stranger asked, supporting her delicate frame with an arm, while the policeman tries to sooth the child, now weeping bitterly.

"None," the famished woman replied; "we were turned out on Monday."

"Great Heaven! and this is Wednesday; where have you been since?"

"A poor neighbour gave me shelter on Monday night, and on Tuesday we slept in the Green Park; to-night we could not, because of the rain."

"And she has evidently been well cared for,"

thought the stranger, looking at her delicate hand; "the child, too, is not of low parentage. It is, I fear, the old, sad story."

The woman wore no wedding-ring, but the child called her mother.

The little party were in motion now, the girl clinging to the skirt of her parent's dress, and taking the policeman's hand. He spoke very kindly to her.

"I've got some bread and meat in my pocket, if you can eat it," he said. "I generally bring a bit out to carry me on till morning. Here."

He produced a piece of newspaper containing two thick slices of bread and butter, with a slice of cold beef between them.

"Eat away," he said, giving the child one piece, with half the meat, "and you, madam, would feel better if you could eat a little. Don't say no. You're quite welcome to it."

The woman shook her head in refusal of food for herself, but thanked him with an expressive look for what he had given the little girl, who was devouring her portion with avidity.

"Can't swallow," the policeman said, understanding her gesture; "that's often the case when you have gone too long without. However, we'll wake them up at the workhouse. Make them give you a cup of warm tea or a little broth."

"Can she get that?" asked the stranger, eagerly.

"Can she? I should say so," the officer replied. "They know me there; I don't take them any troublesome people. It's only a case of this sort I leave my beat for. She must go into the sick ward—the infirmary."

"You're a good fellow," said the stranger, as gratefully as though the man had rendered him a personal service, "and I wish it were in my power to reward you."

Here he came to a stand. The woman began to grow faint again.

"We shall never get her there," he said; "she must be carried."

The policeman, after looking around to see that his sergeant was not near, pulled out a small flat bottle.

"It's rum," he said, drawing the cork and inserting the neck between her teeth, "strong as brandy, and better to drink. That's it; a little more—the lot of it will do you good. Feel better now?"

The poor woman, revived for the time by the powerful stimulant, tried to walk again. That she had no strength was obvious. The stranger rather carried than supported her.

He had not too much physical power just now. Perhaps he was weakened by hunger, for he cast a wistful look at the bread and meat the child's mother had refused.

"You take the child, and give her to me," the officer said. "I see you are not over strong; but hire a cab, that's better."

A four-wheeler, drawn by a tired horse and driven by a man muffled up in a shapeless mass of coats and rugs, and only visible as regarded eyes and nose, came slowly over the bridge. Like his horse he was tired; he even used his whip in a tired sort of way.

"Cabby!"

The horse pulled up with a jerk by the kerb, the driver poked his head nearly half an inch out of its muffling, and looked at the group.

"It's a hospital case," he said, interrogatively, "eh?"

"No; it's to the work'us."

"Who'll pay me?"

"Them as has the right—the parish—and perhaps the inspector will, and charge it upon 'em."

"Not as I'd say anything if I never got the fare," said the cabby, getting down, "'cause it's clear the poor critter wants a lift. Put her in the back seat—that's most comfortable. Better sit side on her, sir, to keep her head up. Now, my little gal, get in. Lor', how wet you are, and what a state my cab'll be in."

He shut the door, mounted the box, the vehicle rattled away, and the tired horse, seeming to understand the necessity for action, went at a pace that astonished his master.

"This is a curious fare," said the driver, Jacob Primrose by name. "I've druv a four-wheeler for a few years, but, blow me, if I ever had sich a strange inside. There's a sick woman and a wet kid, a real bobby, and a swell out o' luck; and I s'pose I shall get eighteen-pence if I takes two shilling's worth o' trouble a getting it.

"Not as I've done a bad day's work," he ruminated, "the last job in pertickler. Lor', he were a queer un. 'Cabby,' ses he, 'I'm so tight that I can't see a hole in a ladder.' Leastways he meant that, only he put it flowery. 'Take me to the Haymarket,' ses he, 'and look arter me while I has a cup of coffee.'

"Thinks I, 'You'll get dropped into, if you ain't careful, flashing them diamond rings and that thick chain on your weskit.' And it's no use making a row in them kaffees. I alwas thought they was called cafes, but he said kaffee, and being a swell he oughter know—but lor' it's wonderful how he knowed what he was a-doing.

"Tight—well, perhaps he were," he mused; "but if he were he were precious artful. I seed him twigging another swell cove as were having champagne with one o' them pretty uns. He speaks to her, and the other takes it up. Then they gets rowing, and has a bit of a scuffle, and I'm blessed, jist as nice as ninepence, if my customer don't lift a pocket-book out o' the swell as was with the gal.

"Then out he comes and jumps in.

"'Drive,' sez he, 'like anything.'

"He chucks me half-a-suvrin'—off goes I. Out comes the other swell.

"'My pocket-book!' he sings out. 'Stop thief!'

"I begins to funk then, and drives up Piccadilly and into May Fair, the other fellows follering in a 'ansum. Mr. Hansum runs slap agin a post—down goes the horse, open flies the door, and out comes the swell.

"My customer stops me—gets out sober as a judge.

"'Would you know me again?' sez he.

"'Think I should,' sez I.

"'Then,' sez he, 'don't recollect me if we ever meet again.'

"And away he walks; and directly he's gone I sez to myself—

"'If that a'in't Grant, the detective, I'm a Dutchman.'

"And sure enough it was.

"Ah!" speculated Jehu, flicking reflectively at his horse's ear, "I've heerd as how he's a perfect demon when any wanting's to be done; and I dessay this swell was only a swell mobsman. He was picking himself up as I druv back, and I heerd him say—

"'Confound it! I know him now. Unless I checkmate him in another way, the loss of the book will be utter ruin. He must have tracked me, curse him! and I, fool that I was, did not recognise him.'

"'It's bad when it's like that,' thinks I.

"And says he—

"'Grant does not know David Eastlake yet.'

"Lor'! he looks so vicious and white over it that I thinks to myself—

"'If it was me I shouldn't want to.'

"And then I comes back this way and picks up this fare. Sich a cabful! And perhaps to-morrow I'll have the First Lord of the Treasury a-riding where the sick woman's a-sitting now. But, lor'! sich is life. And here's the work'us'."

The cab stopped.

The passengers had not had opportunity for conversation. The policeman had asked a few questions of the child, but obtained only incoherent replies.

Her name was Florence. That was all she knew, except that people called her mother Mrs. Lake. The poor creature seemed to feel herself under protection.

Once or twice during the journey she raised her head from the stranger's shoulder, looked gratefully into his face, and pressed his hand.

He returned the pressure kindly.

The constable alighted first, to obtain admission. While he was so engaged, Mrs. Lake spoke to the stranger.

Her faint, low voice had a touch of sweet pathos in it.

"You have been very kind to me, sir, and I wanted kindness. I have no friends—no kindred, but those who would shun me."

"That is bad, indeed. I would it were in my power to do more for you; but I am poor."

The woman pointed to her child.

"Don't let her stay in the house," she said. "Do me this one last favour. We are strangers, and shall never meet again; but I feel you will do what I ask. The kindness will be great."

"What can I do?"

"Tell me your name."

He answered without hesitation—

"Philip Bartlett."

"By the morning," said the woman, in a sorrowful, pleading whisper, "she will be motherless. I want her taken to a house the address of which is in a letter I have here. There is another letter, also, of which I ask you to take charge—it is my history. Here—keep it, guard it, protect her. A dying mother asks it in Heaven's name."

Not for an instant did Bartlett shrink from the heavy responsibility so strangely forced upon him.

"I will," he said, "as best I can, protect her. This I swear, by all that is most sacred."

She made an effort to convey his hand to her lips.

"Flo will be so lonely and so unprotected. Heaven send her father will be kinder to her than he has been to me!"

"Her father! Has she a father?"

"It is written there. Keep your promise—a mother's dying prayer will be a blessing for you."

Philip Bartlett took the wondering child in his arms.

"My life will have a purpose," he said, pushing the tangled hair from her beautiful, infantile face; "she will be something to live for—something to love and work for."

He kissed her tearful eyes, and set her down, as the policeman came back, having by dint of strong argument persuaded the clerk to make room for yet another casual for him.

Philip lifted the woman in his arms, and bore her inside.

The matron had been sent for, and stood by in waiting.

"Poor dear," the matron said; "but it isn't so bad as you thought, sir. It's cold and tiredness. I have seen many much worse come round in the warm after a little hot broth. She must not go into the ward just yet; bring her into my room. I have got one poor girl there already—she seemed so decent that I had not the heart to put her in with the casuals."

"That woman's too kind," thought the policeman; "she will get the sack."

Philip took his burden into the matron's room, where she was placed on a sofa.

Her hand went to her bosom and brought out two letters.

These she gave to Bartlett, and spoke one word—

"Remember."

"I shall," he said, reverently. "Fear not; little Flo will be my only care. I will be a father to her—a brother."

The mother's eyes closed, her head fell back.

Florence rose and clung to her. The matron gently lifted the child away.

"Come in the morning," she said to Philip. "You seem a friend of hers, but go now. She must have her wet clothes changed. This is nothing but faintness. I shall soon bring her round. The child must go into the ward. It's quiet now, and she would do more harm than good here."

"Not from me," murmured the mother; "don't send Flo from me."

"Very well," said the matron, soothingly, "she shall stay. Be quiet, my dear—don't worry mother."

The matron's quiet, firm voice subdued Flo, and she sobbed silently.

"I shall come and see you in the morning," Philip said to her, and caressing Flo, he pressed her parent's hand, and withdrew with the policeman.

"You don't seem to have anywhere to go," said the policeman. "Hadn't you better stay here?"

They were in the hall now.

"No," said Philip, with a gesture of distaste; "not in the workhouse. I have a friend who will give me a night's lodging if I knock him up."

"Far to go?"

"To Stockwell," Philip Bartlett replied.

"That's a journey on a night like this," said the constable. "However, you have got yourself to please, not me. But it seems a queer start a chap like you taking charge of a stranger's child."

"I daresay it does," said Bartlett, bitterly. "Humanity is such a singular piece of goodness that such an act must seem altogether wrong."

"Well, it's no light burden to undertake."

"Perhaps not."

"And you will get nothing by it."

"Nothing—there you mistake. The world with all it's worth could not give me a tithe of what I shall get from that poor child."

"You're slightly off your nut," thought the policeman, but he asked, "What's that?"

"Her love," Philip Bartlett replied—"the sweet, pure faith of a young, unsullied heart; something true and deep. No fickle fancy that will change with the weather. That child has saved my life."

"How's that?" inquired the startled official.

"Had I not met her and her mother I should have been dead and quiet in the Thames by this time," Bartlet said. "Had I not undertaken to cherish her I should now be on my way back to take the leap I was prevented taking before."

"That's a bad thing to do at the worst of times," the constable observed. "There's plenty of things a young fellow like you could get up to."

"Tell me one."

"Got a good character?"

"Why, yes. I never disgraced it."

"That's all very well; but could you get a reference?"

"Doubtless."

"Well, then, join the force," said the policeman. "The pay ain't much, but it's regular, and there's a little to be picked up now and then; not that I ever get much, though people have a great idea we make a lot."

Philip grasped the speaker's hand.

"For the suggestion, thanks, many thanks," he said. "The idea never struck me. When am I to apply?"

"In the morning. Get a letter from the clergyman of your parish and another from a respectable householder. The more the better," the constable replied. "Send in a written application to Scotland Yard; you might get taken on before the week's out. We are rather short of men just now in our division."

"Then I shall apply for your division," said Philip Bartlett. "Come, I have a friend in it already."

"Have you indeed? Who is the man?"

"Yourself."

"That's right enough," said the constable. "I took to you somehow, for it ain't many you'll find willing to do a good action. You'll get on in the force ; you are a scholar, I should say ?"

"My education has not been neglected," Philip Bartlett said, smiling. "I have enough and to spare of dry knowledge, which I never yet found useful. I thank you very much for the idea, and shall instantly apply."

"Very well. If I am in the way I will give you a hint or two. My name's Rugby — John Rugby."

"Mine is Philip Bartlett. So we know each other."

"I must get on now," Rugby said. "The sergeant will be looking after me. Good-night."

"Good-night."

"But, here. It's about ten to one you will pass ; so we shall be chums. If I can lend you half-a-crown or so, no offence meant."

"None taken, Rugby. The pride that would prompt me to refuse a manly, thoughtful offer would be insolence. Here is the fact—I have not a penny in the world."

"Well, there you are, then," said John Rugby— "there's four shillings ; and if I never get it back I will never judge a man by his face again'"

Philip thanked the gruff, kind-hearted constable with an eloquent look ; he would have spoken, but the words choked each other in his throat.

The stalwart form of John Rugby strode away, and Philip with swimming eyes turned towards the nearest coffee-house in quest of a lodging.

Four shillings is not much, but it stood between him and despair.

He had often scattered ten times that sum in a single evening's amusement ; he knew its value now.

He hired a bed for sixpence ; there were two beds in the room, and the room itself was small, he could hardly stand upright in it, and the space between the bedsteads left hardly standing place for the washstand, over which hung a looking-glass ; but the bed was clean, and the chamber had no other occupant than himself.

"I can get you a cup of coffee, if you like," said the man who conducted him upstairs.

"I should be much obliged to you."

"Anything to eat, sir ?"

"A French roll, if you have one."

"Yes, sir—have it in two minutes."

Philip undressed. There was nothing in his pockets but a soiled handkerchief, and the two letters which Mrs. Lake had given him.

The first was addressed—

"Mrs. Seawell, Bilus Court, Hampden-street, Camberwell."

"Seawell ?" he reflected ; "the name does not seem entirely strange to me. Let me see !—I remember now. The boy I had to look after my ponies was named Seawell ; his father is a street scavenger, and lives in Bilus court. What connection can Mrs. Lake—a lady, clearly—have with the wife of a scavenger ?"

The other letter was not addressed, and he put both under his pillow as the man entered with the tray.

The hot coffee and light bread came as grateful to his appetite as did the soft, clean bed to his tired body.

"Call me at six," he said, as the man retired, and then he lay wakeful, wondering what eventful history was hers who had come so strangely in his path.

His last thoughts when sinking to sleep were upon Mrs. Lake and Flo.

Then a dream haunted him dimly. In it he recognised the girl he had seen sleeping on the floor of the matron's room when he assisted Mrs. Lake into the workhouse.

She was unquestionably a daughter of the poor—a work-girl ; but the entire expression of rest and plaintive innocence on her face had fixed itself in his memory.

At six he rose and went to the workhouse. He was admitted.

The porter remembered him, and conducted him gravely to the matron's room.

Philip had no occasion to ask what had occurred. He felt it.

The door opened, and the matron, subdued and rather sad, beckoned him in.

Mrs. Lake lay on the sofa, calm and still. She was dead ; but when the placid features were uncovered, she looked as if she was calmly sleeping.

Little Flo, upon her mother's breast, had sobbed herself into insensibility, but clung to her parent, and, in her slumber, sighed out deep, quivering moans of piteous pain.

The sight was very touching. The sleeping child clung to the dead woman, who had expired so quietly that the poor work-girl in the corner had not awakened.

"She went like an angel," said the matron, reverently. "She never spoke after I put her dry things on and made her comfortable. She tried to take a little broth, but could not swallow it."

"I see," said Philip, softly ; "fatigue and starvation have done their work. She must have suffered much."

"How thin she is !" said the matron, "thorgh such a pretty figure that she don't look so. She's been a long time dying, sir, and it's fatigue and starvation, as you say."

"I promised to take the child to a friend," said Philip, speaking with emotion. "She belongs to me henceforth."

"Lor' ! sir, are you related ?" asked the matron, in surprise.

"Yes, by the common tie of humanity, and the closer bond of desolation," said Philip Bartlett. "I am alone in the world—so is she. I want some one to love, and she is in need of a guardian."

"May she be a blessing to you, sir, for it is a noble thing you are doing. Are you going to take her home ?"

"Not yet. The person whose address her mother gave me will have care of her for awhile. I shall take her when I am prepared."

"Let her stay with me to-day," said the matron, whose motherly heart warmed towards the orphan. "She will want to stay with her mother, poor pet !"

"I shall be grateful for your care of her," Philip

Bartlett returned. "She, of course, will not be treated like an ordinary pauper."

"Like my own child, sir."

"Thanks." Bartlett caressed Flo's pretty hand as he spoke. "Heaven bless you, Flo! You have come to me like a gift from Paradise; you have taught me to have strength and turn from despair. I will keep my promise to your mother, I will indeed."

And so in the matron's room of a workhouse Philip Bartlett accepted the trust left him by the poor dead woman who wore no wedding-ring, and who had left her history and child to a stranger.

## CHAPTER III.

A MORNING IN THE POLICE COURT—REFRACTORY CASUALS—THE CRIME OF POVERTY—AND HOW THE PRISON HELPS THE WORKHOUSE IN THE MANUFACTURE OF A VAGABOND.

THE workhouse clock striking seven was the signal for the casuals to be awakened, and the motley mixture of destitution and ruffianism was soon to be cast adrift upon the world once more.

To some the sound was welcome. They longed to get their task done, and get out of the loathsome atmosphere. Others uttered savage curses as the pauper attendants entered bringing in the clothes.

"Number nineteen," said the keeper of the ward. "Wake up."

"That's me," said Tike. "Chuck it here, and take this bloomin' thing you calls a shirt."

The young thief stripped himself, and rolling his shirt up tightly, flung it at the man, who threw back Tike's bundle of rags.

"Where's my walet?" inquired Chimbley Joe, sitting up. "I'll be glad to get my things. 'Cause mine's a shirt, mine is. These is made out of old bed-ticks, jiggered if they aint."

The distribution of garments did not occupy much time. The number on each ticket was called out, and the bundle flung to its owner, who in turn threw back his borrowed shirt.

In most cases a curse or an oath accompanied the returned garments. Some were sent back in savage, sullen silence. One or two quiet "thank you's" were heard, but only one or two.

Gilbert slept heavily. The voice of Alick woke him.

"Come, it's time to get up," he said. "Here's your things. I sung out your number; still damp they are," and, he added, looking over them, "and dirty."

"Is yours?" asked Chimbley Joe.

"Worse than his. And we came in clean last night."

"I'd do a tear up," said Tike, who had dressed himself, entirely indifferent as to the condition of his garb, "if it was me. Only take my word, I'd have another suit afore the day's out."

"So I will," said Alick between his teeth. "They can't send me out naked."

He set to work deliberately and tore his clothes into shreds. The task of demolition was not exten-

several sizes too small for him, and the remnant of a calico shirt, were all he had to destroy.

"hy are you doing that?" asked Gilbert.

"I want some new ones, that's why," Alick replied. "It ain't the first time they have served me like this."

"That's seven days for you, no error," said Chimbley Joe; "but a new soot is cheap at that. I'm in with you, I am."

In less than two minutes his clothes were in strips.

"There," he said, having a wild dance amongst them with nothing on but a rug, "let 'm take it out o' that; my pal and me goes together, don't we, Alick? Shan't we look well in spank new fustin, with fash'nable buttons—boots and all—hobnails and toe-plates? I'd do seven days on my head for that lot."

"Don't tell anybody if you gets fourteen," said Tike; "'cause you might."

Chimbley Joe surveyed him with unutterable scorn.

"What, ain't you going to do a tear up?"

"Make no mistake," laughed Tike; "I've had enough of the jug to last me a week or two."

"Well, you are a sneak; you wasn't called a Tike for nothing. If we wasn't here I'd give you a oner that would make you see double for a month."

There might have been a quarrel, but just then one of the attendants came in to call the boys in to the bath room to dress.

He entered at the moment when Gilbert, hardly understanding what had been said, and not knowing whether he was doing right or wrong, had demolished the second leg of his trousers, and torn his coat down the back.

"At it again, eh?" said the attendant. "That's the little game, is it? Three of yer. All right, just you foller me."

Alick was slightly pale, but quite composed. He knew the risk he ran, and had shrunk hitherto from contact with the law. He knew how wide a space the prison cell puts between hope and redemption.

"Don't be frightened," he whispered to Gilbert. "They won't hurt you. I'll say I did it."

"What will they do to you?" Gilbert demanded.

"Not much—not more than I can stand to, anyhow. It will only be another kick back into the gutter; but there's harder stuff here than they can break."

Chimbley here set up a grotesque imitation of a clown's salute, and danced like a wild Indian in his blanket.

He had no dread of prison. It was food and lodging for a time, and he got a new suit of clothes by it.

Untutored, and altogether in a state of semi-barbaric ignorance, the boy had nothing to keep him honest but a rude sort of affection for his pal, Alick. He recognised Alick's superiority by instinct, and liked him better than he liked Tike, or he might have been Tike's pal, and taken to thieving.

"We's going

"Well?" growled Tike.

"I should like to hit you hard over the heye, and, blow me lucky! if I don't, too, the first chance I gets."

"I'd let you have a domino, if you wasn't here," said Tike, viciously. "Think I'm going to be fool enough to tear up, 'cause you does? Just wait till I git you in the street."

"And if you touch him," said Alick, turning upon Tike with the resolute quietude peculiar to him, "I will give you something to remember."

Tike muttered a sullen defiance, but it died away before Alick's sturdy look. Tike was an elder and a stronger boy, yet he dared not say much to Alick. The latter had perfect mastery over the wild young crew with whom he associated.

"Shouldn't a' gone tearing up," said Spitalfields Boozer, who was smoking a morning pipe, and attiring himself at leisure. "You are sure to get it hot. What's the odds if yer clothes ain't comfortable. You gets used to it in time."

He rubbed himself in a way that suggested his philosophy had been gained by experience. Alick made him no reply, but followed the pauper with Gilbert. Chimbley Joe danced after them, and at the door executed a step that elicited a roar of laughter and applause.

"A lively cove he is!" commented the Boozer, between two satisfactory whiffs. "Though I've seen many a livelier cove snivel at the Old Bailey; but then nature's nature—what's the use?"

He did not seem to expect a reply, but knocked the ashes from his pipe, and rubbed them out with his naked heel.

He then, with much deliberation, began to arrange a badly-soiled and well-ventilated sock, which he dropped with an execration, and began to rub his heel. A tiny morsel of tobacco, not being quite extinguished, had adhered to his heel and scorched it a little.

"Thought you was going to give us a step," observed Tike, with an ugly leer.

The ill-grained lad seemed to take a malicious pleasure in seeing his fellow-creatures in trouble or pain.

"Never saw yer move so quick before, Spitalfields," he added.

The Boozer growled out something unintelligible between his teeth.

"Halloa!" cried the Tike. "Here comes Crank-and-Oakum. Now we gets our toke and our work."

"And skilley," rasped the Boozer, for his voice had thickened in the night. "Hay is never very dry, and sleeping on a bag of it in a ricketty shed, with a coarse rug for sole covering, is not healthy, even for a pauper. "Hot and thick, sometimes, but not so good as we get in prison. They know how to make it there."

The individual termed Crank-and-Oakum—the overseer or taskmaster, more properly—came to turn the crew into the yard, where they were counted and provided with bread.

At the same time a large tin vessel, not unlike a barrack mess-kettle, was brought in by two paupers.

"Skilley; hot and smoking. That's your pretty sort. Fill your hand and warm yer inside for a thank'ee; then pull yer inside out at the crank for it. Skill—ey!"

This is a polite rendering of one out of many graphic remarks made while the gruel was being ladled out.

It was evidently a luxury, and hands were rubbed joyously together in anticipation of the comfortable warmth to be derived by holding the hot basin.

An epicure could not have tasted a choice dish with keener relish than did the casuals take their first mouthful of the rough and insufficently-boiled dilution of oatmeal.

In the majority of cases this sip was toyed with some time before being swallowed. Its effect was exhilarating. The gruel was praised.

Gilbert and his companions did not come in for their share yet. They were before the master of the workhouse, a very formidable personage to pauper boys, but in every other respect nothing very astounding.

"I think you have been here before for the same thing," he said, fixing a stern eye on the irrepressible Chimbley Joe.

"Werry likely, and good luck to yer," that youth replied. "P'raps I'll be here again; I did it last time, 'cause I collered the scratch, and had to eat such a lot o' brimstone that I'd a-struck like a lucifer match if I'd a-rubbed up ag'in the wall."

"Why did you destroy your clothes on this occasion?"

"Did a whater?"

"Destroyed your clothes," said the master of the workhouse.

"Done a tear up, you mean?"

"Yes."

"Well, there was such a many holes I didn't know which one to dodge into," said Chimbley Joe; "and knowing what a good sort you are, I thought I'd jest ask you to recommend me a tailor."

"Why did you tear up your clothes?" the master asked of Gilbert.

He did not answer. Privation had unnerved him, and he had not courage to speak.

"I will tell you," said Alick, "they were wet and dirty, that's why, and—and—I tore them."

"You tore his clothes?"

"Yes."

Alick hesitated before telling an untruth.

"No," said Gilbert, "no—please, sir, it was me."

"Very well, that will do," said the master of the workhouse; "and now, sir, you seem an audacious young rascal—why did you tear yours?"

"They were not fit to wear. I want to get work, and I couldn't if I went dirty."

"That will do."

"Give them things to wear," the master said, turning to the porter; "let them have breakfast and do their task, then give them into custody. We can't have the parish money wasted on a lot of vagabonds who abuse our kindness in this way."

"I know you must do your duty, sir," said Alick, respectfully, "and I don't ask you not to: but, sir,

*One sportive youth smote the Gorger on his hat while others converted his back into a drum.*

if I died this very moment I only wanted to get clothes so as to have a chance of getting an honest living."

"I daresay; we know all about that," the master

of the workhouse returned, grimly. "You will get clothes, and something else in the bargain."

"Him as sot in the rabbit-hutch promised me a' pair o' boots," said Chimbley Joe. "Will I get them——

"Wait and see."

"Thank you."

The boys were taken back.

The porter, who seemed to feel for the poor lads, cautioned them as to their behaviour before the magistrate, and went to find clothes for them. He provided each with a clean shirt, a suit of fustian, and a pair of strong boots.

"Seven days is a long price to pay for them," said Alick; "but I can try again for work when we come out."

Chimbley said nothing, he was wholly engaged in admiring himself.

"Wonder what fustin's made of?" he observed, after a pause. "It smells."

Gilbert, poor little shivering lad, was glad to dress and eat the breakfast served him. Alick ate his in silence, and disdaining the lighter task of oakum-picking allotted to his companions, went to the crank and worked manfully.

"I shall be nothing in their debt," he said; "two hours of this work will pay for such a lodging and such food—for the clothes there is loss of liberty and disgrace. I shall not owe much."

"You have a sweet prospect," said Tike, who stood by his side at the crank.

"You have a long tongue—keep it to yourself."

Tike made a grimace aside and said no more.

The porter kept an eye on the boys till they had finished work. Two policemen were waiting for them then.

The captives were being led across the yard at the moment the female casuals were about to leave. One of them stopped with a cry, and turned pale on seeing Alick.

"Poll," he said, dejectedly; "this is worst of all. I didn't want her to know. I didn't think to see her here."

The girl flung her arms round his neck.

"Oh! Alick, what have you done?"

"Now then," interposed one of the policemen, "out of the way here."

He pushed her roughly.

"If you want me to go quietly," said Alick, "don't do that again; she is my sister. Don't you cry, Polly. It's only for tearing up my rags. But how is it you are here?"

"We lost our work, and had to leave our lodging."

"Then you have got no home?"

"I shall have a nice situation to-day in a milliner's at the West-end."

"That's all right," exclaimed the lad, with a sigh of deep relief, "work's everything; go away now, Poll. Don't let people see you crying; besides, it will make me as bad. There, kiss me and go."

"Oh! Alick, what will they do to you?" the girl cried.

"Not much; it's nothing wrong, you know. Go away, like a good girl. I shall see you in a few days."

The police urged their captives forward. Polly followed, sobbing bitterly.

Philip Bartlett, who had been loitering about the workhouse, saw the incident, and feeling interested

The party arrived at the police-court, and the lads were given into the gaoler's care. He locked them in a cell.

Polly, not being allowed to follow, had to remain in the working-room. In spite of her anxiety for her brother's welfare she felt a curious interest in the company assembled.

There were the usual cases—theft, burglary, night assaults upon foot passengers, drunkenness, and disorderly conduct.

The company comprised witnesses and persons interested. Some few were defendants and prisoners released on bail, and these were the liveliest of all.

Philip Bartlett was there, and surveyed the scene reflectively. There was food for contemplation —a study of strange life phases. Many a face had its miserable history written upon it.

"I hope they won't send my poor man to prison," said a woman who bore traces of most brutal ill-usage; "I shall have to go to the workhouse if they do. He is kind enough when he's not had a little drop too much; and I did aggravate him."

Two puny squalid children were with her, one at her knee, the other hugged close to the bosom.

Five minutes afterwards the poor creature was pleading hard for her husband. She forgave, but the law would not. He was sentenced to three months' hard labour.

"Our little home will have to go, and there is nothing but the workhouse for us," said the wife, in tears. "I am sure, sir, if you let him go this time he will never do it again."

"The law must take its course," said the magistrate. "It is a great hardship that the poor wives and families of these ruffians suffer because of their ill usage. But an example must be made. Remove the prisoner."

The woman clung affectionately to the man who had knocked her down and beaten her the night before.

He threw her off, and cursed her savagely for having got him into trouble.

The next case came on.

Some few night charges were disposed of, and then the refractory casuals were called in.

The gaoler, going to the cell, was struck by the expression of Alick's face against the grating. It did not seem the same, so great a change had come over it since he had been in captivity.

Gilbert, taking example by Alick's calm courage, did not seem so nervous now. The first dread had passed.

He began to feel that he had done nothing very wrong, and wondered what sort of a place the police-court was, and whether the magistrate was, to any remarkable extent, dissimilar to other human beings.

Chimbley Joe was still irrepressible. He chaffed the gaoler till he set that functionary on the broad grin, offered to toss him for a new hat, asked him why he walked about without a tile, and who did his mangling.

Even in court he did not sober down, but entered

"Unkiver your 'ed afore his wushup," said a dignified constable.

"All right, old son," said Chimbley, in an audible whisper, and winking at the official. "I'll tell her just to keep it on the hob till you gets round the beat. It's the second arey, ain't it?"

"Take your cap off," said the officer, reddening. The court was tittering and it hurt his dignity.

"She wears ribbons in her cap. All serene. I knows her," Chimbley continued.

The man snatched Joe's cap off, and pulled his hair rather smartly in so doing.

"Now then; don't you hit me," said Joe, with the air of a martyr. "Look here, I shall give you in charge for assault. Didn't nobody see him do it?"

The magistrate, resting from the fatigues of his morning's work, had ended a short conference with his clerk and returned to duty.

He looked stern and bilious; his breakfast had not agreed with him. We, of course, do not hint that the prisoners suffered in consequence.

"What is the charge?" he asked.

"Refractories, sir, destroying their clothes in the casual ward."

The three boys were placed in the box together. Philip Bartlett, watching them with interest, saw the pretty, anxious face of Polly close by Alick.

"The same charge for each, is it?" asked the magistrate.

"Yes, your wushup."

"What is your name?"

"Alick Thorne, your worship."

"What are you?"

"Anything; I have no trade," the boy replied, unflinchingly.

"Nor occupation?" demanded the magistrate, gruffly.

"No settled occupation, your worship," Alick replied. "I wish I had."

"How do you live?"

"As best I can. Doing odd jobs now and then."

"Where do you live?"

"I have no home, and my parents are both dead."

"Ah! I see, a confirmed vagrant, clearly," observed the magistrate. "You have been to school?"

"Not since mother died, sir," said Alick.

"Hum! It seems a pity to see a boy of your age and apparent intelligence in such a position," the magistrate remarked, with a short dry cough. "I am sorry to say that the charge on which you are brought up is of frequent occurrence. How old are you?"

"Sixteen, your worship."

The bench then addressed Chimbley Joe, leaving Alick in suspense.

"What is you name?"

"Joe Morriss, I is called, your worship," he replied, with a mirth-provoking wink at the nearest constable.

"What are you?"

"A cove who does the cath'rin wheels."

"Do what?"

"Cath'rin wheels. Don't you know, sir? I runs alongside a 'busses, and does summersalts, head-over-heels, and gets ha'pence chucked to me."

"And have you no other means of obtaining a livelihood?" the magistrate asked.

"Do a what, sir?" demanded Joe, with another wink at the constables.

"Getting a living."

"I did have, sir. I took a crossing, only Irish Mike nailed my broom. He's bigger than me," Chimbley Joe replied.

"Where do you live?"

"Lor, sir, nowhere. Father bolted long ago—he's a sweep he is—and mother lives along with Bill Jenkins, the coster. I can't live with them, 'cos they wollops me."

"A dreadful picture of profligacy in low life," observed the magistrate. Profligacy in high life might not have seemed so objectionable. "How old are you?"

"Fourteen next Janivary."

The bench left him in suspense also after this reply, and went to Gilbert.

A course of questioning elicited some information that excited considerable surprise.

So far as could be gathered from his story, told with childish incoherence, the boy had been placed at Norwich in the care of a labourer's wife, who had died in the workhouse, leaving no clue to his birth or history. He was taken to the workhouse school, but ran away because he was ill-treated.

"What was the name of this woman, your supposed mother?" the magistrate demanded.

"Bennett, please, sir."

"Bennett. And that is all you know?"

"That is all, sir."

"Hum! that is all, is it!" said the magistrate, as he scanned the boy's slender figure. "You are very young, and it is a shocking thing to see you so early on the road to prison; in fact, I do not know what is to be done with you. Is the master of the workhouse in court?"

"Yes, your washup," said the individual alluded to, stepping forward.

"I think," said the magistrate, "we cannot do better than leave him with you, and place the matter before the board. He must be kept from the streets, from crime. He is only twelve years old."

"I am willing to take charge of him," the master said, "acting on your worship's advice and subject to the board's decision."

Chimbley Joe, having nothing better to do, wondered whether any other than a woodenheaded opinion could be extracted from a board.

So far Gilbert's fate was settled. He had no voice in the matter, or, with his own experience at the Norwich Union, he would have preferred going to prison.

He was removed from the dock.

Philip Bartlett, actuated by some curious motive, entered the particulars of Gilbert's history in a note-book.

"As for you," said the magistrate to Joe and Alick Thorne, "you are both old enough to be aware of the nature of the offence committed. I am reluctant to make prison cases of them, but the guardians must be protected. You are each sentenced to seven days, and in the meantime I will consider what can be done with you afterwards. I feel morally convinced that two strong, healthy lads need not pursue such a course of life as you seem to have pursued."

"Your worship does not know," said Alick, speaking out boldly and clearly, though with much emotion. "No one but the homeless, destitute, and friendless can tell what we have to endure. I have tried for work, offered long hours for mere bread, meat, and lodging; but, though I was never in a police-court before, I have not got a character. That's where it is, sir. If what I have done is a crime, I have been driven to it."

"I cannot allow such things to be said here," the magistrate observed. "An industrious lad can always find work. There is no excuse for such conduct as yours—idling about till your garments are too ragged for use, then destroying them for the purpose of getting others at the parish expense. I have given you a lenient sentence, and hope you will reform."

"Reform! Give me a chance—" Alick began, eagerly, when, at a signal from the bench, he and Joe were taken out.

Polly Thorn hung weeping on her brother's neck; the two poor children of misfortune loved each other dearly.

She, as he did, felt the disgrace more keenly than the punishment, for the sister would have its stigma on her, too.

Alick soothed her bravely.

"It's only for seven days, so don't cry, Poll," he said. "Kiss me, and bear up. I shall get over this, and something may turn up when I come out. Remember, Poll, I have kept my promise to mother. I have done nothing wrong. I have fought through it all—hunger, and rags, and the workhouse—and now there is the prison. They are trying very hard to make a vagabond of me—very hard, but they won't. I'll try and try again, and, Heaven helping me, I shall get out of the gutter yet."

This was the hope—the noble wish that gave the street boy courage. He had resolved to rise—cast away the fetters of obscurity and adversity. He was determined with heroic spirit not to be driven to crime.

───

## CHAPTER IV.

THE PIG AND PORRIDGE POT—WHEREIN TOOK PLACE AN INTERVIEW BETWEEN DAVID EASTLAKE, ESQUIRE, AND JAMES BURKETT, ALIAS THE BOSKER—AT WHICH ASSISTED MR. NICHOLAS SLIME, ALIAS THE GORGER.

IN the New Cut there was a doubtful turning leading to a nest of intricate alleys, and occupying a remote position.

In the doubtful turning was a public-house known as the Pig and Porridge Pot.

An ordinary wayfarer suffering with thirst would not have been tempted to slake it by the inviting aspect of the Pig.

In fact, the house did not depend upon the custom of ordinary wayfarers. It had a select connection of its own, and thrived on it.

Yet Dan Garnett, the landlord, did not seem to do an active trade.

He spent most of his time leaning on the counter in familiar chat with a familiar customer, and inevitably with a short clay pipe in his mouth, and in a general condition of shirt sleeves and unshaven grime.

The frequenters of the Pig and Porridge Pot were of a peculiar type. Very short hair, thick cloth or sealskin caps, ponderous boots, muscular legs in tight corduroys, bird's-eye kerchiefs and bull pups.

Occasionally an interesting group of this fraternity might have been seen ornamenting the wooden cellar-flap, which, from its elasticity of nature, was often chosen as a spot for the display of a vigorous dance, terminating with a shrill whistle and playful bonnetting of the nearest spectator.

A little before twelve o'clock, on the morning after Alick and Chimbley Joe went to prison for "tearing-up," the wooden cellar-flap outside the Pig and Porridge Pot was occupied by two human oddities, one a man of middle height, built like a giant, with a massive, resolute head, and deep-set eyes—a quiet, desperate, but not a savage face.

He wore the usual tight corduroys, a thick moleskin coat over a blue guernsey, and his head was protected by a sealskin-cap.

A man who made a picture that would not have been complete without a bull-dog. You looked for it by instinct, and there it was at his heels—a big, strong brute, bandy-legged, and ugly.

Not a nice animal to look at, or have smelling round your legs, but a dog that loved its master, and would have died for him.

The man was James Burkett, the Bosker—a burglar, a daring criminal, who defied the law, and laughed the police to scorn.

His companion was a character evidently; tall and huge, and gaunt, with a slight stoop in his round shoulders, and tremendous feet. He had a long meagre face and hungry eyes, and he had an appetite of such terrific capacity that he had been nick-named "the Gorger."

Though of the Bosker class, Mr. Slime — the Gorger's proper name—did not affect the Bosker style of dress; he was original in that respect at least.

Some circumstances of earlier life, or a peculiarity of fancy, made him cling to fashionable garments.

The fashionable garments he at present wore had some difficulty in clinging to him. His trousers had shrunk, and kept a respectful distance from his boots.

His boots were ventilative, and his arms need not have come quite so far through the sleeves of a coat ever so much too short for him.

He would persist in wearing a hat, and the habit got him into a lot of trouble. It was always battered.

If he bought one in the morning, he was sure to knock the crown in and graze his nose by going violently against a low doorway, or blundering head-first against a lamp-post.

He wore long hair, except when misfortune brought it into the hands of a Government barber, and this, with a black hat, broad-brimmed and battered, gave him an appearance more singular than distinguished.

He had another characteristic—he always wanted to borrow sixpence.

"Think he'll come, Jem?" he asked.

"Think!" the Bosker rejoined. "He never broke his word yet. Twelve, he said, here at the Pig, and here at twelve he will be."

"Does it want much to it?" said the Gorger.

"About five minutes," replied the Bosker. "Why?"

"I thought there might be time to have a snack—just a crust of bread and cheese. I'm awfully hungry."

"What! again? You had breakfast, didn't you?"

"Just a couple of bloaters and a saveloy," the Gorger replied, in a whining tone of voice. "The bread wasn't much, for there was two of us to half-a quartern, and Jack was hungry."

"Very well, go and do justice to the name you've earned, and gorge if you want to. I shall stay here."

The Gorger hovered about uneasily. He seemed to have something on his mind.

"Jim?" he said, nervously.

"Well?"

Jim was in the act of lighting his pipe, and the match went out when he spoke.

"You couldn't lend me sixpence, I suppose?"

"Go to the devil! I've got something else to do with my sixpences," replied the Bosker, indignantly. "I lent you one yesterday."

"I got a little pork and greens with that."

"You had sixpence on the wipe you pinched."

"I got some more pork and greens with that."

"And you sold the ticket for sixpence?"

"The pork and greens were very nice, and I had a little more," the Gorger explained.

"Talk about a wolf, it must take several wolves to make a Gorger," the Bosker observed.

He gave Nicholas Slime the sixpence, and Nicholas Slime entered the Pig and Porridge Pot to spend it.

"Let's have a bottom crust," he said, "with a bit of Cheshire, and a pint of half-and-half."

Burkett, with his hands in the deep pockets of his coat, stood smoking moodily, and reflecting meanwhile.

"I wonder what's the game now?" he thought. "David Eastlake ain't coming here for nothing; some job like the last I suppose, nigh by. I've never got the sound out of my head. The poor beggar's shrieks and his white face, it shook me; but he stood by and laughed like a devil."

While the Bosker waited cogitating, a cab, driven by Jacob Primrose, stopped at the corner of the street, and a gentleman got out—a gentleman, and a proud one, in spite of the rough and shabby garments which clothed him for the nonce.

"If that isn't him Grant follered," muttered

Jacob, looking at the half-crown just paid him for a shilling distance, "I'm a Dutchman, and if I'm a Dutchman I'm a fat-headed fool, all breeches and no brains."

Jacob took his growler away, on the look out for another fare.

The stranger walked down the New Cut, went down the doubtful turning, and into the Pig and Porridge Pot, without noticing the Bosker.

He passed through the bar, nodding carelessly to Dan Garnett, who stood marvelling at the way the Gorger threw bread and cheese down his throat.

The Gorger had an immense mouthful when the Bosker, entering, slapped him heavily on the back, and said—

"He's come."

Nicholas Slime, the Gorger, made a painful bolt, and swallowed a large piece of crust.

"Don't, Jim," he said; "you might choke a fellow."

"Choke the Gorger!" said the Bosker, with a derisive laugh. "Pooh! you could swallow the whale that took a fancy to Jonah without hurting yourself. Leave that, and come with me."

The Gorger did not believe in leaving it.

He grabbed the remains up in his hand and followed reluctantly.

The Bosker, with Cruiser, the bull-dog, at his heels, entered the room into which the stranger had gone.

It was a curious apartment behind the bar-parlour, with which there was ocular communication by means of a small panel in the wainscoting.

The stranger sat opposite the door, with his dark eyes fixed full upon Burkett, who settled his gaze as steadily on the stranger, and took a seat facing him.

Mr. Nicholas Slime slunk into a corner, and took sly bites of bread and cheese, but he did not look happy.

The stranger did not shift his glance for quite a minute, but not once did the Bosker quail.

The stranger's glance, keen, searching, accusing, would have sunk into and caused to tremble the soul of a man less resolute than Burkett.

"If they keep at that," thought the Gorger, "blessed if they won't petrify each other, like himages at a penny wax-work. What heyes the swell have got."

"James Burkett," said the stranger, "you told a lie to me."

"David Eastlake," said the Bosker, as quietly, "I did not."

"Insolent," said Eastlake, rising, in an attitude of menace. "You dare speak so to my teeth?"

The bull-dog had its fierce eyes on Eastlake's throat, and it gave a low, deep growl.

"Quiet, Cruiser," said the Bosker; "your voice is not required in the matter. Keep your seat, Mr. Eastlake; we ought to know each other, and should not waste hard words or use big threats. Sit down, and say what you want and what is wrong."

Eastlake resumed his seat in sheer surprise.

"Really," he said, with a sneer, "there is an improvement in my respected friend since we met last. He was then a savage ruffian, valuable only for his brute courage and fidelity, now he advises me with quite a distinguished air."

"Bah," said the Bosker, smiling in scorn, "that style of prate is stale. The aristocratic villain, always cool, refined, and devilish, is out of date; he belongs to tradition and the stage—so does the Bill Sykes type of my class. You affect to treat me as a barbarian brute—a mere thing to be hired and paid."

"Indeed, we grow interested—this is an age of progress—we hear an eloquent burglar," Eastlake replied, with a sneer.

"Half the instinct, nerve, capacity, and talent that are required to make a skilful burglar, would, if properly applied, make an honest fortune and a cleverer man than you, Mr. Eastlake," the Bosker retorted.

Mr. Eastlake smiled and thanked him for his compliment.

"To succeed we have to encounter and overcome every obstacle that mechanical science can effect in the matter of strength and skill," the Bosker continued. "We must baffle the vigilance of a body of men trained expressly to watch us, and to hunt us down—an untaught ruffian, with nothing but brute courage at his back, could not do this, Mr. Eastlake."

"Silence with my name. Curse you, I do not want to be known."

"Very well; but you need fear no one here. Dan Garnett can keep his tongue between his teeth, and that big, shivering cur is safe enough."

"Is he the one you depend upon for assistance?" asked Eastlake, looking doubtfully at the Gorger.

"Yes. He don't look very brave; but he would put a knife through a woman's throat, or run his own hand in the fire, if I told him to, wouldn't you, Nick?"

Nick, with an inward shiver, replied in the affirmative.

"Subdued into obedience, I suppose, by that peculiar moral power some men possess over others," said Eastlake, with an almost imperceptible mocking intonation of voice. "Is it so?"

"Perhaps the influence of a stronger will, acting on a mean, cowardly, and sensitive heart—something of the kind you fancied you possessed over me at one time."

"Was it fancy?" Eastlake demanded.

"Entirely," said the Bosker. "You have no power over me. You are not so much like the devil as you believe. Some men are proud of their demoniac capacity for sin. You are."

Eastlake grew hot with internal rage. The burglar had measured his character to an atom.

"But you are only a gentleman in appearance with a ruffian's heart," said the Bosker, "and not sufficient pluck to do your own dirty work. Keep your seat. I should not strike you; but Cruiser might fly at your throat before I could stop him."

The caution checked Eastlake, who was rising again.

"The exchange of compliments had better end,"

he said, "and we will commence business. See, however, that your dog is quiet. I will shiver his skull should he dare to touch me."

He laid a loaded pistol on the table, and the Bosker laughed.

"Put it away," he said. "The dog will not touch you until you touch me, and if you hurt Cruiser I would brain you. Now to business. What do you want?"

"This. You told a lie to me about the boy. You said he was safely out of the way."

"So he was; in the care of a woman who always does her work by putting them out of the way," the Bosker replied.

"She failed with this one, then?"

"I saw him dead."

"She deceived you," Eastlake said. "The child that ten years ago my cousin sent to Norwich I saw yesterday in the police-court charged with tearing up his clothes. The one you saw dead was a boy belonging to some poor wretch who could not afford to pay for it. This one, Gilbert, is alive."

"Well, is that my fault?" the Bosker demanded.

"It is," Eastlake returned, quietly. "I know the scheme perfectly. You thought by keeping him alive to always hold a terror over me and trade upon it."

"Think so, if you like," the Bosker growled; "but you know I always kept my word and did what I was paid for."

"Wisely. I am not a man to be trifled with. You would not play fast and loose with me, knowing how swiftly treachery would bring the horrors of the Old Bailey and the hangman to you. James Burkett, the burglar, the criminal, the murderer, would not deceive—"

"David Eastlake, the forger, criminal, and murderer, too," the Bosker retorted. "In point of moral character we are equal, I think. I know as much of you as you of me."

Eastlake, pallid of face and trembling with rage, started.

"See here—say that you charge me," the Bosker continued. "Speak about the deed you saw by the river side, that first placed me in your power."

"I remember," said David Eastlake, musingly; "the gentleman you garotted died where you dropped him, and you pushed his body deep into the river slime. It was low tide then, but in the morning the water had risen, and your victim was hidden."

The Bosker wiped the perspiration from his forehead.

"What of the girl," Bosker said, "who was dragged out of the Surrey Canal? She was with child, the coroner on the inquest said. I could have found the father and the murderer."

"Charge and counter charge. However, she went in by accident."

"Accident!" the Bosker exclaimed. "Like the kick that broke her forehead. She struggled to land, asking your help—that was accidental."

"Go on."

"Where is your cousin, the father of Gilbert and a little girl?" continued Bosker.

"You ought to know, since you helped me take him to a madhouse," retorted Eastlake.

"With a certificate of lunacy legally obtained. Where is the woman whom you drove from place to place, denying the validity of her marriage, and hunting her to despair?"

"She," said David Eastlake, quietly, "saved further trouble by dying two nights ago in the workhouse. We shall have to look after the girl."

The Gorger shivered. The diabolical coolness with which Eastlake spoke of his infernal work made Mr. Nicholas Slime nervous.

"Died in the workhouse?" repeated the Bosker.

"Yes. The woman had a strange fear of me, and would do anything to keep out of my way. I terrified her once," Eastlake said, with a cold, cruel smile; "frightened her into thinking she had done a very punishable thing. The fool believed me and fled, even giving to me the pocket-book containing the certificate of her marriage and the letters written by my poor cousin."

"You got them?"

"Every one, and lost them again."

"Ha!" cried the Bosker, starting in his turn.

"Richard Grant," said Eastlake, between his teeth. "You know him."

"Well," said Burkett, smiling faintly, "has he got the book?"

"He has, but must not keep it."

"What is it worth to you?"

"I will give five hundred pounds for it," David Eastlake replied.

"You shall have it," said the Bosker, toying with a heavy yet flexible life-preserver. "Mr. Richard Grant is a gentleman for whom I have more admiration than affection; he is the only man who has been able to teach me what it is to have anything like a sense of fear. You shall have the book if he has it about him."

"Very well," said Eastlake, seeing by the Bosker's savage eye that his black heart was in the work. "That is settled. Get the book anyhow; if he does not carry it about with him, find the hiding-place. And now, about the children."

"Well!" exclaimed Burkett.

"The boy Gilbert is, as I told you, alive and in London," Eastlake continued. "I saw him at the police-court yesterday. He was taken back to the workhouse; the magistrate had a merciful fit, and would not send him to prison. I have every reason to believe he will not stay in the workhouse, since he ran away from the Norwich union."

"Well?"

"We cannot hide the dead," said Eastlake, and the Bosker shivered slightly. "Murder, unless done very well indeed, will out. Now the only way to safely remove an obstacle is to do it slowly. Killing is a great work of art; one blundering ruffian, with no sense of fear or thought of remorse, can butcher a fellow creature, but the trail of blood is sure to find him."

"Well?" said the Bosker again.

"The boy must be put away by degrees," said Eastlake, in a tone so quiet, pitiless, and deadly that the Gorger went cold to the ends of his long fingers. "He must first be lost—that is to say, so mixed with young street thieves, beggars, and ragamuffins that his identity cannot be traced. You must be his tutor. The stages to death are easy—from hunger to theft, petty theft; from that to more daring crimes; in time the desperate felon, killing a man by the garotte, we will say, or doing bloodshed while defending himself from capture. Life transportation will do. Take your own time over it, but train him so that he will go that way."

"But suppose he will not go that way?" queried the other ruffian. "No amount of training will make some lads dishonest. You can't get them to take the first step, or the rest would be pretty easy."

"If he will not go that way," Eastlake said, "you must do the work more quickly, more surely, and take the risk."

"What do you mean?"

Eastlake's voice sounded like the hiss of a rattlesnake as he said—

"Kill him!"

"Yow—yow!" exclaimed the Gorger, unable any longer to keep his teeth from chattering with terror. "I won't have nothing to do with it—upon my sivey I won't!"

Eastlake turned upon him savagely.

"Don't take any notice of him. He is right enough," the Bosker interposed; "I can trust him with the light work. He could do for a baby with his eyes shut, but he couldn't look at what he did. I understand about the boy."

"Mind this—he must not live to be of age, unless by that time he is in the condemned cell, or in the colonies, with a convict log at his heels."

"Leave him to me," said the Bosker. "Old Gorger here shall take him in hand first when we get him, and Nathan Claws can put him through his paces afterwards, and he will bring him out as fine a workman as ever put a jemmy into a safe."

"Very well. Now about the girl. She is in the workhouse, too."

"So much the better. There will be less trouble to find her."

"But how will you get her out of it?"

"I will manage that. I know the particulars, and can put Mother Wood up to a dodge. Let her say the girl's mother was a friend of her's, and she don't want to let the child stay in the workhouse; the parish will be glad to get rid of her."

"And then?" said Eastlake.

"She can be stolen—sent away—anything."

"Come, you really do improve; you can devise as well as act," Eastlake remarked. "Mind, I do not want any particular harm to happen to the girl. She will be as safe hidden in obscurity as in the grave."

"Quite."

"Should she choose to sink further out of sight by going into crime she can. With that we have nothing to do."

"Nothing," laughed the Bosker. "You have an easy conscience, Mr. Eastlake; mine is not sensitive."

Eastlake gave him a handful of money.

"This day fortnight I shall come again," he said, "and see what you have done."

"I shall not have been idle."

David Eastlake departed.

There were two boys standing in the New Cut as Eastlake came from the doubtful turning.

One had a shoe-black box, the other sold cigar lights.

"Clean yer boots?" said the shoe-black, pointing at the toe of the gentleman's boot. "Here yer yar, sir!"

"Cigar lights! Box o' lights, sir? Only 'apeney."

"No. Out of the way."

He had not gone ten yards before the cigar-light boy crammed his fusees into his pocket.

"It's him, captain," he said.

"Then after him," said the shoeblack. "Don't lose sight of him. See where he goes; learn his home, his place of residence. Away, and keep the trail."

The shoeblack slung his box over his shoulder and went to the corner of the Waterloo-road, where he spread his mat, arranged his brushes, and knelt as before.

From his position he could command a view of the bridge and the theatre.

There, with his keen eyes scanning every face, he remained, while the fusee-boy went stealthily after Eastlake.

That gentleman had no suspicion of that ragged street boy's strange vocation.

The Bosker and his companion at the Pig and Porridge Pot were silent for a moment after Eastlake's departure.

"Look here," the Bosker said, displaying the money. "That's only a little of what we shall get. Don't sit there with your teeth chattering, you cowardly fool. Here, get some brandy, drink it, and listen to me. I'll set your work in order for you."

He hurled a sovereign at the Gorger, who picked it up and hurried to the bar for brandy. He wanted to get nerve, for he could see the Bosker was bent on some desperate purpose before the night was out.

"A nice little task," Jim Burkett cogitated. "A boy to be driven to the gallows or the hulks, or to be killed; a girl to be lost in crime or misery; and Richard Grant to be settled. Settled's the word. He knows too much for me. I shall have to do for him sooner or later, and it had better be done at once."

The Bosker played with his bludgeon again. His look grew intensely savage.

"To-night Richard Grant will enter Nathan's den in disguise," he said. "He wants to catch me. He shall. Come, Cruiser. Mr. Nathan's den is not a wholesome place for people who are not wanted. I think we shall be able to settle Grant to-night."

The bulldog followed. The Bosker went with Nicholas to see Nathan Claws, the thief trainer and receiver of stolen goods, a grey-haired, treacherous wretch—half Englishman, half Jew—a man who must have inherited his soul from a demon.

He was known as the modern Jonathan Wild.

## CHAPTER V

A HAUNT OF SIN—THE BOY VAGABONDS AT HOME —THE THIEF TRAINER—A NEW PUPIL.—CAPTAIN JACK THE SHOEBLACK.

THE shoeblack who had sent his companion on the track of David Eastlake stayed for some time at the corner of the Waterloo-road.

He did not do much in the way of trade.

He was only a chance shoeblack, and had a member of the red brigade in active competition with him.

The red member flourished till he changed his corner, which he did in consequence of seeing a pair of muddy Wellington boots coming across the road towards him.

"Not if I know it," said the red member to himself. "Clean them boots for a penny. No—make somebody else happy."

So the youth changed his corner, and the long Wellingtons went to the chance shoeblack.

"Want 'em cleaned, sir? Yes, sir."

The boy set his customer's foot on the shape prepared for it, and began his task industriously. It was hard work.

"Sticky mud this, sir," he said.

"Yes, Jack; it came from the river-side."

The shoe-black dropped his brush, started, and looked up at the speaker.

He saw a massive, not unhandsome face, with a dark and thick red beard round it.

The man was dressed like a cab-driver, and wore a black and white worsted comforter.

"I thought you had more nerve, Jack," the stranger said. "Pick up your brush and polish away. I have not much time to spare, but want to have a word with you."

"All right, sir; I can listen," said the shoeblack.

"Did you keep watch?" the stranger demanded.

"I did."

"He came?"

"Yes," the boy replied. "To the Pig and Porridge Pot at twelve o'clock."

"Whom did he meet?"

"Slime and Burkett the Bosker."

"Good," said the man who looked like a cabdriver. "Who is after him?"

"Little Dan."

"You are sure of the man?"

"The one you described, sir—tall, proud-looking, with glistening eyes."

"Right. Is the Bosker still in the neighbourhood?"

"I think so. He has not come this way yet, but I believe he is going to Nathan's."

"I will be there too. Keep your post for an hour or so, Jack. I shall pass again by then, and want to know what you have seen."

Jack put the finishing touch to his second boot, then touched his own cap.

Any passer-by would have thought them merely a shoeblack and his customer in the ordinary way.

Jack received twopence for his work.

"Grant," muttered the boy, as his customer strode away, "and on the look-out for the Bosker.

Should they suspect him at Nathan's I would not give much for his life."

"Hallo!" yelled a coarse voice behind him. "How much yer made to-day, captin?"

"Hallo! Tike—not much; fivepence, I think. No, it's fivepence 'apenny. I had the odd 'apenny from a swell with thin patent boots on—cracked they were, and mended with a needle and thread. He said he had no more change."

"Poor beggar!" said Tike, rattling his own pockets, "it's like 'em. A 'apenny would a-done him more good, most likely. I've had a bloomin' day."

"Have you?"

"Fine," responded the Tike. "I did Cheapside and St. Paul's Churchyard this morning in some new togs. It was a spree—no mistake! I didn't try arter handkerchers. I pinched a purse, though."

"Much in it?"

"Seven pound odd and a flimsy," replied the little scoundrel. "It was a lady coming out of a draper's with her purse in her hand. I twigs it d'rectly. She'd got a parcel, too, and a bag. So I just drops a bit o' orange peel, and goes down whack right in front on her."

"Did she drop it!"

"The whole blessed lot—parcel, bag, and all. She gives a squeak, and down goes all the things. I rolls on the purse, and flicks it up my sleeve. Of course I gets up, rubbing my elbow, and limps away."

"Didn't no one twig you?"

"No, there was sich a crowd o' people pushing by, that I was down on Ludgate-hill and in a bus afore she half got over her fright."

"And you got seven pounds?"

"Seven pounds eleven and a tanner."

"It would take a long time to earn that," said Captain Jack, with a sigh.

"More fool you! Catch me sticking here in the mud cleaning boots all day, and p'raps not get enough for a tuppenny doss and a penny starver. Look at me. I'm going to have a tuck out; the joints are just up at the cook shop t'other end o' the Cut—hot plum duff and all; make no bloomin' horror!"

"How much will a dinner cost?"

"Well, a big plate o' meat's sixpence, taters a penny, greens a penny, plum duff a penny or tuppence, and beer a penny, if yer likes. That's if you sit down; it's cheaper in paper at the counter," replied the Tike.

"Nearly a shilling," said Jack; "that's about as much as I shall earn all day long, and there's mother and the little uns will want it. I don't get money so easily as you do."

"You ain't got pluck enough," the Tike observed, contemptuously. "Just listen; I only come out the other day, slept in the casual same night along of Alick and Chummy—that's Chimbley Joe, you know; we calls him Chummy sometimes."

"I don't know him."

"Yer don't know Alick. One of the pretty silly sort Alick is—'ud rather go hungry than crib anything."

"Well, Tike," said Jack, "if we are hungry sometimes, we are never afraid of a bobby nabbing us."

"Ain't you!" laughed Tike. "Mr. Clever Alick's doing seven days for his lot, 'cause he teared up his rags in the casual. So is Joe—wonder how they'll like it!"

"Ain't you afraid of being caught?"

"Not me. 'Sides, if I is, old Nathan keeps my coin till I comes out again. Why don't you have a try?"

"At what?"

"Pinching. No error, it's the best game out if you ain't caught."

"And what if you are caught?"

"Why, you have another go when you get loose. I do. Tell you what; just come and see old Nathan. He'll talk that rot out on yer, and teach yer how to pick yer own pocket without knowing it. It's better than this shoeblacking for a few mouldy coppers."

Jack shook his head irresolutely.

"Nathan wants a few 'spectable ones for omnibus and train plants," Tike said. "You twig wot I mean?"

"No."

"Why, you goes out with a swell mobsman, gits into a 'bus or a train, sits aside a lady or gent; he sits opposite. You picks her pocket, and he covers you so as you ain't seen. You'd just do for that."

"Don't tempt me."

"I don't want to tempt yer," said the Tike. "I only wants to tell you wot you might do. If you like shoeblacking and starvation better, why stick to it. I should like you for a pal"

Jack shook his head again.

"Wery well," the Tike continued. "Only, if you'd make your mind up, I'd take you to old Nathan and get you sworn in. There's a plant tonight, when you might get your hand in. I shall be there arter I've been to the theatre. Tell you what. Try this for another hour or so and see how you gets on. If you think it's better than pinching, stick to it; if not, come along of me."

"I will try it for an hour or so," said Jack, as though he had made a sudden resolution; "but I am nearly sick of this miserable style of life."

"Like a good many on 'em, I tried all sorts of things," that arch villain the Tike continued, "every odd job—holding horses, running errands, carrying parcels, selling things, begging, singing, every way; but, lor', it was not a bit a use. Lots o' men are glad to do odd jobs and hold horses, run errands, and all that, and there's too many selling things as it is. Can't all get a living. And they locks you up for begging same as thieving. I had lots o' months at different times for vagrancy. Then they called me inkorri-something."

"Incorrigible."

"That's it," said the Tike. "And gave me three. So, thinks I, I shouldn't get no more for pinching, and when I comes out I took to pinching. I ain't in prison a bit oftener."

"But wouldn't they have kept you in the workhouse?"

"Who's going to that place," said Tike, savagely, "to get kicked and cuffed about and fed on skilley

—not me—or get apprenticed out to some dirty snob, p'raps, who makes you do all the work and whollops you? Not me. No error."

"They could put you in a reformatory."

"What's that but a prison; and don't you have to work hard without getting much," cried the Tike, indignantly. "Ain't the rules like prison rules, and they can whip you just the same, and they send most on you to sea. I don't go to sea to come home as poor little Tim Walker did, with his back all in gashes with the cat-o-nine-tails. I'll live somehow."

"Well, Tike." said the shoeblack, "it may be true all you say, but I should be sorry to think there is no chance of earning an honest living."

"You've tried, ain't you?"

"For many a long day."

"And you're hungry?" demanded the Tike.

"Very often."

"So have I been; but I don't do it again. There's plenty o' rich uns can afford to lose a bit. I've made ten pun to-day, 'cos I shall get two pun ten for the flimsy from old Nathan—it's a tenner."

"How will he pass it?"

"Easy enough. The lady as I pinched it of might think she lost it, and there'll be a reward p'raps. Then he'll send some cove with the flimsy, and some flash sovereigns, and p'raps get five pun."

"A dangerous trick," said Jack.

"It's werry often done. Or p'raps Nathan will give the flimsy to a swell, one of the mob, and it'll be changed and a hundred miles away afore it's advertised."

"That's how it's done, is it?"

"You don't know half the dodges we're up to in getting rid o' things as is pinched," said the Tike. "'Taint likely we let 'em be seen in London, when we know the bobbies is arter 'em. You should just come to Nathan's and see a little."

"I will," said Captain Jack, "to-night; I'm sick of this. We will be pals."

"Will you?" said the Tike. "That's the sort. I ain't got a pal as I cares for, 'cept the Boozer, and he's too fond o' drink to be up to much; but he's a rummy old beggar, though—makes yer larf sometimes. Alick's no pal; he wouldn't pinch a bit if he was starving. Chummy's getting nearly as bad, 'cos he sticks to Alick, but I'd lay a tanner old Nathan haves 'em both some day."

"Will you take me to-night?"

"Yes. At least, I'd better not to-night."

"Why?"

"Well, keep it dark; I expect a row on," the Tike replied. "Yer see the Bosker's wanted, and p'raps there'll be a detective arter him. The detective's been blown on."

A quick flash of Captain Jack's eye told that the news startled him.

"What will they do with him, then?" he asked. Tike shuddered.

"Shouldn't like to tell; only it's easier to get in than out of Old Nathan's place," he said. "Hullo! here comes Burkett and the Gorger; they're going to Nathan's now—I'm off."

Tike lit a clay pipe and went up the New Cut,

passing Slime and the Bosker, with whom he exchanged a nod.

The Gorger, as usual, was going in for a good feed.

He had purchased a long string of saveloys, which he was munching greedily, forgetting that it is not considered polite to dine in the street.

His appearance was hailed with a shriek of delight by a score of boys, who bore down upon him like a swarm of bees.

One sportive youth hit him over the hat with a broom, while the others proceeded to convert his back into a drum.

The Bosker laughed and walked on.

He had something else to think of besides paying attention to the Gorger's misfortunes, and he knew perfectly well that the hungry individual would overtake him.

Meanwhile the wretched Gorger was battling with his assailants, but he had not only the boys to contend with.

The Bosker's dog lingered and took a fancy to the disengaged end of the string of saveloys, and gobbled more than half of them up before the Gorger was aware of the catastrophe.

"I'll have your lives you warmints!" he yelled, striking out at the boys, and kicking viciously at the dog. "Only wait awhile, I'll settle with you one by one."

"The Gorger! The Gorger!" shouted the boys. "Yah! who stole a workhouse child's breakfast? Who robbed the poor widow of her market basket? The Gorger! The Gorger!"

Slime's blood was up, and he looked round for some heavy missile to hurl at his tormentors, but there was not even a stone he could lay hands upon, and after seeing how futile it was for him to remain, he dashed through the crowd and followed in the footsteps of the Bosker.

"If I ever should rise to be a regular detective," thought Captain Jack, when the fun was over, "I would look out for Tike; he's a greedy, ill-conditioned thing—spiteful, and altogether bad. He will be a second Gorger. There is something better in Burkett; he is no cur."

He had watched them on their way as far as he could see.

"To Nathan's," he said; "that's the game. Tike did some service in saying what he did; Grant might have gone into danger."

Captain Jack, the "watcher" (or "policeman's nose," as he is sometimes termed at the present time), sat on his box and kept on the look-out for the detective.

He did no more trade that day; the red brigade boy having seen the big muddy boots cleaned, returned and took up a position that successfully interupted Jack's custom.

Jack did not mind. He waited patiently till the boots reappeared; they were as muddy as before. Jack was deep in the pages of a story when the boots stopped before him.

"Clean your boots, sir—yes, sir," he said, as before.

The book was folded and thrust into his box, and his brushes were at work in a minute.

"Don't go to Nathan Claws' to-night," he muttered.

"Ha!" said Grant, starting. "Have you heard anything?"

"From a boy in the gang. You have been betrayed. The Bosker expects you."

"Thanks," the detective replied. "I shall be on my guard; but I shall go. Can you whistle through your fingers?"

"Loud as any boy living."

"Be outside the place at nine o'clock, then. You will see me enter. If I do not come out by a quarter past whistle through your fingers twice and go away."

"Go away?" queried Captain Jack.

"Yes," said Grant. "I shall be safe, and do not want you to be seen."

"I understand."

The disguised detective was moving away when the boy stopped him.

"Sir," he said.

"Well?"

"Have you such a thing as a silk handkerchief about you?"

"Yes."

"Will you give it me?"

"If you want it," said Grant, in surprise.

"I do," Jack replied. "Don't let anybody see you give it to me, but drop it as if by accident as you go along."

The detective went on marvelling at the boy's motive. He knew Captain Jack did not want the silk handkerchief for the sake of its value.

He went about ten yards, then dropped the silk. Jack and a young fellow in corduroys both started for it at the same instant. Corduroys reached it first, but Jack snatched it away.

"Now, then," said corduroys; "do you want a prop in the eye?"

"Hold your tongue, you fool," said Jack. "We can go halves, can't we?"

"All right," said corduroys, with a knowing leer. "I see you know your way about."

"Just so," returned Jack, quickly. "I wasn't born yesterday."

"No fear," laughed corduroys. "Where's the leaving shop?"

"Old Nathan's."

"I know. All right; see you to-night?"

"Yes."

They parted, corduroys going away with the full conviction that he had been talking with as rascally a young vagabond as himself.

"A clever lad that," said Grant, to himself. "He will turn out well one day, and be an ornament to the profession. He is the best watcher we have, and takes to detective work by instinct."

Before nine o'clock Captain Jack had taken his shoeblack-box home, and, with the handkerchief in his pocket, was on his way to the thieves' haunt kept by Nathan Claws.

He went fearlessly through the slums between Lambeth and the Borough, and stopped at a street where stood a rag shop, a barber's, and a public-house, within a few doors of each other.

At nine precisely Richard Grant, differently dressed, went into the rag shop. He passed Captain Jack, and a signal was exchanged between them.

Captain Jack noticed that about this time an unusual number of people were either thirsty, had rags to sell, or wanted shaving. Very few could have wanted their hair cut; that, in the majority of cases, seemed to have been done free of expense.

The boy, watchful and curious, stood loitering and reflecting on the strange, furtive faces passing by.

There was the sneaking, shabby lad, shuffling and on the alert, creeping into the rag store; the grinning, hardened ruffian, repulsive and of reckless aspect, lounging into the barber's; and the well-dressed, gentlemanly fellow, with quick, shifting, restless eyes, strolling leisurely into the tavern.

But whether sneaking lad, hardened ruffian, or more refined and gentlemanly rascal, all were birds of prey alike.

All had one common rendezvous—the thieves' kitchen, running underground parallel with the cellars where Nathan Claws stored his rags.

To this the rag shop, the barber's, and the tavern were all entrances and exits. It was a strange place altogether and very near the waterside.

When Grant entered the rag shop he saw Nathan himself behind the counter, apparently busy with a large scale full of bones. He looked up. Grant said something in a low tone and went into a small room at the end of the counter.

A peculiar glance shone in Nathan's deep-set orbs.

"Becky!" he called.

A heavy, slovenly woman, with a flushed, dirty face, and strong Jewish features, came forward.

"You can shut the shop. We sha'n't do any more businesh to-night."

The woman replied with a scowl. Nathan slunk through the small room and into another on the other side of the passage.

Becky closed the shop. It might have been noticed that at about the same time the barber came out and put up his shutters too, leaving only the door a little ajar. He had quite a number of customers.

"What hash you got?" asked Nathan of Grant.

"A few fawneys and a ticker," said the detective, gruffly; "and don't come none of your tricks of knocking the price down. I left old Joe Levi 'cause of that."

"Old Sol ish a sharp trater, pherry, but he dosh not know his customersh," said Nathan. "I am phair to mine, and give the mosht I can. Upon my soul and poty I pherry often get nothing py it."

"So Leary Jock said."

"You have known him long?"

"Known him long? I should say so," Grant replied. "We did our first tramp on the everlasting staircase together."

"Ah! Leary Jock ish a good lad, brings me lots of trifles. He knows mine ish the pest shop."

"So he said," replied Grant. "Is he in the kitchen now?"

"Yesh. Would you like to see him?"

"Yes, if you think it's all right."

"Ah! itsh right enough."

Grant produced a watch, with chain and seals, and two handsome rings. Nathan took them eagerly.

"Pherry handsome, pherry. I will test them and bring you the prish ; that ish the way," he said. "Lots of businesh to-night—lots of businesh."

He opened a trap-door. Grant descended by a flight of steps, and when he reached the bottom of the steps the trap fell.

"Moshish," said the Jew, clasping his hands, "what a bold un! What a treadful thing! They will kill him."

The cellar into which Grant had gone was dark at first ; but faint streaks of light came through the chinks of a door near at hand.

This he pushed ; it gave way, and he stood in the thieves' kitchen.

He saw a sight that, daring as he was, sent a chill to his heart, for he stood alone, a stranger and a spy, hated by the lawless crew before him.

There would not be much hope, not much mercy for him, should they discover his disguise.

A long table, made fast with iron legs screwed into the floor, ran the length of the room, and round this, on bags and boxes of various descriptions, sat a hideous throng—boys and girls, men and women, well-dressed mobsmen and cadgers —truly a sad and motley group.

The singular fancy which prompted all to meet in this horrible and loathsome den was no other than that here they could indulge safely in conversation relating to their exploits with no fear of a stranger or a spy listening to or betraying them.

There was a plentiful supply of drink, and most of the male portion of the company had pipes or cigars.

The females, with few exceptions, drank gin.

The anecdotes, related and listened to with zest, were horrible to hear.

Mere lads talked of crime with infernal relish, and felt proud of the applause given by older sinners.

The Bosker and his inseparable companion, the Gorger, were there, and with them a man of Burkett's stamp, but younger and less powerful.

This was Leary Jock.

He rose as Grant entered.

"A pal o' mine, mates all," he said, "and a stunner, though he comes from the other side o' the water. He was with me when we cracked the sheriff's crib."

This introduction ensured the new-comer a welcome, but by this he was not deceived.

He went and sat with Leary Jock.

Old Nathan came down soon afterwards.

He brought a bag of money and a list, on which was entered the various articles he had received from the company.

"Businesh first," he said, beginning with the mobsmen. "Ah! my tears, you have been doing some goot work. But I shall not pay one before the others, 'cause them as have peen unlucky will pe envious of them as have peen lucky. I shall take tree at a time into the counting-house."

He jingled his bag of gold, and beckoned three into another compartment of the cellar. The door to this room was of iron.

The three were paid. He first named the articles, then the price.

It was a peculiarity that none murmured at the sum given.

After the mobsmen came the more successful burglars and footpads, for even vice has its grades.

The man who is steeped to the lips in crime holds a prouder place among his associates than does the new beginner.

"Now te Posker and Nicholas, with Leary Jock and te new pupil," said Nathan, appearing at the iron door. "Gootnish me! I shall spend all my monish."

The men he had mentioned rose and went to him, and the iron door shut with a loud click.

Grant did not need to look at the Bosker's or Leary Jock's savage faces to see his danger ; but he was prepared.

"What did you bring?" asked the Bosker, whose hand was on the bludgeon in his pocket.

"A watch and some fawneys," said Grant, quietly.

"Is that all?"

"That is all at present," replied Grant.

"Then it's not enough," said the Bosker, with a savage laugh. "We never betray our pals here, Richard Grant. You are in the way."

"I am here," said Grant, setting his back against the wall, so as to face the Jew, "and I knew I was betrayed before I came. So I brought this with me."

He produced a loaded revolver and a short bludgeon, heavy and flexible, not unlike the Bosker's.

The Gorger dropped to his knees with a howl of terror, and crept behind Old Nathan. Leary Jock drew a clasp-knife, and the Bosker and Richard Grant eyed each other fixedly.

The detective did not seem at all astonished at the position in which he found himself. One thing alone disconcerted him, that was the presence of Burkett's bull-dog.

"You had a pocket-book from a friend of mine," Burkett said, swinging his bludgeon slowly up and down. "I want it."

"And I want you," Grant retorted. "So come quietly."

The Bosker laughed savagely again.

"We have got you," he said, with deep ferocity. "I have been hunted by you long enough, and I sha'n't give you the chance of hunting me again. You can't escape. Even if with that pistol you were to kill all here, there are enough in the kitchen to take care of you."

"In less than two minutes more," said Grant, "if I am not outside, this den will be besieged and gutted from roof to ceiling in search of me. You surely did not think me idiot enough to come like a sheep to be butchered in the shambles?"

"I think," said the Bosker, slowly, "that all the men you have brought would never find so much as a finger-nail of you unless we like to let you go."

Grant smiled in stern mockery.

He saw that his threat had made an impression on Nathan Claws.

*Like a swarm of bees they attacked the Gorger until he rolled in the mud and howled for mercy.*

"Since you will not come," he said, "it would be madness to try to take you under the present circumstances, but it is also madness in you to attempt to bar my way out. I hold six lives here. I have gained some knowledge. I wanted to see the thieves' kitchen, and the thief-trainer, Nathan. I can wait for you, James Burkett," and turning suddenly, he seized Nathan Claws by the throat.

"Now show me the way out," he said, putting the muzzle of the revolver in Nathan's ear. "Don't try to break away. Don't let a hand be raised against me. My finger is on the trigger. Come!"

"Save me!" screamed Nathan, in terror. "Ton't let him co, he knows too much. Save me—he tare not plow my prains out."

"He will not," said the Bosker. "Cruiser, seize him!"

At the words the dog leaped right at Grant's throat.

The brute did not reach it, but fell bleeding, with a bullet from the revolver in his body.

Grant's blood was up, and so was the Bosker's.

"The next for you," said Grant, still retaining his grasp of Nathan. "The third for my friend here if he does not take me out."

Grant fired a second time.

The Bosker avoided the bullet by dropping to his knees, and it struck the faithful bulldog, who, though badly wounded, was again going to the attack.

The Bosker hurled his bludgeon full at Grant's head, and he instinctively held up his hand to guard himself.

The bludgeon struck his wrist, and dashed the revolver from his grasp.

It fell upon the hammer and went off. The bullet lodged in the lower extremity of the Gorger's back.

He howled with pain, and ran round the cellar on his hands and knees.

The Bosker closed with Grant, and Nathan broke away.

"The water cellar," said Nathan. "Let him co, Purkett—let him co."

At the words "water cellar" Burkett wrenched himself away, and leaped back to the wall.

Grant, bewildered for the moment, stood motionless, looking round to see whence to expect the infernal treachery he was warned of by the demoniac looks and gestures of his foes.

He had not long to wait.

A click—the sound of a spring bolt shooting from its socket—and the floor went from under him like lightning.

There was a brutal laugh, as, with the desperation of despair he clung to the floor, then a brutal blow that made him release his death clutch, for the Bosker stamped his iron heel on the detective's hand.

The white face disappeared.

A heavy, sullen splash as the detective's body fell into water.

Then came a wild cry, and impenetrable darkness around poor Grant, for the trap had closed.

The deed was done!

Four men looked at each other, two in savage triumph—two in terror.

Hark!

A shrill whistle, such as a thief would give between two fingers.

Another, shriller than before.

Crash!

Nathan and the Gorger clung to each other with chattering teeth.

Crash!

Then came a prolonged, terrific hammering at the outer doors.

A wild flight ensued. Wantons and ruffians were struggling for egress.

Crash!

Wantons and ruffians have disappeared. The long table on its iron legs had sunk through the boards, and in its place had come a piece of level flooring, like the rest.

Crash!

The door had given way.

Lights were out now, and voices silent.

There was not a sound. Solitude and darkness reigned.

Crash!

Now came a tramp of many feet.

Lanterns flashed on sombre uniforms and determined faces.

It was time for all who had done dark work to hide.

The police, with Captain Jack at their head, were seeking to save or to avenge their comrade.

---

## CHAPTER VI.

OUT OF THE WORKHOUSE AND OUT OF PRISON—LITTLE FLO IN DANGER—THE CHILD-STEALER AND THE CROSSING-SWEEPER.

ALICK THORNE and Chimbley Joe, not having been convicted before, suffered their seven days in the House of Detention.

This, although the mildest form of prison, they did not find a pleasant place of residence. It struck Alick that a month of it would be quite enough to break a sensitive heart, and send a prisoner not sensitive either mad or desperate.

He remembered having heard Tike speak of it as torture.

It was.

Deadly oppressive—soul-subduing—spirit-crushing. Grim, cold, repellent cruelty. Pitiless, passionless coërcion.

The silent system.

The clang of the ponderous iron gate as it shut upon the file of prisoners just hauled from the van went sinking like a knell into Alick's breast.

Even the irrepressible Chimbley Joe was quieted—he was not used to it yet.

Their names and the charges against them were entered in the prison book.

"Another step," thought Alick, bitterly. "They are getting on with their work. A pauper last night—a companion of thieves to-night—used like one, punished like one, treated like the vagabond I do not want to be."

A stalwart gaoler, with a face like a mask, touched him on the shoulder and beckoned him to follow.

He turned to press Joe's hand; but that was not allowed. The gaoler pulled him away.

He was placed in a cell, called in mockery a waiting-room. There was a wooden stool in it; but nothing else.

The gaoler left him, and locked the door without saying a word.

In this place he was kept half an hour, and the boy, with his face in his hands, sat brooding over the wrong done to him by society.

It was the first time in his life he had ever felt what it was not to be at liberty.

That half hour of suspense and solitude seemed an age, and the sound of the key turning in the lock was welcome.

The gaoler beckoned him out, and Alick obeyed with a shiver, for he felt cold and sick at heart.

This time the gaoler took him to another cell, which was narrower than the first, and had no stool in it.

Here he was left again, and still no word spoken.

Alick could have shrieked, as the echo of the gaoler's footsteps died away.

The proud spirit, which quailed at first, now began to rise, and in the loneliness and darkness of the narrow cell he paced to and fro like a young tiger in captivity.

"For this," he said, plucking angrily at the coarse collar of his fustian jacket, "for this wretched garb I am shut up here. They could not treat me worse were I a felon or a murderer. What will come next—what new indignity?"

Half an hour passed.

The silent system gains in cruelty by degrees, and many a strong man has been heard to weep during confinement in the second cell; so far the system is good, when it works upon a brutal nature —it may break that.

On such a boy as Alick it would have a different effect.

After the first minutes of despair and weakness there was a sense of wrong—a thought that he had not deserved so much punishment.

Despair faded and a vindictive longing for revenge succeeded.

"What I have done," he said, between his teeth, "I did with a good motive. I wanted nothing but a clean suit of clothes, so that I might get work. I cannot tell a lie, and when asked where I have been I must say—in prison. Who will have me then—who will have me then?"

So he paced to and fro, brooding savagely and moodily.

The system was doing its work. The fight between Society and the boy was going on.

There was good stuff to make an experiment upon—stuff with which to make a good and honest man, or as dangerous a vagabond as ever defied law and cost Society as much trouble and expense as would help a dozen poor and honest men.

The bath came next. He had just left the workhouse, and was clean. He told the gaoler so, but he opened the bath-room door and said—

"Get in."

Alick obeyed.

The bath water was not clean, but he made no complaint, he was helpless as yet in the fight with Society.

Bathing over, he was taken to the cell that was to be his home for seven days.

It contained a washing basin, a stool, a small board on a trestle, and such conveniences as were absolutely necessary.

There was also an open three-cornered cupboard, a roll of cocoa-nut matting, in which were a blanket and a rug, the whole being strapped to the wall, a Bible, a single gas-jet, a card of prison rules, a bell-handle, a coarse towel, and a hard piece of soap.

One rule on the card was to this effect—

"The purpose of solitary confinement is not punishment, but to prevent contamination."

The boy bit his lip in scorn at the mockery.

"I suppose I shall be let alone now," he thought, mechanically opening the Bible.

Hard and bitter as he felt, the simple, solemn words soothed him.

He did not feel the injustice less keenly, but he he could bear it better. He had been taught piety early.

His gaze was attracted from the text to some pen and ink notes on the margin. These notes were continued throughout the book on the edges of the leaves.

Some curious, some startling. Many a wretched inmate of that cell had given a brief touch of character in a few words.

"It's the first time I have been here," wrote one, "and they say it's for vagrancy. What made me a vagrant? My poverty—and to be poor is a crime in the eyes of Society."

"Written perhaps by some poor lad like myself," Alick thought; "only poor at first, then driven fierce and desperate like I feel now."

The next note read—

"I wish I was dead and in my coffin."

Another ran thus—

"Never despair; they won't hang me, and I will have something for this dose."

The next at which he looked said this—

"Too poor to live, too proud to beg for life, I cannot die in prison. I go out on Monday. At night there is the river."

This, written in a delicate, well-educated hand, told a sad story.

The writer had seen better days; he was crushed by despair, driven to crime by poverty and the law.

Perhaps he kept his word and died in the Thames. Perhaps he lived on, past despair and hope alike—a desperate, callous criminal, being revenged on Society for what it did to him.

The governor and the House of Detention officials were almost universally condemned in these strange marginal notes.

We have not selected the worst, but those we have given will suffice to show that prison discipline is not so humanising, chastening, or satisfactory in effect as we could wish.

The chaplain, a meek and worthy old gentleman, who, to judge by his appearance, was certainly not so well paid or cared for as were the stalwart, coarse, and callous officials about him, visited Alick in turn.

It was evident he did not know with what crime the boy was charged, for he addressed him in terms that seemed stereotyped—hoped reflection and solitude would bring repentance and make him express contrition for his sin.

"It's a long lane that has no turning," thought Alick, when he was alone again, "and perhaps I have come to the worst now. I will have another try when I get out. The seven days here won't seem so long after it's over. After all, I might have come here for doing worse than I have. I wonder how Joe's getting on?"

Joe was getting along very well by this time.

He had stood his first hour's confinement in the cells without caring much.

He whistled several nigger tunes, and began several more before the gaoler stopped him.

Then, not to be done, he whistled them all over again in a whisper, and did a dance with his boots off.

The bath delighted him, but he demurred at the soap.

It was a new piece with sharp edges.

"You couldn't lend us a knife, old man, I s'pose?" he said, to his gaoler.

"What for?"

"Jist to pare the edges off," Joe replied, with a friendly wink. "My skin's delikit, don't you see, 'cause they give the chaps hard water in the casuals, and the hard water gives the casuals chaps."

"Get in!" the gaoler growled.

"All right, old man," Joe said. "You wouldn't be in a hurry if it was you. I say, just lick round the edges. Your tongue must be rough by the way you speak."

"Get in, I tell you!"

"Wery well. I s'pose you'd chuck me in clothes and all if I didn't, wouldn't you, like you did that cove the other day? If you did, I'd have you hup like he did, and get yer hexposed in the papers."

"If you ain't in the bath in two minutes," said the gaoler, "I'll help you to undress in a style you won't like."

"Thank you; but you are too good-looking for a walet. Are you the cove as is going to take the hangman's berth when he kicks the bucket?"

Here he finished undressing himself, and leaped into the bath with a splash just as the gaoler made an angry clutch at him.

"I will take you before the governor if you are insolent," the gaoler said, "and see how you will like an hour or two in the black hole."

"Thank you. I say, what makes you stop in prison? Won't they let you out?"

He got no reply to that.

"I s'pose you wears that dress so as they should know you if you was to run away?" Joe continued. "I should like me and a lot more to have you out on the fifth of November day. We should get lots o' ha'pence."

The gaoler retired, smiling in spite of himself.

"Talking's not allowed here," he said, when conducting the youthful prisoner to his cell.

"Wery well," said Joe. "Don't you holler, then, if talking's not loud."

"Silence!"

"Well, why don't you shut up?" Joe demanded. "I've as much right here as you, I s'pose? Prisons was built for such as me, wasn't they?"

"If I have to speak again—"

"I don't want you to speak to me," Joe interposed. "You can go if you ain't proud o' my company."

Then he dived into his cell.

"What's that?" he asked, kicking the roll of cocoa-nut matting.

"Your bed," the gaoler replied, grimly.

"My bed?" Joe exclaimed. "Well, a crammer 'ull never choke you. Why, you've been and nailed the matting out of somebody's passage and calls it a bed. How's it fixed?"

"You will find that out."

"When am I going to have dinner?" asked Joe. "I ain't had nothing to eat since morning—then it was toke and skilley."

"Wait and see."

"Bring us a crusty bit, old man," said Joe, who was neither to be cajoled or threatened into silence. "I'll do the same for you some day."

Taking into consideration their relative positions, this was kind.

The chaplain found Joe as irrepress'ble as the gaoler had.

"What did they bring me here for, then?" Joe asked, when the clergyman had tried to impress upon him the evil of the way he was going. "I was never in a prison afore."

"But you have committed a crime."

"Well, I teared my rags—not as they wanted much o' that—if you calls it a crime."

"You put the parish to some expense," said the chaplain, trying to show the boy in what degree he had been wrong.

"Well, I ask you, sir, what was I to do?" Joe rejoined. "If my clothes had a-fell off I should a-been collared by the bobby for walking about with nothin' on, shouldn't I?"

"Collared by the bobby?"

"Yes. Nailed by the peeler, don't you know?"

The chaplain tried to explain that he had no right to be in such a ragged condition.

"That's just wot I thought," said Joe; "'cause I've heard o' poors-rates and sich like—which is money as people pays to the work'us specially to find them in togs as wants 'em. And you see, sir, there wasn't much left o' my trousers; they was that wentilated that I had allus a strong draught runnin' up my back."

"They would have taken care of you in the workhouse—brought you up to some trade," the chaplain observed.

"They wouldn't, sir. You see they said I'd got no parish."

"No parish! How was that?"

"'Cause I was born while mother was on tramp —looking arter father," Joe replied. "He was dead, but she didn't know it then. And they wouldn't have me in the workhouse. You see I was born in a ditch that belonged to two parishes, and neither on 'em would have me. Bill Jenkins—he was a tinker then, he is a coster now — made mother's 'quaintance and married her after I was born."

"Why does she not support you?"

"You see, sir," said Joe, his eyes filling involuntarily with tears, "she took a kind o' dislike to me, and when Bill and her gets drunk they both wollops me if I goes a-nigh 'em, so I prefers picking up a bit o' grub out o' doors."

"Where do you sleep as a rule?" the chaplain demanded.

"Nowhere, sir; I ain't particular—railway-arches, and the dark 'uns down the 'Delphi, under a cart, or anywheres—sometimes in the casual, when it rains."

The last words told a tale of the complete aversion in which our poor hold the workhouse; under an archway or a cart was preferable to the "casual." Joe only went to the casual when it rained.

"How long have you been houseless?"

"Allus since I can reckilect, 'ceptin' when I worked for Jarvis the sweep. That's why I am called Chimbley Joe."

"What do you mean to do when you go from here?" asked the chaplain, touched by the simple pathos of the last reply.

"Dunno, sir; jest what I best can. Take a crossing, p'raps; matches isn't no spec now, and there's too many trying fuzees. Oranges is worse, and flowers is no good, 'cause nobody will buy 'em of boys. Men gets all the odd jobs, such as horses and parcels and messages, and most shoeblacks belong to the ragged school."

"Have you no idea what to do?"

"Not till I tries, sir. P'raps something 'ull turn up. I'll stick to Alick; he knows better than me," Joe replied.

"You have a friend, then?"

"Yes, sir; Alick's my pal. There's Tike; but he's a thief, and I don't want a thief for my pal."

"That is right," said the chaplain; "respect honesty and walk in the right path."

With which and the usual homily the chaplain retired.

Soon after this the gaoler entered again. This time he brought a square tin can containing rather less than a pint of gruel. He also brought a small brown loaf, weighing about half-a-pound.

"If I was in a coffee-shop," said Joe, eyeing the loaf with much distaste, though he was very hungry, "and they wanted a penny for this, I'd chuck it at 'em. Why, it's worse than the casual; we do get it white there, and new, sometimes."

"The tin will be fetched in half an hour," said the gaoler. "And you must make your bed at eight; the gas goes out soon."

"Take it with you," said Joe, "if you like. Only bring me a candle; it would be something to stir up the skilly. Crikey! if the Gorger had this for supper wouldn't he do a howl?"

He bit the bread, and masticated it slowly.

Either the baker or the ingredients were not too clean, for the bread was decidedly dirty, and a famishing dog might have wagged his tail in contempt at the gruel.

It was thick, certainly, and so far claimed superiority over that provided for the casual poor at the workhouses; but it was coarse, rough to the palate, badly boiled, and without sufficient salt to redeem its bitter flavour.

Nothing less pungent than the very keenest hunger sauce made it go down Joe's throat.

"It's enough to take away a fellow's appetite, this is," said Joe, picking from the loaf sundry bits of black that could never have belonged to the vegetable kingdom. "Not that there's too much on it; but what there is is wery strong."

But he ate it and drank the gruel out of one corner —he had no spoon—cleaned the tin out with his finger, and then entered into the mysteries of the cocoanut matting. Fixing it up in anything like a shape for repose was a difficult thing to the uninitiated.

"They might give a cove a piller," said Joe, after he had succeeded in hanging it, by means of iron rings in the matting and hooks in the walls, at about the height of three feet from the stone floor. "I could do without a bolster, but they might give a cove a piller; then ag'in they mightn't—and they don't."

"It's a doss, this is!" he said, when the matting was arranged properly across the cell. "All sides and no middle. My head'll be as high as my feet, and the rest o' me nowhere. I should like to give what it's worth and git the change out o' fourpence. Carry me out! here's a lark."

He indulged in some acrobatic performances, taking a short run from the back of the cell, then a flying leap over the bed, till he caught his toe in the matting and went crash against the door.

Then he undressed and retired, tucked himself up comfortably, and began to sing.

"Stop that," said the gaoler, coming in.

"Ain't you fond o' moosic?" Joe asked.

"You will sing a different tune if you don't obey orders," the gaoler said, savagely.

"Obey who? You're name ain't Orders, is it?"

"Be quiet, or we shall have to punish you."

"Thank'ee; don't trouble yourself. Good-night, old man," said Joe, blandly. "I say, what's that handle in the wall for?"

"That's the bell."

"Wot's it for?"

"To ring if you want anything. Don't you see the rules?"

"Of course. I ain't got dust in my eyes," Joe said. "So I'm to ring that, am I?"

"If you ring without occasion you will be punished," said the gaoler.

"That's a treat, that is," Joe returned, elevating his eyebrows. "I'm to ring the bell if I wants anything, and if I pulls it, and you don't think I wants anything, I'm to get it hot. You're a nice fellow, you are."

The gaoler retired muttering, but so amused that he grinned as he walked down the long white-washed corridor.

Chimbley Joe, light hearted and irrepressible, soon went to sleep.

His last thoughts were of Alick, whose slumbers were of a fitful nature, as he laid awake for hours, pondering what he should do when restored to liberty again.

He was thinking of his sister Polly, and he felt sure she would be at the gate waiting for him when he went out.

Throughout the long night, save when he dozed, Alick heard nothing to break the painful stillness but the monotonous ticking of the prison clock, and the distant articulations of its bell chiming the quarters.

He was awake and pacing his cell when the gaoler entered in the morning; his breakfast he left untasted, and did mechanically what he was ordered to do.

Chapel time came—he saw Chimbley Joe there; each wore a numbered brass ticket on his arm, and went to chapel with a line of felons, walking single file and ticketed.

He could not speak to Joe, could not press his hand; silence was the order, and Joe was in front of him—a burglar, a pickpocket, and a maker of spurious coin, awaiting their trial at the sessions, being between them.

There were some few visitors in the place of worship, and the door was guarded by gaolers. The sermon, delivered in a low, almost inaudible voice, by the chaplain, was listened to attentively; then they were marched back again to their respective cells.

This, with an hour or so each day in the exercise yard, the exercise being a continual walk, and still the same eternal silence, was the routine of each day till the miserable week was gone.

Liberty came at last.

Never had the cold sun of a wintry day seemed at once so beautiful and so sad as it did that morning to Alick as he stood with Joe at his side, the prison gates behind him, the world before him; glad to be out of the grim stone building, but with a heart as heavy as lead.

Alick looked round eagerly for Polly, but she was not there.

He had dwelt upon the thought of her wistful face looking for him—pictured how she would come to kiss him and press his hand, to whisper love and comfort to him, and to say she could think of him without reproach or shame.

But she was not there.

He only saw a throng of curious faces, on the watch for friends expected out of prison; he only saw these, and the police, looking at the rest and at him, making a mental note of his appearance, so that they might know him again.

"Come, Alick, old boy, don't be down in the mouth," said Joe. "What are you looking like that for?"

"Polly's not here," Alick replied, mournfully. "I don't know where to find her."

"Never mind; we'll look after her. We're out now, and it's over."

"It's over," repeated Alick, drawing a long, deep breath. "Yes, it's over, Joe, and we're out of prison, without a penny or a crust, with nothing but our workhouse dress. And," he added, striking his breast, "a wretched hardened feeling here. They are trying to make a vagabond of me, Joe. They will make a devil if they don't take care."

"Drop that, Alick," said Joe. "I don't want my old pal to give way in that style. Don't think of playing Tike's game. It's a dangerous one."

"Only if they drive me to it, Joe," Alick returned, with a hard glitter in his eye, "only if they drive me to it. But look here—see how we stand to-day. We've not a bit of food, and no chance of getting any. And then, behind us is the cursed prison and the police, who know us now. I've been there, and they'll hunt me from place to place, till I'm the vagabond they want to make me."

"No fear; they won't interfere with you," said Joe, consolingly.

"They had better not, but they will," Alick responded. "I've heard many a poor wretch tell how, after he'd once been convicted, they've been down upon him, watching and hunting him out of every place where he'd got honest work—doing their duty, they said, by telling the master what he'd been. It's hard, Joe—it's hard. I want to get out of the gutter, and they won't let me."

"We'll have a try, anyhow," Joe remarked, cheerfully. "Come on, I knows what to do. We'll get a broom a-piece and take a crossing, one at each end, and I'll get something to eat."

"How can you, Joe? We haven't got a penny."

"Never mind, come on; you're the only pal I cares for, and I don't like to see you down. Let's go and do what I said, then look out for Polly."

The poor little lad just out of prison in a workhouse dress had a heart of gold, and his faithful affection for his pal showed itself as he took Alick's hand to hurry him on.

They went over Blackfriars Bridge to Lambeth. Joe stopped when in sight of a rag and second-hand clothes shop near the New Cut.

"You just stay here," he said to Alick, "and wait till I comes to you."

"Where are you going? What are you going to do?"

"Just mind your own business," Joe replied. "Don't ask questions that don't concern you. Just wait and see."

The wretched street boy had resolved upon as noble an act of self-sacrifice as ever graced a story of higher-sounding heroism.

He set off at a run.

He was not gone two minutes, and he came with two new birch brooms.

"There!" he said, setting one in front of each foot. "Fine uns, ain't they? I got the two for sevenpence, and now there's elevenpence to carry us over to-day and to-morrow, if we don't have no luck."

Alick looked at him from head to foot, wondering how he got the money.

A thought struck him, and he moved one of the brooms aside.

Chimbley Joe's feet were bare—naked.

"Joe," he said, huskily, touched by the lad's devotion, "you shouldn't have done that."

"Shouldn't done what?" Joe cried, laughing. "Now, then, just stop that crying, or you'll set me off, too. I can do as I like, I s'pose! Chuck the broom away if you won't have it—that's all."

"Joe, you shouldn't have done it. I am the biggest and the strongest. I could better bear to go without boots than you could."

"No, you couldn't," Joe said. "You can get work, p'raps, but I ain't big enough; 'sides, I can get 'em back. I left 'em at the dolly-shop for eighteenpence, and I can have 'em back for two shillings, if I gets 'em the day after to-morrow. So let's go and get a crossing. There's lots o' mud, and we are sure to pick up some coppers."

Alick took a broom in silence. He could not speak, for his heart was too full.

They chose a crossing in the Westminster-bridge-road.

They had a lucky day, for Alick's great civility and Chimbley Joe's drollery attracted attention; coppers were given freely, and by nightfall they had earned a shilling.

Just as they were going Alick got a horse to hold outside a public-house.

The owner of the trap, a sporting man, gave him sixpence.

" Now we have got the boots," he said ; " we've only spent twopence, so there'll be threepence left after we've paid two shillings for the boots."

"So we can," Joe assented, "and I'll be glad, 'cause my feet are cold. But how about the lodging ; we don't want to go to the casual ?"

"Perhaps Jacob Primrose will let us sleep in his cab yard," said Alick ; " he is a good sort."

" P'raps he will. Let's go and see."

"And to-morrow I must see where Polly is," Alick added. " I don't like her not being there waiting for us—it looks strange. You see, she is pretty and poor, and out of work, and I knows what happens sometimes when it's like that."

They had to go some distance to reach Jacob Primrose's cab yard, and were proceeding down a dark and lonely street when they heard a cry.

" Don't take me away, please," said a child's voice, pleading piteously. " You said I was going to papa's—Mr. Bartlett's papa. Don't take me away !"

" Hush ! you little wretch !" responded somebody, with a growl. "Hold your tongue. I'm very hungry, and I'll eat you if you don't shut up."

" It's the Gorger," said Chimbley Joe, stopping and looking at Alick. " The long brute has got hold o' some little girl. Let's stop him."

Then came another cry—

" Mamma—why did mamma die ?" wailed the child's voice. " Don't let him take me away."

" He shall not," said Alick, loudly. " Hallo ! there. What are you doing with the child, you lanky villain ?"

The street was dark and near the river, and the boys could see nothing yet.

But at the sound of Alick's voice the child's cry rose to a shriek.

Then came an oath from the Gorger, the sound of a savage blow, a piteous moan, and then silence.

The two boys ran forward towards the spot where they fancied the Gorger and his helpless victim— little Flo—must be.

The sound of Alick's voice brought a number of ragged urchins from the tumble-down, evil-smelling houses.

" Bravo !" cried Chimbley Joe. " Now we'll have some fun. Boys, the Gorger's prigged a little gal. Follow me and my pal, and we'll let the lanky villain have what for."

With a whoop and a cry the whole pack started forward.

Dashing round a corner they came upon the Gorger with little Flo in his arms.

He was making rapidly for a turning leading to an archway, in the jet black shadow of which washed and surged the filthy tide of the Thames.

" Quick !" shouted Alick. " After him, boys, or he will drown the little girl.'

## CHAPTER VII.

THE RESCUE OF LITTLE FLO—JOHN RUGBY ON DUTY—A LOST CHILD IN LONDON.

IT did not take the crowd of street arabs long to reach the fugitive.

Light of foot, and with the additional activity of a good design, they overtook him before he had time to reach the archway.

That the Gorger's purpose was a sinister one there could be no doubt.

His howl of rage as Chimbley Joe seized his ragged coat tails, and another youth hurled a dead cat full in his face, attested to the fact that his designs against little Flo were malicious if not murderous.

" Drop her, you beast !" Alick cried, dashing his broom in the Gorger's face.

The Gorger let the child go, and endeavoured to make his escape, but the boys had not half done with him yet.

Like a swarm of bees they attacked him, until he rolled in the mud and howled for mercy.

" Let me go, or I'll be the death o' some o' you," he yelled. " It's her temper—the little vixen—it's her temper. She's a bad gal, and always runnin' away from my sister, her poor mother, that loves her. Ow !—ow ! It's 'ard for a man to be sat upon when he's tryin' to do right."

" Ow !—ow !" cried Joe, in derision. " Why 'ere's the Gorger doin' the water-cart bizness. You're a nice take-down, you are. So she's your sister's child, is she. Just hold on to her a minute," he added, to the boy who had charge of little Flo, "and I'll fetch a bobby. P'raps the Gorger will tell him the same tale."

At this moment Nicholas Slime, the Gorger, saw his chance.

The boys were looking everywhere for a policeman, and just as the loud, measured tramp of an officer on his beat was heard he started to his feet and fled like a hare before the hounds.

" Hallo !" said Joe, "that's a caution. The Gorger's got long legs, but I didn't think he could run like that. Never mind. Let the lanky brute go. We've got the little gal right enough, and she's a lot better off than when we found her."

The strange boys, finding that their services were no longer required, gave a shrill yell of triumph and vanished amidst the gloom and darkness of the gruesome neighbourhood.

The policeman passed, not seeing the group of children in the gloom.

The lads had acted on impulse. They had saved the child, but had not the least idea what to do with her.

Only, as the friendless cling to the friendless, they thought of taking her somewhere with them, and protecting her.

" You are all right now, you know," said Joe, as

little Flo looked at the two boys in bewilderment. "The wicked man sha'n't touch her any more, he sha'n't."

Alick took one hand, Chimbley Joe the other. They led her out of the dark street, talking kindly to her the while.

"Where did he bring you from?" Alick inquired.

Flo did not know.

"What's your name, eh?"

"Flory, please."

"What else?"

"Flory Lake."

"Poor little thing!" said Alick, as though the knowledge of her name increased his interest. "Have you got a father?"

She told him she had not.

Only a mamma, and mamma was dead in the workhouse.

"That's the way with most on us, somehow," commented Joe. "Mothers dies in the workus, and we don't seem to have no fathers. Seems to me there ain't so many fathers about as there oughter be."

By dint of questioning further they elicited some information, told with childish want of clearness; but the name of Papa Bartlett, Seawell, and Sam figured frequently. They also learned that she liked Sam.

"Blowed if I ain't struck a bright!" said Chimbley Joe. "Perhaps it's Sam Seawell—don'tcher know, him as comes from Biler's-court, and works in the skinyard down Bermondsey."

"It may be," Alick said; "but that is a long way to take her at this time of night."

"Well she must go somewhere."

Tramp—tramp.

The policeman came round again and Alick hailed him.

"Now, what's the game?" he asked, coming towards them with his bull's-eye open.

Chimbley Joe left Alick to tell the story.

"So Nicholas Slime had her, eh?" said stalwart John Rugby, glancing kindly at the child. "I wish you had kept hold of that nice young man; he ought to be taken care of, for the benefit of his health."

Then he looked more attentively at Flo.

"Why it's the child I took to the casual with her poor mother, who died," he said, under his breath, "and my new mate promised to take care of. This is a rum go."

"Going to take her to the station-house, sir?" asked Alick.

"Yes, till I see what's to be done," John Rugby replied. "Come along, little gal; don't be afraid of me—I've got lots of little people like you about at home."

At this moment a cab with a gentleman inside rattled sharply down the street.

He saw the group formed by the policeman, Flo, and the boys, and putting his hand through the trap in the top of the hansom, signalled for the cab to stop.

He got out in the road instead of on the pavement, paid the driver, threw a curious glance at Flo, and walked slowly down the street.

"Hullo, Rugby!" said Jacob Primrose, whose cab it was. "Got another case for me?"

"No, Jacob, unless you want an addition to the family; it's the same little 'un we had the other night."

"'Lor, now; is it?" exclaimed the cabman. "Bless her poor little heart! You ain't going to take her to the workus ag'in, surely?"

"No. I know the man that's taking care of her, I think, so I shall just keep her at the station till I can send to him."

"Poor little mite!" said Jacob Primrose. "I'm blest if I ain't a good mind to take her home with me. I was a telling the missus about her 'tother day. And sez she, 'Jacob, any man as wasn't a brute would have brought the little lambkin home.' And sez I, 'Well, Rachael, old gal, so I would if I'd a thought you'd a liked it. Only you might a thought it queer like.' But it's a cold place in the station-house."

"So it is," said John Rugby.

"And," said Jacob, "when a man's got seven on 'em all lying in two beds in a row, another one don't make much difference. I'll take her if you like. She'll have a warm bed for the night."

"Do," said Rugby, "it will be better for her. These lads found her with Nicholas Slime, the Gorger. He was making off with her somewhere."

"Ah!" said Jacob, emphatically. "He's a beauty, is Nicholas Slime. He ought to have been put out of the way of doing mischief long ago. Hollo, young shavers, what's your game?"

This was to Alick and Chimbley Joe.

"We were looking out for a doss," said the latter, "and thought of coming down to you to ask you to let's turn in in your yard."

"Were you? Very well, trot along then," said the cabman. "Tell Mike I shall be there as soon as you."

"Thank you, Mr. Primrose," said Alick.

"You're a good sort," said Joe, "and no bloomin' horror. Come along, Alick, old boy. Won't I take a sleep out o' some clean straw and a horse-cloth."

Gladdened by the prospect, he was going away with Alick, when John Rugby called to them and they turned.

"Here's a tanner for you for taking care of the little gal," he said.

"Thank you, and may you never know what it is to be hungry," said Joe. "The tanner's welcome; though we didn't think o' getting nothing when we stopped Nicholas Slime. He got more than a tanner's worth for his share."

Jacob got down to exchange a word with the policeman.

"Did you see my fare?" he asked.

"Yes."

"Well, now it strikes me there's something strange about him."

"Why?" demanded the constable.

"You remember the night when we first saw this little un," said Jacob Primrose.

As he spoke he took the heavy cape from his overcoat, and wrapping Flory in it placed her in the cab.

"Yes," said Rugby.

"Well that same swell had a turn-up with Grant in the Haymarket."

"Grant—our detective?"

"Him and no other," replied Jacob Primrose.

"How was that?"

"Perhaps it ain't my business to tell, but I seed all about it," the cabman responded. "I only know that the swell lost a pocket-book."

"Well?"

"Just a morning or two afterwards I druv him down as far as Watchorn's, corner o' the Marsh Gate. He was done up in different togs then, but I knowed him ag'in."

Rugby became interested.

"Where were you taking him to-night?" he asked.

"Down to the railway arches," he said.

"That's where Nicholas Slime was going with the child," said Rugby, struck by the coincidence. "I must keep my eye on him."

"So will I," said Jacob, with more than necessary emphasis; "and if that ain't him a-lurking about the end of the street I'm a Dutchman."

"It is," Rugby observed, softly. "This is a go, Jacob! Drive along quietly, and keep your eyes open. I should like to see his game. Don't seem to take any notice of him."

"Not me," chuckled Jacob Primrose. "I gets up as early in the morning as most people does; and I ain't about on a cab all day for nothing. If we don't get fly to his game, make a note of it, and call me a hass."

He drove slowly away, after Rugby had promised to fetch Flory in the morning. Flory went quietly with Jacob; his homely, fatherly kindness won her confidence, and he had promised that she should see Papa Bartlett in the morning.

Rugby went down another turning on his beat, hoping to intercept David Eastlake on the way, and have a good look at him.

The policeman reflected deeply but was also on the alert.

Walking about hour after hour in the silence of night, and alone, is apt to make a man reflective, and the policeman grows by habit a creature of meditation.

The nature of his profession is such as tends to give him watchfulness and capacity to study character.

John Rugby was always starting a theory of some possible crime; he begun one now.

"There's queer things done nowadays," he reflected, "some on 'em so queer you can hardly believe 'em. It's suspicious Nicholas Slime stealing the child, then the swell coming down and hovering about."

Here he emerged into a turning, from which he could see the street down which Jacob had gone, preceded by the stranger.

He saw the outline of the cab, and some distance behind it, following cautiously, he saw the stranger.

"Ah," said Rugby, feeling his lantern in a self-congratulatory sort of manner, "then I was right this time; I thought I smelled a rat."

He went as far as he dared without leaving his beat, at the end of which he met his mate, whose beat comprised the arches, the river-side, and the street where Jacob Primrose lived.

"Coleman!" he said, after they had nodded to each other as policemen invariably do, no matter how many times they met in the course of the night.

"Well, Jack."

"Just walk after that cab, and see if the swell follows. Do it quietly."

The other's instinct was roused.

"Is there a game on, do you think?"

"Nearly sure. There's a little gal inside the cab —do you twig?"

"Is that his caper? All right."

"Take a good look at him."

"Right."

They parted.

Coleman turned on his bull's-eye, and appeared to be minutely surveying keyholes and shutter fastenings, which he had seen were safe five minutes before.

His light went as if unintentionally over Eastlake's face. The constable only caught a momentary glimpse, but it was enough. He would have known that face again anywhere.

"Good night, sir," he said, civilly.

"Good night."

Eastlake, not suspecting how closely he was being watched, followed the cab, which stopped outside Jacob's yard.

"Mike!" said Jacob.

A sleepy-headed ostler opened the gates and appeared.

"Did you send two boys here, sir, telling them they might sleep here," he asked.

"Yes; all right," said Jacob Primrose. "Have they come?"

"Yes," the ostler replied. "I let them in, 'cause I thought if it was a lie I could turn them out again when you came. They're snoring like young porkers now."

"Take the cab," said Primrose.

Jacob lifted Flory out and carried her into his house, which was by the side of the cab-yard.

The cabman was a small proprietor. He had contrived by steady industry and sober habits to buy four horses and two vehicles—a four-wheeler and a hansom.

Eastlake entered the name of the street and the number of Jacob's house in a note-book, and the constable Coleman, watching him closely, saw him do so.

Then Eastlake turned back, and passing the railway arches he halted and went slower, as if looking for someone.

The lanky, sinister face of the Gorger peered out of the shadow.

"Hist!" he said.

Eastlake paused.

"How did you manage to lose her?" he asked.

"A lot of boys set on me," the Gorger whined. "I had her safe enough."

"Curse them!" Eastlake hissed. "Why is not Burkett here?"

"He's hiding, sir. The police are after him."

"Where is he hiding?"

"At the Pig and Porridge Pot," the Gorger replied. "He told me to tell you he can't stay after to-morrow; it's getting too warm for him. Thank you, sir; very kind of you, I'm sure."

The Gorger chuckled, and spat on some silver Eastlake let fall into his hand. The Gorger began to whine again, and Eastlake took the cue directly his voice changed, and acted as though giving alms to a mendicant.

The cause was that John Rugby passed them with his heavy, stalwart stride. They did not see him till he stood within a few yards of them.

"I might nab him," thought Rugby, as the Gorger slunk away; "but it would be no good. I may do more by keeping quiet."

He watched the well-clad form of David Eastlake till he faded out of view, and then went tramping heavily on.

"What the game is I can't see," Rugby meditated. "The little gal's got something to do with it. So the Bosker's hiding at the Pig, is he? That's worth knowing. We don't lose sight of him. I'll set a man on to look after his health to-morrow, and another to watch Primrose's house, to see if our swell comes again. And I'll have a talk with Bartlett. Perhaps he will know a little. I'll go to him directly I get off duty."

Philip Bartlett, who had been nominated, but was not yet appointed to a situation in the police force, was staying with a friend.

He had taken Flory from the workhouse and placed her in charge of Mrs. Seawell, the woman with whom the child's unhappy mother had resided some time before her death.

With Mrs. Seawell Flory's mother had left a locked box, as security for money as yet unpaid for rent and food.

Bartlett left the child with her, promising to pay for her subsistence and to redeem the box as soon as he got his situation.

He thought Flory was in perfect safety, never dreaming that Eastlake had set his agents to work.

Nicholas Slime, instructed by the Bosker, had found out where Flory was, and enticed her from the street when she was playing with Mrs. Seawell's children.

But for the interference of Alick and Chimbley Joe the child would by this time have been in Eastlake's power or at the bottom of the Thames.

Gilbert had again ran away from the workhouse, and was supposed to be wandering about the streets in a state of destitution.

## CHAPTER VIII.

WHITECHAPEL DICK AND HIS WONDERFUL INVENTIONS—A FAMILIAR FACE IN A CURIOUS CROWD—DAVID EASTLAKE AND THE CHEAP-JACK.

AT the corner of the Kennington-road on the broad space which was neither road nor pavement, there stood on the day of little Flo's rescue a huge caravan.

It was painted yellow, and the horse was invisible. Anyone given to the solution of difficult problems might have set to work pondering how the animal, whether horse or elephant, ever did contrive to set the cumbrous house on wheels in motion.

But the horse—it must have been a horse, for the shafts were too big for a donkey, and not large enough for a camel—was invisible.

We suspect that the keeping him out of sight was an artful dodge on the part of the caravan proprietor, resorted to in case the police should request him to move on.

He might have considerably the best of an argument by simply telling them to move his caravan for him if they objected to its being there.

That caravan caused quite a commotion in the vicinity.

Several horses, seeing it sideways, shied at it, and 'bus drivers continually fouled each other through looking at it when they should have been looking after their own business.

A doctor's boy damaged his master's income, and gave several of his master's customers another chance, by standing staring at it open-mouthed when he ought to have been delivering his medicine and pills; in fact, the active errand-going youth of Lambeth, and a few from far away places, were fairly represented in the group gathered round.

It caused sad neglect of juvenile duty.

A tremendous picture, with either Daniel or Van Amburgh in a den, with a liberal number of lions, tigers, and leopards, all bearing a remarkable family resemblance as regards spots and stripes, was too much for the juvenile strength of mind.

One instance was deplorable.

A Lambeth devil, belonging to a Lambeth printer, who was the proud proprietor of a Lambeth local paper, stayed picture-gazing while on his return from the City. Under his arm he had a copy of all the daily morning and evening papers, in the absence of which the Lambeth local could not come out, and the editor tore his hair, dashed the paste pot against the wall, and swore that he would have that boy's life with the editorial scissors.

Street boys were in force—shoe-blacks, paupers, and crossing-sweepers being largely in the majority—Alick, Chimbley Joe, Tike, and a lad called little Dan, amongst the rest, intent in observation of the lion's den picture, and another on the other side of the caravan, on which were painted a fire-king, a giant, a dwarf, and a fat woman.

"Wonder when it will open," said Joe, who had got his boots again, "and whether it'll be a 'apenny or a penny."

"A penny—sure to," said Tike. "Think they'd show a fat woman for a 'apenny; tain't likely."

"Dunno," said Joe, "it all depends. They had a spotted boy up the road once, with a mermaid, and lots o' things. They used to charge a 'apenny all day long, and a penny at night. 'Cause at night you might feel the spots to see if they was real; but they wouldn't let you in the day-time."

"I should a' gone at night then," said Tike. "Hullo, here come's the bloke. I don't think it's a show at all. It's a cheap-jack."

The door, which had been shut hitherto, now opened, and an individual showed himself.

He took a leisurely survey of the crowd, and the crowd took an eager scrutiny of him.

He bore this scrutiny with much self-possession, and a certain consciousness that he was worth notice.

He was a handsome, tall, and well-built fellow, of about five-and-twenty, and had a singularly proud carriage of the head, which was altogether very much above the style of a cheap-jack or a showman.

There was nothing vagabondish about him, either.

He wore a splendid, semi-military costume—a dark-blue, closely-fitting frock coat, with black silk epaulettes, a braided collar, and plain buttons.

This, set off by a rich crimson sash, dropped carelessly round a waist as small as a woman's, gave him a strikingly distinguished appearance.

He wore, also, a velvet cap, with a heavy gold tassel, and this, with buckskin breeches, and a dashing pair of high-polished leather boots, with gilt spurs, completed his costume.

"Come, ladies and gentlemen," he said, his white teeth gleaming through his black moustache as he smiled pleasantly on the expectant throng, "there are not fifty yet, and I dare not display a single one of my wonderful curiosities to less than that number. I am sorry to see so many kind friends waiting, but I cannot do otherwise. It is the express condition under which I travel with a commission held under his Imperial Majesty the Great Mogul."

Some believed this, and they respected the speaker. Those who did not believe laughed, and thought him witty, but either way he grew popular.

The fact that he wanted an audience of fifty soon spread, and more than fifty were shortly assembled.

"Wonder what he's going to do?" said Joe, who was always wondering. "He looks fine, don't he, Alick?"

Alick did not notice the remark. His glance, roving from the master of the caravan, had caught sight of a pale, frightened face in the crowd.

It was Gilbert.

Childlike curiosity had conquered childish terror for the time, and he had a vague hope of seeing Alick in the crowd.

"Where have you been?" asked Alick, elbowing his way through till he reached Gilbert, "and what makes you tremble so? They can't hurt you."

"But I ran away," said Gilbert, clinging to Alick's hand.

"Well, never mind," said Alick, "you were not obliged to stay against your will."

"The policeman will take me there again."

"No fear," said Alick. "Stay along with me. Keep in the crowd; nobody will see you."

But somebody had seen him.

The Boozer, who had taken up a position against the lamp-post at the corner, where he could at once see the show and lounge at ease, felt his hat gently lifted from behind.

He turned his head, but did not change his attitude. He could not afford to do that. A certain projection of the post suited his back admirably for rest.

"Spitalfields," said a voice, in hollow and hungry tones, "what luck?"

"Luck!" Boozer replied. "I haven't seen it. Here's my last arf pipe o' bacca, and if I knows where to get any more, hang me!"

He said it with total unconcern. His voice never changed. It was a rasping sleepy wheeze, always ending with a heavy sigh, as though speaking were a trouble and the sigh an expression of relief at having got over it.

"I spent my last tuppence in a snack," said the Gorger, more hungrily than before. "It's bad luck, Boozer. We are unfortunit, and yet there's a little cove a walking about as 'ud be a mine of gold to look at."

Boozer did change his attitude this time, and almost went down backwards. He had been standing in an easy heel and toe position, which did not afford much support when he moved his back.

"A mine o' gold," he wheezed, shifting his cap by a circular pressure of the hand, thereby gently allaying a general irritation. "What do you mean?"

"We might tumble over it, Boozer, you and me," the Gorger replied. "It's a little casual as were in the wurkus one night last week."

Boozer seemed to listen with the whole of his shaggy head.

"A little casual!" he said. "I was in the casual every night last week, and this week, too. Wot's he like? Wot does it mean?"

"He's worth his weight in gold, I tell you," the Gorger said. "I'd get a handful to-day if we could show him."

"Lor!" gasped the Boozer, knocking the ashes out of his pipe and into the Gorger's eye. "Tell us where it was. Per'aps I seed him?"

"It were last Friday," said the Gorger, wiping his optic with the tail of his coat; "and be more keerful o' your dust next time. It were last Friday. You'll pr'aps remember it. Him and two more was taken up for tearing their togs."

"Then," said the Boozer, emphasizing his words with a heavy slap intended for Nicholas Slime's shoulder, but which he dodged, "then I know the wery kid. He were with Tike and young Chummy and another one—Alick they calls him. And there he is with Alick now."

He pointed Gilbert out to the electrified Gorger, who thought of a hundred ways at once for getting possession of the boy, but could not hit upon one practical plan.

"I've got it," he said at last. "He ran away from the workus. Keep your heye on him for a minit. I know the fakement."

"Very well," wheezed the Boozer, lazily. "Only don't be gone too long, unless you've got a bit o' bacca to leave."

The Gorger felt in his waistcoat pocket, from which he produced two plug-like pieces of the weed.

Boozer crammed them into his pipe, and producing a lucifer from his waistcoat pocket, lit it, and went on smoking.

"I couldn't do no more than give him the best I had," commented Mr. Slime, as he slunk round the corner to a public-house. "Them two quids has lasted me a week, very nigh. What the heye don't see the 'art can't grieve about. Boozer 'll smoke 'em and enjoy 'em."

He went into the public-house and asked for a pen and ink, also a sheet of writing paper and an envelope.

He was known at the bar.

"This is the boy we want," he wrote. "Don't let him go. We mightn't get another chance. I send him with the note as a plant.

"NICHOLAS SLIME."

He put this in an envelope, which he addressed to—

"James Burkett, Esq.,
　　"The Pig and Porridge Pot,
　　　　"Dinkin's Court."

"He'll go like a little hinnocent dicky bird into the net, he will, and the Bosker will settle him afore the morning," the Gorger mused. "Poor little chap! But it'll be putting him out on his misery, and save him knowing a deal o' trouble in the world."

Mr. Nicholas Slime walked back to the place where the caravan still stood.

The Boozer had resumed his former position by the post, and was calmly enjoying his smoke.

"Better wait a little," the Gorger thought, "till away from the young beggars. They is fly, might be up to the fakement—they tumble to thing in a minit."

Boozer agreed with the suggestion.

"If," said the keeper of the caravan at this point, "I were to tell you all the strange and marvellous incidents connected with my career, you would smile at me in doubt. Yet, so much is truth stranger than fiction, that—"

"Where's the lion?" sang out Chimbley Joe.

"The lion?" said the showman, quietly.

"Yes, wot's the good o' showing us a picter if yer ain't got nothing inside?"

The crowd laughed; but the showman remained perfectly cool.

"And the fat woman!" shouted Tike; "what have you done with her?"

"Did yer eat the giant?" said little Dan, lighting a fuzee, which he dropped on to the finger of the doctor's boy. "And where's the dwarf?"

"My friends," said the showman, "not to give free and true replies to your very natural questions would be to bring upon myself the stigma of being an impostor. My explanation is simple. The giant quarrelled with the dwarf about the lady, and the giant, being a native of the Fiji Islands, actually ate the dwarf, who did not agree with him."

"I should think not," said Chimbley Joe, "it 'ud make me dreadfully sick. Then what's come o' the fat woman?"

"The last time I saw her," said the showman, gravely, "was during my stay at King Dahomey's court."

The crowd gave a yell of derisive doubt.

"To which I went with my wonderful curiosities," the showman continued. "I gave the king my giant and the fat woman, and the king gave me his beautiful slave, Leola. My lions I sold for a thousand guineas each to the Zoological Gardens, after they had dined on their keeper and tried to make a breakfast of me."

This was greeted with another yell.

"If you doubt me," said the showman, "all you have to do is to pay a visit to the Gardens and see for yourselves. Meanwhile, let me introduce to you the first of those marvellous curiosities which have made your humble servant, Whitechapel Dick, renowned throughout the universe."

"The last time he was here," said Chimbley Joe, in an audible whisper, "I seed a hospital wan going along full of people."

"What was they a-doing?" asked little Dan.

"They was incurables, 'cause o' hearin' him say them long words set 'em on a trying to say 'em too, and they broke their jaws over it."

"That little boy will never get along in this world," said Whitechapel Dick, bringing out an Indian basket, which he placed on a platform in front of the caravan door; "and now, gentlemen, if I were to tell you that this—"

He opened the basket, and the crowd watched him anxiously.

"If I were to tell you," he continued, "that this is a remedy for all the ills of mortal flesh, you would very properly say I was—"

"A awful fibber!" interposed somebody in the crowd.

"Thank you, the term is graphic," said Whitechapel Dick, "but expounds the sentiment exactly. I wish to impress one fact upon you."

He paused, and the crowd craned their necks and strained their eyes.

"My object in coming here is not to gain money. See!" he exclaimed, showering a handful of coppers among the throng and causing a wild scramble.

The Gorger tried to participate, his long hand going down upon a penny just as little Dan's foot made for the same coin, and the consequence was that little Dan's foot went crash upon the Gorger's hand.

"Yer little warmint!" he said, aiming a ferocious kick at Dan, who dodged away with the penny, "take that."

The Gorger had a tremendous foot—twelve inches and a little over; in fact, two of them upset a supposed arithmetical fact, and made a yard.

He missed Dan, and caught Spitalfields Boozer, who was stooping for a halfpenny in the mud.

Boozer turned over, and said nothing for nearly a minute; but the working of his eyes told the agony he suffered.

"I didn't mean it," said the Gorger, assisting his friend to rise. "I's very sorry, Boozer, old man."

"So you oughter be," said the afflicted one. "I thought a heliphant had run agin me with his trunk. But lor'! it's about my luck; I always did get more kicks than ha'pence."

The scramble was over. Boozer went back to his post.

# THE
# POOR BOYS OF LONDON
## OR, DRIVEN TO CRIME.

No. 4.]　　　　　**A LIFE STORY FOR THE PEOPLE.**　　　　　[ONE PENNY.

"*A rat—a rat!*" *cried Shakespeare Dick.* "*Dead for a ducat!*"

He had lost his pipe, and now could only rest himself. The Gorger picked up a stray halfpenny from the gutter, and then he stationed himself near to Gilbert.

"To benefit my fellow creatures," said White-chapel Dick, " is my only motive. I am rich. The magnificent generosity of his Majesty the Emperor Napoleon, who conferred upon me the order of

Truth and Honour for restoring the empress to health when every known remedy had failed, has placed me beyond want. I do not want money. See! here is a half-crown, for which I will take two and five-pence."

There was a pause; nobody seemed anxious to invest.

"No buyers?" he said. "Come! two four-and-a-half—a safe speculation on good money. Take it; test it! I will give anybody a pint of beer to take and get change for it. Who buys?"

Still no reply.

"Come!" said Whitechapel Dick. "Two and three, two and two, two and a penny, two shillings. Well, if you won't have that, here's another I can sell for eighteenpence, and give the buyer sixpence for taking it away."

"I'll have that," said Tike, "and chance it."

"Wait till your hair is a little longer, my lad," said Whitechapel Dick, smiling blandly. "People who are in a hurry never get rich. I will sell this half-crown to a respectable person for one shilling. A lady can have the two for one and tenpence."

Still there was no offer. It was thought to be a sell.

"'Tain't a good one," said Tike, savage at having been personally alluded to, rebuked, and laughed at. "'Tain't likely it could be, unless he steals em."

"There's a policeman just behind you," said Whitechapel Dick. "I think he knows you, my lad. Don't run away; it looks bad."

Tike slipped through the crowd, and performed the vanishing trick in double quick time.

"Come, my dear," said the cheap-jack to a girl who stood looking on much interested, "one-and tenpence is the price. Look! here is one. Catch. Pay me out of the change, and you shall have the other."

Half-curious, half-doubting—as woman is sure to be—the girl caught the coin.

She was a fair, pretty creature, and she blushed at being called into notice.

She tripped away, and returned soon with the change.

He took one shilling and tenpence and gave her the other half-crown with the air of a man who had made a profitable bargain.

As the crowd made way for the girl to reach the showman Alick caught sight of her face.

"Polly!" he said, and, forgetting Gilbert, he went after her.

She walked rapidly.

It took him some time to get through the crowd, and Polly was a good distance in advance before he started.

Following her to an old-fashioned church he saw her stop; a gentleman joined her on the instant.

Alick knew him again.

It was the man who had ridden in Jacob's cab when Chimbley Joe and himself rescued little Flory.

"He does not mean her any good," thought the lad. "I'll see."

He walked fast on the other side of the way -- turned, and met them face to face.

"Polly?" he said.

To his inexpressible surprise she did not speak to him, but went on.

She took no notice of his presence, except by a look meaning to tell him not to speak to her again.

"Polly," he muttered, "this looks very bad; a rich gentleman like that can't mean any good to a poor girl. And she's already ashamed of her own brother."

He turned again, and clutched the gentleman's arm.

"I want to know who you are," he said, resolutely, "and what you want. She's my sister, and I'm her brother. So tell me."

"Alick?" said Polly, reproachfully.

"Don't speak to me," he said, passionately. "I haven't seen you for a week, and now I meet you with a man who can't mean any good. He has taught you to be ashamed of me already."

"Very good, lad," said the stranger. "I admire your affection for this lady; but don't be stupid. She is old enough to know whom she can trust herself with, and does not doubt me as you do."

"She hasn't seen so much as I have," said Alick. "I know the world better than she does."

"Then go away like a good boy," said Eastlake. "Take this sovereign, and amuse yourself."

"What, let my sister go with you? No!"

He struck the piece of gold from Eastlake's hand.

Eastlake, expecting further violence, struck Alick with his cane, and the boy was upon him in an instant.

He was strong and big for his age, and Eastlake found him an antagonist not to be despised.

"Rash boy!" he said, "let go. I do not want to hurt you, for your sister's sake."

"Say that you won't see her again, then?"

"Nonsense! Let go."

"Alick—Alick!" sobbed Polly; "don't."

But Alick would. He grew so violent that Eastlake, in self-defence, had to throw him off. He rose again, but, before he could reach his opponent, a policeman had him by the collar.

"I saw it all, the young ruffian," said the constable. "Come along with me."

"No—no!" sobbed Polly; "no—no!"

"I have no wish to prosecute," said Eastlake; "only see that he does no mischief."

Alick acted rashly then.

The policeman would not let him go, and Alick struck him.

"Now it's a case on my own account," said the constable, tightening his grasp, and dragging Alick away. "Come along."

"Save him!" sobbed Polly; "save him!"

"Just now it would be worse than useless to interfere," said Eastlake. "The policeman is bound to prosecute. I will save the lad, however. I will see these men in an hour or so, and a little money will make all right."

"Thanks—oh! thanks."

They went on, he talking to her in a low tone, and between her thoughts of Alick and her bewilderment at what was being said by her companion, she didn't notice which way he led her.

Alick, dragged powerlessly along by his brawny captor, felt more fiercely and bitterly than ever his angry feelings rise against the world.

"They shall have what they want," he said, between his teeth. "It only wants that; let anything happen to Poll, and they shall have such a vagabond as London has not seen yet."

Meanwhile Whitechapel Dick pushed a rapid sale of cheap half-crowns, and gathered an immense crowd together.

Then he introduced the first of his wonderful inventions, which was pills.

"Here is thirty doses," he said, "and with the thirty pills contained in this little box I promise to cure effectually the most obstinate cough. One pill must be taken at night, another in the morning; by the time the box is empty the cough will be gone."

He offered to deposit fifty pounds at any near tradesman's, as security for his word, and sold lots of pills.

When he was about to introduce a second wonderful medicine, Chimbley Joe suddenly missed Alick.

He turned to look for him, and saw him being taken to the police-station.

"Hallo!" he said, "in for it again. What's the bobby want with him, I wonder?"

He followed to see, and Little Dan trotted after him.

"Now's our time," said the Gorger to Boozer; "we shall get him—the other little thieves are out of the way."

He went to Gilbert; he not yet having missed his companions, stood staring at Whitechapel Dick, thinking Alick would return.

The Gorger touched him on the shoulder.

"Little boy," he said, insinuatingly, "would you like to earn a penny?"

"Yes, sir," Gilbert said, glad to have the chance.

"Then look a here. Just run down to the New Cut. Ask anybody for the Pig and Porridge Pot. Give this letter to a gentleman there — Mr. Burkett."

"Yes, sir."

"Don't tell anyone where you are going," said the Gorger.

"No, sir."

"Wait for an answer."

"Yes, sir."

"Then come back to me for the penny."

"Yes, sir."

The poor little fellow started off on his errand.

"Poor little warmint!" soliloquised the Gorger, watching him go. "I hope the Bosker will put him out of the way quietly. I'll go to Mr. Eastlake and let him know. I'll—hullo!"

He stood face to face with David Eastlake.

## CHAPTER IX.

THE GORGER DETERMINES TO HAVE A JOLLIFICATION WITH HIS TWO-PUN-TEN.

"WHO was that boy you sent up the road just now?" Eastlake demanded.

"Him," said the Gorger.

"Him!" Eastlake repeated, suppressing a start. "What, the boy from Norwich?"

Nicholas nodded; and grinned all over his ugly face.

"Good. Where have you sent him?" David Eastlake demanded.

"To Burkett."

"Where?"

"At the Pig and Porridge Pot."

"That will do," said Eastlake, approvingly. "You are a cur, but that fault is counterbalanced by the cunning of your low rascality. Here."

He slipped five sovereigns quietly into the Gorger's hand, and Nicholas Slime as quietly slipped them out of sight, thinking to avoid the eye of Spitafields Boozer, but failed to do so.

"Burkett well knows what to do, I suppose?" said Eastlake.

"I tipped the office, sir, in the letter I sent the boy with," the Gorger replied.

"He will not let him go," Eastlake said, reflectively.

"No fear," the Gorger replied; "he knows too well which side his bread is buttered to do that."

"He will be safe till to-morrow night?"

"Quite."

"See that it is so," Eastlake said, "and tell Burkett to expect me then. I shall be there late; by midnight, let us say."

"I'll tell him, sir," the Gorger replied.

"Do so at once," said David Eastlake, turning to depart. "I have other business in hand at present."

At that instant he caught the gaze of Whitechapel Dick set full upon him.

Both started slightly, and an exclamation rose to the cheap-jack's lips, but he suppressed it.

It was certainly a recognition, but it passed so quickly that Eastlake thought he must be mistaken.

Such, however, was not the case with Whitechapel Dick. He recognised the face, as one he would as soon have looked on as Satan's own, for he had bitter cause to remember it.

An instant, however, and he was going on glibly with the sale of his wonderful inventions, and Eastlake, taking a long and furtive glance at him, went away slowly.

"Impossible!" he muttered; "it cannot be, and yet so like him that could I think the dead can rise from their grave, I should think he had come back to haunt me. I almost fancied he started too; it must have been fancy only."

"I think I can put you up to a good thing, Nick, my boy," whispered the Boozer, in the large ear of his friend, the Gorger; "so let's go an' have a pint of summat warm, and fork out half."

The Gorger did not much like that proposition.

"He didn't give me nothing, Spitalfields; I'm to have it to-morrow night."

"You'll get it this afternoon," said the Boozer, doubling his grimy fist, "if you come any tricks with me, you long, greedy hostrich, wanting to do a cove out of his 'onest earnings; think I didn't see it?"

"See what, Boozer?" demanded the Gorger, with a face as long as a fiddle.

"Why the shiners. A regular handful. Five on 'em at least. I want two-pun-ten, or I lands you one and blows on you arterwards."

Nicholas Slime felt dreadfully uncomfortable, and turned all sorts of colours.

He clung to money with a miser's love for it, but he knew it would be bad to trifle with the dirty brawny vagabond before him.

"You needn't get wild, old man," he said, conciliatingly, "I was only a jokin' with you."

"It's a sort o' joke I don't keer for, Nick, old boy," said the Boozer. "Down with the coin fust, and then joke as much as you like."

So they went into the nearest public-house and called for a pint of dog's nose, which is a mixture of gin and beer.

"Seeing as its cold," rasped Spitalfields, "'spose we make it a quartern to the pint and have one each."

"With a bit of pork pie," said the Gorger, lifting one from the bottom of a plate, which was turned upside down and had a glass shade over it, to keep the flies from making themselves ill; "it's a genuine Pimlico one."

"Close nigh the refooge for destitoot dogs," said the Boozer.

"Now look you, old man," said Nicholas Slime. "Don't go for to spile a feller's appetite."

'Are your's deliket?'

"Like a babby's," the Gorger replied.

"Then, if I was you, I wouldn't eat pork," said the Boozer. "I know as how in a medical book it tells dreadful things about pork. There's tiny worms, as you can only see through a mikriscope, as gets into your wains, and irritates you awfully."

This interesting announcement was made while the Gorger had his mouth full of beer, pork, and pie-crust, and did not add a relish to the meal.

"Nasty beggar!" he said, putting down his pie and going to the door. "I—"

The rest was indistinct.

The Gorger dodged round the corner, with his head down and his hand up to his mouth.

"Thought he would," said the Boozer, placidly taking up the pie and a position by the bar partition where he could lounge at ease; "it's having a himagination, that is."

And he ate the pie which the Gorger had turned against so suddenly.

"Only think," said Nicholas Slime, running back, pale and spiteful, for a little brandy cold, "of the worms irritatin' of you! Why, you seems to be able to eat anything!"

"Always could," rasped the Boozer, pitching a loose fragment of crust down his throat. "Drink up and let's have another—then you can fork out. You'd better do it now, while I think of it—not as I should forget it, but you might."

Very reluctantly the Gorger produced four out of the five sovereigns.

He would have kept two back, but they would have chinked, so he left only one.

"You ought to take one and be satisfied, Boozer, old man," he said, dolefully.

"I know I ought," the Boozer replied; "but people don't always do wot they orter, or I should a seen you doing the tight-rope performance long ago. Two-pun-ten's the figger, so out with the oof." ·

"What, out of four?" gasped the Gorger.

"Gammon! there was five," said Boozer. "I've got a heye like a 'awk. You can't deceive me."

"See," said Nicholas Slime, shaking his pocket with an air of sincerity.

"You wasn't old when you was born," said Boozer, with a leer, "of course not. One suvrin don't chink by itself, does it?"

"Look 'ere, Spitalfields—" began the Gorger.

"Now wot's the use a trying to diddle me? Don't I know you? Ain't I fly to the fakement?" said Boozer, interrupting him. "Two-pun-ten I wants. I was up as early as you this morning."

The Gorger wished he had gone to bed again.

He put down two coins, one by one, slowly.

Then he looked at Boozer and Boozer looked at him.

"Now you ken pay for the lush and the cigars, my pal, and I can pick up the half-suvrin."

The Gorger indulged in a wholesale groan and paid.

There had been at the bar during the progress of this incident a labourer in a flannel jacket.

He came in in a zig-zag, slouching fashion, as a labourer when not at work is apt to come.

He stood in the next compartment of the bar over a pint of six ale, apparently practising the science of involuntary oscillation—that is to say, he balanced himself slowly, first on his heels, then on his toes, and his head swayed to and fro on its own account.

Now the Boozer, having lounged himself by degrees half way along the partition, got against the door without knowing it.

He had had the measure of gin and beer just replenished which he held in his hand, and the door, which did not happen to be bolted, let him through on his back with a tremendous crash.

The labourer, being startled, and just then on a balance of extreme heel, gave way, and dropped bodily upon the Boozer's region of wind.

Exactly that peculiar sound that a road-maker makes when he drops his ponderous mallet on the stones, broke from the Boozer, a snorting sort of gasp, very amusing to hear but painful to the gasper.

"Halloa! mate," said the labourer; "anybody tumbling down?"

He lurched over heavily.

"Tumbling be blowed!" panted the Boozer. "Why don't they keep the blessed door fastened, and you needn't a-come down like a house on a fellow's dinner receptacle."

"I ax your pardon, mate," the labourer said, as he rose and began to sway again. "Fill yer pot again. I'll pay for it."

"Thank'ee; I've had enough," the Boozer growled.

"Just as you like," said the labourer. "I can't do more than ax pardon and fill your pot again. If that don't soot I'm good for anything—stand treat, toss you for it, or have a round outside."

"I don't want no round outside," replied the

Boozer, who did not like the look of the man's muscular arms. "Only you needn't a fell upon a cove."

"Could I help it?" demanded the labourer, running his eye over the Boozer, as if to judge his fighting capabilities.

"Didn't say you cood," said the Boozer, lurching through the door again, taking care to fasten it this time. "Come on, Nick; let's go to the Pig and give Dan Garnett a turn."

The mention of Pig made Mr. Slime want another threepen'orth of cold brandy, having drank which they departed.

They had not been gone a minute before the labourer in the flannel jacket went out rather more zig-zag than he went in, and followed them.

This independent Briton took a deal of the pavement; he went methodically from the kerb to the shop windows and from the shop windows to the kerb, getting much in the way of other passengers, but nobody stopped him.

It might not have been good for anybody's health if they had, for he was a man of middle height, with broad shoulders and a heavy face, and his hands were in his pockets with his elbows sticking out.

In a word, he was the kind of man who could drink lots of beer and sing "Rule, Britannia!" at a free-and-easy, and go comfortably home with a black eye.

"Going to give Dan Garnett a turn, are they?" he muttered. "Very well. I'll give him a turn, too, but I won't trouble him with my custom just yet. His beer might not be good for me."

He smiled once or twice in a self-satisfied sort of way, thinking of the Boozer as the Boozer had looked when he spilt his gin and beer over his own face.

The Gorger soon got clear of his knowing friend the Boozer, and went on his way alone.

The possession of so much loose cash was a new luxury to the Gorger. He was afraid it would not last, so he determined to make the most of it while he could.

"If I was to go about with this lot o' tin," he thought, chinking the gold and silver between his fingers, which were thrust in his pockets, "I should be a mark for them as likes what isn't their own. No; I'll have a jolly blow out this time, if I never do again. Let me see—one and five and seven, that's two bob, and a tanner's 'arf-a-crown leaves two pun seven an' six, an' two pun seven an' six—"

"My eye!" cried a boy's voice at his side, "here's a cove counting of his chips; ain't he rolling a stunning lot in his pocket?"

The Gorger turned round with a scared look, and saw that two street boys were beside him.

"Go home, my little kiddies," said the Gorger, whose teeth had begun to chatter—"go home, my lovely little covies, or you'll have your mammies waiting for yer with the copper-stick."

"Oh, crikey! Hear that, Costy?"

"Yes; ain't he got a nerve?"

"Got a hat, too. I say, guv'nor, don't want to sell that tile, do you?"

"Not without the head in it," chimed Costy Dick, a sharp-eyed, ragged urchin, about up to the Gorger's waist, "'cos he has to double hisself inside it every night to dodge away from his mammy when she brings round the spoonful of treacle for him and the other blessed babies."

"You cheeky young cubs!" the Gorger cried, his dignity touched by their impudence. "Take that, and be blowed to you!"

He made a terrific sweep with his long arm.

Costy Dick and his chum dodged out of the way, and the Gorger, getting his heel on a bit of soft orange peel, slipped along the pavement.

The kerbstone was hard as well as slippery; the Gorger came down with a jerk, his back settling against the sharp edge of a lamp-post.

He did not seem in a hurry to move; his long, lanky legs went wide apart, his heels stuck out, his jaws opened wide, and his hat jumped on to the back of his head.

His eyes watered, and he looked about for his teeth, of which he thought at least a dozen had jerked out.

The two boys danced round him in glee.

"Here's a lark!" said Costy Dick. "Blessed if you ain't a picter. Shouldn't I like to have yer fortygruff took in that hattitude. Take better than old Daddy's that they giv' five bob for a sittin'—only he didn't sit like that."

"Lost any of your chips, old chap?" asked the other.

Very painfully and slowly the Gorger began to get up, with the feeling that the skin of his backbone was sticking to his coat.

The street boys did a new dance round him.

Costy Dick could not resist the temptation to give his hat a settler, which he did with such force that the Gorger suddenly found himself in complete darkness.

By the time he could see the boys had scampered out of sight.

"If ever I catches hold of 'em," soliloquised Nicholas Slime, slowly, as he felt in his pockets for his money, "I'll pull their ears till they squeaks like pigs when they sees a butcher."

The Gorger was savage.

He caught the eye of a policeman who was over the way watching him at that moment, and, like a detected cur, he slunk down a back alley, his shaking knees knocking together as he went.

Evening was coming on, and Nicholas Slime began to feel the gnawings of his never-satisfied appetite.

He had sneaked into the New Cut, and in the shop windows and on the stalls were displayed viands of the choicest kind.

Pigs' feet, mealy potatoes, pease pudding, boiled pork and beef, sausages and saveloys, with other delicacies, that made him instinctively rub his long stomach.

The pork, roast and boiled, was tempting, but the Boozer had spoilt his appetite for it.

He looked at a tempting pile of rich saveloys, and he thought how it would astonish the shopkeeper if he were to go in and buy the whole lot.

Ultimately he made up his mind to buy six pennyworth.

With these in one hand, and a huge portion of pease-pudding in the other, he sallied from the shop.

"I'll stow four away while I eat the other two," soliloquised the Gorger, putting four away in his pocket. "It 'ud look greedy to be seen with the lot."

This was very much to the satisfaction of several hungry-eyed urchins, who had watched his movements with longing eyes, and now came suspiciously close to him as if they had taken a great fancy to following him.

The Gorger was in the enjoyment of the second saveloy when a dirty-faced urchin came tumbling between his legs.

"Now then," cried the Gorger, sprawling out his foot and giving the boy a kick, "where are you comin' to?"

"Couldn't help it; Jim shoved me under," cried the urchin.

"I'll shove Jim," replied the Gorger, angrily turning round, and speaking with his mouth full.

The boys were all standing in the same posture —each had their legs wide apart, and each was taking a sight at him, with their dirty fingers stuck to their dirty noses.

When the Gorger turned round they cried, "Yah! there's a guy," and bolted down a narrow alley.

"Them boys gets precious cheeky," muttered the Gorger, feeling in his pocket for the other saveloys. "Hullo!" he gasped. "All gone, every blessed one on 'em."

Had the Gorger looked down the dark turning he would have seen the four boys engaged in the pleasing task of munching the saveloys they had so dexterously extracted from his pocket.

There was only one alloy to their joy.

They wanted a share of the pease-pudding to complete their banquet.

"Bless'd if I ain't in for it, to-day," muttered the Gorger, ruefully. "If I don't look sharp I sha'n't get nothing out of my two-pun-ten. I'll dodge into this 'ere public, they sells 'ard eggs, an' I can put away ten or a dozen on 'em, with mustard an' salt, while I thinks what else I'll have."

Only a few people were at the bar when Nick Slime slouched in.

A delicious pile of white, shining eggs, boiled hard and ready peeled, were in a dish on the counter, under a glass case, to keep people's fingers from them.

"Ten on 'em," said the Gorger, pointing to the dish.

The barman stared, but a glance at the hungry jowl of his customer sufficed him, and he laid the ten luscious eggs on a plate.

"A pint of 'arf-an'-'arf," was the Gorger's next order, as he took half an egg at one mouthful, while his greedy eyes glared on the tempting pile still left on his plate.

Several famished wretches came in while he was at his selfish meal. Some for half-a-pint of porter, some to beg, some to sell matches, but all half starved, tattered, and pinched.

They could not keep their eyes off the Gorger's feast, and went out with a sigh when they could stay no longer.

Many men—hardened and desperate criminals— had they been in luck as he was, would have offered a share. But the Gorger was as greedy as he was cowardly. He turned his back on them while he ate, determined to enjoy his feed alone.

Presently a boy put his head in at the door and spied him, and the Gorger immediately became the object of admiring observation.

"Oh!" one ragged little wretch cried, "ain't he having a blessed blow-out."

"He's got a fine mouth for cold taters," said another.

"Say, Billy," observed a third, "shouldn't like to be a dead donkey in his way."

"No; he'd eat hoofs an' tail an' all."

"Let's come away, he's eating for a wager."

"No, he ain't; he's a practisin' to see how far he can stretch his innards."

The Gorger found these remarks more free than complimentary, but he stuck to his repast till he had forced down the last mouthful, and had washed his throat down with the beer.

"Emptied the blessed pot an' all," remarked a boy, a dissatisfied observer of the Gorger's gluttony. "Not so much left as you could put in your heye. He can do a gorge!"

"I'll take another pint of 'arf-and-'arf," said the Gorger, deigning the boys no notice.

"Any more eggs, sir?" he asked, smiling as he removed the plate.

The Gorger hesitated and pondered on whether he should make up the dozen.

He counted the money in his pocket.

"Well, they are fine," he observed, with a satisfied sigh; "you may give me two more."

The boys set up a perfect yell.

"Oh! crikey, he's going to have another tuck in," they cried. "Here is the big elephant man from Chiney, wot's been a eating of all the babies, come to show hisself an' bust."

"Now, cut away there," said the barman. "The peeler's at the door."

The boys slipped away like young eels.

But now and then one or two returned to peep at this strange phenomenon, whom they had already nicknamed the Gorger.

At last the Gorger was satisfied, and walked into the open air.

Any ordinary man under the circumstances would have presented a blown appearance, but such was not the case with Nicholas Slime.

He looked as thin and hungry as ever, and a benevolent old lady stopped and looked at him, and meditated whether she should give him a penny or not.

Before she could make up her mind one way or the other, a strange object, with a troop of boys at his heels, came rushing round the corner.

The cause of the commotion was a hatless, ragged, big-headed, wild-looking man, who was known in some localities as Richard the Third, and in others as Shakespeare Dick.

He gained a precarious livelihood by reciting stirring passages from the immortal bard's works, which he mixed up according to his fancy. Shakespeare Dick was never without a wooden sword, which he flourished about during every performance.

"Ha !" he cried, glaring at the Gorger. "What do I see? Are there two Richmonds in the field? A 'orse, a 'orse ; my kingdom for a 'orse."

"P'raps you'd take arf of it for a donkey?" observed Nicholas Slime, with a grin.

"Oh ! speak again, sweet hangel," Shakespeare Dick cried, shaving the tip of the Gorger's nose with his wooden sword. "Oh ! that I was a glove upon that 'and, that I might touch that cheek. Wot's in a name, Romeo. A rose by any other name would smell as sweet."

"Hooray !—hooray ! Go it, Dick," shouted the boys.

"He's off his nut !" gasped the Gorger, aghast at the performance, which, strangely enough, he had never seen before. "Wot's the matter with him ?"

"Hangels and bannisters of grace defend hus," screeched Shakespeare Dick. "Be thou a spirit of earth or goblin—ahem ! not bein' allowed to swear in public, I'll say 'jammed.' Brings with thee airs from 'eaven or—ahem—'urricanes from the lower regions? Be thy intents wicked or charitable? Thou comest in such a questionable shape that I'll speak to thee. I'll call thee King. Father ! —'Amlet ! Oh ! speak to me, and let me not bust in hignorance."

"It'll be a case of bustin' anyhow presently," observed the Gorger, as he dodged the sword a second time. "Poor chap ! he's mad, and orter be in a loonatic asylum."

"Aye ! mad, my lord," roared the street actor ; "but faith you'll find that there is a method in my madness. Oh ! 'Amlet, 'Amlet, wot rash an' hawful deed is this? Just as good, kind me-other, as to murder a king and marry with his ber-other. A rat—a rat ! Dead for a ducat !"

Here he lunged out with the wooden sword and caught the Gorger in the region where apron strings are generally tied, and the lanky one, taken off his balance, fell into the arms of the benevolent old lady, who had not as yet made the offer of the penny.

Nicholas Slime and the ancient party in petticoats performed a frantic waltz, and finally went down with a crash, to the delight of the beholders.

"Oh ! wot a falling off is here," Shakespeare Dick said, sternly. "Gentleman, the dramy is finished. Spare a penny, if you please."

As no coppers were forthcoming the street actor went his way before the Gorger could stagger to his feet.

"This 'ere's a day of haccidents," he groaned, as he regained the perpendicular. "It warn't my fault, old lady. Him with the wooden sword did it."

"If you are a gentleman, you'll help me to get up," the woman said. "Oh ! you long, good-for-nothin' willain."

The Gorger did the gallant with very bad grace, and then slunk away, to find a more genial clime in which to invest the balance of his money.

The labourer before alluded to, going to the corner of the New Cut, stopped at a barrow, at which stood a policeman cracking nuts with a privileged costermonger.

He said something in a low tone to the policeman, and the policeman dropped a handful of nuts into his coat-tail pocket.

"No," he said.

"Yes," said the labourer. "At the Pig and Porridge Pot."

"Then," said the policeman, "we'll nab 'em."

"Thickhead—"

"Eh ?"

"Thickhead—is nabbing the game till he is found."

"Who do you mean ?"

"Grant."

"Ah !" said the policeman, with an air of wisdom, "I see."

"We must have the lot," said the labourer ; "to take one would be to put the others on their guard. I'm very much mistaken if Burkett isn't there."

The policeman shook his head and whistled softly.

"The night man ain't seen him, and I haven't seen him," he said.

"That goes for nothing," the labourer observed. "Dan Garnett's customers are pretty safe. I've seen 'em go into the house, and gone in after 'em, searched every room, and then not found 'em."

"Ah !"

"Keep your eye on the place."

"I will."

All this was spoken in a low tone, and the labourer went on again, but steadily, and with a measured tread now.

"I'm afraid it's all up with Grant," he said, regretfully, to himself. "I always thought he would go too far some day. He had too much pluck—a lot too much."

"Clean yer boots, sir ?" queried a youthful voice.

The labourer paused and looked down.

A shoeblack was kneeling in the road with his box on the kerb.

"Here you are, sir ; do 'em in a minit, sir," said the boy, pleadingly.

The labourer put his heavy bluchers on the box. The shoeblack was Captain Jack.

"Has he been found yet, sir ?" he demanded.

"No, Jack ; but he will be," the labourer replied, in a familiar tone of voice. "Everyone who left the kitchen that night has had a man after him."

"I think it's the Bosker," said Jack.

"Have you seen him ?" the labourer asked.

"No ; but I know where he is. You'll find him, I think, at Dan Garnett's."

"I think so too," the labourer observed. "But how do you know ?"

"About an hour ago I saw a boy coming along, and he asked me the way," Captain Jack replied. "I saw a letter in his hand, and got out of him that it was for a Mr. Burkett."

"Jack, you will make one of us some day," said the labourer.

"I hope so. He was to go back to the corner of Kennington-road to the man that sent him. By the description the man must be Nicholas Slime. He went up the court just now with the Boozer."

Grant was being well looked after.

The detectives, who were led by Captain Jack into the thieves' kitchen, had been baffled by the villainous Jew and his accomplices.

Every one of the gang had fled by secret ways before the detectives entered the kitchen, which looked like a rag and bone store then.

Bales of rags and boxes of bones were piled in disorder where the table and seats had been.

The police made a long and vigorous search, but found nothing.

Even the counting-house, as the murder-room with its treacherous trap and iron door was called, was cleared of every trace that might have told the sanguinary struggle which had taken place there.

Nathan Claws was prepared for every emergency.

He knew that the blood marks would betray him were they seen ; but they were not seen.

Some hidden machinery set to work brought out from the bottom of the well a complete floor, which covered the old one, and hid the trap completely.

The police, who sounded every inch of wall and floor, were baffled, and on their return found old Nathan with Rebecca in the greasy parlour behind the shop.

There, also, sat a dark-eyed, beautiful girl—the Jew's daughter.

She looked pale and troubled. Her mother was scared. The Jew himself looked startled by the advent of the police.

"Moses !" he cried ; "what is the matter. Why do you come here troubling a respectable trades-man ?"

"Cleverly done, old Nathan," said the leader of the police ; "but we shall find him yet, if we tear your old house down to its foundation."

"Find who ?"

"The man we seek. Look out ! You are watched."

So with this warning they departed, and Richard Grant was left to a dreadful and apparently inevitable death.

He was not dead yet.

The fall had only partly stunned him.

His hands were maimed, his limbs bruised—only the brave heart was left untouched, but there was no despair in that.

He soon recovered from the shock of the fall, and found himself in darkness, with no gleam of light or sound to guide him.

He had fallen on his side, partly against the wall, and when he was fully conscious, he discovered what the Jew had meant by saying—"The water-cellar."

When the river was at high tide this vault was filled to the height of ten feet with water.

Now, in his reclining position, it reached to his waist, and Grant, therefore, came to the conclusion that the river was at low tide.

He sat still for a few minutes to recover his scattered faculties.

"I see," he murmured, "they thought the fall would kill me, or so stun me into helplessness that I should lie here to die as the waters rise. Not yet, not yet. Courage, Richard Grant. There is hope."

He rose cautiously, and felt carefully about him with both hands and feet.

What was that ?

Groping round the wall his hand touched a piece of iron projecting.

To catch at this and grasp it firmly was the work of an instant.

His arms, though weakened by the shock of falling, still retained sufficient power to lift his body by the help of the projecting iron.

He drew himself up and felt higher still.

Hope ! How it rushed warmly to his heart, giving him life and energy anew, for there was another piece of iron two feet above the level of the last.

Forcing his knee upon the first, he clung to the second, and felt again.

"Life !" he muttered, "life ! They will not destroy me after all. Oh ! for a way of escape, and then revenge."

He found that these projecting irons rose in regular succession up the wall, much in the style by which means of ascent and descent are provided to the street sewers.

There was not much in this to keep him from despair, but it was a chance of escape for a while at least, for by means of the irons he could keep himself beyond reach of the water.

If he could only have space enough to breathe until the water went down again, he might devise a means of escape.

The hot blood rushed to his heart with the new hope of life.

"I know enough to repay them all," he cried, "if I can only get from this horrible hole."

"I will put a rope round his neck," as he rested his swollen hand on the cold iron—the Bosker's iron heel had crushed the flesh to the bone—"and when I have him safe he shall know who has hunted him down."

Detective Grant set his teeth firmly together.

It was too dark for him to see, but he could hear the water slowly rising.

He climbed a step higher, and leaned against the slimy wall.

An hour and more he crouched in that cramped position—crouched with the patient energy of a man who knew he was fighting a silent battle with death.

The water drove him higher still, till he got to the highest projecting iron, and here he was forced to remain, while the gurgling fœtid sewage trickled in his ear, and surged higher, till the noxious vapours almost threatened to stifle him if the putrid waters did not succeed in drowning him.

He had to hold on a long weary time.

How many hours he did not know, as he could not count the weary minutes as they went.

His limbs were stiff and his body cramped.

Once or twice the iron hooks seemed sliding from his grasp, and brave as he was at heart, a clammy perspiration began to bead his face at the thought of falling back into the horrible waters.

Only his head and neck were now free.

The water flowed over his shoulders, and still rose inch by inch. It was horrible!

Richard Grant drew himself up till his knees rested on the rusty iron, but drew back as his face touched the icy wall.

A monstrous rat had dashed swiftly past his very eyes.

Here was a new terror.

Another came, and then another.

The dark slushy bodies brushed his cheeks, and the wretched man knew that the brutes were growing bolder.

And in the darkness he could see their fearful eyes glaring ravenously upon him.

A deep, deadly cry of rage broke from the detective's lips.

How he resolved in his bitterness to take a sure and merciless revenge should he again reach the outer world.

His low, sullen cry scared the huge water rats, and he heard them fall with a splash into the water.

But in a little while they came again.

They came, peering closer into his unqualing eyes, touching him with their soft paws and bodies, and at last one bolder than the rest made a sudden dart, and fixed its sharp fangs in his arm.

Every muscle on the detective's arm writhed.

His whole body was drawn up as he tried to shake the animal off his arm.

But the little teeth were firmly fixed, and began their swift work of tearing the flesh in strips.

Grant could not move either hand or foot to defend himself.

The pressure of the water was so great that had he relinquished his hold of the irons by either hand he would have been sucked down below the seething mass, and suffocated at the bottom of the cellar, to lie there and rot till the rats finished him.

It was this thought that roused him to sudden frenzy.

Bringing his head down to his chest he seized the rat with his teeth by the middle of its body, as a bull terrier would have done, and with one powerful pressure of his jaws squeezed the life out of it.

With a savage force he flung it among his fellows.

The others were crowding near him, but this sudden act scared them away a second time, and before they came again Richard Grant could feel that the water in the cellar was slowly sinking.

It was a glorious hope.

He did not mind the rats when they again attacked him, as he was as savage as they.

He had one arm free now, and seizing the nearest rat he dashed its brains out against the walls.

Another and another shared the same fate.

The detective was mad with frenzied strength.

He knew not how long the battle lasted, but when it was over, and the remainder plunged into the waters, he uttered a hoarse cry of triumph, and defied the worst to come.

By degrees, as the waters subsided, and he began to feel the benumbing effects of the cramp and chills to which he had been so long subjected, his strength went from him, and a stupor overcame him that seemed like the stupor of death.

He roused himself suddenly.

He was letting go his hold. One hand still clutched the iron.

He smiled with grim purpose, and, shaking the moisture from his drenched and shivering form, slowly crept down the iron stands.

The floor of the cellar was still a foot or more deep, but Richard Grant did not mind that.

He waded through it boldly.

An idea had occurred to him, and he asked himself the question how the water found its way into the cellar.

He waded on till his progress was arrested by the growing deepness of the water.

While he waited for the tide to go down, he groped about the dark, dank walls, in hope of finding more of those projecting irons.

He felt one presently, and, crawling further on, found another.

His detective sagacity was excited now.

The irons did not go up the wall, but along it.

He was certain that they were placed there for some purpose, and that purpose the guidance of human footsteps.

Placing his feet on the iron, he stood upright, felt another above his head, and holding this with both hands, stepped along the wall.

The mode was difficult and dangerous, but Richard Grant was not the man to be daunted after what he had seen and endured.

He crawled along the tortuous way till he got into a tunnel-like passage, so narrow that he was forced to go on to his hands and knees to enter it.

It was half-filled with water.

But by keeping his head near the arched roof he contrived to get air enough to breathe, and halfway along the narrow tube he paused.

The low rushing of waters sounded behind him.

He tried to look in the direction he had come.

His position was one of imminent peril.

To be overtaken by a flood would be speedy death, for there was no way of escape if once that narrow passage was blocked up.

The detective set his teeth harshly together.

It was hard to die now without a struggle, yet perhaps if he turned back he might yet escape.

He hesitated, but only for a moment.

During which time the chances of life and death were swiftly weighed in his mind, and he decided not to turn back, but to go on, taking the risk, whether it led him to liberty or his doom.

He pushed on further, and found that the water was increasing in volume.

Now and then he had to dart through it, for it flooded to the roof; but with his head once more free he breathed anew the hope of escape.

After one of these suffocating immersions he put up his hands and felt no roof.

A joyful cry escaped him.

As far as he could reach there was no obstruction over him, and with difficulty raising himself he stood upright.

A draught of air, pure by comparison, came down the shaft.

He felt for the irons which instinct told him were there, and soon found one.

Mounting this he reached another, and then another.

Weak as he was he could have laughed in gladness.

He imagined when he reached the top he should find himself in the open street.

That he was mistaken he surmised at once when he felt an old and broken wooden trap above his head.

A slight push enabled him to raise it.

He forced his way through, and springing to his feet, found himself in a room of a riverside house.

"Free—free!" he said, in wild joy. "Safe! Now for escape and revenge!"

## CHAPTER X.

THE OLD HOUSE BY THE RIVER-SIDE—FOSKY MIKE, THE RIVER RAT — THE ROOM OF DEATH.

It was a dreary-looking building by the water-side; Grant could see that by the first look he gave through the broken windows.

He did not give a thought to the dangers that might menace him in the house.

Indeed, it seemed deserted.

He was seeking for a means of egress when a ponderous door was thrust open, and a human being appeared, at sight of whom Detective Grant instinctively crept back.

The stranger was a tall, powerful man, with broad shoulders and tremendous arms and limbs.

A rough, shaggy cap was drawn over his immense head, and his legs were encased to the thigh in thick leather boots.

His coat was of dark velveteen, with a band over his shoulder, and he had a thick belt round his waist.

When he saw the detective he paused abruptly, and a sinister look settled on his scowling face.

"Hallo!" he roared, with the voice of a bull; "who the devil are you, and what do you want here?"

Richard Grant took the measure of his man before he answered.

"A man like yourself," he said. "Help me from this place. I have no wish to stay."

"I daresay not," replied the man, laughing. "But I'd like to know how you came here, first?"

"Not to seek you. I came by the trap."

"The trap?" repeated the man, and his features underwent a sudden change.

"And how the devil did you get there?" he cried, with a savage emphasis in his voice.

"By accident," replied Grant. "I fell into the sewer, and found my way here."

"Oh—oh! fell into the sewer," said the man. "Ha—ha! that's a likely tale, my friend; and pray what did you see on your way here? Plenty of rats, eh? Dead cats and dogs, and that sort of thing, eh?"

The man's voice trembled, though he tried to hide his visible agitation.

"I did see plenty of rats," Richard Grant answered. "I am glad I saw nothing more—they were enough."

The man laughed with more assurance; he was better at ease.

"Yes," he remarked. "I daresay you found 'em enough; they're bad companions in a dark cellar with the water rising up to the top brick, eh?"

Strong as the detective was physically, he shuddered.

"You may as well tell how you got down there," the man said, after a steady survey of Grant's features. "I like to know my visitor's secrets—and you won't do yourself any harm by telling me."

Grant hesitated, as the man might be a confederate of the Jew, Nathan Claws.

"Why should it concern you?" he asked.

"Oh! nothing; only I like to know, that's all."

"Do you not know of any place from which I might find my way into the sewers?" Grant demanded.

"Well, yes; I do know of one or two, though they don't think I know so much about their secrets," the man replied. "There's Nathan Claws' place for one."

"The very man," Grant replied, quickly. "It was from his den that I went down into the sewer."

"Whew—ew! And what, pray, was the reason why old Nathan wished to get you out of the way?"

"My name will be sufficient. I am Grant, the detective."

"I've heard of you," replied the man, slowly, "and you must be a fellow of nerve to tell your name to a stranger in this place; but as I've nothing to do with old Nathan or his set I sha'n't stand in the way of your getting out again."

Even with the delicious prospect of sweet liberty before him Grant was cautiously reserved. He had accurately taken the standard of the man before him, and knew he might at any moment be dangerous.

"I shall not be sorry to get out," he said, "I am faint with my journey hither."

He paused as a sudden thought struck him.

"The way I came led to that den of crime," he exclaimed; "would you offer any opposition to my taking some men with me by the same way?"

"No—no, Richard Grant. I don't care about letting people get there through my place. I shouldn't have thought either that you'd want to go that way again, though I have travelled it often. It would be a trick on Nathan, though," he added, with a grin. "Ha! you'd give something to know what I know, and see what I've seen about that place. There's many a secret crime they think hid under the river that I could tell them a different tale about."

"It might be worth your while to be paid for the information," said Grant, the detective.

"No; go your own way about your work. I'll not meddle with it."

"May I know your name," asked Grant. "It might be in my power to befriend you some day."

"Well, I'll tell you. My name's Fosky Mike; the

River Rat some people call me. I do all sorts of business down the sewers and on the river. More than I should ever tell you, Richard Grant."

"I have no wish to learn your affairs."

"And if you should ever have to hunt me down, don't come here," said Fosky Mike. "You'd never find me; but you'd find the death you've this time escaped. Yours is the first detective's foot that has ever crossed this threshold. If it ever crosses it again, it will be the last. You would not see me, but such a death would fall upon you that would rive your heart for days, while your life was driven inch by inch out of you."

The two men looked steadily into each other's eyes. Neither shrank from the gaze.

Fosky Mike broke the silence.

"This is the way," he said. "Good-night!"

He opened the door and Grant followed him.

Mike saw him through with suspicious attention.

The man's mistrust was well concealed, but the detective knew there was something on the premises he did not wish him to know of.

At the present time Grant did not concern himself much about it, though at any other time his professional instinct would have induced him to endeavour to discover what it was.

Fosky Mike, who still watched him narrowly, led him along another room as dilapidated and tumble-down as the one they had just left.

There was a dirty, broken flight of stairs at the end, up which he motioned the detective to ascend.

"To the left," he said, as Grant touched the top stair.

There were two doors—one to the left and one right in front.

Something in the quick command of Fosky Mike roused Grant's suspicions, and he thought he detected a shakiness in the man's tone, and with him an impulse was an act.

Great as the risk was—though he knew he placed his life in jeopardy—he resolved to open the interdicted door.

Making a false stumble on the top stair he put out his hands and forcibly struck the door.

It opened and he went sprawling in, and sprang to his feet.

With one keen glance he had taken in the view of the room—a low-roofed, smoke-grimed den, with some rude benches falling to pieces with age.

On one of these was an object that arrested him as he was about to retreat.

The prone form of a young and lady-like woman with hair and garments drenched.

She lay in the rigid repose of death, her dark tresses falling dishevelled over her pallid brow and bosom.

While he was gazing at this unexpected sight, Fosky Mike's heavy hand was laid upon his shoulder, and he was swung completely round.

The livid, passionate visage of the River Rat confronted him—the brows knit, the lips compressed, the eyes gleaming in sullen fury.

"To the left, I told you!" he said, in a whisper, hoarse with fury. "You are a dead man, Richard Grant!"

The detective stepped back a pace.

His cue was taken on the instant.

"Why, man," he said, with a laugh, "do you think I am likely to tell tales about a dead woman? Bah! you must be a fool."

Fosky Mike regarded him uneasily.

A low gleam of suspicion lurked in his cunning eyes, and at that instant he looked murderous.

"Yes," he said, presently, "she is dead. No harm in a dead woman, eh?"

"None," Grant replied. "I've helped to fish many a one from the river when we've been out at night."

"Ah! so have I. At least, I've done it alone. I like the dead."

Grant looked him full in the face.

"The reward tempts you," he said.

"Reward?" Mike almost shrieked. "I touch money for handling the dead? Once I had a fair young wife. I took her from the cold, dark river dead, in the first week of our married life."

"A suicide?" Grant asked, moved by the man's strangeness of manner.

"A murder!" Fosky Mike hissed between his teeth.

"Do you hope to discover the murderer?"

"I know him," the man replied, in such a tone and in such a look that the detective instinctively recoiled.

He changed the subject.

"This poor creature is young," he observed, going nearer the body; "young and delicate, too. She seems a lady born."

Fosky Mike edged himself between him and the pale form.

"Have you seen enough?" he asked, abruptly.

"Quite."

"Then see no more, if you would leave this place alive."

Richard Grant was about to retire with the mental intention of some day solving the mystery of that horrible house and its strange occupier, when a fancied change in the features of the woman arrested him.

With two quick strides he was beside her.

"She lives!" he cried; "her lips move. We are in time to help her back to life."

Fosky Mike gave a savage, sullen cry, and then with a panther's leap he threw himself on the detective, his eyes glaring into his.

"Will you shut your eyes and depart?" he asked, fiercely grappling him by the throat.

"Not till I have solved this mystery," cried Grant, keeping his gaze fixed on the fair, beautiful face of the young creature. "Back! As I am a man I will see this to the end."

"You will see no more on earth, then," yelled Fosky Mike. "Richard Grant, you have seen more than living man beside myself shall see, and for that I swear you shall never go from this house alive."

His powerful arms girded Grant as if he had been a giant and the detective a child.

Still, weak as he was, his iron courage rose in his giant's breast.

He gripped his antagonist by the throat, and forced his head back.

In their deadly struggle for mastery their limbs became locked, and the veins on the temples of each swelled up like cords.

At ordinary times Grant had the strength of a lion, and would have risked little in a contest even with such a giant adversary as the River Rat.

But now he was weak and cramped, and though he had fixed Fosky Mike by the throat, he felt his strength going slowly and surely from him.

They struggled to the door.

The detective's grip was still deadly as a vice.

Fosky Mike, half-strangled, held him with one hand, and with the other dealt him such fearful blows in the chest that the breath seemed driven from his body, and, with the blood weltering to his lips, he sank to the boards.

Then his powerful assailant lifted him in his huge arms.

"Down there," he cried, the foam falling from his lips ; " down, and tell the rats what you have seen."

He kicked open a trap in the broken floor.

Richard Grant felt himself hurled violently down.

He tried to clutch at the edge as he fell back. A fearful blow on his head stunned him, and he went down crushed, bleeding, and helpless into the dark chasm beneath.

Hark !

A sound falls upon his ear.

The trap has fallen.

But a cry, the familiar cry of human voices, reaches him as he falls.

It comes from the river side.

And as a death dizziness whirls his brain, he fancies he distinguishes the voices of Captain Jack and his boy band.

## CHAPTER XI.

THE ATTEMPT ON THE LIFE OF LITTLE GILBERT —WHITECHAPEL DICK INTERFERES WITH THE BOSKER'S PLANS.

THE Bosker was snugly ensconced in a secure part of the Pig and Porridge Pot when the letter brought by poor little Gilbert was put in his hands.

He read it eagerly, and a sharp look of satisfied cunning gleamed from his cruel eyes.

"Where's the little kiddy that brought this note ?" he asked of the young girl who gave it to him.

"Upstairs, waiting for an answer."

"I'll come up," growled the Bosker.

Finishing the liquor remaining in his measure, he got up from his chair and followed the spruce waiting-maid into the parlour where little Gilbert was standing.

The Bosker looked without remorse on the hapless victim whom he was paid to strangle or leave with his throat cut.

"Are you the little boy who brought this note ?" he asked.

"Yes, sir," Gilbert replied.

"Come with me, and I will give you the answer."

He put on his fur cap, and went forth from the Pig and Porridge Pot, little Gilbert timidly following him.

"Keep close to me," said the Bosker. "Come along. Don't be frightened," he said, as Gilbert rather lagged behind.

Gilbert crept closer ; but he did not like being too near.

An instinct seemed to warn him to keep away.

The Bosker led the way towards Kennington.

He went through all the dark and narrow turnings, taking great care to keep Gilbert by his side.

He had not seen a pair of keen eyes watching his movements as he came from the Pig and Porridge Pot.

The eyes in question belonged to Captain Jack, who, after he had seen which way he took, experienced a great disinclination to trade, even at the most remunerative rate of pay, and, having slung his box on his back, went quickly out of sight.

The Bosker had got into a very secluded part of Kennington when a labourer, turning a corner, ran full up against him, and, with many drunken apologies, stumbled on his way.

At the first encounter the Bosker had felt in his pocket for his bludgeon ; but as the man stumbled off he replaced the deadly weapon in its concealment.

Little Gilbert sidled up to him as they were going up a dark turning.

"Please," he said, "I don't know where you are taking me."

"All right ; come along," growled the Bosker. "Soon be there."

"But I'm to take back the answer and earn a penny."

"I've got a bran new sixpence I'll give you when I get home."

The Bosker said no more till they stopped at a lonely house in an out-of-the-way place where extensive building was going on.

He tapped three times against the shutter. The door presently opened, and the Bosker led Gilbert in.

"Take care of this little boy," he said, to a gaunt, ill-looking woman, who stood in the passage, "till I come back to-morrow."

"No, no," Gilbert cried, running to the door; "I don't want to stay—"

"Get back !" the Bosker cried, pushing him savagely away.

The woman caught the terrified boy in her arms and held him securely, and the Bosker went out, slamming the door after him.

And Gilbert was immured in that lonely house to await the coming of the man who had paid to see him laid still in death.

The Bosker was there the next night half an hour before the time appointed by David Eastlake.

The latter came to the moment of his appointment. He smiled a cynical, cold, deadly smile when the Bosker told him they had the boy safe.

"Let him be brought in here !" he said.

Gilbert came in pale, and his cheeks wet with his tears.

He had been crying all night and day.

Young as he was, he feared something worse than his captivity.

*Away went Nicholas Slime with a yelling crowd at his heels.*

When he saw David Eastlake he fled to him for protection, and clung to his knees, asking him to save him from the other, not more a ruffian than the cold-hearted, hardened, gentlemanly villain.

Eastlake put the boy quickly away from him.

"Take him to the other room," he said to the Bosker, significantly; "I will come and see him presently."

He caught the Bosker's eye.

"When all is over," he added, in an undertone.

The Bosker took Gilbert by the hand, but the boy was frightened and would not go.

"Help me—save me!" he cried, appealing to Eastlake.

The pallid miscreant heard him pitilessly.

He was too great a craven to join in shedding the boy's blood, but he wanted to see him still and cold in death.

The Bosker put his hand before Gilbert's mouth and lifted him with brutal force from the floor.

"Shall it be strangling," he said, getting closer to Eastlake, "or shall I cut his throat?"

"Curse you! do as your murderous instincts prompt you," exclaimed Eastlake, starting back aghast. "Do not ask me how it is to be done."

"I thought you would like to have it done your own way," rejoined the ruffian with a grin.

"Tamper not with me," Eastlake said. "I care not so that it is done well and quickly. When I see him cold and stiff I will give you your price."

"There's lots of ways," said the Bosker, holding the struggling boy under one arm. "There's smothering in the bed, like Charlotte Winsor used to do, but he's almost too big."

"Take him away!" hissed Eastlake. "When it is done send for me."

The Bosker nodded his head, and took Gilbert from the room.

The place he carried him into was a sort of back kitchen, with a window opening on to a narrow yard.

The window was screened by double shutters, which were yet in their place, and effectually shut out all but the faintest ray of light.

Burkett sat little Gilbert on his feet, and shut the door.

"Don't make a noise," he said, in a low, husky tone, for the brutality of his intended deed touched even his callous nature. "What I'm going to do will be good for you."

Gilbert writhed out of his grasp.

"I won't stay here," he cried. "Help! Oh! will no one help me? I shall be murdered!"

"Yes, that's just it, my little boy, and you may as well take it quietly. It'll only be the knife at your throat, and it'll be all over in a twinkling."

Spellbound, and for the moment mute with terror at the atrocious savagery of his captor, Gilbert staggered back; but an instant after, with a shriek for mercy that curdled the ruffian's blood, he fell at his feet.

"Oh! no. Mercy!" he shrieked; "don't kill me —I never—did—did anyone harm; oh! mercy— mercy."

Eastlake heard the shriek, and his face went livid and cold.

The pale, pleading face of the boy was before his eyes, and he pictured him writhing under the Bosker's knife.

"The fool!" he muttered, striding quickly to and fro; "he might have taken more quiet means than that."

The shrieks ceased. The boy became quiet, a cold sweat stood on Eastlake's cheeks.

He thought the deed was done.

The boy's cries had ceased because, inspired with a strength beyond his years, he had broken away from the Bosker's grasp as the ruffian was forcing him down.

Burkett had taken out his clasp-knife, and with his knee on the boy's quivering chest, was opening the broad blade with his teeth, when Gilbert wriggled from under him, and with wild frenzy kicked at him with his feet.

The Bosker was on one knee.

With an oath he tried to grasp Gilbert's foot, but the boy struck him suddenly in the mouth and knocked the knife out of his teeth.

There was just light enough for the Bosker to see Gilbert make a rush at the knife.

With a curse he sent out his huge, heavily-booted foot, and struck Gilbert a fearful blow on the head.

Another moment and the Bosker's knife would have been torn from the boy's trembling hold and buried in his throat; but as the Bosker leaped on him the two shutters were sent down with a crash, and the woman who had let them in threw open the window.

"I won't have murder here," she cried. "Run, boy, for your life. They may kill you out-of-doors, not here."

She caught Gilbert by the hair of his head and dragged him through the window.

Eastlake dashed in at that moment.

"Is it done?" he asked, huskily.

"Look!"

The Bosker leaped through the window like a baffled hound.

"I will wring your neck for this," he muttered, savagely, as he dealt the woman a blow that felled her as if she had been shot.

He stayed a moment to pick up his knife, which he had dropped, and then hurried after Gilbert, who, with the swiftness of a deer, was fleeing for his life.

It was quite dark, and the few lamps but faintly lighted up the lonely spot.

And, it being late, no one was about.

Even the night policeman was away from his accustomed beat.

Little Gilbert fled, with palpitating heart, in the hope of meeting some one to save him from the savage clutches of the Bosker, whose fierce curses he could hear as the ruffian gained upon him.

He did not know in which direction he was running, and the last hope of escape was gone when he fell, weak and helpless, at the door of what looked in the darkness like a large shed.

We have said it was a late hour, so late that nearly everybody had gone home.

Whitechapel Dick, like the rest, had finished his sales for the night, there being no more people abroad to buy his wares, and had taken his caravan to the remote corner of a piece of spare ground, preparatory to turning in for the night.

Whitechapel Dick was, from some unexplained cause or other, very fond of gazing on the stars.

It was one of the curious fancies that marked him out among his fellows.

On this eventful night he was standing on the steps of his caravan, gazing meditatively at the sky, when he was startled by feeling something come with a bump against his caravan.

Looking down, he saw the huddled form of little Gilbert crouched at his feet, and hoarsely whispering for mercy.

One glance was enough for Dick to understand the business.

He saw at his knees a little boy, panting, breathless, and trembling in deadly fear, his chattering teeth expressing his terror as he crouched under the steps of the caravan, as if they would hide him from his pursuer.

Whitechapel Dick saw this, and he saw, too, something else.

He saw a burly-looking ruffian, armed with a large bludgeon, hurrying up to the boy, and, having a naturally intuitive mind, he was at no loss how to put a proper complexion on the matter.

So when the Bosker came blustering up, calling Gilbert the foulest names, and promising him what he would give him when he got him home, Dick put his hand inside his caravan and took hold of something that the Bosker did not see.

The Bosker was a little tamer after he caught sight of Dick.

"Come here, you whelp!" he growled, getting closer to Gilbert. "I'll teach you to run away like that."

The boy shrieked and upraised his white face.

"Save me! He'll kill me!" he cried, in a frightened whisper.

"Kill you, will he!" exclaimed Whitechapel Dick. "Don't be afraid of that, my boy; we don't allow any killing here."

The boy crawled closer to him, conscious that he had found a protector, but still fearful of the Bosker's savage power.

Whitechapel Dick patted him softly on the head.

"Now then, my fine fellow," he said to the Bosker, "what may you please to want?"

"That boy," the Bosker replied, his hand tightening on his bludgeon; "he's run away from home."

"Oh! no, please, sir, I haven't. He wants to kill me. Don't let him come near me with that big knife."

The boy's terror was acute.

"Be calm, my lad," said Whitechapel Dick. "I'll not let him touch you."

A hard glare of savage malice shone in the Bosker's eyes.

"I've come for him and I mean to have him," he said.

"Indeed! Then let me warn you not to attempt anything of the kind while I am here," replied Dick, his fine, expressive eyes kindling.

"What's the lad to you?" the Bosker asked, fiercely.

"Nothing; but I mean to protect him," Whitechapel Dick observed.

"Then I'll settle you first and take him afterwards," the Bosker cried.

Giving a quick look round to see that no one was near, he sprang on the steps.

Gilbert uttered a cry of terror, and fell into a dead faint, while the Bosker poised his bludgeon ready for a fearful blow.

His blood was roused, and almost blindly he sprang upon Whitechapel Dick.

"Curse you! take that," he said, as he dealt a blow full at Dick's head.

"Thank you, take that instead," was Dick's quiet answer.

In the twinkling of an eye he drew from behind him a long, keen sword, which was whirled round the Bosker's thick skull as Dick stepped nimbly aside.

It flashed before the ruffian's eyes, and then the flat of it struck him such a fearful blow on the forehead that he reeled, and, staggering some distance, fell with a thud.

"I thought you would not like that," observed Dick, quietly, as he put his sword inside the caravan.

Burkett was up on his feet in an instant.

The blow had only partially stunned him, and all the passionate savagery of his nature gleamed from his bloodshot eyes.

His open knife was in his hand.

"I'll drive this to your heart, curse you!" he cried, as he bounded up the steps.

Singularly enough Whitechapel Dick only laughed. He did not even put forth his hand to reach his sword.

The fact was he saw what the Bosker could not see, that others had arrived on the scene.

The Bosker only knew of their presence when he was rudely seized from behind, as his foot was on the top step, and the knife was struck from his hand. And while the strong arms of the disguised labourer held him powerless a pair of handcuffs were adroitly slipped over his muscular wrists by Captain Jack.

Whitechapel Dick clapped his soft hands together and laughed airily.

"Excellently done, gentlemen!" he exclaimed; "most capitally executed—as neat as ever I saw anything done in my life."

The Bosker bestowed upon him such a glare of ferocious hate and fury as only a baffled tiger might give forth.

"I will pay you for this some day," he muttered, grinding his teeth and struggling at his fetters.

"No use, Burkett," exclaimed the disguised detective. "It's all up with you now."

The Bosker turned his sullen gaze upon the speaker and Captain Jack.

He said nothing, though his lips moved in silent curses, for at that moment he caught sight of the white face and skulking figure of David Eastlake.

## CHAPTER XII.

CAPTAIN JACK AND HIS BOY BAND ON THE SEARCH FOR RICHARD GRANT—THE RIVERSIDE BY NIGHT.

IT struck Whitechapel Dick when, after the Bosker had been led away to the station, he lifted Gilbert in his arms and carried him tenderly inside the caravan, that the pale, delicate face, with its sad, careworn expression, was familiar to him.

Old memories came stealing to Dick's heart, and an unbidden tear stood in his eye.

The boy's wan features recalled scenes and faces whose very remembrance he had long ago striven to crush from his heart.

Whitechapel Dick had had a strange, eventful history, and his lips were closely locked upon secrets that would have startled the world, who saw in him only the cheap Jack and professional showman.

A young girl was at the entrance to the inner compartment of the caravan.

She had been disturbed by the scene outside, and was standing by the doorway with pale, anxious face when Dick carried in the senseless boy.

She asked no questions when he told her to nurse him back to consciousness.

Whitechapel Dick was a man of very few words when not engaged in bandying them with an audience from the steps of his caravan.

Silent and thoughtful, he offered few explanations of his sometimes eccentric conduct.

And the young girl, who was his sole travelling companion and attendant, and served him with the fidelity of a singularly true and self-denying nature, had learned the wisdom of never seeking to penetrate the causes which dictated his acts.

She was not above seventeen years of age—gentle and delicate in feature, supple and slender in form.

Her eyes were large and lustrous, but had a melancholy look in them that became more melancholy when the owner of the caravan was the object of her gaze.

She served from choice, and because she was alone in the world and he was kind to her. She would not have stayed with him for hire or wages, however large.

There was a deeper bond between them, and if Dick suspected her feelings towards him, he was too honourable to take advantage of them.

A huge black dog lifted his noble head as Dick laid Gilbert down, and it licked the boy's thin hand and face.

It would have bounded up, but a look from its master restrained it.

Whitechapel Dick busily aided in restoring Gilbert to consciousness, and when the boy's fears had been allayed, and he had been given some nourishment, Dick had him placed in their softest bed.

"He will be refreshed by a night's sleep," Dick said to the young girl. "Do not disturb him too early, Minnie. His system has received a severe shock. 'Tis a comfort to think they've laid the scoundrel by the heels, for I verily believe he was bent on murdering him."

Saying which, Dick lighted a long meerschaum pipe and sat down to enjoy a quiet smoke.

In spite of the terror he had endured, Gilbert slept heavily till morning, and was only awoke by the bright sun streaming in at the little curtained window of the caravan.

Dick had long been up and astir.

He came in when he saw the boy was awake, and spoke kindly to him, asking him questions about his home and friends, all of which Gilbert answered as he had answered at the workhouse and in the police-court.

The story, slight as it was, interested Dick by its pathos.

"My poor little boy!" he said, gravely; "and what are you going to do?"

Gilbert burst into tears.

"I'm sure I don't know, sir," he said; "every one seems against me—and I've no home, no friends."

"You sha'n't say that any longer," cried Dick, his heart warming towards the friendless boy; "you shall stay with me—I'll be your friend, this shall be your home, we shall travel about the town and the country, and when you are tired of staying with me you must tell me so."

Gilbert thanked him with the gratefulness of a full heart, as it was long since he had met with a word of kindness. He burst into tears again, and let his head fall on to Dick's hand.

That evening Dick took his stand in a more fashionable quarter.

He was dressed well for the occasion, and in his elegant costume looked exceedingly handsome and noble.

Gilbert was beside him, watching his every movement with the faithfulness of a petted dog.

It was yet early, and no crowd had collected about the caravan.

One or two carriages passed by, and many of the fair occupants turned their heads to take a peep at the graceful figure of the good-looking showman—a mark of honour which Dick rewarded with his most brilliant smile.

All at once a change came over him.

His features went ashy pale, and a mist swam before his eyes.

A creeping chill stole over his frame.

He had caught sight of a face in one of the carriages—a fair, girlish face, with bright blue eyes and hair of the purest golden tint.

A face as lovely as it was mournful, but it held him mute and breathless.

She was leaning back in the carriage as it passed.

An elderly gentleman was seated opposite her, and was paying her some compliment when she caught sight of Dick.

In an instant the gay look went from her eyes, with a stifled cry she put up her arms, and then sank back in the carriage.

Breaking from his entrancement, Dick was about to dash down the steps when the carriage-blind was suddenly closed.

He heard the gentleman's voice calling to the coachman, and the vehicle rolled rapidly out of sight.

As if he had been stricken by a heavy blow, Dick reeled helplessly back.

"Heavens!" he exclaimed, his hands striking hard against his temples. "Do I dream? Is it her face, or have I looked again upon the dead?"

Minnie came and linked her arm in his.

She drew him with womanly tenderness inside the caravan and wiped a tear from his eye.

"Minnie," said Dick, hoarsely, "let me go forth. I should choke if I shut myself up to-night."

But presently he calmed down, and that night Dick did a roaring business.

Never had he seemed so light-hearted, so full of buoyant spirits.

Never were his sallies known to be so witty and successful.

But after the evening's excitement was over, and the glare of the many lights was darkened, Dick sat alone in his tiny chamber, brooding in moody, silent bitterness, his arms folded across his breast, and a terribly mournful look on his face.

．　．　．　．　．　．　．　．

Captain Jack, after he had so cleverly tracked the Bosker, and seen him securely marched off in safe custody, put aside his blacking and brushes for a while, and went with several of the boy members of his gang on an expedition that had been planned some time previous, and under his leadership was now decided upon.

This was an excursion down the river to a lonely old habitation on its banks at Southwark, which was believed to contain some secrets, the discovery of which would repay them for their venture.

It had first been projected by Chimbley Joe, who, ever on the alert for mischief, had proposed getting into the place at night to see what was to be seen.

The proposal had been submitted to Captain Jack, whose keen instinct being aroused by the description given of the place, had determined upon going with them.

Chimbley Joe, Tike, and a lot of others, always ready for any fun, were of the party, which was made up by the street boys of Captain Jack's band.

Chimbley Joe gave information where a barge was to be got off Lambeth, and in the darkness of the night the whole party got safely on board and pushed off.

Keeping along the muddy banks, so as to avoid being seen by the river police, who, though they could do Captain Jack no harm, were not bound to let him proceed on his way unless he showed the authority for his expedition.

When they were almost opposite the Temple gardens Captain Jack heard the measured plash of oars.

The police boat was coming towards them.

"Get down, all of you," he whispered.

The boys quietly stowed themselves out of sight, while Jack, lying flat along the edge, paddled the barge in amongst some others that were moored to the bank.

By this ruse they escaped the vigilance of the police, who rowed by, not suspecting that there was such a case under their very nose.

Before they were fairly out of sight the barge, with its living freight, was again on its way.

Chimbley Joe could hardly be restrained from indulging in a yell of delight.

"Crikey!" he exclaimed, "them bobbies have poor noses not to smell us out, jigger me if they haven't."

Here he did a shuffle with his feet on the very edge of the deck, till he came to grief by the barge giving a lurch and dousing him headlong into the river. There was more mud than water just there, so he was not much hurt.

But he was precious dirty, and he grumbled extremely thereat.

"I'd make them blokes what has all the money wash these banks clean if I had my way," he said, scraping the mud off his clothes.

"Now then," sang out Tyke, "don't fling the mud in my heye."

"Silence! all of you," spoke the voice of Captain Jack. "We're near the house."

A dingy, crazy-looking old pile it was, built more of wood than of bricks and mortar.

It seemed trembling to its foundation with age and rottenness; but Captain Jack shrewdly suspected that it was stronger than it looked.

"How are we to get in?" whispered Tyke.

"Up there," Chimbley Joe replied. "There's a chink you can all get through. I tried it once—got up there and looked in."

"And what did you see?"

"Nothing," Chimbley Joe replied. "My foot slipped, and I tumbled all the way down, and if it hadn't been for a man pulling me out of the mud I shouldn't never have got out again."

"Up, boys!" cried Captain Jack, suddenly, addressing his band; "we must get in at any risk. See—there's devil's work going on there—quick, or we shall be too late."

Captain Jack's exclamation it was that had reached Richard Grant as he fell.

The dizziness went from the strong man's brain, and he staggered to his feet.

The boys were not long in getting into the old place, but the entry was effected so quietly that the detective began to fear he had not been seen or heard after all.

Still, with the latent hope of life, he listened for the least sound.

Footsteps came gradually—soft, stealthy footsteps, and Grant knew that the boys were inside the house.

Springing against the wall, he cried, fiercely—

"Help!—help! This way. I am under the trap."

That cry saved him.

Captain Jack had heard the struggle between him and Fosky Mike, but the detective's disappearance had been so complete that he did not know where to look for him.

When he heard Grant's cry it sounded feeble enough from within.

He threw himself against the decayed wainscoting. "Are you here?" he asked, kicking at the woodwork.

Grant replied by battering furiously from inside.

"Don't let any one escape from the house," Jack shouted to the others.

Half the boys posted themselves at different points, while the rest, with Jack, made a noisy onslaught on the wooden panels, and in a few minutes forced them in.

Then, pale as death and weak as a child, Grant came forward.

He took Jack's hands and pressed them in his.

"You have given me life," he exclaimed, "for you have rescued me from this accursed place; you are only just in time—a few minutes longer in this hole would have finished me."

"There's a man upstairs we want,"he continued; "some woman is in his power. Let us mount before he escapes."

Fosky Mike heard the noise made by the boys as he was bending over the pale form of his inanimate prisoner.

Standing erect, and with the veins rising like whip-cord on his forehead, he heard, with set teeth and clenched hands, the boys batter down the panels and release the man whom he had hurled down the trap to die.

The boys were at the door before he seemed capable of action.

Then, with a wild, delirious cry, he lifted the girl's form in his arms, and sprang with her to the door.

Captain Jack and his boy band had just got outside when the door was flung wide open and Fosky Mike appeared on the threshold.

Giving a yell like a wild Indian, he sprang upon Captain Jack.

With one hand he grasped him by the hair of his head, and, lifting him bodily off his feet, hurled him into the room.

Before Jack could spring to his feet the stalwart figure had leaped past him, past the detective, who, too weak to grapple with Fosky Mike, met his vindictive glare of fury with quiet, steady triumph—past the boys, and up the creaking stairs, till he stood on the roof of the building overhanging the water.

Captain Jack and his band were after him, nimble as young deer.

They were only in time to see him rest for a moment on the edge of the roof—to hear the vicious curse he flung back at them—before he had lifted the senseless girl in his arms, as if she had been a child, and cried, as he held her helplessly above his head—

"Take her from me? Ha! ha! You shall take me as soon."

Then there was the flutter of a dress, and a splash came from below.

Fosky Mike stood alone on the parapet.

Laughing hoarsely, as they rushed forward to seize him, the River Rat leaped after her into the dark river.

A sickening crash attended his fall.

He had gone headlong against the side of the barge moored by the boys.

They saw him put out his arms, as if to clutch the senseless girl, and then he sank from their sight.

But in a moment the still white face of the young girl rose to the surface.

"Get down to the barge," cried Captain Jack, who saw her rise, "while I go after the girl. We must leave the ransacking of this old place till another time."

The boy coolly threw off his coat and cap and took the terrible leap into the river with safety.

He rose beside her as she sank for the second time, but, diving, he seized her dress, and brought her once more to the surface.

The boys were soon on board the barge, and Captain Jack, with his pale burthen, was helped from the muddy waters.

"Push off!" Grant said, as they laid her tenderly down. "There may yet be time to save her life."

He knelt beside the lifeless girl, and raised her hand. Tenderly he scanned her features.

"Heaven help her, poor creature!" he murmured. "She seems past praying for. But I have seen the apparently dead brought back to life when all hope has long been past."

He grew strangely interested in her as he chafed her cold hands and frozen cheeks.

Somehow the idea grew upon him that he had seen her before.

Her wan face was familiar to him, yet he could not remember where or under what circumstances he had met her.

Of one thing he was glad—he had got her safely from the power of the River Rat.

With that individual's fate he did not further trouble himself, beyond waiting for a few minutes to see if he rose again, but as he did not the barge was slowly propelled to the river police-station, where his fair charge was given into proper hands.

Richard Grant waited to hear the result.

A joyous feeling arose in his heart when he was told that she lived—that there was a chance of her being brought back to life.

"Thank Heaven!" was Richard Grant's exclamation. "I will learn her history, and while I live she shall not want a protector."

He went back to the barge, where he had left Captain Jack.

"I shall not return with you," he said. "I have reasons for not being seen alive just yet. Should anything come in your way," he added, with a significant look at Jack, "don't forget to inform me of it."

"At once," replied Captain Jack.

"Share that amongst the boys," Grant continued, giving Jack some silver; "and, remember, silence on the events of this night."

"Trust me," Jack replied.

"We must have them all, Jack—all."

Jack nodded, and the detective went ashore.

"Push off, boys," Jack said; "it's getting chilly, and my bath has made me cold. Some hot coffee and rolls will do us all good."

"Yes, and I'm blowed if we sha'n't get summut else to do us good," retorted Tike, "if we stay much longer in this old barge. We sha'n't have none of them precious bobby-coves poking their noses here presently, and axing us where we came from—oh! no, not at all."

"Shut up," said Chimbley Joe, whom the mention of such a banquet for breakfast had driven into ecstacies; "ain't we going to have a stunning blow out? My heye! hot rolls and coffee. Wouldn't the Gorger like such a feed?"

Soon after the tide turned they left the barge safely in the place where they had taken it from, and were in a cosy coffee-house eating such a breakfast as they had none of them indulged in for a very long time.

## CHAPTER XIII.

### THE GORGER'S TROUBLES—A STREET FIGHT AND A TAILOR'S DUMMY.

NICK SLIME'S troubles for the day were not yet over.

Whichever way he turned some fresh misfortune stared him in the face, and at last, when his money was knocked out of his hand while counting it, and appropriated, he leaned against a lamp-post and wept.

"What's the matter now?" gasped a well-known voice. "Well, I'm blest! ain't you dead yet, Nicholas?"

"Yes, I am," said that worthy, pulling himself together. "Wot, you, my covey? Why, Booser, old man, I 'as been nearly murdered."

"Mur—oh—ow! you don't mean that anyone have a been trying that game on, old pal?"

The surprise of the Boozer was immense at seeing the state of his chum, and in such a short time, too.

"Yes," said the Gorger, giving an involuntary shudder at the remembrance of his late perils. "If yer is coming to have a snack, I'll tell you all about it when we gets inside—I am hungry."

"Come on, then," answered Spitalfields; "I was going to have a drink, but them little cusses foxes me, hang 'em!"

"Shall we go in here?" whined the hungry Gorger, who was thinking more of his enormous appetite than of his chum's tale of woe.

"You'll stand treat, old man," Nick Slime whined. "They collared my two pun ten, besides a bob or two."

"What?" exclaimed the Boozer, in surprise and alarm.

Surprised to hear that he had been robbed, and alarmed at the idea of having to pay for a feed for the Gorger.

He knew too well by experience what it cost to satisfy the glutton by his side.

Then, again, he thought, if it had not been for the Gorger he would not have had any money at all.

So taking all things into consideration, he made up his mind to "stand treat."

"What are you going to have?" asked the Boozer, as they entered the public-house indicated by the Gorger.

"I doesn't care, Spitals, old boy; some 'arf-and-'arf."

The Boozer immediately called for a pot of the required drink, and also a screw of tobacco.

But the Gorger was not contented with that.

He wanted a snack—a very large snack, too.

His hungry eyes swept around the place, and he saw nothing that would satisfy his greedy appetite.

But there were some small plates of cold meat on the counter, of which he took two, with the addition of half-a-loaf of stale household.

"I ain't 'ad any grub for a long time," said the Gorger. "How much have you got?" he added.

"About one pun seventeen and a tanner."

"Lor!" exclaimed the Gorger, glaring round, as much as to say, "Then I can have some more."

But the Boozer could not see it.

He paid for what they had, lighted his pipe, and said—

"Come on."

The Gorger followed very reluctantly.

He certainly felt anything but satisfied with his snack, but he slouched on behind the Boozer, with his hands in his greasy pockets, chewing a piece of tobacco, supplied by the ever-generous Spitalfields.

"You haven't told me how you got on since I left yer, Nick, old boy."

"Well," answered the Gorger, who was glaring hungrily in the window of a dirty cook-shop, "we had better get out of the way for a few hours. Wot say, old son, shall we slope to old Nathan's?"

"That's jist where I was a-thinking o' going when I seed your ugly mug, only, don't yer twig, I is sneaking down the slums out o' the way o' the blessed peelers.

"Yer see I have had a little plant on with Mike the Cabby. There was a fussy old lady hailed him who had a nice little dog.

"Well, I opens the door, and sez I—'Shall I hold yer dog, mum?'

"And she sez—'No.'

"'Dog a-going on the box, mum?' I sez. 'If so, I'll mind him for a pint.'

"Well, the old lady sez—

"'Very well; but mind and take care o' the darling pet.'

"I puts him on the box, jumps up by the side of Mike, and he drove off.

"Then, I sez, 'Mike, I wants the tike—a real one, no error.' So he sez, 'Well, halves.' 'Yes,' I sez, 'if you can help me get the little brute orf the box, he kicks so.' 'Well,' he sez, 'stay quiet a minnit and we'll do it.'

"'Now,' he sez, 'Spitals, just let him go. Then when he jumps orf the box, you run arter him, don't you see? He runs round the corner, you goes round the corner, too; but you doesn't come back, nor the dog either.'

"Well, I twigs. So I lets go o' the dog. The minnit he feels himself a bit loose he gives a kick, and struggles a bit.

"I pretends to hold him, but he gets away, rushes across the road, and I jumps down and rushes arter him up the street; he cuts round the corner, and then bolts orf full rate.

"I thought now was my time; but, lor! they sets up such a hollering and shouting arter the dog that it skeered him.

"The old lady was searching arter him, offering half-a-crown for anyone as would bring her dog back.

"In course there was a rush. I gets knocked over and rolls into the gutter. At that moment the dog come tearing along; he rushes quite close past me, so I clutches at him and collars hold on his tail.

"Lor', yer should have heard him yell. He snapped at my fingers, so I lets him go again.

"'Never mind,' I thought, as I saw him rush down a turning, 'I knows where he'll go, there's no thoroughfare there.'

"Well, when I gets into the street where he was, I thinks I had got him safe enough. He could not get out; I knowed he'd have to come back.

"I waits and down he comes; I stretched my arms out, but he knowed me and would not come anigh.

"He crouches up in a doorway. I made a grab at him, he snarled and made a grab at my fingers, and caught hold o' my thumb, too; look a-here," he said, "what do you think o' that?" displaying his shapeless, grimy thumb, which plainly showed the marks of the dog's teeth.

"Well, I'm jiggered!" ejaculated the Gorger, in some surprise.

"But I didn't care for that," continued the Boozer. "I cuddled him up under my arm, and sloped round the corner.

"I should a' got orf all right 'ad it not been for them little cusses, Chimbley and his chums; they sets up a howling and hooting in sich a manner they werry soon brought the peeler down on me.

"'Hi—stop!' he calls out; 'you'd better give in I've nabbed yer.'

"You can guess how I felt. I commenced to funk and felt my knees knocking together. I was a thinking o' what I could say when the little cusses sez—

"'Why don't yer coller him? He wants to nail the tike.'

"'No I doesn't,' I roars out; 'I am going to take it back to the old gal.' But he didn't see it. He makes a grab at me, I drops the tike, the little cusses picks him up, and trots back to the old lady. Well, seeing as I 'ad lost the dog, I wasn't a going to let him nab me, so I takes my hook, and had only just come round that ere blessed corner when I knocks up agin you."

"Lor' where is you?—ow! Oh! lor', they're at it again."

The Gorger found his speech cut short by receiving a slap in the eye from a dirty piece of orange peel. He knew too well from whence it came, as the throwing of the orange peel was followed with a yell of delight from a chorus of juvenile voices.

"Yah! who nailed the dog?"

"What cheer, long legs? I thought yer was in the work'us long ago."

"Smash his hat," shouted a third.

"Yah! boo. Who nailed the kid's toke?" put in a fourth.

"Spank 'em in the heye with a lump o' mud," shouted another.

And, suiting their actions to their words, they sent the Boozer's hat flying, and caught the Gorger such a fearful blow on the ear that he heard trains whistling for a week after.

Then they yelled as only a crew of the London street boys can.

The great, cowardly Gorger would run miles rather than face that wild crew behind them.

"What are we to do?" whined Nicholas, as the boys' hooting became more fierce, and the mud was flying about in all directions.

"I knows," said the Boozer; "let's give them young wretches the slip, and then go to the riverside. We isn't far from old Terry's boats. He'll let us have one on 'em. What say, Nicholas, old son? Suppose we takes one o' the old chap's boats, rows up to old Nathan's, goes in the secret way, and lays up until to-morrow, 'cause I is horful tired?"

"And I am horful hungry," said the Gorger, laying great stress on the awful, as though it were impossible to describe how hungry he really was.

During the time they had been arranging their plans the wild little vagabonds kept up a continuous howling, which grew more fierce, and the missiles became more violent, when they thought the worthy pair would not notice them.

Quite a crowd of loiterers of nearly every age and class had commenced to accumulate, gaping, and wondering what the boys were hooting those miserable objects for.

Chimbley Joe, who was, or appeared to be, the leader of the young urchins in this little bit of fun, as they termed it, very soon enlightened the wondering loiterers upon the cause of their hooting.

"Why, don't you see," he said, in answer to several queries put to him by the before-mentioned loiterers, "they are two big, cowardly sneaks? That long-legged one collared a little boy's bread and butter, and the other is a dog prigger, so we think they oughter be pelted!"

"Did they?" said several at once. "The ugly great brutes! Let's pelt 'em!"

Then there ensued one of those noisy squabbles too often seen in the streets of London, which commences by hissing and hooting.

As the rioters got warm, so did they get more courageous, and, heedless of both passers-by and shop windows, they commenced pelting the unlucky wretches in a most shameful manner.

It was enough to strike pity to the stoutest heart to look upon the pitiable faces of the Gorger and the Boozer.

What to do they did not know.

To have run would have brought the noisy crowd upon them in a very short time.

As it was, they kept very wisely under the protection of the shop windows.

The Gorger's terror was something awful to behold. Big drops of perspiration rolled down his cheeks, and when he beheld the crowd coming towards them he commenced to blubber like a great child, which, as may naturally be supposed, caused roars of laughter.

"Nick, old boy," said the Boozer, who had a little more courage than his friend, "let's make a run for it. We shall never get out unless we does."

"All right, Spitals."

"Now, then," said that worthy, "follow me."

And he started off at a run.

The Gorger, finding himself alone, did not seem to relish it.

He made a desperate rush, and shutting his eyes to keep out the mud, flung his long arms about.

In so doing he unconsciously seized upon a tailor's dummy that stood at the shop door, and whether he thought that he had captured one of the boys, or that the shopman had sprung suddenly upon him, are matters only for conjecture.

Somehow or the other the dummy became attached to him, and the Gorger could not shake it off.

Yelling with rage and terror, Mr. Nicholas Slime fled at a headlong pace, followed by a crowd of hooting boys and a policeman ; but he outstripped his pursuers, and left them to return to the place where the row began.

The policeman, whose knowledge of London boys was extensive, slipped round a corner as soon as possible, and the urchins, with the spirit of mischief still in them, began pelting each other.

It so happened that one youth hurling a piece of mud at a friend caught a rather swellishly-dressed young fellow on the cheek.

The swellish young gent had two or three friends with him, and being himself by no means a coward, he immediately stepped in amongst the crowd and singled out the fellow who had thrown the piece of mud.

"Do you know what you have done, young fellow ?" he said, walking quietly up to the aggressor.

"No ; nor don't care," was the insolent reply. "Shouldn't keep your jaw in the way, then you wouldn't get a clout intended for somebody else."

"Oh !" he said, coolly, "then you don't intend to apologise ?"

"To what ? 'Tain't likely."

And he gave the swellish one such a blow that it fairly put him on his back.

Certainly for a gentleman he had an enormous amount of courage, and instead of him calling the police, as was expected by many, he got up and gave the mud-slinger such a lift under the left ear that he was felled like an ox in the shambles.

A fight immediately ensued, which in a few minutes became general, the friends of either party joining in as if by magic.

"Here's a row," Chimbley Joe said, as he joined his companions. "Where's the Gorger ?"

"Dunno," said one—Hungry Sam, the rat-catcher, they called him.

"Go it," said another, "let's settle Ikey Bob, the flash 'un."

This elicited some surprise, and attention was immediately directed to that individual, who was no other than the swellish gent who had got up the fight.

We mention his name because he will play a very prominent part shortly, but we will for the present leave them all, hoping they will enjoy the fight, and return to the Gorger.

The Gorger having discovered that he had nothing more terrible clinging to him than a tailor's dummy, contrived to get rid of it, and to reach the Boozer, when they set off towards the waterside at full speed.

Arrived at the moorings of old Terry, as they termed him, they looked about to see that they were not watched, when the Boozer caught sight of an old man sitting in the bow of a boat engaged in the industrious occupation of "splicing" a rope.

The Boozer walked towards the old man and told him in a few words how the case stood.

It was not the first time by many he had aided some of the band, and, therefore, did not hesitate to do so now ; he knew that he was always well paid for his services.

That was all he cared for.

Pointing to a rather light, square-sterned boat, he motioned the two pretty-looking objects to enter, which they did, Nicholas Slime seating himself near the stern.

As may be readily supposed, he knew no more about rowing than an elephant, and that pleasant task fell upon the Boozer, who did it very clumsily.

However, the boat made pretty good way, as the tide favoured them.

"We are lucky !" he muttered, at the same time missing his stroke, causing him to strike just the top of a little rise in the water, and sending about a pint in the Gorger's face.

Now, it so happened that that gentleman was doing a slight snooze after the fatigues of the day, and the sudden dash of the cold water was like an electric shock to him.

He gave utterance to one dismal howl and fell upon his back in a fright.

"Well, you are a nice sort, Spitals, old man," he spluttered.

"Couldn't help it."

"Where are we ?" demanded Nick Slime, gazing round in a vacant manner.

"Wery near old Nathan's."

"Lor' ! are we ? I am glad. Ain't it fine to think we got away from them young varmints like this. Won't I have a snack, for I am hungry," the Gorger said, reflectively, by way of a finish.

"I should like a drink, too," said the Boozer. "Never mind, here we are at any rate ; five minutes more and we shall be in Nathan's."

The Gorger's eyes commenced to brighten at this, and pulling himself together a bit he sat up, looking awfully dignified.

He little knew what was in store for him before the next five minutes had elapsed.

The tide was rather low, so they had to thread their way among the barges, within a few feet of the slimy, filthy mud, that lies all along the bank, when the tide is down.

A few yards ahead of them there were a number of wharves — old, rickety, tumbledown-looking places—and under one of these there was an aperture that either led to a sewer or some cellars under the wharf.

It seemed almost impossible to be the latter, as when the tide was up it must have been filled with water. Be that as it may, there was something peeping from this rather large opening very much like the dirty faces and rough heads of the street boys.

"Carry me out," said a well-known voice. "Here they come."

This alluded to the unlucky Gorger and his friend.

Mr. Nicholas Slime was still in his dignified position, and was in the act of making some comment ; he thought he heard the bottom of the boat grate on the shore.

"Ow—where is yer going, Boozer ?" yelled the frightened Gorger.

"Yah, boo ! here we are again. Lug him out, Sam. Come on, lively ; that's it ! Oh ! here's a bit o' luck—here's a lark," came in reply, and

Chimbley Joe and his comrades actually danced in the mud, their delight was so great.

The Gorger felt at least a dozen willing hands pulling him out of the boat. Down he went splash. He struggled frantically to free himself, but all to no purpose ; those who held him did not intend to let him go.

"Yah, hi, ho-o-o-o-o ! Spital. Ho-o-o—he-e-elp m-m-e-e, little cusses—o-o !"

He found his speech cut short at that instant by a handful of mud, and then a dirty hand went smack across his eyes.

The cowardly Boozer no sooner saw his friend in a fix than he rowed off with might and main, but he did not gain much by that, for two or three caught sight of the sneaking thief leaving his friend in trouble.

They gave a shout, and sent enough mud after him to knock him off his seat.

Then the Gorger in his struggles happened to place his huge hand across one of the boy's faces.

The boy was grinning to a most dangerous extent at the fun, but when he found his mouth full of mud he yelled—

"You dirty beggar ! I'll give you something for that."

So he did.

He caught the Gorger by the legs, while two others clutched him by the arms, and a third caught hold of his hair, and nearly pulled it out by the roots.

"Now," said Chimbley, "jist give a hand, and let's chuck him in that ere soft pool."

"Ow ! p-p-le-ase don't," said the nearly-suffocated Gorger. "Me-r-mercy !"

"Chuck him in," shouted the boys.

And without more ado they lifted him as well as they could.

"With a one, two, three !" shouted Chimbley.

There was a gurgling yell, a loud splash, and a floundering of big feet.

Then all was still.

"The Thames peelers ! Look out, mates !" sang out one of the boys.

At that cry they disappeared as if by magic, leaving the Gorger sinking lower and lower.

He had sunk underneath save just his chin and face.

"Help ! Oh ! help !" he shouted, as he gave one last desperate plunge.

And then Mr. Nicholas Slime sank from mortal gaze.

---

## CHAPTER XIV.

GILBERT AND HIS NEW HOME—DAVID EASTLAKE AGAIN—THE CHARGE BEFORE THE MAGISTRATE —WHITECHAPEL DICK IN COURT.

THE policeman who had taken Alick in charge locked him up in the station all night, and brought him up in court the next morning.

It was not often he had a case, so he was glad of the opportunity of distinguishing himself.

Puffed out with dignity, self-importance, and padding, he took his place as accuser and prosecutor.

Alick had passed a weary night, but it was not because of the closeness of the hard cell that he could not sleep.

The boy's proud spirit was wrung by the humiliation of his position.

Besides, he thought of his sister, whom he had striven to protect.

Bitter tears had coursed down his cheeks all night, but he dried his eyes and showed no signs of weeping when he was taken before the magistrate.

David Eastlake had not kept his word.

He had promised Polly that he would see Alick safe.

But the accomplished scoundrel, besides having his time so occupied with the affair of Gilbert as scarcely to give a thought to Polly's brother, was in no humour to trouble about setting the proud-spirited boy free.

Alick was in the way, so he let him take his chance.

Alick stepped proudly into the dock when his name was called.

He felt that he had done no crime ; why, then, should he be ashamed ?

Nevertheless, his fair cheeks tingled as the eyes of the people in court were turned upon him.

The magistrate, as well as the rest, scanned his youthful countenance to seek the expected signs of juvenile depravity and vice, but, baffled by the quietness of his demeanour, the magistrate addressed the policeman—

"What is this charge, policeman ?"

The peeler breasted himself like a turkey-cock.

"Assault, your wushup, an' theft."

"Theft ?"

"Yes, your wushup ; I was on duty yesterday, when I saw him attack a gentleman in the street, and try to steal his watch."

Alick cast a look of proud scorn on the lying policeman, and the magistrate looked round for the prosecutor.

"Is the gentleman not here to charge him ?" he asked.

"He was in too great a hurry to leave me his name, your wushup ; but he said he'd be here this morning ; hows'ever, I saw the attempt."

"What did you see ?" the magistrate demanded.

"When I came up, your wushup," the bobby replied, "the prisoner had got hold of his watch-chain, and was trying to twist it off, and when I took him into custody he flew at me like a tiger."

"We will take the charge of robbery first," the magistrate said, checking the bobby's exuberance of zeal. "Did he succeed in getting the watch ?"

"No, your wushup, because—"

"Let us hear no becauses—did he steal anything ?"

"No, your wushup."

"I did not attempt to steal anything," Alick exclaimed, his eyes filling with tears at the imputation of dishonesty. "I never wished to take anything yet that did not belong to me. The constable has spoken falsely."

"Tush—tush," exclaimed the bench, "we can't have police officers abused in open court."

"Sentence me if you will," cried Alick, who was

not to be frowned down. "I can bear that—any punishment, but I never yet did a wrong action. They were taking away my sister, and I interfered. The gentleman struck me, or I shouldn't have struck him."

"And you struck me," interposed the policeman, maliciously, "or I shouldn't have brought you here."

"Then the case resolves itself into an assault upon you?" interposed the magistrate.

"Yes, your wushup. He struck me in a most vicious way, and—"

"Is anything known of him?" the magistrate said, interrupting the man in blue.

"Oh! yes, sir; he's been to prison before to-day; and he's known to be the associate of thieves."

"It is false—" Alick began, when he was stopped by the bench.

"He was sent to prison only the other day," continued the policeman, who seemed to take a malicious pleasure in getting Alick into trouble.

"What was the charge?" asked the magistrate.

"Tearing up his clothes, your wushup—him and a lot of young thieves; they give us a deal of trouble."

"Humph!"

The magistrate looked sternly at Alick.

"I should have been inclined to deal leniently with you, but the constable's evidence alters the case. I shall be compelled to send you back to prison."

"It is an injustice and a cruelty," Alick cried. "I never yet did wrong. But I am fast being driven to crime. Whatever I become society must take the blame."

"A hardened criminal!" exclaimed the magistrate, shocked at what he considered Alick's depravity. "You are committed to prison for seven days. If you come here again we will try what a reformatory can do with you."

With crimson face and flashing eyes Alick turned towards the magistrate.

"I have not deserved this punishment," he cried. "If I had been a criminal I could not have been treated more harshly. I have striven to be good. There is no chance and I will give up the attempt. It shall be for something when I am brought up again."

"Take him away!" exclaimed the magistrate, waving his hand.

Alick was led from the court to undergo his unjust imprisonment, and the policeman, whose false statements had sent him to prison, retired, satisfied with his triumph over the defenceless boy.

. . . . . . .

Gilbert got on very well in his new sphere of life.

Whitechapel Dick looked well after him, and Minnie behaved towards him with a true woman's kindness.

They were quite a happy family—Dick, Minnie, Gilbert, and the faithful dog; and, as the caravan roamed from place to place, Gilbert never grew weary of the change in his existence.

His good-hearted protector did his best to make him happy.

The chief difficulty was to overcome his fear of the Bosker, whose burly form haunted him still.

Night after night he fancied the ruffian at his bedside with the murderous knife at his throat.

When Dick had given the evidence that he did not doubt would send Burkett on his travels across the herring-pond, the orphan boy became more assured.

The Bosker was duly committed for trial.

He was so well known, and had been so long wanted, that there was quite enough proved against him to send him away for several years.

But his sentence would have been light in comparison with his crimes if Richard Grant had kept out of the way.

He entered the Old Bailey on the day of Burkett's trial.

The ruffian had, by the help of Nathan Claws, engaged counsel to defend him, and was behaving with the utmost hardihood, when the prosecuting attorney announced a new witness.

Nathan Claws, who was in court, materially helping the defence, for the Bosker was of use to him and his establishment, could not believe his ears when Richard Grant entered the witness-box.

The Bosker had been leaning moodily on the dock, and did not notice the detective when he first took his place.

But when he heard his voice he leapt up as if he had been shot.

Glancing wildly round the court, he fixed his bloodshot eyes on the pale features of the detective.

And the two men stood silently looking each other in the face.

Not a word did the Bosker utter; all the terror of which his coarse nature was capable was depicted in his countenance.

His eyes started from their sockets; his tongue, parched and dry, clove to the roof of his mouth; and his limbs were paralysed and trembling.

The effect of Grant's appearance was not less on the Jew thief-trainer.

His livid face was beaded with sweat, and his claw-like hands worked as if smitten by a palsy.

For some minutes he was unable to move.

But when he regained the power to do so he stood erect, and muttered, shaking like a leaf—

"Great Heaven! the dead has come to life."

He dared not look again; but, leaving the Bosker to conduct his own defence, he turned towards the door.

Richard Grant's voice, commanding him to stay, froze the very marrow of his bones, and arrested him as the outer air fanned his bloodless cheeks.

He tried to take a step forward and leave the precincts of the court, but a hand was laid on his shoulder, and he was led back a prisoner.

The depositions of Richard Grant were soon given.

They told with fresh effect against the Bosker.

He related how and why he had ventured into the den of infamy of which Nathan Claws was the chief, and told what had befallen him there.

The attack—the murderous descent into the sewer—his escape.

He told what he had seen while at Nathan's place, and the two trembling villains were newly indicted.

An indictment charging them with the deadly crime of murder.

Richard Grant meant to have his revenge.

Revenge for what he had endured in the water-cellar under the thieves' kitchen in Nathan Claws' house.

.      .      .      .      .      .      .

Since the evening when the face in the carriage had occasioned Whitechapel Dick such unwonted emotion he had been more moody and reserved than before.

Perpetually he was gazing at the occupants of carriages, in the hope of again seeing the fair girl whose features haunted him night and day.

Minnie, although she saw the change which had come over him, forbore to question him anent its cause, and Dick kept his secret within his breast.

But the tireless quest took him often to more aristocratic neighbourhoods than that from which he had derived his nickname.

Hitherto without any result rewarding his patient search.

Early one morning, when he had pitched his caravan at its old corner by the Kennington-road, little Gilbert had been sent on an errand for him by Minnie, and was tripping lightly along, glad to do his protector any service, when, looking in at a window, he caught sight of the white face of David Eastlake.

All his old terror returned at the sight, and he would have fled back to the caravan.

But Eastlake, with a hard smile upon his thin lips, took him by the arm.

"I want you, my lad," he said. "Don't run away."

Gilbert struggled to get from him.

His terror was so real and acute that Eastlake saw he would have no chance of getting him to go with him.

People were gathering about them, so he adopted a sudden and wicked resolution.

Twisting Gilbert sharply round, he contrived to let fall his handkerchief, a silk one, which dropped at the boy's feet, and was instantly trodden upon.

He had seen a policeman a little way off, and he waited till he came up.

"What's the charge, sir?" the man asked. "Lock-up case?"

"The young rascal!" Eastlake replied; "he has tried to pick my pocket. I believe he has stolen something."

"No, please; I haven't done anything," Gilbert replied, his eyes filling with tears. "Let me go home."

"I daresay," remarked the policeman to Eastlake; "like to go home, no doubt. A precious lot of young thieves about here, sir. Better make sure whether you've lost anything."

"My silk handkerchief is stolen," Eastlake replied.

"Hullo!" cried the policeman, picking up the handkerchief, "why, here it is, under the young vagabond's feet. Come along with me. Will you charge him, sir?"

Eastlake could hardly repress a smile of triumph. He had gained his point.

"Yes," he replied, after deliberation, "he had better be locked up."

The policeman crammed his knuckles into Gilbert's neck.

"Now, then, come along," he said, gruffly.

"Oh! please don't take me away. I didn't do it, sir."

"Oh! I daresay—they never does."

"No more he didn't," exclaimed a boy's voice from the crowd; "he never stole it. I see the gent drop it with my own eyes."

The voice belonged to Chimbley Joe, and the policeman turned sharply round.

"Oh! you're one of 'em, are you?" he growled. "Stop till I catch hold of you."

Chimbley Joe slipped away like an eel.

"No, you don't," he chuckled, as the bobby made a grab. "I ain't wished good-bye to my mother yet."

Eastlake handed the constable his card, saying he would be at the station immediately.

"A confederate, doubtless," he remarked, referring to Chimbley Joe, who was dancing round the lamp-post.

"Oh! yes, sir," said the constable. "Bless you! I knows their tricks; they'd steal the eyes out of your head. We shall nab him presently."

Chimbley Joe bestowed a comical wink on the officer.

"Will you? No you won't," he said. "You ain't paid for washing your shirt yet, and I see you getting in at the kitchen winder, where they had the cold mutton on the table."

"Yah! rabbit-pie!" yelled a chorus of boys.

The policeman looked as if he would like to do great things; but he was powerless to act.

Meanwhile poor little Gilbert crouched in his grip, weeping bitterly.

"Please take me home," he said.

"Take you home! Yes, I'll take you to the proper home—the station."

Gilbert covered his face with his hands.

"Not there," he said, appealingly.

"That's just where you're going to, and no mistake," said the policeman, as he led the lad away. "Come along; and you young vagabonds, don't come anigh my clutches, or I'll put you somewhere very sharp, I can tell you."

"Tike," said Chimbley Joe.

"What's up?"

"That's the little cove as was with us at the casual."

"Well, what of that?"

"Why, they're going to lock him up," said Chimbley Joe. "He never stole it."

"No," said Tike, "and I'm blowed if I won't sarve 'em out. I say, Chummy."

"What?"

"If he don't have that hankercher he can't prosemcute."

"No more he can't."

"I'm going to nail it—make no error. I'll have it out on him, and something else besides, if he's got anything to take."

*" Richard Grant," hissed the Bosker, "your life is in my hands."*

Tike glided away in the wake of Eastlake.

In a few minutes he returned.

"Got it," he exclaimed, displaying the edge of the silk. "Hooray! won't he be staggered."

"It will be a lark, Tike," grinned Chimbley Joe.

"Yes."

"Let's go and tell Gilbert to keep his pecker up, Tike."

"All right."

The two boys had the audacity to walk beside the policeman.

Presently Chimbley Joe whispered to Gilbert.

"Don't you mind," he said, "they'll be forced to let you out in the morning."

"But I'm to be locked up all night," sobbed Gilbert, "and I sha'n't see Dick, and he won't know where I am."

"Dick—who's Dick?"

"The caravan—"

"What — Whitechappy?" Chimbley Joe exclaimed. "Come on, Tike, we'll soon tell him about it. Good-bye, don't be down on your luck. They can't hurt you."

The two boys ran off, and soon told their tale to Whitechapel Dick, who listened gravely and in silence.

When they had told him all, he dressed himself with scrupulous care, and went to the police-station.

He was willing to bail Gilbert out, but the inspector refused.

"He'll be up in court presently," the official said. "You'd better go before the magistrate if you're his friend."

"Thank you," replied Dick, "I will."

There was silence in the court when Gilbert was brought in.

His pale face and delicate looks attracted much sympathy from the spectators, but not from the magistrate.

In the eye of the bench all who stood in the prisoner's dock were guilty criminals, and Gilbert was set down as a youthful proficient in sin and hypocrisy.

When the charge was stated, the boy burst out sobbing, and, protesting his innocence, let his head fall to the rim of the dock.

"Is anything known about the prisoner?" asked the bench.

Whitechapel Dick stepped forward.

His handsome face was pale, and his eyes shone with unusual brilliancy.

"Yes," he said; "he is known as a friendless orphan boy, alone in the world, an alien in society, but not an outcast. The boy's mind is pure and uncontaminated as yet. Heaven only knows whether it will be allowed to remain so."

"What is your object in interfering?" the magistrate demanded.

"To befriend the boy," Whitechapel Dick replied. "I wish to see him saved the misery and suffering of a night in a dark, cold cell—saved from the evil influences of prison companionship. His mind is gentle now; I would keep it so. It will grow hardened soon enough, as his acquaintance with the world increases."

"The charge against him is a serious one," the magistrate observed.

"It is trumped up—from what motive I cannot tell, except that the boy has been already greatly persecuted."

"I don't see how I can help him," said the magistrate.

"There is no prosecutor present," Whitechapel Dick said. "I will be bail for the boy's appearance."

The magistrate mused.

"What are you?" he asked, presently.

"A vendor of cheap goods."

"Your place of business?"

"Various. I remove from place to place. My caravan holds my stock-in-trade. My horse draws my house and goods."

"A cheap-jack!" exclaimed the magistrate. "How can you expect me to listen to your proposition? You pay no rates; you have no settled abode. The idea is preposterous."

"It is for the boy's good," Dick urged.

"Nonsense," said the magistrate. "He will be well looked after."

"Will you not take bail?" Whitechapel Dick asked, pleadingly.

"Impossible. Were you a responsible householder it might be done. We should never know where to lay our hands on you."

Dick's face flushed.

"I do not hide from sight," he replied. "And, as to my calling, it is that of an honest man."

"That may be. We cannot listen to you," said the magistrate.

"I will put down any amount you like, to be forfeited if I do not appear with the boy."

"No, the ends of justice might be frustrated."

"Justice!" Dick exclaimed, bitterly. "Is it justice that deals so harshly with a child like this? His looks would plead for him if this were, as it should be, the hall of mercy."

"Please, your worship," exclaimed a policeman in court, "I've seen the prisoner afore. He's one of the casuals. His clothes was tore up last time he went in the ward."

"I thought as much," replied the magistrate. "These are the people about whom such an outcry is made. We've heard enough of the harsh treatment of the poor. It will be well when those who are so fond of interfering in what they do not understand will take pains to arrive at the true character of the casual poor. In all my experience I have found them the scum of the earth. No system is of avail with them—they are incorrigible."

"The system by which they are supposed to be reformed is not a humanising one," Dick answered.

"It is the system, sir," continued Whitechapel Dick, in impassioned tones, "that drives the helpless poor to the streets and imprisons them for being there.

"It is the system that makes crime preferable to poverty, because the punishment of the poor is worse than that of the criminal.

"It is the system which inures young minds to filth, infamy, and every vice; which leaves the helpless unhelped, the starving unfed; that gives a stone when asked for bread.

"It is the system that gives power to pampered officials to fatten their own bodies while paupers perish at the workhouse gate; that shuts the sickly and dying in wards that are worse than vaults; that leaves the pauper sick in the care of bed-ridden wretches, who cannot even help themselves.

"It is the system, sir, which in the midst of our

boasted civilisation fills our prisons because of its cruelty, which is a disgrace upon a Christian land, which cries out with heartbreaking voice to Heaven for help against those who deny even bread to the poor."

There was a buzz of admiration when Dick concluded, and every eye was fixed on his excited face.

Little Gilbert looked gratefully towards him.

The magistrate and the court officials were for the moment dumb.

The silence was broken by Chimbley Joe.

During the whole of Dick's speech he had been in ecstacies.

"Stunning!" he kept whispering to Tike; "don't he know how to give it 'em."

He could not repress his feelings, and flinging his cap up in the air he electrified every one present by calling out—

"Horoay! give it him like that agen, and I'll stand on my 'ead free gratis for nothing."

The magistrate's face flushed with anger.

"Take that boy into custody," he said, "and bring him before me for contempt of court."

Several policemen dodged after Joe, but he was too nimble for them.

At the first sight of the magistrate's eye fixed upon him, he got some faint idea of the extent to which he had committed himself, and, before any of the police officers could get to where he stood, he had bobbed under the legs of the spectators and slipped out of the court.

Once safe outside those dreaded precincts, he stood defiantly on his head, till, catching sight of a blue coat and helmet, he went tumbling base over apex after a passing omnibus.

The zealous policeman made one or two attempts to grab him, but Joe's nimble heels bespattered him with mud every time he came near, and at last he got a lump clean between his eyes.

This effectually blinded him.

And before he could recover his sight Joe had made good his escape.

The magistrate had determined to make an example of Chimbley Joe, and he could not conceal his chagrin at his escape.

"A strange thing," he observed, testily. "A boy offends against the rules of the court, and slips out before any one can lay a finger on him. At that rate one might be assassinated on this bench and have no surety that the murderer would be taken."

He bent his ruffled gaze on little Gilbert, and if he had been previously disposed to deal leniently with the boy, he would not have done so now.

"Take him back," he growled, savagely; "he is remanded."

"Why, you ain't got the wipe!" sang out Tike, unable to keep his secret longer.

This time the bench seemed staggered by the audacity of those in court.

"Who was that spoke? Bring him here," he exclaimed.

One of the policemen dashed at Tike, who, conscious of the slip he had made, bore the look of a saint.

"Come along," said the policeman, taking him by the collar.

"Me! What for?" gasped Tike. "I ain't done nothing."

"All right, we know you. Out you come."

"Why, I ain't said a word—have I?" demanded Tike, appealing to those who stood near him.

Fortunately a burly mechanic helped him out of his scrape.

"It was a boy behind me, I think," he said.

A great many boys were behind the mechanic. The policeman scanned their faces, but could not discern which was the culprit.

Besides, he was almost certain that it was Tike who had spoken, and the magistrate was getting angrier and redder every second.

Any capture would be better than none.

"Sure, an' you've got the wrong sow by the ear," remarked a tall, gaunt Irishwoman.

The policeman began to look foolish, and Tike tried to wriggle away.

He had the missing handkerchief tucked inside his boot, and didn't want the disagreeable honour of a search.

The attention of the court was at this juncture drawn towards Whitechapel Dick.

He had reached over to Gilbert, and took his delicate hand.

"I presume," he observed, "that in the absence of criminating evidence, the charge against this boy will not be persevered in."

"I shall allow no conspiracy to defeat the ends of justice," replied the magistrate, resolved not to part with his victim.

"But the policeman has no proof," Dick urged. "The handkerchief is missing, and there is no prosecutor. Really there exists no foundation for the boy's detention. I must ask that he be set at liberty."

Even then the magistrate would have resisted Gilbert's discharge, but Richard Grant came in at that moment, followed by Captain Jack, the latter still wearing his shoeblack's dress.

"What does that boy want?" asked the magistrate, as Jack got close to little Gilbert.

"I am a witness, sir. May I be sworn?"

The oath was administered.

"Do you know anything of this case?" asked the bench.

"Yes, sir; I saw it all."

"Saw the boy steal the handkerchief? I thought as much."

"Not that, sir. It was never stolen. The gentleman dropped it under his feet."

"How?"

"Purposely."

The magistrate scanned Jack's intelligent face.

He was in doubt whether to believe him, when Detective Grant spoke a few words to the magistrate in a low tone.

"I must believe this evidence," the magistrate said, casting a quick glance at Jack; "the boy is discharged."

Whitechapel Dick bowed, then he took Gilbert's hand and led him from the court.

As Dick was leaving Captain Jack said something

to him in a low tone, and whatever it was it caused him to start visibly.

His handsome face blushed to the temples, and he laid his hand quickly on Jack's shoulder.

"A word more—a question," he began.

But Captain Jack, respectfully touching his forelock, hastily left him.

Those who witnessed this little episode supposed it bore reference only to the shoeblack's evidence, but Whitechapel Dick returned to his caravan with a new secret, like a flaming sword, in his heart.

---

## CHAPTER XV.

CHIMBLEY JOE GOES IN SEARCH OF ALICK AND GAINS BAD TIDINGS—THE MEETING OF HUNGRY SAM THE RAT-CATCHER AND CHIMBLEY.

BEFORE the Thames Police could get their boat safely upon the bank, Chimbley and his chums were out of sight, and on their way to Lambeth. Now the excitement of the little adventure with the Gorger was over, Chimbley, for once in his life, commenced to think a little.

He wanted Alick. Where could he have got to?—what could he do to discover him? were Chimbley's thoughts.

Without Alick he felt lonely and miserable. To him Alick was more than a friend; he looked to him for advice and protection.

So he finally made up his mind to make a general search for his missing friend.

He shouted to the boys, who were enjoying themselves in a fine little game of (in their language) "follow my leader."

"Have any of you seen anything of Alick?" he asked, when he had got the noisy crew round him.

"No!" was the response, from a chorus of voices.

"Where is he?" shouted one.

"He's hooked," replied another.

"Oh! he's sloped," said a third, who rejoiced in the name of Nat the Nicker. "He's got too proud for our company; we ain't flash enough for him. He's a sneak, that's what he is."

"Now, look a here," said Chimbley Joe, calmly, "say sich a thing again and I'll put my fist in your heye; 'cause, you see, Alick's a good sort, an' wouldn't leave old chums for anyone. He's been collared, and I means to say we oughter go and look for him."

"Yes, o' course," all shouted.

"I will, for one," said Chimbley.

"And me, for another," said a little, fair-complexioned boy, with a wondrous curly head of hair. Of course, like the rest of the boys, he had a nickname. Not being able to find him a better one, they called him Curly; certainly it was a most suitable name for him.

"Well, s'pose three or four of you goes in different directions, and try and diskiver what's become of him," said Chimbley Joe. "I'll go down the bankside and up the bridge."

"And I'll come with you," said Curly, who had rather a liking for Chimbley.

"No," said Chimbley; "I'll go by myself."

Then the boys dispersed, each taking a different direction, and Chimbley went alone.

He had walked about for nearly an hour, questioning every crossing-sweeper, shoeblack, and boy with cigar lights that he knew, but could gain no information.

He was about to return to see if his companions had gained any tidings of his friend Alick. At that moment a little dog came bounding up to him.

"Why, Ruff, what brought you here?" said Chimbley Joe, patting the dog affectionately. "Where's your master, old boy?"

He very soon discovered where he was.

For he saw one nicknamed Sam, a rat-catcher by profession, emerge from a baker's shop, with a currant roll in his hand.

"What cheer, Joe, old pal? You look down in the mouth. I was just coming to look for you. I've got something to tell you that'll make you stand on you head for a month. What, you won't grin at that piece o' information. Well, have a lump?"

He said this as he kindly offered Joe a piece of his roll, which Joe refused.

"No, thank you, Sam; I've got the hump," said Chimbley Joe, dismally. "I'm looking for Alick. We have not seen him for a long time. I'm afraid he's been collared."

"Jist so. That's jist what's happened," said Sam the rat-catcher. "I've been up and knows all about it. He's got seven days; but that'll soon blow over, and by the time he comes out you'll be able to gladden him, when you knows what I've got to tell you. Fizzing, and no mistake; just like you read about in tales. Secret passages and all that. There's no blooming herror about it."

"What do you mean?" said Joe, in wonderment.

"Why, I'll tell you; but I only wants you to know, 'cause the other boys would split on us, don't you see?" Sam explained. "I have a been out rat-catching to-day, and I've been jolly lucky; I've earned a half-dollar, besides perks, w'ich I've got here," he added, displaying a rat-trap, in which were several live rats. "Fine uns, ain't they? I shall take 'em to Jerry, the dog fancier, to-morrow; he'll give me tuppence a piece for 'em."

Had Joe been in his usual spirits it is not at all unlikely but that he would have inquired how much they would have given for a whole one, as they were going to give two pence for a piece; but he did not. He felt too gloomy, on Alick's account, to say or do anything.

"Well," continued Sam, "I've been in some o' the oldest wharfs about Whitefriars; talk about catching rats, never 'ad sich a day in my life afore; why, Ruff was killing 'em six at a time."

Chimbley Joe looked down at the dog as though he did not believe it; but the dog wagged his tail in such a confidential manner that Chimbley felt bound to credit his master.

"Arter we had done rat killing," Sam continued, "I thinks, well, s'pose I goes eel-hunting. The tide 'ad jist started to run down, so there was a nice chance o' getting some eels. Down we goes on to some timbers, then into the mud, but not a blessed eel could I get. Presently I misses my dog. I called

Ruff, and whistled, but no good. I gives another whistle, and up he comes covered with mud. He looks at me, barks, and off he runs again, but into such a funny place. I was allers afeared to go there before, 'cause, don't you see, I thought the mud wouldn't bear me, and I didn't like the look o' the place; it's hawful dingy and dark, and when I looks, where d'ye think I was?"

"Don't know," said Joe; "where?"

"Why, jist where old Pat Waggar was murdered."

"Lor, you don't say so; didn't you feel dreadful bad?"

"Well, I just did," Sam replied, "but then I thinks there's no one as 'ud hurt me, so I made up my mind to foller the dog, and I did. What do you think I diskivered, old boy?" he said, looking wonderfully mysterious, and slapping Joe on the back.

"Don't know," said Joe, "what is it?"

"Why, a secret cellar."

"My heye—won't it be fine?" said Chimbley Joe, with a delighted grin.

"Yes," continued Sam, not heeding the interruption. "I sees a little hole, where the dorg had disappeared, which was only big enough for me to crawl through, and then I grazed me back. I didn't stay long gaping about; I thought I'd fetch you and Alick, if he'd a-been here, and we'd all go together and look at the crib. I ain't a coward, you know that; but I didn't care about being there alone, so I calls Ruff, marks the place, trots orf with my rats, and meets you just in time—so wot are we to do?"

"Pr'aps it would make a snug crib for a doss of a night," Joe responded, "and, if it's dry, why it 'u'd be better than the casual, any day; s'pose we goes and looks at it."

"Just what I thought," said Sam the rat-catcher. "Don't tell any o' the other boys; let's keep it dark until we finds out all about the place. We can't go now, 'cause it's too dark, and we mustn't go in the day time, 'cause that would be too light. But you and me can go and have a bit o' grub and a doss tonight out o' my money. Then we can get up early—say about four o'clock—take the dog and rat-trap, and see what the place is like."

"All right; but I ain't got any money," said Joe, ruefully.

"Wots the odds about that?" Sam rejoined. "I've got enough for the two on us," he said, as he led the way to a low coffee-house, where they might get a cheap tea.

"What say, chummy? Shall we take two o' these herrins in with us. No charge for cooking. No extras."

"If you like," said Chimbley, too modest to say yes, though he was very fond of a herring when they were to be had.

Uncultivated as the boy was, he could not directly ask for anything he might fancy if he had not the money to pay for it.

But Sam, taking it for granted that he would like one, picked out two full-roed herrings, for which the man wanted an extra halfpenny, vowing they were the best he had with him.

Satisfied with their bargain, the boys dived into the

before-mentioned coffee-house, and were very soon, as Chimbley Joe termed it, doing a "fizzing tuck out."

After this they adjourned to a "model lodging-house," where they put up for the night.

Sam awoke first, and thinking that it must be getting late, he called Joe.

They immediately dressed and started off to make further discoveries concerning the secret cellar.

Keeping a good look-out, to see that they were not watched, as the hour was much earlier than Sam had anticipated—and they well knew how suspiciously the police would regard two ragged boys being out at that time of the morning—they soon reached the water side.

Then they felt safe.

"Now," said Sam, "we must thread our way among the barges for some time, then dive in amongst that timber, cut under the old wharf, and there we shall be at the rummy crib."

"I'm glad Ruff is here," said Chimbley, "cause he will make a row when there's anyone near."

"Yes, he will, I can tell you," Sam replied. "See him stick his ears up and whine if anybody comes."

"But where was he?" asked Chimbley, "all night, I mean."

"Why," answered Sam, looking proudly at his dog, "he stayed out on the door-step. He allers does that; if I was away for a week I believe he'd stay outside for me; so it wouldn't do for anyone to try their games with me, 'cause the dog would soon tell tales. That's why I takes him about; he ain't up to much, 'cos he's so little, but to me he's worth his weight in gold. He's true bred, and a stunning rat-catcher."

"Carry me out! Look where the dorg's sloped to," Joe cried.

"Yes, that's the hentrance to the crib; fine, ain't it?" said Sam.

"Lor?" said Chimbley, making a dead stop, and gazing round in wonderment, "this is a stunning place, and no herror."

"Now, Chummy, jist pick hup that stick as is lying at your feet, I've got one and my knife," said Sam. "Have you got one?"

"Catch me without a skewer."

"Well, then, follow me," said Sam. "Crawl down on your 'ands and knees in through the hole, and keep close to me in case anyone should be inside."

"All right," said Joe, doing one of his original shuffles in the mud while Sam was getting through the hole.

He was very soon followed by Chimbley Joe, who was so anxious to get inside that he could hardly refrain from helping Sam with the end of his stick.

"It strikes me that that is an opening," said Sam, pointing to a dark square mass, that might have been a door in its time, but so covered with cobwebs and dirt that it was impossible to say whether it really was anything more than a dark corner of the cellar.

"It's a door," said Sam.

"Is it?" queried Chimbley. "Shouldn't like to have to open and shut it. Guess you'd find yer heyes bunged up for a month with dirt."

"Can't open it, anyhow," said Sam, who was puffing and blowing from the exertion he made in trying to pull the door open.

"Just get your knife, Sam, and shove it in that ere crack, till you makes it large enough for me to put this stick through."

"But," said Sam, "you can't. There's an iron plate the other side."

"Never mind about that," Joe replied. "We'll soon knock that off."

As soon as Sam got the knife in the woodwork of the door, it commenced to give way, and Chimbley had the gratification of thrusting his stick through the aperture.

By this means they soon broke a large piece of the panel away, which was dreadfully rotten through old age and the continual dampness of the atmosphere, and by hammering with the thick sticks they quickly effected an entrance.

They then had to ascend three or four stone steps, which led to a large, stone-floored vault.

"Here's a bit o' luck!" said Chimbley. "Wot's that? I heard summut go click then, jist as I put my foot through the door."

"Most likely a rat," Sam returned. "Look at 'em scampering away. Come here, you brute!"

He said this as he administered a tremendous blow to a rat that passed close by him.

The hit was effectual; it brought the rat down dead without a squeal.

"Oh! that was a clout," yelled Chimbley, with delight.

The dog had managed to kill two or three, and then Sam felt contented.

"Now," said Chimbley, "be careful, 'cause I'll swear that there was something clicked jist inside."

"All right."

But it was not all right, for no sooner had Sam put his foot on the spot indicated by Chimbley, than the click was heard again.

Instead of Sam springing from the spot to where Chimbley was, he stood wondering what it could possibly be.

While he stood thus, there was a sound very much resembling that of a pair of dirty, rusty hinges being put in motion, by the opening or closing of a trap-door, or machinery, which ended in a loud, grating noise.

Then Sam felt himself held firmly by the waist, and the flagstone that he stood upon commenced to move from under him.

"Help me, Joe; I am going down."

Greatly to the surprise of Joe, and the delight of Sam, the stone stopped as though unable to move.

In the confusion and fright this unexpected event had thrown them into, they had not noticed what it was that held Sam so tightly; but now they had an opportunity, and Sam very soon understood the nature of the thing that held him.

"Joe, I've been caught in a man-trap," he said, dismally.

"Ugh! crikey! my! it's a wonder you warn't killed, Sam," said Chimbley Joe, who had heard many awful tales about man-traps, but had never seen one before.

Not so with Sam. He had seen traps of every kind made for a similar purpose.

"Come here and help me," said Sam, who was ghastly white.

He was no coward; but the narrow escape he had had was enough to make any boy turn pale.

"Yes; but look at this ere hole. What's the meaning of that?" said Joe, as he pulled at one side of the trap to release his friend.

"Darn it!" returned Sam, who was thinking of a way of getting out. "Give me my stick; that's it. Now, then, put your foot against the other side, and pull with all your might. That's right," he said, as Joe pulled the great iron row of teeth from Sam's side.

"But what are you going to do with the stick," demanded Joe.

"Why," said Sam, "if you'll hold the trap away from my back I'll put the stick along the edge of the teeth, and then I can force it back and get out, otherwise the teeth would stick in me.

As they forced the trap back into its former position, they noticed that the flagstone resumed its place.

"That's all right. Carry me out if it ain't."

"Yes," said Sam, as he stepped away from the trap, "it's a very cunning bit of machinery, but it don't trap me again."

"Nor me either," Chimbley Joe remarked, shuddering.

"But how was it that it didn't hurt me?" said Sam.'

"Why," said Chimbley, "because, don't yer see, it's rusty and won't work."

Chimbley Joe had spoken correctly; the trap was a piece of machinery made for some devilish purpose, though what that purpose was no one could tell."

It was a fixture, that could plainly be seen, and when stepped upon by anyone it would close immediately, just above the hips of any ordinary sized man, and cut him in two, if it was in proper order.

It had not been used for many years, that could plainly be seen, nor had the cellars, by their appearance.

The most strange part of the affair was that when the iron teeth met, after going through a person, the large stone upon which it was fixed would drop in a slanting position.

So that whatever might have got into the trap, after being cut through by a double row of iron teeth, would slide down the slanting stone into the sewer below, then the stone would resume its place.

The trap would not open of its own accord, but had to be reset by human hands.

"I should like to examine the thing," said Joe.

"Not now," said Sam. "Plenty of time for that. And if ever we should come to live here, why, we'll oil it and set it in workin' order."

"Yes, so we will," replied Chimbley Joe, who was surveying the apartment, for they had no time to notice anything before.

The chamber in which they found themselves was certainly one of strange construction.

It was a style of architecture very rarely seen now-a-days. The walls were of stone, the roof vaulted, and supported by large pillars.

At one end there were three small stone archways, but only one had any entrance.

That they walked through.

They saw nothing beyond a small cellar, so dark and murky that they had to strike a light to see their way across it.

"Well," said Sam, "what do you think o' the crib?"

"Fizzing," replied Joe, who was indulging in a fugitive breakdown at that moment. "Anyhow, I shouldn't like to be here alone. Crikey, shouldn't I get the blues."

"Now we must see about starting back, cause, don't you see, its getting late, and this place ain't over sweet," said Sam the rat-catcher.

"No, and a little breakfast wouldn't do us any harm," answered Chimbley, as they returned to the entrance.

"Mind the trap," said Sam.

"Make no error, I shall be werry careful that it don't mind me as long as I am capable o' taking care o' my sweet self."

Then, thrusting his hands in his pockets, he gave a very comical look round at the vault, as though he did not feel inclined to leave it, exclaiming—

"Well, this is a luxury, Sam. You oughter have a putty medal for finding this crib. Won't Alick jist be off his nut with delight. I s'pose you'll want to be leader of the Poor Boys o' London for finding 'em this place?"

"No," said Sam; "Alick's a better fellow than I am; he understands more than me. 'Nother thing, he can read and write, and the boys mind him; they wouldn't me."

"Just so," said Joe. "You an' I don't think as how we can do much till he comes out, excepting to tell some o' the boys that we can depend on. No shoplifters or prigs you know in our band—they must all be honest who join the Poor Boys of London."

"What a fine name for 'em, Joe. Where did you 'ear that?"

"Why, Alick used to say that."

"Ah! he's a clever feller, and I likes him," said Sam; "but come along, or else we shall be twigged."

They had made their way out among the barges again, and were very soon in the street; seeing a coffee shop near at hand, they entered and called for coffee, which Sam paid for.

"I'm going rat-catching to-day again, so you'd better leave me here, and go and see Curly, Lanky, and Birchy, cause they's a good sort. Tell all on 'em 'cepting them as you can't trust."

"All right," answered Joe, who was amusing himself by leaning back in his seat, throwing back his head, and jerking crumbs of bread into his mouth; one stuck just at the top of his throat, stopping his little game, and making him feel uncomfortable. He clutched at the coffee cup and took a draught to wash the crumb down, but soon felt the folly of that, for the coffee was scalding hot, and it went down his throat, taking the skin off his tongue, and burning him all the way down, which caused his eyes to water so that Sam asked him what he was crying for.

Joe, being in a nasty spiteful humour, at that moment wouldn't tell him the real cause, hoping that he might be served the same, for he said—

"I was thinking of poor Alick what's in prison."

"Never mind, old boy, he'll be out soon."

And Sam took a good pull at the coffee.

Joe nearly fell off his seat with delight as he watched his companion's face.

It went very red, then he gasped, his eyes commenced starting, and then, as he gave a gulp, the water streamed down his cheeks.

"What are you crying for?" laughed Joe, who was unable to keep himself still, his mirth was so great; and in his delight he threw his legs about in such a manner that he kicked Sam awfully in the shins.

"Why, I thinks it's a pity you ain't in prison with him—he—he—he," said Sam, mockingly. "You are a sneak, and just you keep them long arms o' yours still. You've kicked me in the shins, and now you've given me a smack over the mouth with them scraggy fingers. They are long enough for a rang-e-tang."

"They are long enough to reach a rat-catcher's nose if he's cheeky," said Joe, suggestively.

"Keep a civil tongue in yer head, and meet me in the Whitechapel-road against the church; I'll treat yer to the Sun," said Sam. "We don't oughter quarrel, yer know."

The Sun was a short name for a minor theatre in the Whitechapel-road, properly titled the Royal Sun.

There most Whitechapel butcher boys went to spend their evenings, the actors playing such things as suited the taste of the audience, and caused the before-mentioned butcher boys to do rehearsals when their masters' backs were turned, and also to get stage-struck every now and then.

"All right," said Joe.

And they parted.

Chimbley Joe soon found such of his companions as he wished to let into the secret, and telling them to meet him under one of the railway arches near the Borough-market, trotted off to get his broom.

He did not do much trade, however, as he had to meet the boys under the railway arch, and he never liked to keep them waiting.

When he arrived there he found them engaged in a game of buttons, which they had picked up goodness only knows where, as their own clothes were innocent of such useful articles.

Curly, who was in the act of throwing a nicker at a button, caught sight of Chimbley.

He partly turned round, and said, "Wot cheer, Chimbley."

And letting fly the nicker, he caught a youth called Birchy a tremendous blow on the ankle bone.

"Who done that?" cried the enraged Birchy, who was christened that delightfully uncommon name by the boys because he manufactured birch brooms.

"Curly did it," said a little sneak, because he was afraid of getting a spank for it from the huge fist of Birchy.

"You did, did you? Then take that," growled Birchy, aiming a blow at Curly, which caught him in the eye.

"No fighting," said Chimbley, "'cause I ain't got no time to spare."

"Wot did you tell us to come here for, then?" said Curly, rather wild at having a smack in the eye.

"Dry up, and come round," said Chimbley, in an authoritative tone of voice. "Now, look here, are you all a mind to stick to Alick, hold aloof from Tike and his gang, keep your mouths shut and be honest, and go on as we should all along—no turn-coats or peaches? If you'll say you will, why, I'll tell you what Sam has diskivered."

"Tell us!" shouted the boys.

"Why, it's a fine place under the wharves," said Chimbley, speaking low in case any one should be near, "and we can all go and live there without troubling the casual any more. You won't want to stop in the streets all night, and when Alick comes out he'll tell us all what to do. Now then, can you keep it dark, all of you?"

"Yes," the boys replied in a breath.

"All right," said Chimbley Joe; "then meet me and Sam to-morrow down the Lower Marsh, Lambeth, and we'll go and make a home for the 'Poor Boys of London,' and a refuge for those who would otherwise be 'Driven to Crime.'"

## CHAPTER XVI.

THE BOSKER IN DISGUISE—TIKE'S VILLAINY— THE RECOGNITION BETWEEN RICHARD GRANT AND JAMES BURKETT UNDER WATERLOO-BRIDGE.

PRISON walls were not strong enough to confine such men as Nathan Claws and the Bosker.

Bribery had something to do with softening the gaolers' hearts, and although there was a great outcry nobody was to blame when the cells which had held the precious pair were found vacant.

There was a dreadful row about the affair, but pursuit was baffled for the time, and no one seemed to know where to lay hands on either of the criminals.

The Bosker kept himself quiet for a few days at Nathan's; but his savage nature soon commenced to feel tired of the quiet life he led there; not only that, he wanted money, and Eastlake would not give it him because he had failed in his attempt to take Gilbert's life.

"Money I must have," he muttered, as he paced up and down the thieves' kitchen, which was nearly deserted on account of the time.

"If Tike should come in send him after me," he exclaimed to Nathan, "to the Pig—you know. I'm going out. I feel choked in this den."

He had not gone far when he met Tike shuffling down the street.

Tike made a dead stop, and gazed at Burkett in amazement.

"Do you want me?" said the little thief, in some surprise.

"Yes, come with me," the Bosker replied, and they moved on towards the park.

"Now look, here, Tike; you're well up to the canting dodge, ain't you?"

"Yes, I can cry as natteral as a blessed babby," said Tike, grinning.

"That is well," the Bosker replied. "I am going to show you a house across the park. I want you to watch this house well; notice everyone that comes out, and when you see an old gentleman with a little bit of white whiskers, follow him. Try the mumping lay; do it well, mind, and if he should take pity on you and give you some money, ask him if you might go and get the bits of bread and meat. You know, of course, what to do?"

"Trust me for that—make no error."

"Listen, then," the Bosker replied, "there's a kind-hearted old housekeeper there, and if you get the right side of her you'll most likely tumble into a berth as odd boy for the servants. If you succeed let me know. Mind you, I want you to sleep in that house before the week is out. You can if you like, but if you breathe a word of what I've said I'll twist your neck."

The boy turned pale; he knew too well that the Bosker would keep his word.

"All right," Tike replied; "and, of course, you want me to let you in?"

"Just so. Now you understand. Go, then; that's the house," the Bosker said, pointing from the corner of the street to a magnificent building; "take this, and keep good watch."

He handed Tike some coppers, and returning across the park, wended his way towards Waterloo-bridge.

Meanwhile, Tike was lurking round the house, keeping his eyes well open, and taking careful stock of everyone that came or went from the house.

"I must make myself look jolly miserable and hungry, else they won't pity me!" he said, deliberately taking off one of his boots, and, placing his foot in a dirty puddle.

This action caused a chill to go right through him, making him look as white as a sheet.

"That'll do," he muttered, as he commenced to shiver with the cold.

He replaced his boot, shrugged up his shoulders, and pulled a most pitiful face; he then turned his eyes up, until only the whites could be seen, causing the water to run down his cheeks like large tears.

Seeing a gorgeous flunkey coming up the area he ran to the gate.

"Please will you give me a piece o' bread?" he said, in most pitiful accents.

"No. Go away," said Jeames, indignantly.

He had no feeling for the poor starving wretches in the street while he could get plenty at his master's table.

Tike began to cry so naturally that the passers-by turned to see what was the matter.

"Oh! do-o-o-o! please," he sobbed, "there's me and a little sister and my poor mother starving."

An elderly gentleman passed Tike at that moment, and was about to ascend the steps when he heard Tike's pitiful half-broken sentences.

He turned, and inquired what was the cause of the disturbance.

"Boy beggin', my lord!" said the gorgeous one,

touching his forehead, "and he won't go away. Shall I fetch a policeman, my lord?"

"No," was the stern reply.

The old gentleman was a kind-hearted man himself, and knew very well that there was plenty in his house to spare for the poor.

"What is it, my little man?" he asked, kindly, and Tike then repeated the tale about his sister and mother.

"Take him down," said the gentleman. "Give him something to take to his starving parent and sister, and tell Mrs. Miller to give him half-a-crown."

Tike felt ready to dance with delight when he found himself in the kitchen, but still keeping a long face he added to his pitiful tale.

At the same time he told a story that he had been trying to get a place to clean boots, or do anything, and so won the heart of the kind housekeeper that she was determined to try and give him work, therefore she told him to call at seven o'clock the next morning.

Tike ran off in high glee to find the Bosker, to whom we will now return.

The Bosker had arranged with Tike to meet him under Waterloo-bridge, and there, strangely enough, he nearly fell over the Gorger, who was darting round a corner of the arch.

The Gorger gave a gasping cry.

"If it's you, Burkett, he yelled, "and not your ghost, run for your life. Richard Grant has been dodging me the last two hours, and he is on my track now."

An oath rose to the Bosker's lips, but, before he could utter it, Richard Grant, the detective, appeared.

"We meet again, Burkett," he said, "and you had better come with me quietly, or, by Heaven! it will be the worse for you."

He placed his hand inside his vest, but as quick as thought the Bosker drew his life preserver from his jacket pocket, and struck him down.

"Richard Grant," he hissed, "your are in my power. Make up your mind to die. You have hunted me too long already, and I will kill you if you have a hundred lives."

Grant saw the life preserver descending, and involuntarily closed his eyes.

At that moment there was a shrill yell.

The Gorger received a blow under the chin from a broom wielded by a boy.

Another youth seized one of his legs and threw him backwards, while a well-known character, named Wild Paddy, danced up in quick time, and dealt the Bosker such a terrific blow over the head with a stick, that he dropped the life preserver and rolled over.

In an instant he was on his feet and away, the Gorger following on his track.

Then up came Captain Jack, with a number of boys at his heels.

"I should have been up first," Captain Jack cried; "but I slipped. There goes the Bosker."

Richard Grant drew a pistol from his pocket and fired.

The Bosker still ran on, and a yell of defiance

escaped from his lips. He reached Nathan Claws' den, and lay quiet for some days.

But, like all hardened criminals, he grew bold again.

The Bosker, a wretch named Joe Lewis, alias the Burker, and another ruffian, rejoicing in the appellation of Leary Jock, met by appointment one evening at Nathan's.

They had business on hand, and they sat talking until Big Ben struck eleven.

Thinking all was quiet and safe, they prepared to depart.

The Bosker procured a bludgeon, and then they wended their way, each keeping a sullen silence, until they heard the tramp of some persons approaching.

In a few seconds the new-comers arrived in sight.

"It's all right," said the Bosker; "two of the flash captains, I suppose."

"I thought perhaps it was the crushers," muttered the Burker, in reply. Moving a little closer to one of the strangers, the Burker stared at him, as though he had a slight recollection of having seen him before.

"Know one of 'em?" said the Bosker, inquiringly.

"I think—"

At that moment the tallest of the two individuals partly turned his face.

The Burker caught sight of it and turned dreadfully pale, proving that whoever the man might be, he had some strange influence over the ruffian.

"Something up," said Leary Jock. "I'll wager there'll be a row atween 'em, and am just going to foller 'em, 'cause, don't you know, I likes old acquaintances, 'specially when I haven't done anything to be afeared on," he continued, sarcastically. And he strode on, giving a knowing leer at the Burker.

Burkett and the Burker continued their journey, and Leary Jock followed silently in the wake of the strangers.

Perhaps it is necessary to give a description of these "gentlemen."

One was tall and well built, with a military bearing and fine features, dark hair, and a massive pair of whiskers and moustachios. By his general appearance anyone would have taken him for a military captain or colonel.

The other was much younger, rather fair, slender, and gentlemanly in his conversation.

He was speaking in a low tone to his elder companion.

"I tell you what it is, major," he said, "give them up I will not."

"This," answered the major, as the other termed him, "is no place for us to settle anything in that line of business. If you will be kind enough to come with me, I have a snug little apartment close handy."

"With pleasure," said the younger person.

"This way," said the major, as he led his companion to a house not far from Drury-lane, and, producing a latch-key, he opened the door and led the way to a room up stairs.

A strange feeling crept over his companion as he

entered. He felt anything but comfortable in a dark, dreary-looking house, with such a man as the one before him, and knowing they were not friends.

But shaking off the feeling of fear, he followed the major upstairs to a nicely furnished apartment.

Leary Jock, who had remained in their wake, found himself shut outside, but that did not matter to him at all.

He felt curious, and a dozen doors would not have kept him from entering.

He was a wide-awake customer, and he never did anything desperate or got himself into trouble by letting people know too much.

In the present case he slowly surveyed the house, and looked about, to assure himself that no one was near.

He produced a bunch of something very much like crooked pieces of wire, but to him they were very useful.

He selected three of them, and carefully putting them one at a time in the lock, had the pleasure of finding the lock give way and the door open.

"Well done," he muttered, as he entered the passage.

Taking his boots off, he took from his pocket a pair of list slippers, and, putting them on, he crept upstairs as noiselessly as a cat.

Arriving at a door at the top of the landing, he stopped and listened.

He could hear voices, but could not exactly catch any distinct words. He would have caught something more than words had the major known he was there.

Leary Jock then placed his ear to the keyhole, and heard plainly what was going on.

"Captain Hamilton," said the major, "I do not wish to get out of temper, but unless you hand over those notes you won from me at the club we shall fall out."

"Never. I will suffer anything sooner. No, Major Carleton; I know you at last. You have had your run. Your game is up. I have a long account to settle with you. I told you that some time or other I would bring you to the gallows. Now I can do it."

"Beware!" hissed the major, his eyes glaring murderously. "Do not dare me too much, captain."

"Bah!" laughed the captain. "I tell you, major, I know more than you imagine."

"You know more than is good for you."

"Stuff, I tell you, major. Let me now depart."

"Not until you give up those notes."

"Look you," said Hamilton, coolly. "I shall not give up the notes. I know they are of no use to me. I plainly tell you they are forged, and you know it. I also know of that little affair with Raymond. How did you kill him? Not in duelling, as you wished us to believe. No, Carleton; he was murdered, and by your second—you know it—and I can prove it. I also have in my possession the cards that you played with at the time you won the two thousand, or rather cheated the gentleman out of it. And I know that a certain gentleman, a captain, some little time since, was kicked out of a club-room for being a blackleg and impostor. He was obliged to fly no one knew whither. He is forgotten in time, and a stranger comes amongst us. He appears to be a gentleman of fortune, and he is liked by all in the club, with an exception—that is myself. I never forget or forgive. And I recognise the stranger, under the name of Major Carleton, to be the same vagabond and villain, Captain Ge—"

"Hold!" shouted the major, "I will hear no more."

His face went livid, and the veins stood out like cords upon his forehead.

He looked a perfect demon as he stood thus confronting his enemy, who had also risen from his seat.

Captain Hamilton felt he had said too much, and this feeling was confirmed when the other spoke.

Stifling down his passion a little, the major said—

"Hamilton, I am sorry for you; but you know too much, and your last words are your death warrant. I must and will possess those notes, my pocket-book, and cards. You hold my life in your hands, therefore I must silence you!"

Hamilton sprang back.

He saw his danger by the look in the other's face, and he made his way to the door, but the major had locked it, and put the key in his pocket.

"Now," he said, a deadly gleam shooting from his eyes, "are you willing to give up those things, and leave the club?"

"Never! I still defy you. You dare not harm me, people would hear."

The major answered him by a low, devilish laugh, and, producing a pistol, said—

"You shall see—you have defied me. My life is in your hands while you live, and I—"

"No, no, for Heaven's sake! don't fire," cried the young captain.

"I intend to; I am very sorry, but it is your own fault."

Captain Hamilton saw it was useless to ask for mercy, so he gathered all his strength for the emergency.

Looking round, he saw an officer's dress sword hanging from a hook in the wall.

With a cry he sprang forward, and, drawing the weapon from its scabbard, turned and faced his enemy.

"Now, pitiless wretch! murderous hound! I will defend myself to the last," the captain cried; but the major only laughed.

As the captain came bounding forward, Carleton fired, and the report was followed by a shriek of agony from Hamilton.

He was mortally wounded.

That shriek the murderer never forgot, sleeping or waking, night or day.

Likewise, he could never drive the dying man's stony gaze from his memory.

The young captain did not fall, but still supported himself against the wall.

He tried to stagger forward, and get at his murderer, who stood regarding him with a grim smile of satisfaction.

"Monster!" said the dying man, "you have triumphed, but, remember, your time will come; hide my body where you will, it shall bring you to your grave."

"Oh!" he continued, "for ten minutes' life—oh! Heaven, 'tis hard to die like this. No," he screamed, "I will not die. Who dares to say I shall?"

He staggered forward, and the major recoiled, as if expecting that the wounded man would yet have his revenge.

It was something horrible to behold the young man, raving like a maniac, with the blood pouring from his body, and the sword still grasped in his hand, as he came towards the villain.

"Ha, ha, ha!" he laughed, "you fear me now. Yes, and well you may. I intend to mark you. Look, look at your face now. You are branded— branded. I will not leave you even in death."

In the last throes of death he raised his sword, and, before the major could move out of his path, he slashed him across the temple, making a gash some inches long.

Even then he did not appear to be satisfied, for he caught the major by the hair, and looked horribly into his face.

The major tried to disengage Hamilton's hand from his hair, but to no purpose.

"Help!" yelled the major, the perspiration pouring down his face as he felt the young captain grow stiff, and his eyes fix themselves upon him. "Horror—oh! horror. Help, help, help!—oh, help!"

Carleton uttered a shriek and fell to the floor, the young captain falling by his side, a corpse.

The major tried to rise, but the hand still retained its hold upon his hair.

Nature could stand no more.

He was held in the death grasp of his victim.

Another unearthly yell burst from his lips, and, fainting, he lay senseless by the side of the corpse.

Leary Jock, who had been a witness of the murderous deed, found himself shut up in that lonely house with the murdered and the murderer.

## CHAPTER XVII.

SAVED BY THE THAMES POLICE—"DOWN WITH THE SPY"—HOW NICHOLAS SLIME BOLTS AT THE SIGHT OF A HELMET.

IT is high time that, having seen Nicholas Slime, otherwise the Gorger, alive and well, we should tell how he escaped drowning.

As the police boat arrived, a wave caused by a steamboat that passed at that moment, washed over the would-be grave of the unfortunate Nicholas, and left no traces where the occupants might find the embedded wretch.

They had given it up for a fruitless search when the Gorger, in his last effort, thrust his huge fist through the mud.

One of the police, turning his head, caught sight of the dirty hand waving about frantically.

"There's the poor devil's hand sticking up, like a signal of distress," he said.

They rowed back, and the Gorger was lugged out in an instant by three or four strong arms, and pulled into the boat.

A more pitiable sight was never seen.

He was one mass of mud, and the men could not have told his face from the back of his head, but for his huge nose, which stuck out like a pick-axe.

His eyes, ears, and mouth were all stopped up with mud, and the police proposed that they should row out into deep water and duck him.

They were about to carry out their proposition, when a voice called on them to stop, and a boat with one occupant pulled alongside them.

"All right, mates," said the boatman, "he's a friend o' mine. Some young warmints pushed him off a barge."

The police were glad to get rid of him, and gave him up without making any comment.

The poor Gorger was dragged from one boat to the other, quite unconscious of what was going on.

The boatman then pulled out into the middle of the river, and, taking up a tin pot which was used for bailing the water out of the boat, dipped it in the Thames, threw the water over the Gorger's face, and washed the dirt from his eyes.

The liquid seemed to refresh the poor wretch, and he looked at his preserver with gratitude and surprise in his dirty eyes; then, drawing a long, deep breath, he gave a spasmodic kick, and, hitting the boatman in the stomach with his big foot, sent him sprawling over the seat, and lodged him on his back in the bottom of the boat.

"Nicholas," he said, after getting up, "don't you know me, old son?"

"B-o-o-o-o!" the Gorger began to bellow; "where am I? B-o-o-o-o!"

"Stop that b-o-o-ing. You are all right."

"Am I?" he said, in a feeble voice.

"Don't yer know your old friend!" inquired the boatman, helping him on to a seat.

The Gorger looked at him wonderingly, and then looked round frightened, as though he expected to see his young tormentors close behind him.

"What! is it you?" said Nicholas, in utter amazement.

"Yes, it's me," returned the boatman.

"Boozer?" gasped the Gorger.

"Boozer, your old pal," laughed that worthy.

"You was a sneak to leave a cove," said Nicholas Slime.

"Them little cusses pelted me with stones and mud," said the Boozer, savagely, "and a lump stuck in my heye; then they shoved the boat off, and I couldn't see where I was going. When I catches hold on 'em I'll wring their necks."

"So will I."

"We'll go to Nathan's, where you'll be able to get a new rig out," the Boozer suggested.

"I'm jolly hungry," said the Gorger, in the way of reply, scraping the mud off the knees of his trousers, as he sat, and flinging it in the water by handfuls— by accident he pitched a piece in the Boozer's eye.

For which the Boozer gave him a dig in the left ribs with an oar, and the Gorger walked very stiff towards Nathan's when they landed.

There came a general shout of laughter as the unfortunate Nicholas entered the thieves' kitchen.

But a smile of pleasure came over his face when he saw the large blazing fire, round which a score of ill-looking fellows were sitting drinking and smoking, and Nicholas Slime's eyes wandered round the apartment in search of something to eat.

"Vell, Mr. Slime, vot have they been doing with you ?" said the old Jew, grinning.

"He looks slimy enough now," said one of the fellows turning round, thinking that he had said something witty.

"Come and have a drink," said another, pushing a huge can towards the Gorger.

He took the proffered vessel and said, in a long, drawling tone—

"I ain't had nothin' to eat all day."

"You'll find some grub over there in a parcel," said a third.

The Gorger made a clutch at it, and seating himself on a bench, began a furious attack on the cold bread and meat.

When he had finished his feed he emptied the crumbs out of the paper into his palm, and threw them down his throat,; then, clutching the can of beer which he had forgotten to return, he took a long draught.

Rubbing his stomach in a manner which denoted that it was filled at last, he walked up to old Nathan and said something to him in a whisper.

"Yesh, my poy, you shall have a brand new suit."

Nicholas Slime seemed very satisfied with his arrangement with the old Jew, and went into another compartment to divest himself of his dirty clothes, wash himself, and put on the new togs, all but his hat—his much cherished tile—which he brushed up carefully.

During his absence, the clamorous voices of the inmates of the den of infamy were suddenly brought to hush by the appearance of a stranger.

A tall, slender, handsome youth, of gentle bearing; his brow was massive and with hair rather inclined to curl ; his complexion was dark, though his hands were small and white ; his countenance was pleasing and engaging, though in his large black eyes there was something resolute and commanding ; a small, black moustache added to his noble look.

As he stood in that den of thieves he looked like a prince among a legion of demons.

He surveyed the scene with a searching look, and his glance fell on Leary Jock ; as the latter met the young intruder's piercing gaze he turned deadly pale.

The stranger beckoned him.

As Leary Jock approached his knees knocked together, and he shook in every limb.

Leary Jock's face relaxed, and beads of perspiration rolled down his cheeks as the stranger whispered something in his ear.

Then he staggered to a seat and hid his face in his hands, while the rest of the gang looked on in amazement.

The stranger must have known the password to get in, but he did not know any of them there at present but Leary Jock.

Nathan Claws looked at him inquiringly.

The stranger answered his inquiring glances by a defiant look, which showed he was not frightened to be there alone.

The Jew made a sign to the men.

"A spy !" cried one.

"Down with the spy !" shouted a chorus of rough voices.

They all rose and made a rush towards him.

The stranger crossed his arms on his chest and gave a defiant laugh as they came towards him, brandishing huge knives and sticks.

They made a dead stop as they saw that cool deliberate act.

There was something mysterious about this stranger that the men could not make out, and, though anxious for his life, they seemed to admire him for his cool courage.

Nathan Claws urged them on, and at last they surrounded him.

Still he did not move.

Just then the Bosker entered with the Burker. The latter, seeing the young stranger, fell back two or three steps, his whole framework shook, and his face turned a ghastly hue.

Then the Burker whispered something in the stranger's ear, and the stranger whispered in return.

"A spy !" again shouted the fellows.

"He's no spy, but one of us," said the Burker.

Then the motley crew returned to their seats, and the stranger went into a corner and seated himself on a stool, where he could see and hear everything that passed.

The Bosker took no notice of anything, but only asked for the Gorger, and that illustrious individual made his appearance.

"Well, you sneaking whelp, where the devil have you been ?  I expect David Eastlake here soon," the Bosker said.  "And I shall want you to go with Burker, as I can't go."

"All right, I'll look after him," said Nicholas.

"That's just what I want you to do."

"Jim," said the Gorger, in a very plaintive voice.

"What is it ?" answered his companion.

"'Ave you got a tanner to get some bread and cheese with ?" Nicholas demanded, who always thought of his stomach before he went out on dangerous business.  "I ain't had nothing to eat all day."

"You liar," cried the Bosker, in a rage.  "You have just had enough to fill a hox."

"It was only a snack that filled up a little corner."

Just then David Eastlake entered, who put an end to their argument by calling the Bosker aside.

The stranger's face underwent a peculiar change when Eastlake came into the kitchen.

He got further into the dark, and watched his every movement.

"I have seen that girl again," said Eastlake, in an undertone, to the Bosker.

The Bosker looked at him inquiringly.

"What girl ?" he asked.

"Little Flo, sister to that young brat, Gilbert, that you have been paid to quiet."

"Where did you see her ?" inquired the Bosker.

"At Jacob Primrose's cab yard, playing about with his children."

*"Take that, you coward!" Alick cried, bringing down a blacking-box on the top of the Tike's head.*

"I know the place," said the Bosker.

"Then you must have her silenced to-night. You know my meaning?" Eastlake said, looking the Bosker full in the face.

"Yes ; but I can't do it to-night."

"It must be done."

"I'll put it in the hands of my friend the Burker."

David Eastlake did not care who did it as long as he could be rid of the children, and, agreeing that the Burker should do the job, he gave the Bosker a purse of money and left.

The young stranger had heard everything that passed, and as Eastlake left the thieves' kitchen he rose and followed on his track as silently as a shadow.

The Burker went on his murderous errand, with instructions from James Burkett, followed by the Gorger, and they soon reached the abode of the good-hearted cabman.

Everything was hushed in the dead stillness of midnight.

The inmates had all retired to rest, and were sleeping peacefully, without a thought of trouble befalling them before the morning.

The Burker scaled the wall, and got to the back of the house without the least noise, while the Gorger kept a look-out, to signal if any one appeared.

The Burker soon clambered over the sheds, and gained the window of the children's bedroom with the agility of a monkey.

Quietly opening the window, he stealthily crept to the bedside where his innocent victim lay, unconscious of what was about to befall her.

One of the children started as he pulled the bedclothes aside.

He clutched a life-preserver, and a malicious glare shone in his eyes.

It would have been the child's last cry if it had made any noise to rouse the inmates ; but it turned over and went to sleep.

Clutching hold of little Flo, he made for the window ; but the child awoke, frightened, and finding herself in the arms of a stranger, she shrieked at the top of her voice.

"Silence !" he hissed, between his teeth ; " if you utter another sound I'll murder you."

Again and again she shrieked, and Jacob Primrose, his wife, and the rest of the inmates, looking terribly frightened, rushed into the room.

Like a tiger the Burker leapt through the window, and jumped from the shed to the ground.

He reeled and fell with the shock ; but he still held his victim tight.

Before he had time to recover and gain his footing he was surrounded by the occupants of the house, in great disorder.

The Burker looked round for the Gorger ; but he was nowhere to be seen.

He had sloped when he saw a shiny helmet appearing round the corner, the owner of this helmet wearing a blue coat with bright buttons.

The Burker clutched his life-preserver in one hand, and holding little Flo in his other arm, made a rush at the people.

He forced his way through them, and was making his escape through the gates, when he was caught in the arms of a policeman.

"Philip Bartlett !" gasped the Burker.

"The very same," returned the policeman, looking at the child wonderingly, as though trying to bring to his mind where he had seen her.

He sprung his rattle for assistance, and in less than five minutes six or seven of his brother officers came to his aid, one of them bringing the trembling Gorger with him.

----

### CHAPTER XVIII.

ALICK'S RELIEF—THE MEETING BETWEEN CHIMBLEY JOE AND ALICK—THE HAUNT OF THE POOR BOYS OF LONDON.

THE seven days had expired.

Liberty was at hand, and in a few more hours Alick would be free.

Free !

How that word seemed to echo through his heart, and caused the blood to rush to his pale and wan face.

"What am I to do ?" he thought, as he paced to and fro in the cell. "Certainly it is something to have freedom, but yet," he muttered, "friendless, homeless, without any means of a livelihood, watched by the police, and shunned by those who could help me, what have I to live for, and for what reason have I been so treated ? Firstly, for wanting that which I have a right to—the chance of earning a honest livelihood ; secondly, for attempting to save my sister from a fate worse than death."

Throwing himself upon his hard seat, he gave way to his grief, and wept bitterly as he thought how he had tried to gain a honest living, but had been prevented.

Soon, however, he was aroused by the gaoler, and shortly afterwards he was breathing the fresh air of a fine spring morning.

He gazed eagerly round as he came out, hoping that he might come across some person he knew ; but he could see no one.

He turned sadly from the gate, with his face flushing every now and then, as those who saw him emerge made some coarse and unfeeling remark, forgetting what their own feelings would have been had they been within hearing of such ill-timed jests upon anyone dear to them placed in the same position as the poor homeless boy.

Alick had not proceeded far before he heard a well-known voice calling him by name.

"Alick—Alick ! Here he is."

And the next instant his hand was caught in the grasp of Chimbley Joe, who danced with delight at seeing his friend, and Alick's face beamed with joy as he beheld a number of his companions waiting to greet him.

"We should a-come up to the gate and waited for you on'y that good-looking peeler wouldn't let us stop there," said Sam the rat-catcher.

"How are you, Alick ?" said a little effeminate voice. "You haven't spoken to me yet."

And Alick beheld the small tearful face of Curly looking up into his.

"I didn't mean it," Alick said, extending his hand to the good-hearted little fellow, who was crying to such an extent that Chimbley thought he never could get his face into shape again.

Poor Alick felt very much inclined to cry himself, as he had not expected such a greeting.

Certainly it was only by a set of rough street boys.

But the poor uncared-for fellows really made such a fuss with him that he could hardly control his feelings.

Chimbley and Curly made more fuss than all the rest.

They were half-laughing, half-crying.

It pained Chimbley to see how Alick's form had wasted in such a short time.

"Come on," he said; "we have got something to tell you that'll make you glad."

"Where can we go to?" asked Alick.

"We'll show you. Don't be so down in the mouth, or else you'll set me off," said the kind-hearted Chimbley.

Then he related the whole circumstances concerning the underground home they had discovered, and concluded by saying that it was—

"All through Sam and the little dog, Ruff. But we couldn't do much. We wanted you to come and tell us wot to do. But we have got the floor clean, and Pug gave us a lot o' mats. Earthenware Ned brought a lot o' his stone mugs and basins, 'cause he's had a lucky week at hawking, so he handed over wot he had left to us. Then we puts a farden, and some on us a happeny each together, for him to get more."

Alick listened with pleasure to the graphic account given him by his companion of the new home.

"But how shall we get there?" demanded Alick.

"Oh! that's easy enough," said Chimbley. "The tide is low, and we've got two entrances; so we're all right."

Here the boys' attention was attracted by the yelling of their companions.

"What cheer, Ikey!" shouted one.

"Hullo! Flash 'un," shouted another.

The person to whom they were addressing these remarks was the same flashily-dressed young gent who figured in the fight at the time the Gorger and the Boozer were being hunted.

It was the unfortunate Ikey Bob, the swell.

He had become acquainted with a simple-minded country girl, who had a little money, and thinking there was a chance of getting something out of her, he pretended that he had fallen desperately in love, and was pitching an awfully strong tale when he unluckily came in contact with the Poor Boys.

They saw at a glance the strength of the whole affair, and thinking they would spoil his little game for once, they began shouting after him, causing the country girl a great deal of surprise and himself to feel very uncomfortable.

"What does it mean?" she asked. "Do they know you?"

"I, my dear; aw! 'taint likely."

Chimbley, who heard the reply, could not stand it, so he left Alick to join in the fun.

"Aw!" he said, mocking Ikey, "you do, only you're too flash to notice us."

"Saucy young scamp!" he said, as he made a clutch at Chimbley.

But missing that young gentleman, he caught the unfortunate Curly a blow that sent him reeling into the gutter.

That was the worst thing he could have done.

The London street boys are ever ready for a bit of fun at some one else's expense, and to take any notice of them only encourages their persistence; but to strike one of a gang is more than they can stand, and so Ikey, the swell, found it.

"Well I'm blowed," said Chimbley, "jist look at that. Why you big, ugly cur, to hit a little 'un like him. Carry me out, you oughter to be bonnetted."

"Yes, let's bonnet him," said at least half-a-dozen boys at once.

And it was no sooner said than done by the young urchins.

The luckless Ikey discovered that he had his hands full.

He was not a coward; but what could he do? To strike boys of their age would have been mean and despicable, if he could have caught them.

"Yah!" yelled the wild troop, "who starched your collar?"

"Don't believe him, miss; he's a sneak!" cried one Arab.

"Let's christen his tile!" shouted Chimbley.

Away went Ikey Bob's hat flying, and his tormentors uttered a yell that nearly sent the country damsel into fits.

She thought they were certainly going to murder him.

But they contented themselves by kicking his hat about until they got into such confusion that they commenced to kick each other instead.

Chimbley had just received a kick below the knee-cap, that made his eyes water dreadfully.

A little doctor's boy, who happened to be surveying the scene with immense delight, stood rather near Chimbley when he received the kick, and Chimbley not being able to discover the real culprit, thought he would wreak his revenge upon the looker on.

"Now then, Buttons, what do you want?" he said.

"Nothin'," said that individual, his dignity hurt by the insult to the buttons that he prized so much.

"Take it and go then," said Chimbley; "don't stand there wasting your master's time, and letting his patients die for want o' their physic."

"S'pose I can stand here if I like?"

"S'pose you can't. You was grinning at me, and I'm a good mind to give you a hiding," said Chimbley Joe.

"Try," said Buttons, putting down the basket, and looking wonderfully brave, at the same time feeling ready to cry with fright in case Chimbley should try.

"Why, you under-sized, skinny-looking rasher o' bacon, I'd take the buttons off on you in two minutes, you shrimp, I would," said Chimbley, looking all the contempt he felt.

"Gar on!" said the doctor's boy, making a feint at Chimbley; "go and comb your hair."

"Say it again," said Joe, looking desperate.

He said it again and got something for his trouble.

Chimbley hit him smartly under the chin, and then he squared up to Buttons.

"You have got my monkey up now, and you'd better look out," said Joe.

"Wait a minute," said Buttons, "I ain't ready," and he made a great fuss of tucking up his sleeves, delaying the fight as long as possible.

The boy was a rank coward, and he would have given anything to have had an opportunity of running away.

Presently he thought of a good excuse.

"You just wait till I come back; I must make haste with the medicine now."

"He wants to sneak off," said some of the boys, who, in anticipation of a fight, had given up tormenting Ikey Bob. No sooner did Ikey see the boys' attention called to the expected "mill" than he picked up his battered tile, and, calling a cab, drove off with the young lady, who felt flattered at having a ride in a hansom.

Meanwhile the boys gathered round, cutting off all chance of flight.

"Give him the coward's blow," said one.

Chimbley Joe walked quietly up to the boy and hit him slightly on the shoulder, then turned to walk back and take his place, when he caught such a stinger on the ear that it took Chimbley's hearing away for a minute or two.

"You little coward, to take me unawares! Come on!" he gasped.

The boy, thinking it safest to fight now he had struck Joe, squared up rather awkwardly, and after a little of very excellent scientific sparring on the part of Joe, and a clumsy flinging about of the arms on the part of the doctor's boy, they had a "set-to."

Two or three boys had collected round Buttons to second him, so that there might be fair play.

"Crikey!" yelled Curly, "that's a hot un', right on the sneezin' horgan, too. Well done, Chummy!"

"That's good, go it, Buttons!" shouted one of the other boys; "hit him where he puts his bread-and-butter."

They went at it right and left; but Buttons was no match for Chimbley.

He skipped round his opponent, landing him one on the nose, then planting a heavy left-hander on the ear, and finally winding up by giving him a blow in the "wind," which sent the unfortunate little boy flying over his basket, where he lay gasping for breath.

"He's done—he's done!" shouted the boys.

"Bravo! Chummy, you have licked him."

And away they all scampered to Lambeth, where they met Captain Jack, who greeted Alick much in the same manner as the others had done.

"Go to the new home," Captain Jack said to Chimbley Joe; "I have got something rather particular on hand. Tell the Boys I shall want them when I come. I shall not be long after you. Sharp is the word, as I expect someone down here presently," he said.

Chimbley led the way towards the new home, telling the boys to come in two or three at a time, observing that he, Alick, and Sam would go in first.

Alick quite enjoyed the strange way of entering, but said nothing until he found himself safely inside.

Then he stood still and gazed around in wonderment at the strange scene before him.

The furniture consisted of a number of mats, a few empty casks, and two or three long egg-boxes.

A lamp hung by a chain from the roof, and gave a smoky light to the place; a large iron stove, placed in the centre, provided the boys with the means of cooking, and at the same time gave them the pleasure of a fire, that greatly added to the comfort of the place.

A box, made from the wood of several egg-boxes, served them for a table, and completed the domestic arrangements, as it also served as a receptacle for provisions.

"There, think we have been lazy?" said Chimbley, when he saw Alick had done his survey.

"No," said Alick; "you have been very clever to get it done at all."

"Yes. Why, don't you see, there was a lot on us, and Flash Harry came and gave his services—he helped, so did Sam the rat-catcher, Captain Jack, Birchy, and Curly, and with the assistance of the other boys we got the place fit for you."

The boys, who were reclining in various attitudes upon the mats, pieces of carpet, and straw, heartily welcomed Alick, and two or three of them hastened to get him something to eat

By the time they had the meal ready, the remainder of the boys had entered.

Alick never felt so happy in his life before. He enjoyed his meal, and asked some of the boys to sing a song.

The boys did so willingly; one or two played tin whistles, and they had quite a concert.

The best tin whistle player was playing a beautiful dance, and Chimbley, unable to resist, did a magnificent breakdown, that brought down thunders of applause from his companions.

Chimbley had never before found such an opportunity of displaying his talent in dancing, and very few of the boys knew really what he could do in that line.

Just as Joe had finished his dance, Captain Jack arrived, and cast a searching glance round the place.

"I want five of those," he said, "whose turn it is to come out. Dan, I want you for one. Now I want four more. I require two cigar-light boys, two shoe-blacks, and one crossing-sweeper. The Bosker has a plant on, and I mean to spoil his game. Alick!"

"Yes," replied the lad.

"You will take charge of the second division, and be in command here when I am away. I will put you on the Bosker's track. Come with me, and we will talk the matter over."

The required boys were not long in getting ready and following Captain Jack, who took them to their respective posts, with instructions not to leave until they were ordered to do so.

They all remained faithful to their task, and never left their allotted posts until relieved—one keeping watch upon the caravan that held Gilbert, while others shadowed the every action of David Eastlake, who still went his dark road of ever ceaseless crime and villainy, little dreaming the way in which he was followed, and his every action marked.

He, in his evil doings, did not know how strangely the hand of Fate would work his ruin, and bring upon him well-merited punishment.

Meanwhile Alick and his followers were on their way to Kennington, with instructions how to act in case they caught sight of the Bosker and his gang.

## CHAPTER XIX.

TIKE IN THE HOUSE—THE BURGLARY—DEATH—ESCAPE OF THE BOSKER WITH THE BOOTY—AN ATTEMPTED MURDER.

TIKE, acting upon the directions given him by the Bosker, returned to the house of Lord Harleyford.

He could, if he liked, make himself very agreeable, and he did so on this occasion. In less than a week he became quite a favourite with the servants, with an exception—that exception was the butler.

From the first time of his seeing Tike he took an immediate dislike to him, and he did nothing but find fault with everything he did, much to the disgust of the housekeeper, who had a wonderful liking for Tike.

" He is a clean, hard-working, tidy lad, and she did not care for a dozen butlers," she said.

Strange to say, the feeling was mutual between Tike and the butler.

Tike hated him, and had it not been for the fear of getting kicked out, as he termed it, he would have insulted him upon one or two occasions.

The rest of the servants he liked—two especially —they were the valet and lady's maid.

They were extremely kind to Tike, and he often regretted having entered the house with such evil intentions.

At times his better nature would get the upper hand of him, and almost cause him to warn them of the Bosker's villainy; but Satan had too great a hold upon him, coupled with the threats of the Bosker, if he did not make haste and succeed in getting the housekeeper to let him sleep there, and the large amount of money that worthy intended to give him after the deed. All helped to work upon him and crush out what little good feeling he had in him, as will presently be seen.

For a very short time we will leave him, while we follow the fortunes of the Burker and the ever unfortunate Gorger.

Philip Bartlett could hardly repress a smile at the comical figure of the Gorger, but turning to the other men, he told two to take the Burker, and two others to look after Mr. Slime.

" Go on," he said, " I will follow shortly."

Greatly to the consternation of the Gorger, he felt himself dragged roughly by the collar to the station-house, but with the Burker it was quite a different affair.

He struggled awfully to get away, and it was with the greatest difficulty they could keep their hold upon him.

However, he became quiet after a time. The policemen thought it was because he found his attempts useless to get away ; but they were mistaken, it was merely a blind.

He was possessed of such strength that he could have defied four policemen to have held him, while he had the use of his hands.

He was hoping the crowd of followers would disperse before they arrived at the station ; if so, he would, when they least expected it, break away.

There was one thing in his favour—the two policemen with the Gorger were nearly out of sight, they had got so far in advance ; and then he beheld with delight the crowd go on in front.

They made for the station-house and blocked up the doorway, to the immense delight of the fat officer who had the pleasant occupation of being on night duty.

He had been taking it easy, and had gone to sleep with his head upon the desk. At every nod he dipped his nasal organ in the ink pot, to the great delight of a lot of juveniles who congregated round the doorway for the special purpose of taking a farewell glance at the miserable-looking Gorger.

The Burker walked along as quiet as a lamb until within two or three minutes' walk of the station; the policemen, by mutual consent, finding him so passive, slightly relaxed their hold to relieve their fingers, which were cramped through remaining so long in one position.

At the same moment they turned the corner and entered a dark, dreary-looking street, with a brick wall, about seven feet high, on one side.

The Burker caught sight of this, and thought there was a chance of escape open to him.

He guessed that there was a large garden the other side of the wall, so, drawing himself together, he gave a tremendous twist, jerking the police half round, and, dropping to his knees, caused them to loose their hold upon him.

Then he sprang to his feet, and, clutching the nearest bobby by the throat, dashed him to the earth. With a terrific leap he mounted the wall and was over the other side before they had recovered the surprise the daring act had caused them.

" Shall we follow ?" said number one.

" Can't," said bobby number two. " How are we to get over the wall ?"

" Don't know," said the first, and they stood looking at the wall, as though that mass of dirty bricks and mortar could help them in any manner.

" I know," said number one, " I'll bump you up, then you can easily jump over."

But bobby number two didn't see it. To be over the other side of a garden wall with a desperate burglar was not exactly the thing, and then again, he thought, had he not broken away from two ?

It was well for them they did not follow, for the Burker was a desperate man, and valued human life as nothing.

Meanwhile, the Burker made his way across the garden and over another wall. Gradually he slunk back to Nathan's without interruption, and going into the kitchen he told the Bosker what had happened.

Burkett uttered a frightful oath, and springing to his feet he glanced fiercely at the Burker.

" Curses ! why didn't you brain the crushers," he

said, "or silence the child before they took her away?"

Bold and fearless as the Burker was, he shrank from the Bosker in fear.

"I would have done it, Burkett," he said, "only they were too quick; seven to one is heavy odds. Don't you see, old pal, I did my best; I could do no more," he added, quietly.

"Your best is bad enough then," replied the Bosker, with an oath, his passion so great that he appeared to be in the act of striking the Burker. "Curse you! and where have you left that cowardly great baby, the Gorger?"

"I think they have nabbed him."

"Then curse them also!" said the Bosker, springing to the table, and snatching up his bludgeon he confronted the Burker.

"Joe," he said, "you are a friend and member of the gang, and so is the Gorger. He is my own pal, one who has a hand in everything that I do, and though he is a coward I will not see him taken. And yet you escape and leave him to the crushers. I tell you, Burker, you had better see what you can do to save him, or it will be worse for you."

The Burker had kept a dogged silence during the time the Bosker had been speaking; but when Burkett threatened him, and accused him of being a coward, he could scarcely control his feelings.

Had it been anyone else, he would have struck him to the earth for one-half of what he had said; but he knew it was more than he dared do—not because he absolutely feared the Bosker, but he being chief and king of the cracksmen, the Burker would have had the band upon him for daring to lift his hand against Burkett.

He almost forgot all this as Burkett finished his speech.

His passion nearly mastered him, and producing a horrible sling-shot from his pocket, he said—

"Burkett, I never yet let a pal be taken; but in this case I could not help it, and if you say another word, I'll see what I can do to make you repent it, even if I suffer the penalty of the water cellar."

Burkett glared fiercely at him, but thought he might have unjustly accused him.

"Put down that shot, Joe," he said, "and don't say any more. Help me to get that lubberly great infant out of trouble, and then I have a plant on."

"No," said the Burker, quietly; "as you cannot trust me, why, don't take me for a pal any more. I shouldn't like to go if I thought you set me down for a coward."

Burkett felt sorry that he had said so much.

Bad as the two men were, they had a certain amount of honour in their own way, and they were as easily hurt in their feelings as men who get their living honestly.

"Never mind, old pal; tip us your flipper," said the Bosker. "I was a bit rusty; but I didn't mean anything."

And much to the relief of the other portion of the gang, who had been expecting to see a fight, they made it up and were soon drinking together.

They had not been so engaged very long before Tike came in.

He looked wonderfully clean and tidy, and many of the ruffians seated round the table stopped him and asked a number of questions, all of which Tike took no notice of, but passed on to where the Bosker sat.

"I sleeps in the house now," he said, with a knowing leer. "I did last night, and I do so again for the future."

Burkett smiled a grim smile of satisfaction.

"Look out next Wednesday," he replied. "I shall be there shortly after midnight. Let me in, and you can gain admittance to some of the other rooms."

"All right," answered Tike. "Make no blooming error, I'll have it all square, then have a row with the butler, and his lord—lord— What do they call him?"

"His lordship," answered the Bosker.

"Oh! that's it," said Tike, "and he's going to slope—not his lordship, the butler, I mean—so he's packed up a lot o' swag. He didn't think as how I knowed he'd got it. And I knows where he has put it, too."

"Ha, ha!" laughed the Bosker; "we'll save him the trouble of carrying it away. You go now, Tike, and don't forget; but you had better come on Tuesday night, and I'll settle the matter then."

Tike then departed, and returned to the house where he had received so much kindness.

And for what?

Why, to betray his master, and to assist a desperate band in robbing the house.

Burkett made arrangements with the Burker, and, at the same time, swore that the unlucky Nicholas should be liberated.

But, however, he waited patiently the issue of the police-court proceedings. Early in the day, to the surprise of all, the Gorger came to Nathan's, looking awfully hungry.

The Bosker was glad to see him out of prison, though he had not much feeling for anyone. He did not like to see the great harmless booby always in trouble.

"Well, you big, ugly idiot, and so you've been nabbed?" said the Bosker.

"Yes, Mr. Burkett, and I am hawful peckish," Nicholas Slime replied, and his hungry-looking eyes glanced round in search of something to eat.

"How did you get out, you great cur?" demanded the Bosker, in his pleasant tone of voice.

"Why, I'll tell you in a minnit, only I am desperate hungry."

"Go and have something to eat, you glutton, do, and make haste. I want you, do you hear?" the Bosker said, with an oath.

"Ye—yes, Mr. Burkett. I am a-going to make haste!"

After the Gorger had satisfied his appetite he returned to the Bosker and the Burker.

"Well, Joe," the Gorger exclaimed, "how did you get away?"

"It would want more than two country boys dressed in blue to take me," said Lewis, laughing.

The Gorger then told Burkett that he was brought before the magistrate; but the police, not being able to clearly prove that he had been aiding the man in abducting the child, he was discharged.

"And now I shall want you on Wednesday," said the Bosker. "There is a little plant on, and see if you can't keep out of the claws of the crushers, and when you've got your share of the swag, don't let people take it away again."

"No, Jim ; I'll have a rig out and a watch, and you'll take care of the rest," the Gorger replied.

Tuesday came ; they then began preparations. Burkett collected his tools and a dark lantern, and carefully packing them into a parcel, they awaited patiently the coming of the following night.

It was arranged that the Boozer and another of the gang should keep watch in the street, and the Gorger was to be at the back of the house.

It happened to be a corner house, with a side entrance, and large stabling ; at the back, therefore, they would require someone to be in the yard to keep watch, while Tike was to lead them over the place.

The Bosker arose as eleven o'clock struck and proposed to depart. The others had already gone, excepting the Gorger, who was drinking strong brandy and water to give him courage.

They departed from Nathan's together, but did not go the journey in company.

Each took a different direction, but they agreed to arrive at the same time.

"Go," said Burkett to the Gorger, "and learn all you can ; keep your eye on the bobby, and discover how long his beat is. Remember you keep your place, in case we should be prevented from coming out the same way we go in, and if we should have to come out the back way, and you're not there to help, I'll throttle you."

Nicholas Slime shivered, for though the Bosker spoke coolly he knew he would keep his word.

Midnight came, dark and dreary, a thick mist floating overhead.

The wind moaned through the stately trees in the park, and swept in fearful gusts round the corners of the now almost deserted streets.

The rain then commenced to fall.

It spattered against the lighted windows of the late public-houses ; it spattered in road puddles, and dashed against cab windows, as the wheels rolled through the slushy streets.

Burkett and his companions cared not for the rain, it was just such a night as they would have wished for.

They met as agreed, but it being too early, they dispersed again, to walk round and meet this time at the house they were going to rob.

The gin palaces commenced to close, late coffee houses, cafés, and ice-shops alike shut their doors, and sent their over-worked domestics to seek a few hours' rest, before the busy, bustling business commenced again.

Half-past one chimed from the neighbouring churches.

All was quiet.

A policeman stood in the shelter of a doorway out of the rain, which was still falling fast, little dreaming that while he leaned there half-asleep there was a daring robbery being committed almost under his very nose.

The worthy trio met again, and going to the side of the house, they saw the Boozer, who was lolling against an iron post.

"You are late, Jim, but it's all square," he said, "and the bobby is nearly asleep round the corner. I've seen nobody else, only two or three half-starved devils of boys, and they are gone now."

"Will the cab be here ?" asked the Bosker.

"In ten minutes," replied the Boozer.

"All right, then. Now, Nick, climb the wall and be ready," said the Bosker.

And, helping the Gorger over, he returned to the front door, where, giving a low whistle, he waited for some minutes.

Soon the massive door slowly opened, and the white face and trembling form of Tike appeared.

"Hush !" he said, "be silent ; I've got it all ready !"

The Bosker entered first, followed by the Burker. Taking their boots off, they put on list slippers, and silently followed the Tike. They then ascended the stairs and entered the drawing-room, packing up all that came in their way.

The Bosker then told Tike to lead them to the plate chest.

"There, that's the room," whispered Tike, his teeth chattering with fear.

The Bosker, with very little difficulty, opened the door and entered, Joe following close behind with the already well-filled bags.

"Show the glim !" whispered Burkett, and immediately there was a light upon the scene. They then saw the chest, and found it to be awfully heavy.

There was a low whistle from the street.

"That's the safe signal," said Burkett ; "so as that is the case I'll just look inside these cupboards."

He produced some skeleton keys, and was soon engaged in a rather hard task.

"Curse the locks ! I'll swear there's something good here, or they wouldn't be so careful."

"Better come while it's safe," said the Burker.

"No !" replied Burkett, "I'll have what's in here. Help me, Joe ; give that young cuss the glim."

But the young cuss, as he termed him, was not there—he had gone to look round, and before he returned they had got the door open. A sight met their gaze that made their eyes water with the anticipation of the booty they had before them.

"We've got a haul this time," laughed the men ; but their laughing was cut short by the sound of signals from the watchers.

"One, two, three," said Burkett. "That's a sign there's immediate danger. We had better take the chest first."

They did, and found it almost too much for them ; but they managed to get it outside safely.

A cab very slowly passed the door at that moment ; but the cabman, seeing them with the box, immediately stopped.

They put the chest inside, and told him to wait round the corner.

They then re-entered the house, and began hastily packing what things they could lay their hands on into the bags.

Meanwhile the danger signals were being repeated every few seconds.

'We've gone too far to retreat," said the Bosker, with a dark scowl ; "so let them look out who interfere. We'll go out the back way."

Almost before the words were out of his mouth heart-rending shrieks filled the air, causing them to drop one of the boxes, which made a great noise.

Then followed the sound of hasty footsteps, and the rushing of people to where the shrieks came from.

Shriek after shriek came pealing through the house, then came a springing of rattles outside, and the rush of heavy feet.

"Our game's up !" said the Bosker.

He produced that favourite toy of his, the bludgeon, and the Burker clutched a fearful instument of death, the sling-shot.

"Take what you can and follow me," said Burkett. " I have got the barkers with me," he said, producing a brace of pistols, as he bounded down the stairs, followed by the Burker.

The whole household was rushing about in all directions.

Footmen, coachmen, and the female portion of the domestics, with scared looks and scanty coverings, were grouped upon the stairs.

They uttered a yell of fear when the two ruffians came bounding down among them.

Away went the terrified domestics, helter-skelter, knocking each other down in their flight.

But the male portion of the servants were called to their duty by the loud, commanding tones of his lordship, and they attempted to bar the way of the burglars.

Several policemen now appeared on the scene.

" Let me pass, or it will be the worse for you !" said Burkett.

" Give in !" said one of the police, drawing his truncheon.

He was knocked down by a blow from the Bosker's bludgeon, who then fired his pistols at the others, and retreated to the back dining-room window.

In rushed more police, who were brought on the scene by the firing of pistols.

The Bosker muttered the most fearful oaths, and dashing the back dining-room shutters open, sprang into the yard.

The Burker followed his example, but had no sooner put his foot to the ground, than he felt himself gripped fiercely by the collar, while Burkett was held in a similar manner.

They stood like savage beasts, glaring murderously upon the three policemen who held them.

" Your game's up ; it's no use, you'd better come quietly."

" Let me go," said the Bosker, in a hoarse voice, struggling to get away ; but the officers held on like grim death.

Finding that they didn't intend letting him go, the Bosker dropped the canvas bag he had held in his hand during the struggle, and gave a low whistle.

" You needn't whistle for your pals ; they're taken long ago," said one of the officers.

Burkett did not reply, but, twisting himself round, he broke away from one, and before the other could use his truncheon, Burkett struck him heavily upon the head with his bludgeon, and sent him stunned to the ground.

As the policeman fell, a long form came from a dark corner of the yard.

It was the Gorger.

He had been lying full length in the shadow, and so escaped notice.

The Bosker snatched up the bag, and then turned to help the Burker ; but he did not require it.

The instant he felt himself taken, a murderous look shone from his eyes.

" Let go your hold !" he said.

The policeman's only reply was to feel for his truncheon.

The Burker did not speak again, but, putting out all his brute strength, he threw the policeman against the wall, and by so doing he had him at arm's length.

Then, with his right hand, he swung the sling-shot round his head.

There was a whizz as it circled in the air - the next instant it had descended with a dull thud, and sunk into the brain of the unhappy policeman, who fell just as the Bosker was about to help his companion.

The other policeman called loudly for help, and sprung his rattle.

He saw it would be useless to attempt to stop two such murderous wretches.

" Come on !" said the Burker, in a husky voice.

The Bosker was deadly pale. He had not expected to find the police waiting for them at the back, and he thought they might escape without using any violence.

"Come on," he said to the Gorger, who stood shaking in every limb.

"Ow-ow-ow—o-o-o—ugh ! I am coming ; ain't it hawful ? Why, Joe has committed mur—aw—o-o-o—"

He saw the Bosker's eyes turned upon him in a very unpleasant manner just then, and he knew by their look that he dare not finish the sentence.

" Say that again, and I'll brain you as well," said Burkett.

Meantime they had made their way into the street, and running madly, followed by the police, they escaped round the corner, where the cab was waiting.

Luckily for them the cabman had not been suspected, so they sprang inside, and told him to drive off at full speed.

---

## CHAPTER XX.

### LEARY JOCK FOLLOWS ON THE TRAIL OF DAVID EASTLAKE.

WE cannot do better than give the reader a view of Leary Jock's position behind the door, where we left him in a state of horror at the terrible scene he had witnessed.

At the best of times he was anything but the most courageous person in the world, and in the present case he was so frightened that had he been discovered he could not have moved.

There he sat, shaking in every limb, and his teeth knocking together and rattling like dice in a box.

The lateness of the hour and the death-like

quietness of the house, combined to inspire him with terror.

Then, again, like most people, he was superstitious, and he thought he heard someone walking about, for there were strange noises breaking the calmness of the night.

He thought he heard a struggle, followed by a most unearthly groan, and his hair began to rise—the perspiration poured down his face—his eyes became fixed, and appeared to be starting from their sockets.

His imagination became at length so strong that he thought he saw the young captain glaring at him as he did at the major in his last death throes; and, to complete his horror, he distinctly heard the patter of feet along the passage and up the stairs; then he saw two fiery eyes glare at him.

They seemed to blaze, and he thought they certainly belonged to a demon.

The eyes came closer still, and as they neared him his horror increased—his tongue clove to the roof of his mouth, and he tried to utter a cry, but no sound came from his lips.

He could not stand any more—he attempted to move down the stairs; as he did so the pair of horrible-looking eyes uttered a yell, and dashed past him.

Something smooth touched his face, but whatever it was, it continued yelling fearfully, and dashed up the next flight of stairs.

Leary Jock thought then that a legion of demons had broken out from the infernal regions, and, giving one hoarse cry, he rolled down stairs head first, and lay insensible, huddled all of a heap, upon the mat.

A few more yells followed his last cry, and then all sank into quietude again.

Some minutes after he had been lying upon the mat, the object of his terror came down again.

It was not, as he supposed, a being from the other world, but a huge black Tom cat.

Certainly it was a nasty looking animal, and it sneaked downstairs, as all cats do after having done any mischief.

He then sat on the bottom stair washing his face with his huge black paws.

That performance being finished, he looked curiously at the leary one, and not being able to thoroughly comprehend the meaning of such a peculiar-looking thing being on the mat, the aforesaid peculiar-looking thing having something projecting from his face in a very prominent manner, which still more astonished Mr. Thomas, who, to ascertain what it really was, ascended the stairs and quietly patted him on the nose; but, finding it immovable, he gave it a final pat, rather harder than the other had been, thereby sticking his talons in, greatly to the disfigurement of Leary Jock's nasal organ.

Perhaps Thomas was then satisfied, for he gave his paw a lick and then bolted downstairs to find some place where he might sleep in comfort till the morning.

But not finding any place soft enough he returned to Leary Jock, and, turning round two or three times, as cats invariably do before they lay down,

he made himself comfortable upon Jock's chest, and closed his eyes in a manner plainly showing he did not feel very sleepy, which he proved by his having a little game at the leary one's expense.

Tommy felt remarkably playful just then, and thinking that Leary Jock's enormous nose was not such a bad plaything, commenced patting it again, and to his delight he saw the nose move slightly at every stroke of his paw.

His delight increased more and more as the nasal organ moved, and at last he got so excited with the fun that he sat on his hind-quarters and smacked away with both his fore paws, until Leary Jock returned to consciousness.

Opening his eyes, he gave a vacant stare at the cat, and then instinctively his hand went to his nose, which was smarting dreadfully.

He seemed to comprehend the cause, for he gave the cat a hoist, and sent him flying over his head, and then started to a leaning posture and listened attentively.

His first thoughts were of flight, but upon hearing the sound of footsteps walking about in the apartment above, he altered his mind.

He wished to see what was going on.

"Perhaps," he thought, "I shall see the end of the fearful tragedy, and then I may discover something to my advantage."

As Leary Jock ascended the stairs day was just breaking, and so enabled him to see what was going on inside the room.

When he put himself in his former position against the door, a shock went right through him; bad as he was he could not look upon the sight that met his gaze without a feeling of terror.

The major had risen to his feet; in his hand he held a knife, with which he had cut his hair away, to release himself from the death-grasp.

But how he had altered! Those few hours had wrought a change in him—his cheeks were sunken, a deathly paleness overspread his features, and his eyes glared in a most unearthly manner.

He was covered in blood; and he stood there regarding the corpse more like a person who had lost his reason than a sane man.

The major cast a terrified look around, and then began with trembling hands to search the body.

A smile of satisfaction lit up his face as he came across the cards, bank-notes, and pocket-book.

"Ha! ha!" he laughed in a low, hollow tone of voice. "Ha! the fool, to dare me in my own den. Ha! out of my path—one the less in society, and no one will know whither he has gone or what has become of him. There is no eye to see, no tongue to tell the tale; and I shall hide him—yes, hide his body."

"Will you, though?" muttered Leary.

The major opened a door leading to a narrow cupboard, dragged the body into it, and securely fastened the door.

He removed the stains from the furniture, then went to the sleeping-apartment to cleanse the blood from his person.

Leary Jock thought he had then seen enough, and stealing down the stairs, he made his way out.

He felt clammy about the mouth, and his nose was awfully swollen.

Luckily an early public-house was beginning to open, so Leary Jock went inside, drank some brandy and water, and, feeling much refreshed, he went his way.

He had not taken a dozen steps before he was overtaken by the major, who stared vacantly at him, as though he had a faint recollection of having seen him before; but Jock had no particular wish to be recognised at that moment, so he turned sharply round and made his way into the Strand.

Here a cloaked figure barred his way.

Leary Jock started; any ordinary circumstance would startle him in his present state.

The cloaked figure neither moved nor looked round, but as the leary one passed him he said, in a clear voice—

"Leary Jock, follow me," and he walked on.

Leary Jock gazed after the retreating figure in wonderment, then a strange look came over his face.

"It's the chief," he muttered. "I must follow."

He followed the stranger, who went up one of the turnings out of the Strand, and after traversing several narrow thoroughfares, he stopped before a well-built, nice-looking house.

He then motioned for Leary to follow him as he ascended the steps. He entered by a key and passed into a room at the end of the hall; by its appearance Leary Jock could see it was a gentleman's study or library.

"I wonder if there's anybody else lives in the house," he thought, and he gazed round as though to seek something by which he could judge; but he could not.

The house appeared to be well furnished with everything that is required for comfort.

Leary Jock was prevented from taking notice of anything more by the stranger, who, with a motion of the hand, indicated that he wished the door to be shut, and by a similar signal requested him to take a seat.

The stranger had already seated himself, and throwing off the cloak and hat, there sat the handsome young stranger who had entered the thieves' kitchen.

He looked searchingly at Leary Jock for a minute or two, without uttering a word, and in such a way as to make him feel extremely uncomfortable.

He could not stand that piercing glance; but at length he was relieved by the stranger speaking.

"Well, you are a pretty looking object, I must say," he observed. "And pray, my worthy friend, where have you been? You look as if you had been scared out of your wits."

Jock shuddered.

"I 'as seen a hawful sight, captain," he said, uncovering his head, and speaking in the most respectful tones; "and I guess it's shook my nerves a bit. Lor'! what a cold-blooded villain that Major G—"

Leary stopped, as though he had said too much.

"Go on," said the young stranger.

"But—but—" he stammered.

"You need not fear, Leary. I already know the cause of your fright."

Jock turned a shade paler, and wondered where the mysterious personage obtained all his information.

"I know murder has been committed," said the stranger; "I also know where the major has gone; but I want you to tell me everything you saw and heard between the major and his victim. I want the truth, mind."

Leary feared him too much to tell him an untruth; and, as briefly as possible, told him what he knew of the affair, with many shudders.

"Now, listen," said the other; "I want your services for a short time. Do as I tell you, and I will reward you handsomely; do as you did last time, and you know the consequences."

"I—I didn't do it, goodness knows it. I—" said Leary, trembling violently.

"Don't lie!" the other said, sternly. "I let you off that time, because you betrayed me through fear. Your accomplice happened to be a bully, with brutal strength and courage, and you feared him too much to attempt to do anything which he did not wish you to; but remember"—his voice became stern, and his eyes gave a deadly glitter as he spoke, that made the low-born cur cower before him—"remember, I have warned once; the next time I strike. Do anything again that I distinctly tell you not to do, and your days will be numbered. I employ you because I know you, and, I believe, saved your life once. You are bad enough, but your companions are worse. But to the point. You saw where the major hid the body?"

"I did," Leary Jock replied.

"And you say that in the hand of the corpse there's a bunch of the major's hair?" continued the stranger.

"Yes, sir."

"Good. Well, keep what you know a secret. I might at any time want you to lead someone to where the body is hidden, and I shall also require your evidence. At present I want your services in another way. You know that black-hearted villain, David Eastlake?"

"Rather," said Leary Jock, "and he knows me too."

"That will do then," the stranger rejoined. "He will start this evening by the train to a country seat of his, where he has a young girl whom he has managed to get there under the pretence of marrying her; and he has set his vile hirelings at work to kidnap a child, of whom you know nothing; she will also be sent to this country seat. Do you understand?"

"Yes, captain," Leary Jock replied; "I have my peepers opened a bit."

He was getting more himself now that there was a prospect of doing a good stroke of business.

"Well, then," continued the stranger, "I want you to follow him. You must disguise yourself so that there will be no chance of recognition. You must keep strict watch over him, dog his footsteps, and let not one action pass your notice; above all, if either of the girls come to harm in any way, you shall suffer for it. That is the reason I send you.

"I will communicate with you, and when you are to return I will let you know," he continued. "Follow my instructions closely, and on your life, mind, do not let him harm the girl or child. Here is some money. Be at the Vauxhall station at six, when David Eastlake will arrive. You must get your ticket and go by the same train, though not in the same carriage. Now you know.

"Take the money," he added. "If you should require more, send and let me know; but, don't fail."

"Trust this infant, captain; it shall be done to the very letter," said Leary Jock.

And, giving a parting wink and a knowing leer, he arose, took his battered hat, and departed.

The stranger mused for a few minutes; he appeared to be thinking deeply, and his thoughts found vent in words.

"Yes, I must now consult the Brethren," he muttered. "David Eastlake is safely watched for a time—now Major Carleton. Ah! he has had his run. It is time that he was either given up to the hands of the law or that he fell by the hands of the vendetta. And then, my poor brother Phi— No—I dare not mention his name; but, by Heaven! he shall be avenged, and my sister too, poor girl."

Here he broke down, and his whole frame shook with emotion; he buried his face in his hands and moaned bitterly.

What fearful wrongs that man must have suffered; and yet, to look upon him, he appeared happy, full of manly vigour and youthful beauty, with a firm, iron will. Certainly he must have some terrible secret locked in his broad breast, now swelling with wild emotions.

But what secret could it be?

We will show all in good time—even his innermost secrets shall be disclosed to the patient reader; but for the present we must follow Leary Jock.

He slunk into an early coffee-house, and waited until the shops were opened.

Then he departed. He knew that he must get one or two things to go with, and, having plenty of money, he obtained some clothes, the fashion of which we should by no means like to recommend.

He also purchased a stick with a tremendous knob to it, in case of accidents.

Then he went to Dan Garnett's to dress and get himself ready.

He would have gone to Nathan's, only he knew they would question him, and as he was forbidden to tell anything, he wisely kept away; in fact, he was so afraid of being seen by anybody he knew that he left Garnett's as soon as he possibly could.

When he came down to the bar Dan hardly knew him again. He had entirely changed his attire, and he now wore a slouched felt hat and had a shade over one eye.

"Something up?" queried Garnett.

"Yes, a little joke on."

"Well, I don't know where you have been; but certainly that's all a beauty, that nose of yours," said the publican.

"Bust the cat," Leary Jock muttered, forgetting that he ought not to mention anything appertaining to the murder, although a remark had been made detrimental to the appearance of his nose.

"Cat! Why, what's a cat to do with your nose?"

"Mind your own business," said Leary Jock, savagely.

He then bolted and slammed the door after him, and it was well for him he did so, for Dan had taken up a pot to shy at his head.

Leary Jock wandered about, not knowing where to go, until it was time for him to start.

In his ramble he found himself in Whitechapel.

He remembered a beer-shop of a very questionable character close at hand, and thought perhaps, on account of the time, the tap-room might be unoccupied by any person.

He signed to the landlord, who gave a nod in return, and going down the passage, that led along one side of the bar, he ascended three or four stone steps, and came to a door in front of him.

It was not the public tap-room, but was kept especially for certain customers, and this explains the reason of Leary Jock going to it.

He opened the door, advanced one step inside, then made a dead stop. The room was occupied, and he took the scene in at a glance.

There sat two of the most villainous-looking beings that ever claimed kindred with mankind.

The instant the fellows noticed his hesitation, one of them arose, with a clay pipe in his mouth, and sent forth a cloud of smoke.

"It's all square, old pal, don't be afeared," he said.

They thought they had found some novice in the profession, and perhaps were likely to get a little out of him; but Leary Jock knew too much for them.

"Thankee, I won't come in just yet—not if I know it," he exclaimed.

The latter part of his speech was *sotto voce*, as he closed the door and went out, to re-commence his aimless ramble.

At length it was nearly time for him to start on his journey, so he strolled on to the platform of the railway station.

People cast many suspicious glances at him, and inwardly resolved not to get in the same carriage if possible.

For this Leary Jock, however, cared but little, and he drew back out of the way as much as possible as he saw the handsome form of David Eastlake ascend the stairs to the platform.

He was followed by a groom, who carried in his hand a small portmanteau.

There was a sinister look upon David Eastlake's face that plainly showed he had some villainy on hand.

He strode impatiently up and down the platform, twirling his moustache; his eyes glistened, and a devilish smile played about his lips.

"Ha—ha!" he muttered, "she is nicely caged. Marry, indeed—ha—ha! I should have enough to do if I was to marry every girl I take a fancy to.

I suppose, though, if she gets away, I shall have her whelp of a brother after me. Bah! I shall find means of putting him out of the way, and that child, too. She will be there by this time to-morrow or next day, and then—"

A murderous gleam shone from his malignant-looking eyes as he hissed these words through his teeth.

" I have tried to get it done ; but the cursed hirelings are either cowards or chicken-hearted," he continued. " I did not wish for her life ; but, not being rid of her yet, I must kill her myself, and remove one more from my path. She is but a child, therefore it will not be much trouble, and—"

A screech was heard as the train came snorting into the station.

Eastlake seated himself in a first-class carriage, and, taking the portmanteau from his groom, told him to return.

David Eastlake was a man without soul or remorse, and when all other resources had failed, and he had to rely on himself alone to commit some desperate crime, he confided in no second person.

But he little thought, as he sat there brooding over his villainy, that in the same train, bent upon tracking him down, was an individual as reckless and as criminal as himself. Nor did he think how fearfully he would have to answer for his many crimes to a power greater than that of man !

## CHAPTER XXI.

SUDDEN APPEARANCE OF TIKE—A ROW IN THE SECRET HOME OF THE POOR BOYS OF LONDON —TIKE FINDS THAT WOOD IS JUST A TRIFLE HARDER THAN HIS HEAD.

THE alarm at the house in which Burkett and the Burker had been so busily engaged was due to Alick and his boy sentinels. Having summoned the police to the scene of the burglary, it was only natural that they should make themselves scarce, for they were too young to cope with such desperadoes.

They then wended their way to the haunt, and by the time they arrived there morning had dawned, and several of the boys were partaking of breakfast, which they had purchased overnight.

Little did Alick and his comrades think they had been followed by that heartless villain, Tike, the cause of all the mischief.

" I'll be even with you," Tike muttered, as he followed in their train. " You ain't to know that I let the Bosker in, and if I do the whining dodge I can get over one of you, at least."

He meant Alick, whom he knew to be a good-hearted fellow, ever ready to forgive even the most degraded of the waifs and strays of mighty London, if he showed an earnest desire to turn honest.

Slinking along like a cat, Tike made himself acquainted with the manner of entrance to the haunt, and then thought it best to rehearse his part before making his appearance.

Meanwhile Alick had been plagued with a hundred questions from those who remained in the cellar, and he was giving a brief account of the

adventure when a startled cry from Sam the rat-catcher caused him to cease speaking.

" There ain't no need to holler out when you see an old pal," said Tike, as he glided into the midst of the boys. " Let me sit down a minute, I'm half-dead with fright."

Alick could only stare at the unexpected and unwelcome guest in speechless amazement.

" How did you find your way in here ?" he demanded, at last.

" Where there's a will there's a way," Tike replied, clutching his waistcoat, and giving vent to a hollow groan. " Oh ! what I'm a-sufferin' !"

" You look like it," said Little Dan, sneeringly.

" It's all very well for you to turn up your nose at me," Tike returned, forcing tears to his eyes. " I got a nice comfor'ble situation, and the Bosker must come and upset me. I've done with him for ever."

" But why did you come here," demanded Little Dan. " Alick has asked the question, and I repeat it. Why didn't you stay behind and give all the information you could to the police ?"

" Yes, and get lagged for my trouble," said Tike, cunningly. " Was it likely I was going to stay and tell 'em I had been a bad 'un ? I want to turn over a new leaf, I do, and that's a fact."

" If you are really in earnest," Alick remarked, a little dubiously, " and mean what you say, I have no objection ; but play us no tricks, Tike, or you will find out that they will cost you dearly."

" Alick," cried Little Dan, springing to his feet, " don't believe a word he says. He has only come here to spy and bring harm upon us. Why don't he answer your question ?"

" Yes," said Alick ; " I must have that, Tike."

" Well," replied the young ruffian, " I'll tell you the truth. When the confusion was at its height I bolted into the street, and seeing you I follered."

As he spoke he shed more tears, and wailed so dismally that Alick could not help pitying him ; but many of the other boys shook their heads, and Little Dan, who was not to be deceived by Tike's display of misery, again besought Alick to turn him out.

" It will be better, even if we have to leave the haunt," he said. " I don't want to be nasty, but I and most of us know Tike so well that we won't trust him."

" Well," Alick replied, " I'll try and settle the matter another way. All in favour of forgiving Tike and letting him stop with us hold up their right hands."

Not a single hand was raised.

" Against," said Alick.

Then every hand went up, and a spontaneous cheer burst from the boys' lips.

" You see," said Alick, turning to Tike, " that the boys, poor as they are, will have nothing to do with you. You must go."

" And the best thing you can do," chimed in Little Dan, " is to go and drop yourself over one of the bridges, with a couple of bricks round your neck, to save yourself comin' to a worse end."

Tike's eyes gleamed maliciously, but, thrusting his hands deep into his pockets, he whistled softly and tried to look cool and collected.

# POOR BOYS OF LONDON

## OR, DRIVEN TO CRIME.

No. 8.] A LIFE STORY FOR THE PEOPLE. [ONE PENNY.

*The Irishman sent the constable's helmet spinning into the air.*

"So," he said, "you won't have me?"

"Not at any price," Little Dan replied, sarcastically.

"Silence," cried Alick, sternly; "just remember while Captain Jack is absent I am in command here."

"That's true enough," said Little Dan, "but I can't help feeling glad that Tike is to be sent about his business. Look at him, with a grin upon his ugly face, but grinding his teeth and working himself into a passion all the time. Ah ! would you ?"

Tike withdrew his hands from his pockets, and before he could be restrained he attacked Little Dan with an open knife ; but ere his arm could descend Hungry Sam lodged his foot in his waistcoat, and Alick, snatching up a box used for blacking boots in the street, dealt Tike a tremendous blow on the back of the head.

"Take that, you coward !" Alick cried.

The knife dropped from Tike's hand, and, rolling over, he lay perfectly still.

"Phew ! that was a near one," said Little Dan, as he scrambled to his feet. " But, I say, Alick, I'm afraid you have killed him."

### CHAPTER XXII.

#### FACE TO FACE WITH DAVID EASTLAKE.

LEARY JOCK had procured a second-class ticket, and seeing one of the compartments in that class only occupied by an old gentleman, he took his seat inside.

The train went on, stopping but seldom, hour after hour, and Leary Jock kept a sharp look out for David Eastlake.

At last he alighted, and Jock, slouching out of the train, followed him at a distance.

Eastlake hired a public vehicle, and proceeded to an inn, where he intended to stay awhile before completing his journey.

At last Eastlake ordered a horse to be brought round, and, vaulting into the saddle, rode off.

Leary Jock had hidden himself until Eastlake had gone.

He then entered the house, went into a small room behind the bar, and ordered some refreshments.

Mine host regarded him rather with surprise for a few moments, but, thinking it was someone a little eccentric, he answered—

"Yes, sir ; always accommodation for gentlemen here."

"Is this the nearest house to the gentleman's private residence that has just started from here ?"

"Yes, sir ; only just across the fields there."

Leary Jock, having refreshed himself, crossed several fields, and climbed any number of gates and stiles, when he came to the private grounds of David Eastlake's house.

He coolly crossed the kitchen-garden, and, breaking through some currant bushes, leaped over the hedge ; but had he remembered the precaution in the old proverb, to "Look before you leap," he would have ascertained that it was the lawn he was springing upon.

He sprung upon something worse still, for he had barely alighted when a hand clutched him by the collar, and, turning, an unpleasant sensation went through him.

He stood face to face with David Eastlake.

"Is—is this a near cut to anywhere ?" Leary Jock stammered.

"Yes, my friend," David Eastlake replied, drawing a pistol and thrusting it into his face ; "unless you can give me a satisfactory explanation of your conduct you will find it a near cut to the next world."

Leary Jock quailed before the weapon.

It had a large barrel, capable of carrying quite an ounce of lead, and David Eastlake's finger was curled round the trigger in a determined style.

"Don't be 'ard on a poor cove," Leary Jock said, as he shielded his head with his arm. "Put that thing down. It might go off by mistake, you know !"

"It will make no mistake if it does go off," David Eastlake observed, with a murderous glitter in his eyes. "Speak out, and tell me the truth. Were you following me ?"

The muzzle of the pistol advanced nearer to Leary Jock's head, and, falling on his knees, he howled for mercy.

"No, sir ; oh ! sir. No, sir," he whined. "Why should I follow you ? It was me as was bein' followed —by the police."

"Oh ! indeed," said Eastlake ; "and pray what have you done to warrant the attention of the police ?"

"Tryin' to pick up a livin'," Leary Jock replied. "I'm a tramp, I am ; and nobody will give me work."

"Your appearance is against you," Eastlake observed. "What kind of work are you most used to ? Robbing hen-roosts, or frightening timid women out of halfpence, I should think. Get up, and look me straight in the face, if you can."

Eastlake put the pistol away, and Leary Jock, much relieved, scrambled to his feet.

"Guv'nor," he said, grinning, "you've seen the world, and knows what a chap is made of as soon as you look at him. Leavin' out the timid women and their ha'pence, I've had a cheap dinner or two in my time."

"I thought as much," David Eastlake returned. "I have a good memory for faces. Where have I seen you before ?"

"At the Pig and Porridge Pot," Leary Jock ventured, boldly.

"Hah !" cried Eastlake, and his hand sought his pocket again. "If you are not following me your presence here is a strange coincidence."

"Which it is," the leary one returned. "I mizzled from London, and why ? There's a chap as is called the Bosker, and Joe Lewis—perfect strangers to you, of course, sir, but they are my pals—well they have got into a bother, so I thought I'd take a 'oliday in the country. The old drum is shadowed by 'tecs."

"What are 'tecs ?" Eastlake demanded.

"What a fool I am to talk to a borned gentleman in that way," said Leary Jock, apologetically. "'Tecs, sir, is detectives."

"Oh ! I understand. And, pray, where is the old drum ?"

Leary Jock could scarcely look into Eastlake's cold, cruel eyes, and continue to play his part, for he knew that he was turning red and white.

"It's a place where we meet," he explained, in a faltering voice ; "but it's gettin' a trifle too warm, so, sir, as I said afore, I mizzled."

"Humph! a pretty story, indeed," said Eastlake. "What would you say if I handed you over to the constable of this village?"

"You wouldn't do that, I'm sure," Leary Jock remarked. "When I sees you at the Pig and Porridge Pot I knew you came there by accident, and if I had had the chance—"

"What would you have done?" Eastlake interposed. "Helped yourself to my watch and chain?"

"No; I should have told you that it wasn't the place for a gentleman."

David Eastlake laughed.

But never for a moment did he remove his eyes from Leary Jock.

"You are a thorough scoundrel, of course," he said; "but I think we may be of some service to each other. If I trust you, will you rob or deceive me?"

Leary Jock commenced a speech in which he hoped that all sorts of horrible things might happen to him if he purloined anything of the value of a pin, or betrayed the gentleman's confidence, when David Eastlake checked him with an impatient gesture.

"Pooh—pooh!" he said. "I am not going to give over the family plate to your custody. I merely want you to keep a watch round the house and grounds, and to give me warning of the presence of any stranger."

"That'll suit me down to the ground," Leary Jock replied. "Give me a little beer and 'bacca, and something to eat now and then, and I'll beat the best watch-dog in the country."

"Follow me," said David Eastlake. "It will be well for you to know something of the inside as well as the outside of the house. But one word before we start. Woe betide you if I catch you tripping. My friend, I think we understand each other. If you fail me in the slightest thing; I will blow your brains out."

"Which it would sarve me right," Leary Jock rejoined.

"Now come with me, then."

The house into which David Eastlake ushered Leary Jock was an old-fashioned and evidently a well-furnished one.

The appointments of the hall made the leary one's mouth water, as several valuable articles met his greedy gaze that would have fitted his coat pockets to a nicety.

Eastlake led the way up a flight of thickly carpeted stairs, and, on reaching the landing, opened a door.

"Step into this room," he said. "I will be with you directly."

Artful and watchful as Leary Jock was, and used to all sorts of traps, he for once forgot that the spider is in the habit of asking the fly to walk into the parlour.

His feet were scarcely over the threshold of the room, which had the appearance of a study, when he felt the boards gliding swiftly from underneath his feet.

Leary Jock threw up his arms, and a cry of horror burst from his lips as the floor divided in two parts, and he went down—down—through horrible darkness.

Perhaps the descent took less than a second, but it was an age of agony to Leary Jock, who, when he found himself fixed in what may be called the neck of a huge funnel, closed his eyes and tried to convince himself that he was the victim of a terrible dream.

The darkness was so dense that it seemed palpable to the touch, and when Leary Jock raised his hands and felt about him, he could discover nothing but a smooth, cold surface, which he naturally concluded was either zinc or iron.

"I'm done for at last," he said, as great beads of perspiration rolled down his face. "This ain't a cell, and it ain't a room. It's like a tube, and the more I wriggles the lower I goes."

The unhappy wretch soon discovered that if he did not wriggle he would choke, for the circular walls of his prison seemed to be pressing upon him.

Leary Jock made a bold bid for life; but all his efforts to secure a holding of any kind were fruitless.

He continued to slide down, until he felt that his feet were dangling free of the tube.

Here was another horror, and the leary one tried to scream for help; but, before a sound could leave his parched throat, he experienced a fall of at least ten feet, and finished the journey by landing heavily upon a hard and rock-like surface.

Leary Jock had been in a good many muddles in his life, but never in such a one as this.

He was fairly caught in his own trap, and so neatly that all hope of escape died out of his breast.

"If I had been a little fatter, I should have choked in that tunnel," he muttered. "This place seems to be a cellar or a dungeon. Ugh! this darkness is awful. I wonder—"

He ceased muttering, for just then a clicking sound came to his ears, as if the spring of a lock had been pulled back.

"Leary Jock!" said a voice.

The owner of that delightful name started, and gasped out—

"Who's there?"

"You may remove that patch from your eye now," said the voice; "disguise is useless. I know who you are, and what you have come for."

"Is it David Eastlake who is speaking?" Leary Jock demanded.

"The same," was the reply. "How do you feel? I hope you did not come down the tube head first?"

"It ain't fair to make fun of a cove in my position," Leary Jock moaned, as he tried to peer through the gloom. "Can't you let me out o' this hole?"

"Certainly," David Eastlake replied; "you shall leave it in a few days, when I give orders for your body to be buried. They tell me that a man can exist without food or water for seven days. I'll look you up in about a week, and see how you are getting on."

"You are joking—you don't mean it?" cried

Leary Jock, wildly. "If you have one grain of pity in your heart kill me out of hand, but don't leave me to starve. The very thought of it will drive me mad."

"Go mad if you like," Eastlake replied, with a cruel laugh. "Good-bye!"

The clicking sound was repeated, and Leary Jock, uttering a scream of anguish, tottered and fell swooning on the floor of his loathsome prison.

## CHAPTER XXIII.

THE BOSKER DOES TWO GOOD STROKES OF BUSINESS, BUT DISCOVERS THAT ONE IS A FAILURE.

THE Bosker sat in the kitchen attached to Nathan Claws' establishment.

As a matter of course he was very much wanted by the police; but, like hardened criminals, he was bold, and stalked under the very nose of justice as murderers stalk in our streets at this very hour.

Then, as now, the police were bewildered when any great mystery claimed their attention.

The telegraph was put to work, bills giving a full description of his appearance were circulated broadcast, the authorities at Scotland Yard put their heads together; but the Bosker, by simply altering his attire, laughed the whole army of police and detectives to scorn.

It must not be supposed that the atrocious ruffian was easy in his mind.

He was nervous, morose, and fidgetty, and when a girl who was sitting near him tapped him lightly on the shoulder he turned upon her so fiercely that she shrank from him in fear.

"How nervous you are, Jim," she said.

"Nervous," he repeated, with an oath. 'I was half dreaming, and when you touched me I thought I was nabbed again. But there, Rose, let us settle the other matter. You must go to the place I tell you of and get the child. I will follow you and—"

"I don't like the job," Rose replied. "Surely I've sunk low enough without turning child stealer."

"Bah!" said the Bosker, contemptuously. "If you choose to turn away a handful of gold do so. I can have the trick done for half the price. If you refuse there is the door. You know what it is to starve in the streets—you know what they are like at night when the wind bites' like the teeth of a dog, and the searching wind mocks at rags and poverty."

"Yes, I know," she replied, "Heaven help me! I know what it all means. Two nights ago I stood watching the windows of a house. Children were going to bed. I thought of the firelight flashing on their cosy beds, and I fancied I could hear the lisping of their prayers. Oh! is there no hope for me?"

The Bosker laughed and pushed a tumbler half full of brandy towards her.

"No," she said, "not that. When I take to drink it will not be for long. I may come to that, and I feel I shall—and then the river! Jim," she added, "would they say a prayer over my grave if I took my life?"

The Bosker did not relish this kind of conversation.

He had a heart of stone, but stone will melt sometimes, and the scoundrel felt a queer sensation he could not understand.

"I don't know," he replied, "funerals ain't in my line. I hope I shall be too late for my own, for I ain't a very punctual cove."

He affected to laugh, but it was a forced, hollow, and uncomfortable sound.

The girl called Rose folded her hands and gazed vacantly at the wall.

Her eyes dimmed with tears, and her lips quivered with inward emotion.

She was thinking of happier days.

She pictured a time when she was happy—happy at home with an aged parent; and then the advent of a handsome stranger, his promises and deceit; she compared the past with her present position and shuddered when she realised how lonely and forlorn she was.

The Bosker aroused her. She trembled at his touch, and glanced around. She had almost forgotten where she was; the scene before her, however, recalled all of it to her mind, and she said—

"I will do it, Jem."

"All right, to-morrow; you know the place."

He then gave her some money to get a few things to go in, for she was in rags.

Nathan furnished her with what she required, and when she re-entered the kitchen the Bosker could not help admiring her.

She was a pretty girl; and she used neither paint nor powder. Her eyes were wonderfully dark, with superb eyebrows, and well-shaped mouth, set off with a set of matchless teeth, and above all, she was a beautiful figure.

Anyone to have seen her in the street, would never have taken her for what she was, even had they been told so. It is not at all unlikely but they would have disbelieved the informant. Truly the closest observer would have failed to notice anything in her to find the slightest fault with; she spoke well, was very grammatical, and had a bearing that spoke of better days.

It cannot be wondered at that the Bosker admired her.

The time having arrived for her to depart, she started on her errand.

Little Flo was playing with some children in the road, and how to get at her was the girl's first thought. Fortune seemed to favour her, for at that moment a "nigger band" came in front of a public-house, close to the cab-yard, and the children, followed by little Flo, immediately ran to hear them play.

By some means the children got separated, and little Flo was alone in the crowd; but, being afraid of getting hurt, she ran to the pavement, and stood close to Rose.

"Are you not little Flo, who is staying with Mrs. Primrose?" she asked.

The child looked up in surprise, and, seeing a stranger, she knew not what to make of it, but she answered, timidly, "Yes, ma'am."

"I thought so, dear," Rose said. "You don't

know me, but you have heard Mrs. Primrose speak of me, have you not—her sister? I have just come from the country, where I have been staying."

This was a bold stroke, but she thought that if Mrs. Primrose had no sister the child would not know. Luckily for her, Mrs. Primrose had a sister, and she had spoken of her to the children and Flo, and even the children themselves had talked about their Aunt Amelia.

"Oh! yes," the child said, innocently. "Mamma Primrose told me about Aunt Amelia, and little Polly always says what a good aunt she is."

"Well, I am Aunt Amelia," Rose replied. "Mrs. Primrose has been telling me what a nice girl you are, and she said that I should find you here. I am going round the corner a little way, so if you like to come, dear, I will buy you something pretty."

"Shall I tell Polly?" Flo demanded.

"No, dear; I can't take too many."

Flo hesitated for a moment. She had an idea that she might be doing wrong, but, looking into the handsome face of her questioner, she decided she would go.

Rose produced some sweetmeats from her pocket and gave them to Flo, but the girl's heart smote her for what she was doing, and more than once she felt inclined to take the child back, and not help in the villainy of enticing her away.

The girl was not hard at heart, as we have seen already; and she conjured up the vision of a little sister at home, but then, again, she thought of the money. How nicely that would help her on; it would at least enable her to flee from the associations which were destroying her, body and soul.

When the child had eaten a few lozenges she began to feel faint and sleepy.

She complained to her conductress, who gave a glance of satisfaction, and said—

"You will soon be all right, I am going to the park, so we will ride."

The child, hardly knowing where she was or what she was doing, felt herself being placed in some vehicle and driven off.

She remembered no more.

"At last!" muttered the Bosker, who was in the cab with them. "I'd better gag her, or she'll squall out presently."

He took from his pocket a scarf, with the intention of tying the poor child's mouth up, but the girl would not allow him to do so.

"No, Jim; no violence," she cried. "I will not allow it."

She took the child upon her lap, and caressed the pale cheeks; then, looking the ruffian full in the face, she said—

"Jim, have you told me the truth? If I thought you were going to harm her, I would take her back, and if you attempted to stop me I would give you up to the police."

The Bosker uttered a savage oath, but, meeting the girl's beautiful eyes looking him full in the face, he cast his own down.

"No, I tell you," he replied; "I am not going to harm her."

"Very well, then," Rose said, "I will trust you."

"You can do so."

"So much the better for me and for you," she said.

The rest of the journey was passed in silence.

The Bosker took little Flo to Dan Garnett's and told him he wanted a room made pretty comfortable, for he had decided to send the child to David Eastlake, in the custody of his faithful henchman the Gorger.

The Bosker was not satisfied.

He determined to kill two birds with one stone.

"I must have the boy before I part with the girl," he thought, "and when they are out of the way I'll make Eastlake shell out handsomely, and bolt."

For a short time we will leave the Bosker to his meditations, and follow the fortunes of Gilbert.

He had never felt so happy in the whole course of his life as now, with his strange protector, and Whitechapel Dick became more attached to the lad every day.

Minnie, too, was kind and gentle, treating him with that sisterly love which the poor little fellow had never known, and he returned it fourfold, for he loved her with all the ardour of his gentle nature.

Gilbert thought Dick was a being to be worshipped, for he was always performing some act of kindness towards him.

Gilbert loved him as he would have loved a father, had he known the pleasure of having a kind parent to watch over him.

He also watched and followed Dick with the faithfulness of a dog, for he could not bear him out of his sight for an instant.

He always felt lonely, and a strange fear crept over him when his protector was away.

He experienced this feeling one day in particular, when Dick had arranged to be away for a short time. Gilbert seemed to cling to Dick as a person would cling to some dear friend whom he was going to part with for ever.

Dick perceived this, and placed his hand upon Gilbert's head in an affectionate manner.

"Why do you appear so loth to part with me, Gilbert, my boy?" he said.

"I don't know, Dick, but I feel afraid to lose sight of you. I wished I might—"

"Go with you," he would have said, only feared that it would be asking too much; in fact, it would, perhaps, be a liberty that would anger Dick. He stopped, and cast his eyes to the ground.

"Finish, my boy," said Dick, kindly, and continued—"I know what you would have said—you would like to come with me; is that it?"

A deep flush overspread Gilbert's face, and, looking timidly at Dick, he answered, faintly, "Yes."

"Not now, Gilbert; but if you like, and Minnie does not require your services or company, you may come and meet me. I shall come across the park from the Marble Arch, about dark; that will be a little walk for you," he replied.

Gilbert looked up with a smile, and, pressing his hand gratefully, bid him adieu.

"Good-bye, Minnie," said Whitechapel Dick; "take care of Gilbert, and don't let him come without the dog; that faithful creature is fondly attached to him, and will protect him from any danger."

Minnie said she would attend to it, and, with a smile of admiration upon her pretty face, she watched him out of sight.

Gilbert passed the day anxiously, and when at last twilight began to set in he prepared to depart.

Taking with him the magnificent Newfoundland dog he made his way to the park.

Gilbert walked to the Marble Arch, but, seeing nothing of Dick, he retraced his steps down the pathway; still he saw no signs of his kind guardian.

He commenced to get alarmed, for while he had been walking about it had become quite dark.

So he started on his way to the gate, determined to go home and see if Dick had arrived. Little did he dream that while he was waiting for Dick in the dreary park he was being watched, and that the faithful dog had already been enticed away by his foe.

Gilbert was proceeding on his way, when he suddenly stopped; he thought he heard footsteps behind him.

He turned to see who was following him, and as he did so he beheld a dark form within a few inches of him.

The place was too dark for him to see distinctly the features of the person, but feeling assured that whoever it was they meant him no good, he uttered a cry.

Before he could repeat it, something like a thick plaister was pressed on his face, entirely stopping his breath and causing a stifling sensation to steal over him.

He heard a coarse laugh break from the Bosker's throat, as that ruffian—for he it was—lifted him from the ground and carried him in his arms swiftly across the park.

Gilbert tried to tear the composition from his mouth, but his strength failed him.

To cry was impossible—a deadly stupor overcame him, his limbs relaxed, and he lay powerless in the hands of his kidnapper.

The Bosker, feeling the boy lay a dead weight, guessed in a moment he had fainted.

He placed him upon the green sward and removed the wrapper with which he had covered the boy's face.

"Trapped at last, my bird—ha, ha!" said the Bosker. "I guess it would give you something if you were awake to feel the nice little plaister being removed. No, bird, you won't fly away again. I didn't follow you all the way from that cart, after waiting four hours, to lose my bird again. No—no."

And he chuckled to himself in a most delighted manner as he carried the now senseless form of little Gilbert to the park gate. He looked cautiously round to see there was no policeman near.

A cab passing the gate at that moment, he hailed it. Jumping in, he placed Gilbert on the seat opposite him, and told the cabby to drive to Westminster.

As he spoke he fancied he knew the cabby, and the cabby thought he knew him, as it appeared from his half-muttered remarks—

"Well I'm blest, if that ain't the very cove as Grant is arter, my name ain't Primrose, that's all."

"Drive faster!" shouted the Bosker from within

"All right, sir," said the cabman, adding—"I'll have him! It's him, I'll swear, that stole my dear little Flo away."

Then he went on muttering—

"Grant's on his track for that, and I'll take good care he don't get off while I've got him safely stowed away in my cab."

He had by this time reached some of the dirty, slums of Westminster. Soon after crossing the bridge the voice of the Bosker bade him stop.

Jacob Primrose, for he it was, brought his cab up with a jerk, causing Gilbert to fall forward and strike the Bosker on the nose with his head.

Burkett's eyes watered to any amount, and he felt inclined to give Gilbert a gentle reminder, but refrained from doing so, in case it might rouse the boy to consciousness.

As the cab stopped, an intelligent-looking boy came along with a blacking-box slung over his shoulder—his hands were thrust into his pockets, and he whistled a plaintive air.

When Burkett alighted from the cab, the shoeblack halted, discontinued whistling, and looked at Burkett and his strange burden in mute surprise.

He then looked at the cabby, and from the cabby his glance went back to the Bosker.

The expression of astonishment died away from his face, his eyes glistened, his cheeks flushed, and with pretended carelessness he commenced to whistle again, but took particular notice of the house which the Bosker entered.

He then turned to the cabby, who had also been careful in his observations.

Certainly they both appeared to be very much interested in the Bosker's business, and each gave utterance, as if by mutual consent, to the same words.

"To the den!"

They then stared at each other, their looks displaying the surprise they felt at the other uttering the same words—

Then a look of recognition passed between them, and the boy spoke.

"Why, Primrose, is that you?" said he.

"Yes, Jack, my boy," the cabman replied, "and I think we can nab him at last."

"I think so, too; he's safe now, anyhow, for a time, at least. But, I say, who was that boy that he has got by his side?"

"Don't know, I'm sure," said Primrose. "He's going to do something with him, I expect; but I'll try and prevent his little game."

"So will I," Jack replied. "If you should see any of our detectives, of course you won't forget to inform them of the affair."

"I should think not. I owes him one for stealing that child—hang him!" Primrose said, as he turned the horse's head, and, bidding Jack good night, he drove off.

Jack started off at a run, and did not stop until he reached a house not far from where Burkett had alighted. He went inside and made some inquiries, but not gaining the information he required, he departed and went to a low public-house. Entering the tap-room, he gave a searching glance round, but among the many dirty faces there he could not find the one he wanted.

He then partially withdrew, when, accidentally dropping one of his brushes, he stooped to regain it.

As he did so, he beheld a man sitting in a dark corner behind the door, who was muffled up, with his hat drawn down upon his brow, and a small measure of beer standing on a cask in front of him.

Jack looked steadily at him for a moment, and by the start the strange individual gave he knew he was recognised ; they then exchanged secret signs, when Jack withdrew and went outside, where he waited until the man came out.

He had all the appearance of a gipsy, and, in fact, spoke like one, until, observing that they were alone, he said—

"Is there anything the matter, that you are in such haste ?"

"Yes, sir, I've just seen Burkett," said Captain Jack ; "he got out of Primrose's cab, with a boy, who I could see had been ill-used, as he was insensible, and the Bosker entered Nathan's with him."

"Can you describe the boy to me ?"

"Yes, sir, I put Dan on watch at the caravan, and he sent up a message that Gilbert—I think that's the boy's name—had gone out, followed by a big dog, and that the Bosker was also following. He had been waiting some hours for the boy, and I fancy, sir, that by the description this is the same little fellow."

"Ah ! then, he means no good," muttered the stranger, as he turned on his heel to depart. "I will see to it, my lad—go to your duty. You, of course, will be ready with your signals as before, for I intend entering again to-night. If I should come out alive I shall not forget you."

Meanwhile what was the Bosker doing with Gilbert—poor innocent little fellow.

Let us follow him and behold his villainy.

He entered Nathan's as usual, but did not go into the kitchen. He passed through the shop, and, turning abruptly to the left, proceeded up a long, dark passage. Stopping at a door on his right, he opened it, and entered a dirty-looking, disused kitchen, with a stone floor.

He rested for a few minutes, but fearing to wait too long there in case Gilbert should recover, Burkett unfastened another door and looked through an aperture.

"That will do," he muttered, "he won't be heard squealing down there."

The Bosker approached Gilbert, and raising him once more in his arms, carried him to a cellar below.

Letting Gilbert drop heavily on the floor, he unfastened a trap, with the intention of throwing Gilbert down, but he changed his mind.

"No," he thought, "I won't do that ; better put him out of his misery first."

So saying he approached Gilbert, who had partially recovered from his swoon.

He gazed round the wretched place in a dreamy manner, until his eyes alighted on the brutal face and form of the Bosker.

A shock passed through him, and a cold sense of fear went to his heart.

The sight of the Bosker had a magic effect upon him. All the recent events crowded upon him instantly, and remembering the Bosker's designs upon him not long since, he sprang to his feet.

A frightful oath escaped the lips of the ruffian on seeing that the boy was confronting him.

It was the very thing he had tried to avoid.

The Bosker would have got him out of the way when he lay insensible without a pang of remorse, but he felt unnerved when the boy stood looking at him in that beseeching manner.

But, however, turning his gaze from that of the boy's, he stepped towards him with his knife drawn, the look in his eyes plainly speaking his intentions.

Gilbert shrank from him in horror.

He understood too well the reason he had been brought there.

What to do to avert his coming fate he did not know.

To die like a dog, away from friends, caged in that dark, damp, cell—to be slaughtered like a beast—was more than he could stand.

The horrible danger he was in seemed to give him strength.

"I can at least make an attempt to save myself," he said, between his teeth, as his quick eye detected the Bosker's bludgeon on the floor.

With a bound he secured the weapon. Flourishing it in his hand, and giving a wild, maddened cry, he sprang upon the Bosker, and struck him several times on the face and head.

"No—no ! murderous wretch, you shall not kill me ! Help—oh, help !" Gilbert cried, in wild despair.

Burkett ground his teeth savagely.

He had not expected this.

"Let go your hold, brat !" he roared, like a wild beast, as he tried to wrench Gilbert from his throat.

Gilbert clung to him with all the wild energy of one battling for life.

The Bosker would have stabbed him there and then, only so unexpected had been the attack that, in trying to prevent Gilbert from hitting him with the bludgeon, he had dropped the knife.

"Will you be quiet, you whelp ?" he hissed, as he tightened his brutal hand upon the boy's throat.

His eyes blazed like red-hot coals, and he ground his teeth horribly.

All the evil passions of his brutal nature were aroused now.

To be struck in that furious manner by the boy rendered him blind with passion, and he would have killed him without the slightest hesitation.

"Ha—ha ! you may cry for help," he said.

At last he succeeded in freeing himself from Gilbert by pressing him backwards, until he was forced to relinquish his hold.

Burkett dashed him to the floor, and, picking up the knife, took Gilbert by the throat.

The helpless boy was swooning again, but feeling the Bosker's hand upon his throat, he attempted to rise, and called loudly for help.

Burkett only laughed, and twisting his fingers in his hair, hissed—

"Die, viper, die!"

The knife was already descending, when the sound of feet was heard in the passage, and the next instant a tremendous dog bounded across the cellar, and giving one deep growl, sprang at the Bosker and carried him to the earth.

There was a fierce struggle between man and beast, and blood flowed from one or the other. Gilbert could not see distinguish from which.

His senses were again deserting him, and all he was conscious of was a crash against the door a confused noise of juvenile voices, and the appearance of a lot of his old friends upon the scene.

He knew that he was rescued.

Then remembered no more, but sank deathly pale and apparently lifeless to the floor.

---

## CHAPTER XXIV.

THE GORGER ON HIS WAY TO THE PIG AND PORRIDGE POT MEETS WITH AN ADVENTURE— THE DIGNITY OF THE LAW OFFENDED—LITTLE FLO IN THE HANDS OF HER ENEMIES.

WHEN Tike returned to consciousness after the whack he had received from the blacking-box, he picked himself up and nodded his cranium sulkily.

"Very well," he said, as he shuffled to the entrance of the haunt, "I'll go, but expect me again soon. When I come back I sha'n't be alone. I'll find means to spoil the look of some of you."

"You will find us here," Alick replied, "and I don't suppose that Captain Jack will be long away. I strongly suspect that he is looking after a few friends of yours."

Tike scowled and rubbed his head again, but he did not waste breath by saying any more, and crept out of the haunt like a whipped cur.

"He's gone and that's a blessing," said Alick. "I can't imagine where Jack has got to. I think that we ought to go and look for him."

A number of the boys expressed their willingness to depart at once, and off they went.

All day long they wandered about without finding a trace of their leader, but in the evening they met Chimbley Joe.

"It's all right," said that youth, "you needn't trouble to hang about any longer. Jack knows what is he about. I'm watching the Gorger. He's in there," he added, pointing to a public-house. "Curly had better stop with me, but it will be best for the rest of you to go back to the haunt."

Alick and his friend took the hint, and Joe and Curly continued to watch the house in which the Gorger was regaling himself on the proceeds of several borrowed sixpences.

At last he emerged from the house, hatless, a little dazed about the eyes, and with a tendency to walk on both sides of the street at once.

At the same time an Irish street comedian appeared and commenced dancing and singing.

The Gorger, not noticing the boys, gazed contemptuously at the performer.

"That must be a jolly 'ard way of gettin' a livin'," he hiccoughed. "His legs are hung on wires, and so

are mine to-night. Hang me! if I don't have a dance myself."

"So will I," cried Chimbley Joe, commencing to throw his naked feet about. "Go it. Keep the pot a b'ilin'. Stick to the Gorger, Curly."

At that moment a policeman turned one corner and a homeward-bound youth the other, and, as if the whole thing had been arranged, the Irishman sent the constable's helmet spinning into the air, while Chimbley Joe brought his broom down upon the head of the passing youth, sending him flying into the arms of the law.

Before the policeman could extricate himself from the wild and frantic embrace of the boy the Irishman had bolted one way and the Gorger the other.

The constable, purple with rage, smacked the head of the youth, pushed him aside, and then turned his attention to Curly and Joe.

They had no alternative but to scamper away, and they did so before the strong hand of the man in blue could be laid on them.

"Oh! Curly," said Chimbley Joe, pulling a long face, "we have lost sight of the Gorger. What are we to do?"

"Go to Dan Garnett's, and keep watch there."

"No," Joe said, shaking his head. "We should only be half killed for our trouble, and besides, it would be acting against Captain Jack's orders. The Gorger will return. This is a favourite public-house of his, and it will draw him back like a penny magnet."

But Joe was mistaken for once.

The Gorger had wended his way to the Pig and Porridge Pot, and thither we will follow him, for he has business there.

The Gorger shuffled sideways through the bar of the Pig and Porridge Pot, so that he should not cause more observation than possible.

The cur was well aware that the "pub" he was now entering was a place of resort for the lowest of the low, and that the many bullies who were always loitering about the bar took a delight in teasing him.

He had reached the stairs, and was about to ascend, when he heard his name called out by the worthy landlord.

"Where are you going, Mr. Slime?" shouted Dan Garnett.

The Gorger could not answer. He was eating a piece of cold meat he had brought in his pocket, and his mouth was so full he could not breathe, and his eyes were starting out of his head.

What could he do? Five minutes more and he would be choked—dead. It was more than he could bear to think of—that the mouthful he was so much enjoying should be his last. Big tears rolled down his swollen cheeks, and mingled with the drops of perspiration trickling from his nose.

Dan Garnett had waited patiently for an answer; but, receiving none, made a rush at the choking Gorger.

The miserable wretch heard him coming, and began to ascend the stairs two at a time, but his flight was brought to a sudden termination.

His pursuer clutched hold of his coat-tail with such a jerk that the Gorger came tumbling head over-heels backwards, crushing Garnett under his huge carcase as he fell.

Garnett hit him in the wind with the heel of his boot, and the suddenness of the blow probably saved the Gorger's life, for it caused him to swallow what he had in his mouth.

"Where are you sneaking to?" inquired Dan, rising from the floor.

"I was only a-going to get the little gal," the Gorger replied.

"Who told you to?" Garnett demanded.

"The Bosker," he answered.

"Oh! very well," Garnett replied. "It is no business of mine, but if you don't make a muddle of the affair it will be a wonder."

Mr. Slime then went to little Flo, whom he found sobbing bitterly, with her head buried in her hands.

"Don't cry, there's a good little gal," said the Gorger, approaching her.

The child looked at the big fellow with a half-frightened yet inquiring look.

"Why am I brought here?" she inquired.

"I am come to take you into the country, if you are a good gal," the Gorger replied, trying to speak in his softest tone, which at most times resembled distant thunder or the roar of an enraged lion, except when he was frightened, and then he changed it into a whine.

Little Flo shrank from him as he extended his hand towards her.

"Come along," he said.

"I don't want to go into the country," she said.

"Come on!" said Mr. Slime, losing his temper.

The child began to cry—she had not been used to such rough handling.

"Where's my aunt, she who brought me here—the one that came from the country?"

The child had taken a great fancy to the girl who had abducted her from her happy home, for Rose's cheerful, kind, and affectionate disposition had won the little thing's heart.

"Come along, there's a pretty little dear," said the Gorger, soothingly.

"But will you take me to my aunt?" said Flo, looking up into his face, the tears glittering in her bright eyes.

"Of course, I will," said the Gorger; "that is just what I mean to do."

The innocent child smiled happily, and they sallied forth towards the railway station.

The pretty, fair face and delicate form of little Flo, in company with such a great ungainly-looking ruffian, caused the people as they passed to look in wonderment at the pair.

The Gorger felt very uncomfortable.

People glanced at him rather suspiciously, and many made remarks about the pretty appearance of the child, and the great, ugly gawky she was with, which did not add to the comfort of her conductor.

He took the nearest way to the station, by cutting through all the back slums, which he was well acquainted with.

There were many people walking up and down the platform waiting for their train to arrive, and all curiously scanned the Gorger.

That object of general inspection and observa-tion did not now heed the sundry remarks that were passed about him, but strutted to and fro as though he was one of the first lords of the land.

The train came in at last, and in due time steamed away on its journey.

When they reached their destination the Gorger, with little Flo in his arms, alighted and looked searchingly up and down the platform, as though he expected to see someone.

"Mr. Slime?" said a man wrapped in a huge cloak, which left his face alone visible.

The Gorger turned and looked inquiringly at the stranger.

"Don't you know me?" inquired he.

"I don't think I do," replied the ruffian.

"You are a fool!"

"You ain't, at all events," Mr. Slime retorted.

"Look here," said the stranger, "my name's Eastlake. I came to meet Burkett, but as you have brought the child safely it is as well."

Eastlake put out his hand to take little Flo, but she clung to the Gorger, as though she rather mistrusted the appearance of the new comer.

David Eastlake's eyes glistened maliciously.

"Who are you?" inquired Flo of Eastlake.

That gentleman did not know how to answer.

The Gorger saw his difficulty, and extricated him from it by saying, "He is your uncle."

"I would rather you took me to my aunt, please."

"Very well," said Eastlake, "he shall take you. I suppose my large cloak frightens you?"

Flo did not reply; if she had told him what she thought she would have said it was his villainous countenance that she did not like the look of.

The Gorger felt quite proud at the preference shown him by the child, and he gallantly took her little hand in his own huge paw. Then they followed Eastlake through several lanes, and across numberless stiles and fields.

Three-quarters of an hour's hard walking brought them to the house.

"Here we are at last, my little dear," said Eastlake, opening the door by the aid of a curious-looking key.

Little Flo reluctantly released her hold of the Gorger as David Eastlake took her hand and drew towards the door.

"My aunt has gone to Mamma Primrose," she said, timidly. "Won't you take me to her?"

"Perhaps," Eastlake replied, laying a peculiar stress on the word.

"Have you got anything to say to Mr. Burkett?" asked Slime.

"No," said Eastlake. "I shall see him when I have settled this little piece of business."

He pointed over his shoulder with his finger, implying that he meant the child.

The Gorger understood him; his lips trembled and his face went livid.

"This is the only job you have done well," said David Eastlake, "and this will reward you for being careful."

The Gorger took a purse full of money and dropped it into his pocket with a grin.

David Eastlake went in and shut the door, leaving the Gorger to amuse himself as he thought best.

"Mine—mine !" Eastlake muttered.

The child began to feel frightened, for the place was very quiet and dark.

"Where are you going to take me?" inquired Flo, as Eastlake dragged her after him down a flight of damp stone steps which led to a large kitchen or rather cellar.

"To your new home," hissed Eastlake.

Florence gave a scream.

She saw the murderous look in his eyes, and guessed his intentions.

"Curse you !" he said, " I will soon put a stop to all your noise."

Again she screamed for help, but the villain laughed at the idea of aid being near.

"You may bawl your little throat sore !" he said, savagely clutching her by the hair.

The child was terror-stricken, for Eastlake flourished a glistening knife before her eyes.

Another minute and it would have been too late for any earthly power to have saved her.

"It must be done !" he hissed, looking at the child.

"Cowardly hound !" said a deep, stern voice, and some one clutched the arm that held the knife, at the same time he was stricken to the earth by a tremendous blow on the back of the head.

His senses seemed to whirl for a moment ; the next instant he had recovered and was on his feet.

The stranger had gone, and so had Flo.

Like a shadow he had come to the rescue of the child, and like a phantom he had vanished.

David Eastlake looked round amazed, for the door had not been opened, and it was bolted on the inside.

There were no other means of entering.

Eastlake started as his eyes fell on a piece of parchment, that was stuck on the wall with a small silver dagger.

As he read the words he clasped his hands to his temples and fell to the ground insensible.

When David Eastlake returned to consciousness his face was deadly pale, and with a trembling hand he drew the dagger from the wall.

Again he read the inscription on the parchment. A spasm shot across his face, and his lips turned a deadly hue.

He tried to laugh, but failed, and only a sickly smile played on his lips.

The inscription upon the parchment was as follows—

"David Eastlake, beware ! Pause ere you go further down the path of destruction ! Advance not one step more in your diabolical work ! Restore the estates you have usurped to their rightful owner, or be sure of our vengeance ! Your every action is watched night and day. This is the first warning of the BRETHREN OF NIGHT—the third will be death !"

He let it fall to the ground, his lips moving nervously for a few minutes, then he rushed to a cupboard, and, taking a decanter of wine, he drank deeply.

As the alcohol began to take effect a fierce light shone in his fine yet evil eyes.

He laughed off the fears that had subdued him for a short time, until all the cold-blooded feelings of his cruel nature were worked up to their highest pitch.

Then he arose and stamped his foot upon the parchment.

"Do your worst, fools !" he muttered. "Think you to frighten me? Never ! No—I have gone too far to retract. Never will I give in whilst an obstacle is left in my way. Think you I shall draw back after going so far? No—no ! if all the fiends doomed to perdition were to rise up against me I would face them—ay ! even then I would finish what I have begun, though I had to steep myself to the neck in crime ! The girl and the boy shall be removed from my path in spite of all !"

His teeth gleamed like those of a tiger anticipating an attack from the huntsman.

He left the cellar and retired to his chamber, where he sat and planned the destruction of the two children again.

Here he evolved a device that would have done honour to Satan himself ; truly the monster in the form of a gentleman had the soul and heart of a fiend !

While he sat alone, brooding over his black villainy, little Flo was carried away insensible by her strange and mysterious deliverer.

He bounded through the nearest hedge and entered a lane, where a dark form approached him.

After a short whispered conference had passed between the two, the first stranger, who still held little Flo in his arms, said, in a calm, commanding tone—

"You know the mission you have to fulfil. Take this child safely to London ; go with her to the chief—he will give you further orders. You have done your duty here. It is well—you understand?"

" I do, your honour," replied the other.

"That will do ; continue to do your work faithfully and all will be well, but play me false—through bribery or anything else—and you know what will follow. I have now to discover what has become of the man the chief sent down here."

With this Flo's deliverer vanished.

Flo, who had recovered consciousness, now timidly set out with her new protector for the village inn, where they could have some refreshment, after which the man intended to carry out his instructions as quickly as possible.

As they walked along a thick-set, sun-burnt man, with restless eyes and dark hair, approached them.

He eyed little Flo and her guide curiously, and, as though interested in their movements, stood and watched the pair enter the inn.

Then he turned away and proceeded across the fields.

He carried a gun under his arm, and a canvas bag hung at his side, so that a casual observer would have taken him for a gamekeeper.

A short walk brought him to the grounds attached to David Eastlake's house.

The fellow glanced about him for a few minutes, to see that no one was observing him, then, entering the private grounds, began with the coolness of an old hand to search for game.

Presently a slight rustling of some dry leaves behind caused him to turn.

As he did so he grasped the stock of his gun, and stood in a posture of defence.

But upon beholding the disturber of the leaves he smiled knowingly, and placed his gun to his shoulder, for he beheld as fine a hare as he had ever seen.

If a dozen gamekeepers had been within reach of him he could not have resisted the temptation to bring the long-eared animal down.

He took steady aim and fired—the hare leapt some feet from the ground, and then fell dead upon its side.

The report of the gun echoed and re-echoed through the lofty trees and over the distant hills as the poacher bounded forward to pick up his prize.

A small yet firm hand gripped him by the collar as he secured it, and the poacher sprang round with an execration—

"Let go!" he cried. "Let go your hold, or you are a dead man!"

A low, mocking laugh answered him, as his captor tightened rather than relaxed his hold upon the poacher, who turned a shade paler than was his wont as he beheld the glittering eyes of David Eastlake.

He saw in an instant that he had no ordinary person to deal with.

"You thieving scoundrel! how dare you enter a gentleman's private grounds?" Eastlake demanded.

"Wait a minute," the man rejoined, shading his eyes with his hand. "I don't think I need make any excuse to you. I know you. You—you are—David E—"

"Just so, but there is no occasion for you to bawl it out. So you are not hanged yet, Michael the Gipsy—eh?—but have come back, and dare to rob me. Well, for your presumption I shall give you up for that pretty affair—do you remember?—double murder they called it, but I do not like ugly names for things myself."

"I did not do it, and you know it; it was treachery, and you dare not give me up for a crime I did not commit."

Eastlake laughed.

"Fool, do you suppose they would believe you?" he hissed. "Why came you here? Who informed you I was in this part?"

"No one, sir," the poacher replied. "I did not come to see you. I didn't know these were your grounds, or I shouldn't a-come here at all. The tribe ain't far off—that accounts for my being here."

The gipsy spoke in a truthful, undeceiving kind of manner, and Eastlake did not doubt him.

Something was going on in the subtle brain of the polished villain, for he stood in deep meditation for some time, ever and anon casting scrutinising glances at the gipsy.

"Follow me, Michael; we may be overheard here," he said, as he led the way towards the house.

The gipsy followed him, wondering what his intentions were.

Eastlake led the way into an apartment, and as soon as they were seated he began speaking.

He had already formed a plan to recapture little Flo and gain possession of Gilbert.

"Are you open to do a little business?" he asked.

"It all depends, sir," the gipsy replied. "We are rather down at present, and a little cash would be of some service, for we are hunted about from place to place, and can earn nothing. But mind you, Mr. Eastlake, no dirty work, for I tell you I will have nothing more to do with it."

A cynical smile played about the face of David Eastlake.

"You are growing respectable," he said. "I know you would not do a dirty action for the world."

"Well, what I do it matters not to you; but I tell you I will not stain my hands with blood for you or anyone."

"Come, come, we will not quarrel," said David Eastlake, as he poured out some wine.

He enticed the gipsy to drink heavily, and then he said—

"Now hark you, Michael, you must do what I require. You need not stain your hands with blood; but what I want you to do must be done neatly, and I will pay you well. This evening a little girl was rescued from me—taken by my enemies. Who she is is nothing to you; suffice it to say, that if that child should get to London it is all up with me—you can guess the rest. Do you remember that boy Gilbert?"

"Well—very well."

"Just so," said Eastlake. "Now, look you—this girl cannot be far away by this time; if you capture her I will give you fifty pounds. I do not want you to harm her. Take her to your tribe; bring her up as one of them—that is all I wish. Now then, there is no time to lose—will you do it?"

A cunning glance shot from the dark eyes of the gipsy as he remembered the little girl he had seen with some one crossing the fields, and he replied—

"I will do it."

"Good," said Eastlake. "When you have her safe come back, and you shall receive the rest of your instructions. There is the boy—you must get him too, if, indeed, he is not already taken by one of my agents; but he must be dealt with in a different manner. Firstly he must be taken out of the clutches of the meddling fools that think to baffle me. Ha! ha! I will triumph yet."

"I understand; these two children are in your way," said the gipsy. "You want them out of it?"

"Exactly so."

"Very well," Michael replied. "The little girl is to be brought up as one of the tribe; let her marry into it later on, so that society would not own her, even if they knew who she was, which isn't likely, as she won't know herself. Then the boy, if he should fall into my hands—he, you say, is the greatest obstacle. Mr. Eastlake, you can trust me, for I have the power to help you; but you must give me my price, and then not only shall the children be for ever removed from your path, but the tribe shall all go away to some foreign land."

" Then that is a bargain—on your oath ?"

" It is."

Had Eastlake been a little less heated with wine he would have seen a look upon the other's swarthy face every now and then that would have warned him not to place quite so much confidence in him ; but his black heart was rejoicing at the prospects of the plot.

He never thought for a moment that he had raised a deep, cunning, deadly enemy in the gipsy.

" Now, how to get possession of the girl is the first thing," said Eastlake.

" That is easy enough."

" You treat the affair lightly. How ?" demanded David Eastlake, with some surprise.

" By mere chance I saw her being led across the fields by a peculiar-looking man," said the gipsy.

" Did you watch them ?" asked his employer, turning slightly pale as he remembered the mysterious letter.

" Well, I did, though entirely without any ulterior intention, and I saw them enter the Shepherd and His Dog."

" Good ! we will have her," cried David Eastlake. " I can see, plainly enough, what they intend to do. They will stay there till about four in the morning, when they will make their way across the fields to the railway station, to be in time for the early morning train. Do you understand?"

" Perfectly."

" Good. Ha ! ha ! How nicely the meddlers will be taken in. Ha ! ha !'

The worthy pair sat and laughed over the anticipated discomfiture of little Flo's rescuer.

In the midst of their conversation David Eastlake fell into a listening attitude, and his confederate watched him closely.

Once or twice Michael the Gipsy fancied he heard something, but he made no remark.

His intentions were, however, to keep a watchful eye upon the gentlemanly villain, for he felt certain all was not right in that lonely house.

Eastlake seemed to read his thoughts, for a cunning smile played about his lips, and he muttered, as he went to the cupboard for more wine—

" I must quiet my watchful companion for a few hours."

He put the wine upon the table and bade his companion drink.

Michael was about to raise the glass to his lips when he fancied he heard a faint scream, and then a noise, such as a person would make in thumping or kicking against a door.

A suspicion flashed through his mind instantly that some foul work was going forward.

With the glass still raised midway to his lips, he looked interrogatively at Eastlake, in whose eyes a sinister gleam shone, and who muttered something more forcible than polite, without answering the inquiring look of his companion.

Then, with some bantering remark, he drank his wine and bade the other do the same.

The gipsy was not so easily thrown off his guard ; he was determined to discover the cause of the noises he had just heard.

How could he ? was the next thought.

In a moment he had formed a plan.

He was aware that he was being closely watched by Eastlake, and if his suspicions were aroused he knew that it might be dangerous to himself.

They had some hours to wait yet before he could attempt to abduct Flo, and noticing the uneasy way in which Eastlake gazed at him, he thought it best to appear as indifferent as possible.

They had been drinking deeply, and presently Michael began to get rather free about the tongue, and hiccoughed and rocked about in his chair.

Then he tried to rise from his seat to reach another glass of wine.

He balanced himself in a very unsteady manner, and, raising his glass on high, he drank the health of his employer.

As Michael did so by some means he lost his balance.

Down he went, the wine spilling all over his face, and the next instant he was lying beneath the table in a state of intoxicated unconsciousness.

Then Eastlake arose from his seat, with a look of deep disgust upon his handsome face as he gazed upon the inanimate form of the gipsy.

He gave the man a kick, to see if he was really unconscious—to make sure that the fellow was not feigning slumber.

" I am safe for a time at all events," Eastlake muttered. " This brute will not wake for some hours. And now to see my pretty bird. I must teach her not to make a noise when I have strangers in the house."

Glancing again at the comparatively inanimate form of the gipsy, Eastlake opened a door, and descending the stairs, he proceeded towards a room from whence the cries of anguish had issued.

Without the slightest hesitation he entered and closed the door behind him, but did not lock it.

It is necessary now that the reader should return to the room in which Michael lay under the table, and watch the actions of the gipsy, which were somewhat peculiar for a drunken man.

He snored until Eastlake had descended the stairs, then he became wonderfully quiet, and when he heard the door close, he sat bold upright and listened.

An expression of grim satisfaction settled upon his swarthy cheeks, and a smile played around his not unhandsome mouth as he hastily drew his boots off and rose to his feet.

His drunkenness had been assumed, and stealing from the room he followed in David Eastlake's track.

For a few moments he was puzzled how to know which was the apartment Eastlake had entered, but the sound of voices soon directed him the right way.

" Viper," Michael hissed under his breath, " you have threatened my life for a deed done by your own dastardly hand, but now I have it in my power to revenge myself. Scoffing, devilish fiend, you shall learn what it is to earn a gipsy's revenge."

Michael opened the door softly and peeped into the room.

Confronting David Eastlake was a lovely but poorly dressed girl.

# POOR BOYS OF LONDON

## OR, DRIVEN TO CRIME.

No. 9.]      **A LIFE STORY FOR THE PEOPLE.**      [ONE PENNY.

"Not yet, Bosker," cried Alick. "Let go your hold, or down you go.'

She was trembling with anger and excitement, and Eastlake, bold villain though he was, quailed before the light of her flashing eyes.

"If you are a man," she was saying, "you will permit me to leave this place. I repent of coming here, for my heart tells me that I did wrong in listening to you. Give me back my liberty. Let me go back to my poor brother, who I know is searching the length and breadth of London for me. Oh! Heaven, what a fool I must have been to believe that you, an educated, wealthy, and accomplished man, ever intended to make me your wife."

"Pretty Polly," Eastlake returned, mocking her, "you came here of your own free will, and here you must stay until I choose to bid you go. You wrong me, indeed. I love you, Polly, as I never loved woman before."

"Back—back!" she cried, thrusting out her hands as he advanced. "Monster, touch me not!"

"What, must I not have one kiss?" Eastlake said, laughing. "Foolish girl, I mean you no harm, but a kiss I will have."

"No—no!" Polly shrieked. "Pollute not my lips. I would rather die than suffer your caresses."

"Fool!" David Eastlake cried, throwing off the mask of the polished gentleman and appearing in his true colours. "Fool! I came here to woo and win you honourably; but since you are so obstinate, you shall learn that my love can turn to hate. You shall never see your brother again—never leave this house alive—"

"You lie!" said a deep voice behind him.

Eastlake stood rooted to the spot, unable to move or speak, and before the sound of the voice had died away he was struck to the ground insensible ere he had time to see who his assailant was.

Meanwhile, Polly stood trembling with fear.

"Fly, my girl," said the gipsy. "Yet stay—can you hide anywhere?"

"Oh! no—no, sir," the terrified girl cried. "Let me fly from this dreadful place—oh! pray let me go."

"Go, then, my girl," Michael said, "across the fields."

"Thanks—oh! thank you, sir," said the girl, weeping, as she hastened from the room and fled up the stairs. "May Heaven deal as mercifully with you as you have with me."

The gipsy waited until he heard the door leading to the grounds open and close, and then he returned to the room which he had previously occupied.

It was evident that David Eastlake had not received much injury from the blow, for he quickly recovered, and glared round the apartment in a terrified manner.

"That dark hound Michael has played me false," he said, as he staggered to his feet. "Let him look to himself. The girl is gone, and Michael—the treacherous cur!—is laughing in his sleeve at the trick he has played me."

His astonishment may be better imagined than described, when, on ascending the stairs and entering the upper room, his gaze fell upon Michael the gipsy.

He lay as David Eastlake had left him, snoring, with his head pillowed on his arm, and the atoms of a broken wine glass around him.

Eastlake could come to no other conclusion than that the gipsy had been innocent of striking him down, and he shuddered as he thought of the mysterious foes by whom he was surrounded.

He drank some brandy to nerve himself, then he gave his sleepy companion a kick in the ribs.

A grunt was the only reply vouchsafed by the sleeper, but Eastlake, after a little trouble, managed to rouse his companion, and Michael, still feigning to be overcome with drowsiness, hinted that it was time he was gone.

Eastlake answered him with a savage growl as he took a heavily-loaded Malacca from a corner of the room, and, grinding his teeth harshly, he prepared to follow the gipsy.

Morn was just breaking, and a gentle breeze wafted across the fields, which passed almost like a sigh over Eastlake's burning brow.

They soon reached a thick hedge opposite the Shepherd and his Dog, where they remained concealed.

At length a noise, like the drawing of bolts from their sockets, sounded upon their ears, and they drew back into the shade.

A man, leading little Flo by the hand, emerged from the inn, and little suspecting what was about to happen, proceeded slowly through the lane, Flo prattling with childish glee about the beautiful appearance of the country.

Eastlake's eyes fairly blazed when he beheld the child and her conductor.

"Curse him! He shall pay dearly for his interference," he said, between his clenched teeth. "Follow me!"

The gipsy followed Eastlake as he quietly made his way to an opening in the hedge, that he might confront the unconscious stranger.

"No violence—we can do it without spilling blood, David Eastlake," said the gipsy, hoarsely.

He understood the deadly look upon Eastlake's face, and thought that perhaps he would strike the child as well as the man.

Luckily for Eastlake he did not, for the gipsy had his hand upon the butt of a pistol concealed in his breast-pocket, and had he attempted to have struck Flo, the gipsy would have shot him without remorse, and so ended the black career of the bold, pitiless villain.

With a savage cry Eastlake bounded forward and confronted Flo's protector.

The stranger stepped back, and, placing the child behind him to shield her from harm, he drew a pistol, and presented it full at the head of David Eastlake.

Michael then came forward and stood by the side Eastlake, who, uttering a savage cry, swung the cane round his head.

The man saw the movement, and pulled the trigger of the pistol, but there was only a faint click and no report.

The cane whizzed through the air, the next instant there was a dull thud, and Little Flo's protector fell bleeding and apparently lifeless to the earth.

"Thus do I crush all that stand in my path, or attempt to thwart me!" Eastlake cried, as he raised the loaded cane again. "Miserable cur, you sought your own fate!"

Michael stepped forward and arrested his arm in time to save the descending blow.

"No more, Eastlake; you have done enough," he said. "If you have killed him, beware, for I tell you I will never work with or for a murderer."

"He is not dead, you chicken-hearted fool. See

if you can remove that brat, and stop her squealing," Eastlake replied.

The lips of the gipsy twitched nervously as he clutched the child by the arm.

She screamed louder than ever, and Eastlake uttered an oath, for he heard the people of the inn moving about.

Michael, fearing they would be discovered, caught the child up in his arms, and sped across the fields with Eastlake.

The poor child fainted from terror, and lay quiet and motionless in the arms of her herculean abductor. When they gained a thicket Eastlake paused.

"Conduct her safely to your camp," he said. "I will see you there, and arrange the other business. Do not leave until I come. You know your part; play it—or beware."

"Have I not promised, and is not—"

"Enough! depart; I will seek you shortly," David Eastlake interrupted, as he turned upon his heel and strode away.

## CHAPTER XXV.

POLLY'S ESCAPE—A PLOT AGAINST A PLOTTER.

POLLY sped quickly across the fields, knowing and caring not in what direction she was going.

All that she thought of in her wild flight was to get away from the dreaded house in which she had suffered so much.

She doubted not but that immediate pursuit would be made, and the very thought increased her fear, and she ran the faster.

But to continue at such speed for long was utterly impossible.

More than once she appeared about to faint from exhaustion, but each time she stopped she fancied she could hear the sounds of approaching footsteps.

Terror gave her strength, and she ran on again, until she was so worn out and fatigued that she sank upon the grassy sward.

"Oh! why—why did I leave my brother for that wicked man, who only meant to do me harm?" she moaned. "What shall I do? There is no house near. This is indeed hard, to be alone in the world, without a friend to help me. Heaven guide me! Oh! my dear brother, what would he say if he could see me now?"

Bitter sobs stopped her further utterance as, with hands clasped, she knelt upon the grass, damp with the morning dews, and wept aloud.

Tears seemed to relieve her a little, and when she ceased weeping she began to reflect upon her position.

To stay there would be folly.

When she arose she discovered that her aching limbs were scarcely able to support her, but still she tottered on, until she found herself at the entrance of a village street.

An old wooden sign of an inn stretched half-way across the road, and she made her way towards the house; but now that she had reached a place of safety her strength failed completely.

Her head seemed to swim, a trembling like that of ague shook her exhausted frame, and, placing her hand to her burning forehead, she staggered forward and fell.

It is impossible to say how long she might have remained in that state but for a friendly deliverer in the shape of an ostler, who was giving a horse walking exercise, which suddenly shied at poor Polly's inanimate form.

"Well I'm blessed—well I'm blowed! If she bean't a dead 'un, poor lass!" he said.

With that he trotted back to the yard, called the boy, who looked surprised at his white face, and enquired the cause.

The ostler pointed to the prostrate form of poor Polly.

"What shall we do?" the boy demanded.

"Wake up the missus," the ostler replied. "Ah! that be the best thing to do lad—come on."

Leaving the horse, they rushed through the kitchen into the inn. The landlady was just rising, and wanted to know the cause of the noise. She opened the bedroom door, and listened to the awful tale of the stableman.

She was a kind, warm-hearted dame, never, if she could help it, letting anyone go away hungry, and the tale she heard greatly agitated her.

"Joe—Joe, for Heaven's sake! wake up," she screamed lustily to her sleeping husband.

"Oh! yes, my dear, I am very sleep—"

Here he snored off again.

This was too much for his better half.

"Joseph, you monster! get up," she cried. "Oh! you brute, to think there's a poor young lady dying outside, and nobody to help her. Joe, you wretch, get up!"

"What's the matter, wife? Somebody dying, eh? Oh, lor'! I didn't know that, my dear," he answered, springing out of bed, his eyes half closed.

"Hurry yourself, you unfeeling brute, and help me to assist the poor lass."

"Yes—yes; I'm coming. I'll follow you in a minute, my dear," he said, now wide awake.

Without more ado his spouse dashed down the stairs, followed by her husband, who shared a part of his wife's good feeling, and was ever ready to help a fellow creature in distress.

The whole of the domestics were already astir, and running about in all directions. But, upon the appearance of their master and mistress, they all proceeded in a body to where the poor girl lay.

The honest heart of mine host was touched by the sad spectacle; his spouse was already weeping, with the corner of her apron to her eyes.

Joseph knelt by the side of the poor insensible girl, and, resting her head upon his arm, he placed his hand to her heart to see if she still lived.

It beat so faintly that at first the worthy landlord thought her dead, but a lengthened application enabled him to feel the slightest possible movement —so slight that he feared it would cease before he could get her into the house.

"Thank Heaven she lives! Help me, my lads," he said.

Everyone breathed more freely, and the ostler, with one or two others, rushed forward to aid Joseph.

Even the little stable-boy nearly stuck the prongs of his fork into the toes of one of the lookers-on when he heard she lived.

The warm-hearted landlady had already made the couch in the comfortable little parlour ready for Polly's reception, and procured something to bring her round, if possible.

The men carried their light burden in with sorrowful faces, and placed her gently upon the sofa ; and while the hostess tried all she knew to bring the sufferer back to consciousness, the ostler was despatched for the doctor.

A number of sympathising neighbours came in to see the strange young lady, and offered to do any little services that lay in their power.

Meantime the patient slowly recovered under the tender care of Mrs. Simmons, the hostess, and presently the doctor arrived and attended to the girl, in time to stop a number of questions that would have been painful for her to answer.

Presently he asked her name.

"Mary Thorne. They call me Polly, sir," she answered, faintly, and then she told a story that brought pity from the female listeners and indignation from the male.

Now we will return to the gipsy and his base employer.

It was the evening subsequent to that on which the gipsy had met David Eastlake.

The gipsies were gathered round a fire, over which was hung a large iron vessel.

Michael sat some distance from the tribe, brooding deeply.

Near him was an old woman—his grandmother, Martel. Her form was bowed by the weight of many years.

She was attired in a mass of discloured rags, and, to complete her strange appearance, a short black pipe was stuck between her parchment-like lips ; she was puffing away with a vigour that would have done honour to an inveterate smoker of the male gender.

Near her, in direct contrast to the old dame, was a young girl, very beautiful, and dressed neatly. She was the intended bride of the gipsy, and she listened breathlessly to every word he was speaking to the old hag.

"Ay, mother, it is sad for me," Michael said ; "but I am in that villain's power, and for my sake you must appear to serve him, or my life would be forfeited before a week."

"Yes, yes," croaked the old women, "he has wronged you, I know, but by all that I hold sacred you shall have a terrible revenge."

"But why do you fear him, Michael—you are innocent?" said the lovely gipsy maiden.

"Mina, it is not him I fear," he replied. "I fear no man ; but his black villainy would stand at nothing, and what chance would I, a gipsy, have against a wealthy gentleman."

"Hist!" said the old crone, "there is a stranger approaching."

The sound of horses' hoofs were heard, and the handsome form of David Eastlake appeared riding into the camp.

A gipsy stepped forward and took his horse, and he walked to where Michael sat with an air of one who feels that he is master.

"Leave us, Mina," said the old gipsy, abruptly.

The girl departed as Eastlake entered the encampment, but not before he had caught a glimpse of her beautiful supple form.

And thoughts flashed through his subtle brain that boded no good to the handsome gipsy girl, as he watched her vanish among the tents.

The determined eye of Michael was watching him closely, and seemed to read his thoughts.

"You have sought us again, my son," said Martel, as she motioned Eastlake to seat himself on a stool.

"Ay, Martel, it is high time I did so," Eastlake replied. "Strange things occur, and everything seems to be against me. Men who perpetrate the vilest crimes seem to fail in anything they do for me. You have her safe?"

"Quite—behold," said the old woman, pointing to a gipsy van closely shut up, and a man standing by the door.

"But mind, Michael, the scheme must be carried out," Eastlake continued, "and I hope you understand what you have to do? Neither of the children shall, upon any consideration, ever see the soil of England again. The girl you must make one of yourselves—marry her to a man in the tribe ; but the boy, when he is your prisoner, you must be very particular with. Make him a vagabond, the greatest villain among your set ; let him be ever within the meshes of the law, so that he dare not attempt to ever return to the soil of England. Do you understand me? Mind—you play me false, and—"

He glanced at Michael, who stood pale and slightly trembling.

The cold, pitiless way in which the hardened villain spoke quite unnerved him, and he longed to be at the rascal's throat.

As Eastlake spoke he gave the crone some money, and her small eyes glistened with avarice as she joyfully gathered up the glittering coins in her skinny hands.

"That is only an earnest of what you will get as long as the children are with you," Eastlake said. "Now, you see, I am willing to keep to my part of the compact, and a very liberal one, too—mind that you keep to yours."

"Have I not sworn to aid you and yours?" said Michael. "It is not so, mother?"

"It is—it is, my son."

"Enough," said David Eastlake, "be ready to depart for London. You know the haunt—seek James Burkett—you are acquainted with him. Take him this packet, you will then be told what your business is. If he has fulfilled his promise, or does so while you are there, come back to me, and prove that he has done his work, and I will pay you, and also save you the trouble of having the boy."

"All shall be managed to your satisfaction," Michael replied.

"That will do. Now, adieu ; Martel, guard well your protégée and the secret I have trusted you with, and I will pile gold in your lap."

With a few instructions to Michael he strode out

of the camp, and, mounting his horse, with an expression of triumph upon his handsome face, rode away.

A change came over the old crone when he had departed.

Her wrinkled features worked dreadfully, and her frame trembled with emotion.

"I will guard the children," she muttered; "they shall be safe in my keeping until the time comes when the doer of this evil shall be thwarted, and the helpless innocents reinstated in their defrauded rights. Curses upon him! But for the power he holds over my son his black career should terminate instantly. Where is the rightful lord? Ah! would that I had our king now to help us. He knew much about these dear innocents and the rightful owner of the estates this monster now usurps."

She bowed her head and murmured to herself in her own dialect.

"His gold—ugh!" she said, glancing at the glittering heap, "there is blood upon it! I could read the awful word murder in his cold and glittering eyes. Yet I will keep the dross, for it will aid me and them, while seeming to serve him."

She secreted the money in her ragged dress, and motioning for Michael to come near, said—

"When do you start, my son?"

"Almost directly, mother."

"'Tis well. Stay not longer than you have need, for I want you here."

"I will be as quick as possible," Michael replied.

"Good; and if you see that poor creature you saved from his clutches, you know what to do. He commands you to take her to him; do nothing of the kind. Find out her whereabouts, and conduct her safely home, wherever it may be."

"I will, mother. Did you notice how he looked at Mina? Guard her well, mother, for I feel certain that he means her harm."

The old woman's eyes fairly blazed as she rose from her seat and screamed—

"He dare not. He should die like a dog!"

Michael took an affectionate farwell of Mina, and started for London.

The next day he was seeking the Bosker.

He soon found that worthy, and they both retired to a private room at Dan Garnett's.

"Well, old pal, how has the world used yer since we last met? We've not had the pleasure of your company lately," said Burkett, as they seated themselves.

"Yes, it is a long time ago when I was among the pals, and now I've come upon business. Here's a letter from that Eastlake," replied Michael, handing the packet to Burkett.

He clutched it eagerly, and perused the contents.

The gipsy could see by the expression of his face that something in the letter aroused his passion, and Burkett began swearing awfully.

"Curse him! I'll see whether it's dangerous or not. I'll do it, curse me, I will!" and he brought his fist down with a bang upon the table.

"What's up, Jem?" asked Michael.

"Everything, I think," the Bosker growled. "I sent a girl to him and he's lost her!"

"But I've got her safe enough though," answered the gipsy, with a forced laugh.

"That ain't all; there's that young whelp that was saved by the imps who call themselves the Poor Boys of London," the Bosker said. "If Grant gets hold of him he'll make him charge me and Eastlake with attempted murder. I tell you, Michael, I'll do it this time, if I gets lagged over it. And then I'll settle accounts with this fine, bragging gentleman, who promises to pay us to do his dirty work, and yet threatens every few hours to give us up to justice. I owe him more than one grudge."

"Then why don't you pay him?" Michael demanded.

"I intend to," said Burkett, with savage glee.

"But venting your spite upon a child is very poor revenge," said the gipsy.

"What do you mean?" the Bosker rejoined.

"Zounds, man, are you such a dullard that you can't read through this polished villain?" replied Michael.

"I don't understand you. Why don't you speak plain?"

"Well, I will try to do so," Michael returned. "I owe David Eastlake a debt that will not be easily paid. Now, if you are of my mind, we can kill two birds with one stone. Are you willing to work with me? If so, Burkett, I promise you such revenge as would have satisfied Shylock. I swear it! Are we together?"

"We are!"

"Well, then," said the gipsy, "can't you see the cunning villain, in the letter I brought you, is only trying to work you up to a certain point? Can't you see that he thinks, by telling you that the boy endangers your life, it will help to make you wish to get him out of the way for your personal safety, and then Eastlake would have a nice laugh at you? He could say that you did the deed for self-interest, and that he had nothing to do with it, and if it was ever discovered, which it would be, the rope would be round your neck—not his."

"Curse him! I see his d—d plot now, but he shall be disappointed," vociferated Burkett, rising from his seat, and again striking the table with his clenched hand.

"And now for my plan," said the gipsy. "As you already know, this boy is a great thorn in Eastlake's side, and he is most anxious to get him out of the way. Well, suppose you say you are not able to murder him, but help me to capture the boy? I will take him to the camp, and pretend the little fellow is lost to the world; instead, I shall look well after him and his interests.

"We could afford to wait patiently until Eastlake is upon the highest pinnacle of fortune," Michael continued—"until his greatest wish has been gratified—then we could bring forth such proofs as would hurl him down to the very bottom of the gulf, never to rise again. Wouldn't that be revenge? Think of it—look at it in a proper light, and tell me if that wouldn't be just and terrible revenge—a revenge that would satisfy the most greedy avenger?"

"Aye, by Heaven! that would be glorious. Can you do it?" asked the Bosker, in great excitement.

"Easily. Are you game to help me?"

"Yes; without a doubt. We'll do it—curse him!" said the Bosker. "I will wait—aye, wait patiently—for such revenge as that. And I can get something—a pocket-book—that will aid us in our vengeance. I and a pal are going to-night to try our best and get it from a fellow that now holds it."

"This is a compact?" asked Michael, with a look of gratification.

"It is, and here's my hand upon it."

The gipsy could hardly conceal his pleasure at having so singularly got everything in his favour; they were still plotting and arranging matters when they were disturbed by a slight tap at the room door.

Michael looked inquiringly at Burkett.

He coolly rose, took his bludgeon from the table, and opened the door.

This caution was unnecessary, for only the boy, Tike, shuffled into the room.

"Well, what message?" growled Burkett.

"It's all right," answered Tike. "They've got Gilbert at the haunt. I saw them take him in. They thought they were doing something clever by kicking me out, but—ha! ha!—I'm a little too cute for them, and know how to use my eyes."

"All right," said the Bosker, grimly; "keep on the alert. Go at once, and keep me well posted with everything you see and hear."

"I'm fly," Tike replied, as he retired.

### CHAPTER XXVI.

DICK'S RETURN — NEWS OF GILBERT — WHITE-CHAPEL DICK'S DETERMINATION — THE BOSKER AND THE GORGER THINK THEY HAVE SECURED A PRIZE.

IT was late on the same night that Gilbert fell into the hands of the Bosker when Whitechapel Dick returned to the caravan.

He had been delayed, and, though anxious about the boy, little dreamed of what had really happened.

A slight knock at the door brought Minnie to the threshold.

Dick regarded her some few seconds in surprise, for the girl had evidently been crying.

"Oh! Dick," she said, "I was so terrified—neither you nor Gilbert returning; and I have been so lonely."

Dick sprang up the steps and clutched the girl's arm.

"Gilbert! what has become of him?" he demanded.

"Have you not seen him?" she said, with a look of alarm upon her pretty face.

"I, Minnie? No. God help him!"

"Then my worst fears are realised," she said, her eyes again filling with tears.

"I can see it all. He has been kidnapped," Dick said, hoarsely, "and I have no doubt but that murderous vagabond has got him again."

"Who do you speak of?" Minnie demanded.

"Do you remember the night when he was hunted under the very wheels of this caravan by that ruffian known as the Bosker?" said Dick.

"Oh! yes, to be sure."

"Well, Minnie, that's the man—but I'll track him!" Dick cried, vehemently. "I'll find the boy, dead or alive."

He finished with an oath, and brought his fist down with a blow upon the table, while Minnie looked at him with fear.

She had never seen him in such a passion before; but it did not last long.

He soon became calmer, though a troubled look still hung over his handsome countenance.

He attired himself in the height of fashion, and never before had he taken so much care over his toilet. Minnie gave him a look of admiration.

"Will you be long, Dick, dear?" she asked.

"No, little one; perhaps not."

"But why do you say perhaps?"

"Because, Minnie, my dear, one never knows what may occur when one is out. If I should not return do not leave this place—when I do come back I will bring the boy with me."

He was about to leave the caravan when a tap came at the door.

Minnie opened it, and, to her surprise, a ragged boy stood before her.

Without waiting for her to speak the boy said—

"If you please is Mr.— Mr. Dick in?"

For the minute Minnie was puzzled how to answer; she knew it would look strange for a master of a caravan to be dressed like Dick was.

"Do you require him?" she said; "or can I take any message instead?"

"I come from Gilbert, miss."

Dick was listening, and at the word "Gilbert" he sprang forward, and said, "Bring the boy in."

Chimbley Joe, for he it was, entered the caravan, and cast a half-timid, half-curious glance about him.

"You come from Gilbert, you said, my boy?" Dick asked, quietly.

"Yes," answered Joe.

"Where is he?"

"Along of us in our house; among the Poor Boys of London."

"How came he there?" Dick demanded, with some surprise.

"Why, sir," Chimbley Joe replied, "we saved his life, and we took him there out of the way, in case anybody should try and collar him again."

"From whom did you save him?" Dick asked, rather excitedly.

"The Bosker, sir."

Then Joe, in a roundabout way, related how Captain Jack had fallen across the Bosker and his victim, how he had summoned the Poor Boys of London, and how Gilbert's life was saved just in the nick of time.

When it came to the part where the boys rescued him from Burkett, Dick's face glowed with admiration.

"Bravo, lads!" he said; "and I sha'n't forget you for it. But tell me, why did not Gilbert himself come and let me know of this?"

"Captain Jack says, 'Don't let Gilbert out for a

few days yet, 'cause he's been knocked about a bit, and he ain't well,'" Chimbley Joe replied. "Another thing he said, 'P'raps there's some sneaking thief on the watch, to get hold on him again.' So I says, 'But they don't though.' 'No,' says the captain, 'when he is well enough some of you go to take care of him.' But Gilbert said he wanted to come and tell you. Now I knowed it would be bad for him to come out. Another thing, he was safer there than anywhere. So I says, 'No; give me a message and I'll go anywhere for you.' Then he told me to come to you, so I trotted off."

"But where is your home?" asked Dick, who had listened quietly to the boy's narrative.

"Under the Thames, sir."

"Under the Thames!" echoed Dick, with a look of surprise.

"Yes, sir; that's where we hang out."

"I don't understand," said Dick. "I will come and see this place of yours at once. Lead the way, youngster, and I will try to make you and your chums happier than you have been for many a day."

Only too delighted at the prospect of having so distinguished a visitor at the haunt as Whitechapel Dick, Chimbley Joe preceded him, but the distance was too great to think of walking it, and a cab was procured.

The vehicle was dismissed in one of the bye streets that led to the haunt, and Whitechapel Dick put himself under the guidance of Chimbley Joe, who walked and looked as proud as a peacock.

In a few minutes Whitechapel Dick found himself in a very strange place, and in peculiar company. He was rubbing his eyes, to get used to the gloom of the haunt, when Gilbert, uttering a glad cry, ran into his arms.

"My boy," Dick said, as he hugged the boy to his breast, "you have suffered terribly. You shall tell me all when we are safe under the roof of the caravan. But there is one thing I should like to know now. How came the dog to desert you?"

"He was gambolling a long distance in front of me, and I think he was enticed away," Gilbert said; "but it appears that when he missed me he followed up the scent until he fell in with Captain Jack and his brave boys."

Whitechapel Dick then turned to the Poor Boys of London, and, after thanking them heartily, rewarded them liberally.

"Now that I know where to find you," he said, "you may expect to see me sometimes, and Gilbert will not forget those who rescued him from a horrible death."

The cheap-jack then returned home with Gilbert, and for a few days he did not stir from the shelter of the caravan.

"This is all very well," Whitechapel Dick said one morning to Minnie; "but as we go roaming about the boy may fall into harm's way again. I must send him to some place where he will be constantly watched, and yet have all the freedom he can desire. Gilbert shall go to school."

Though Minnie did not like the idea of parting with the lad, she could not help feeling delighted at this proposition.

"Gilbert will be a gentleman," she said. "How nice it will be for him to come to us at holiday times, and tell us how he is getting on, and about the fun he has had."

Whitechapel Dick was as good as his word.

He wrote to the principal of a middle class school in the country, and, on receiving a reply, purchased such clothing as he thought Gilbert would require.

When the boy was dressed in his new attire Dick and Minnie scarcely knew him.

"I am quite sure I should pass you in the street," Minnie cried, clapping her hands. "If Dick had tried to disguise you he could not have done better. Why, Gilbert, you are quite a little swell!"

Tears rolled down Gilbert's cheeks, and his heart was too full to allow his tongue to give utterance to the gratitude he felt, but his eyes spoke for him.

In another week Gilbert would be gone, and Whitechapel Dick, not liking to shut the boy up altogether in the caravan, thought it safe to let him walk about the thoroughfares where there were plenty of people.

One afternoon, just before dusk, when the caravan had moved eastwards, and whilst the lad was strolling about, a strange-looking boy, with red hair, and a jacket buttoned almost up to his ears, accosted him.

"You are Gilbert, ain't you?" asked the peculiar-looking youth.

Gilbert hesitated, and looked hastily round, half expecting to see his terrible enemy, the Bosker, close at hand.

"Well," said the stranger, "you don't know me, it appears; but I suppose you know Alick?"

"Yes," Gilbert replied, as his eyes brightened; "I know him very well."

"He wrote something on a bit of paper for you," the strange replied. "I can't read myself, but I daresay you can make it out."

Gilbert took the paper and read the few words written on it; they stated that Alick would be pleased to see him, if only for a few minutes, at the haunt.

When the lad had finished reading he looked up and found himself alone. The messenger had disappeared, and Gilbert stood pondering on what he should do.

"I wonder how Alick knew that I was in this neighbourhood," Gilbert thought. "Perhaps he saw the caravan, but did not like to call. Well, there will no harm in going."

Gilbert, young and innocent as he was, suspected nothing, and made his way to the river.

He was turning a corner, dimly lighted by a lamp, when two men rushed at him.

A cry of terror came from his lips as he recognised the Bosker and Nicholas Slime.

"So," yelled the Bosker, seizing Gilbert by the throat, "I've got you again. What a goose you must be not to know Tike in spite of a red wig. Ha! ha! come along my lad, you and I won't part company again in a hurry."

"No, no!" Gilbert shrieked. "Let me go."

"Go! Of course, you shall go with me," the

Bosker said, grinning. "Another word and I'll squeeze the life out of you."

"Not yet," shouted a voice. "Let go your hold or down you go."

These words were uttered by Alick as he, with Chimbley Joe and Dan, dashed round the corner. Alick swung a broom over his head, facing the Bosker boldly, while the Gorger, seeing at a glance that he would suffer if he remained, glided round the corner and took to his heels."

"Get out of the way," snarled the Bosker. "This is no business of yours."

Down came the broom, and with such force that the ruffian, loosing his hold on Gilbert, staggered and almost fell.

Before he could recover his balance two policemen appeared in sight, and the Bosker, uttering a fearful oath, ran down to the river-side. Leaping into a boat, which happened to be there, he seized the oars and bent to them with a will.

The police sounded their whistles, and the boys shouted as they followed. Presently the Bosker became aware of an unpleasant sight, in the shape of a galley, manned by three of the Thames Police, shooting out into the middle of the river and giving chase.

An outrigger, manned by five strapping young fellows, seeing that something was wrong, shouted to the river police, and hearing that they were hunting a thief, willingly gave their assistance.

The Bosker turned ghastly pale when he found himself so hotly pursued, for he felt all chance was gone now.

He might escape from the police boat, but how was he to escape from the outrigger?

He ground his teeth in savage fury, and muttered the most awful curses upon the heads of his pursuers.

He felt his strength begin to fail, and he knew that he could not hold out much longer.

The perspiration poured down his face, and his hair looked as though he had been ducked in the water. His eyes were bloodshot and starting from their sockets, and his tightly-clenched teeth shone like the fangs of a hunted tiger.

With a cry of delight the pursuers urged their boats on, feeling sure that the Bosker would soon succumb.

The five young fellows saw with delight the way in which they were overtaking him, and this gave them encouragement and renewed strength to continue their exertions.

But they did not know the man they had to deal with.

They were within a few yards of the Bosker, who had been trying, all the time he had been rowing hard, to evolve a plan by which he might upset the outrigger. At last he had resolved what to do; the supreme moment had arrived, and a fierce glitter shone in his eyes.

He had determined not to give in while he could sit in the boat, and, throwing all his strength into one pull, he swung the boat round, and only just in time, for in another instant it would have been too late.

The coxswain of the outrigger discounted Bosker's manœuvre by pulling his left hand hard, and thus getting his boat in such a position that another powerful stroke of the rowers would bring the stern of the outrigger right athwart the bow of the Bosker's boat.

It was very cleverly executed, so the young fellow thought, but he was counting his chickens before they were hatched, for he had done the very thing Burkett wished for.

The young coxswain never thought for a moment of the daring act the Bosker intended to perform, but called to his crew to pull harder.

"We shall catch him now!" he cried.

Each bent to his oar and gave a pull that nearly lifted the boat out of the water, but the next instant they bitterly repented it.

The Bosker, with a grim smile, also gave a tremendous pull at the same moment, and drove the iron plated prow of his skiff into the thin cedar sides of the outrigger.

It was a moment of intense excitement to everyone on the river.

The remainder of the pursuers held their breath, and rested upon their oars, knowing that a catastrophe was about to take place. They were not kept long in suspense.

There was a cry from the men in the outrigger, a crash, a sound of splintering wood, and then a terrible splashing and plunging.

It had ended as most of them expected.

The boat was split from stem to stern, and five young and hearty fellows were struggling for life in the Thames.

A hoarse yell — a laugh full of demoniac fury and exultation—broke from the lips of the Bosker.

During the momentary confusion he had thrown his other pursuers into he was enabled to wipe the huge drops of sweat from his brow.

The Thames Police were still on his track, and several boats followed cautiously behind.

"You'd better give in!" yelled one of the officers.

"See you hanged first!" was the polite reply of Burkett.

As he spoke he leaped to his feet, and knowing that to remain in the boat meant capture, he jumped overboard and disappeared.

The pursuers uttered a cry of surprise.

"Back—back her—back water," said the inspector in charge of the river police. "The prisoner's drowning! We shall lose him after all!" he cried.

Twice had the Bosker risen and sunk.

The third time he came to the surface, and was just going down again, when the inspector caught him by the hands, and attempted to drag him into the boat; but the Bosker was too heavy for him.

"Lend a hand here!" cried the inspector. "Put down the oars; now try and raise him—take care or you'll have the boat over."

He soon discovered that for once in his life he had been a true prophet.

The police, as a matter of course, all crowded to the side of the boat where the desperate burglar was floundering, with his head just above water.

Burkett had waited for this opportunity.

No sooner did the boat cant over on its side than

he became a dead weight upon the inspector, and that individual began to get awfully alarmed.

For the first time a suspicion flashed through his mind that he was being led into a snare.

He saw the error he had made, but too late.

The Bosker was attempting to drag the official into the slimy water.

He called to his men to trim the boat, but he was too late, and he felt himself and men being hurled into the murky stream.

The Bosker, by a sudden wrench, had dragged the unfortunate inspector over the boat.

The police tried to save him, but the boat was over-balanced, and the next instant they were battling with the water.

The Bosker was not the man likely to lose his life without a struggle.

He could swim like a duck and dive like a fish, and the instant he had succeeded in his purpose of upsetting the boat he relaxed his hold upon the wrists of the officer.

He sank several feet, then swam along under the water for some seconds, when, upon coming to the surface, he found himself near some barges, unobserved and almost unheeded in the excitement.

Half-a-dozen boats went to the assistance of the occupants of the outrigger and the Thames Police, and, happily, they were all saved.

"The villain!" cried the inspector, as soon as the police were safely in their boat again; "he shall pay dearly for the mischief he has done. Pull away, my men, we will find him even if we have to rake the bottom of the Thames. Pull away! that's the style. He can't be very far off."

He continued grumbling and growling, though the poor soaked officials did their best to accelerate the speed of the boat.

All eyes were scanning the surface of the water, but they could not see the Bosker.

"P'raps he's drowned!" said a waterman.

"P'raps he is," growled the infuriated inspector, "and a good job too."

"What's to be done?" said one of the officers, laying on his oars, glad to get a rest.

"Goodness knows, I don't," vociferated the inspector. "I think it isn't at all unlikely that he has gone to feed the fishes," he continued; "in fact, I fancy I felt him sink from under me."

But suddenly the Bosker was seen creeping among the coals of a heavily-laden barge, and the boat occupied by the police drew alongside almost immediately.

"Keep back! On your life don't attempt to board the barge!" the Bosker hissed.

"Ha, ha!" laughed the head officer, in derision, "you'd better surrender without giving us any more trouble."

"Never! Keep back, I say," replied the Bosker.

"Hold fast, my men; get the handcuffs ready."

A savage laugh escaped the infuriated Bosker.

"Your blood be upon your own head then!" he exclaimed.

He raised a tremendous piece of coal above his head, and with another mocking laugh he hurled it at the boat; but the aim was wild and uncertain,

and the Bosker, seeing the officers were already clambering among the coals, once more took to the river like a water rat.

He swam to the slimy banks of the river, and, crouching behind a large sailing-boat, took temporary refuge from his pursuers.

He was thoroughly beaten; his hands were sore and bleeding, and his face was most horribly distorted.

He crawled slowly away on his hands and knees, and climbed over the boats and barges with difficulty.

Nature was giving way, yet he dared not stop. He could hear his pursuers not very far off.

He began to bleed at the nostrils, yet he still crawled along, and the police drew nearer and nearer.

"Yield, miscreant!" cried one of the men, springing forward. "You are my prisoner!"

So sudden and unexpected was the demand that the Bosker could offer no resistance for the moment.

His heart almost ceased beating, but this weakness was but of short duration.

Worn out and tired as he was, he would have one more struggle for liberty.

He lifted his two hands to the hand that grasped his throat, but as he did so the officer's iron grip tightened.

He felt those sinewy fingers almost meeting round his windpipe.

He could scarcely breathe.

"Would you mur—mur—der me?" asked the Bosker, with the greatest difficulty speaking the words.

"No," replied the officer. "I would not soil my hands by taking the life of such a cold-blooded miscreant. The hangman will do that."

These words aroused the worst passions in the Bosker's nature, and the thought flashed through his mind, "Shall one man take me? Never—never shall a gaping crowd laugh at my death struggles."

"There is no occasion to strangle me," he said. "I am dying. Pray have mercy. Loosen your grasp from my throat and let me die in peace."

These words were uttered in such a plaintive tone, and with such an appearance of thorough exhaustion, that the officer at once relaxed his hold.

No sooner did the Bosker draw his breath freely than he glanced eagerly around in search of a weapon.

Nothing met his gaze.

Heaving a deep groan he staggered forward, as though about to fall to the ground.

The policeman moved but a pace away, but it was sufficient.

With a spring like a tiger's he flew at the officer's throat, and, hurling him aside, dashed through the others who were coming up to assist their comrade, and fled inland.

The Bosker found the old feeling of exhaustion coming over him again.

"Oh!" he gasped as he fell, "I am dying. Mercy! Help—help!"

Strangely enough he had fallen into a ditch

that ran alongside of the lone house by the river, occupied by Fosky Mike, the river rat.

While the officers were yet following, a grating in the wall opened, and the huge hands of Fosky Mike, who had miraculously escaped drowning after he jumped from the parapet of the lone house, dragged the Bosker out of the reach of his pursuers.

## CHAPTER XXVII.

### THE BOSKER'S ESCAPE—BACK AGAIN AT NATHAN CLAWS' DEN.

FOSKY MIKE'S action completely baffled the police, for it seemed as if the Bosker had been snatched from their clutches by some magical power.

Meanwhile, Mike had dragged Burkett's nearly unconscious form further into the lone house, and watched until there were signs of returning animation.

Never had the Bosker had such a fearful fight for life ; his whole frame and nerves were thoroughly shaken, and many hours passed away before he could speak coherently.

"Long time since I've seen you," said Mike, as the Bosker raised himself on his elbow and glared at his rescuer.

"Yes ; and you didn't expect to see me in this state," Burkett replied, faintly. "I gave them a long chase, though. But what place is this, Fosky ?"

"The lone house on the Thames," said Fosky Mike.

The bare mention of the place to anyone else than the daring burglar would have caused them a slightly disagreeable sensation.

"How did you discover me ?" the Bosker demanded.

Mike gave a peculiar smile.

"Well," he said, slowly, "I guess it was rather an accident. I have a slight interest in that sailing-boat you hid behind, and I was watching it when I saw the police after you. I didn't like to see an old pal in trouble, so I just opened the grating and pulled you through when you fell into the ditch. Are you going to hide here for a week or two ?'

"Not if I know it. No, I'm going to Nathan Claws," the Bosker replied.

He rose from the rude couch he had been lying on, but he was so weak that he could scarcely stand.

"I sha'n't be able to walk to the haunt just yet," the Bosker said.

"No, but you can ride."

"How ? From this place ?"

"Just wait until my blessed friends turn up, and then you'll see," said Mike.

He did not have to wait long before a peculiar sound reached his ears. It came from some part of the building he was in.

Fosky Mike smiled but said nothing, and, placing a whistle to his mouth, he blew three times.

"I shall return in a few minutes," he said, as he rose and departed.

Soon after the Bosker heard voices proceeding from below.

In a few minutes Mike reappeared.

"Are you ready ?" he asked.

"Yes," replied Burkett.

Fosky Mike then led the way down a flight of old, tumbledown rickety stairs.

They passed an apartment on the way, and through the chinks of the door Burkett caught a glimpse of two ruffianly men, seated at a table drinking and smoking.

The River Rat, however, proceeded onward before the other had time to make any comment.

After traversing a number of underground passages they suddenly came to the grating through which Burkett had been safely hauled by Fosky Mike.

But the the tide was up now, and Burkett wondered how he and his guide could possibly leave the place.

A short walk, however, brought them to the river, and Fosky Mike, unmooring a boat from a post, motioned to the Bosker to take his seat, and then, leaping in himself, he plied the oars until presently they ran under the dark hull of a sailing barge.

Greatly to the Bosker's surprise, when he got on board, three bearded individuals came up from the cabin.

They wore dark coarse trousers and blue guernseys, and a cloth cap finished the costume. At first sight they appeared to be barefooted, but a closer inspection proved that their feet were encased in india-rubber shoes, rendering their movements perfectly noiseless.

Silently the barge drifted slowly up the stream, and when they came to a bridge the mast was lowered level with the deck in the same silent manner.

Not a word passed above a whisper.

One thing Burkett had taken particular notice of —namely, the crew obeyed the slightest sign of the captain.

The Bosker was awakened from his reverie by the voice of Fosky Mike, who, for the first time since they had been on the barge, now spoke to him.

"That's your way, Jim," he said, pointing to Nathan's house.

"How am I to get there ? I can't swim ashore," said Burkett.

"You can take the boat," replied Mike.

"But how will you get it again ?"

"Why the devil don't you take what's given to you, without asking a lot of questions ?" Fosky Mike growled.

"All right, old pal, don't get rusty."

"Rusty be hanged ! Take the boat, moor it outside the entrance, and I'll fetch it away when I want it," Mike replied.

Without another word Burkett stepped into the boat.

When he had safely taken his seat Fosky Mike let go the painter, and a few vigorous strokes took the Bosker to the secret entrance of Nathan's house.

He was greeted with a gladdened cry from his associates, who had thought him dead.

They could understand the sufferings he had undergone by the haggard look and paleness of his face.

Nathan came shuffling into the thieves' kitchen, and gave a hideous grin when he saw the Bosker.

"Ah! you ish back again," he cried, holding up his hands. "I ish glad. My boy, you look ill; very—very. This ish bad times. I shall have all my children taken soon. Oh! my tears, my tears, you should be careful."

"Hold your croaking," said the Bosker, "and bring me something to drink."

Just then a young man, attired in the height of fashion, entered the room, and the Bosker rose and removed his cap.

"James Burkett," began the stranger, in a calm voice, "among those present now is a traitor, a blackleg, and a murderer of those of his own gang."

"Is he here?" asked Burkett.

"He is one of you," repeated the young stranger.

"Close the doors and collect the gang," shouted Burkett, in a loud, commanding voice.

His order was immediately obeyed, and the men all stood in a row round the kitchen.

Burkett cast his quick bold eyes along the faces, as though counting how many of the gang were missing.

"Send Nathan here," said the Bosker.

"Oh! my poys, dosh you want meesh?" moaned the Jew, as he came into the room. "Vot dosh you wantsh of me? I ish been like a fathersh to youor. Oh! mine tears, mine tears. Oh! my pitiful sir, dosh you wantsh me?" he added, bowing low to the stranger.

"Take your place with the rest," replied the Bosker.

His deep impressive voice jarred uncomfortably upon the Jew's ears.

"There is Leary Jock and the Boozer absent," he said to the stranger.

"Then the person I want must be here, as neither of those you mention is the man I want," replied he.

"Pick out your man," said Burkett.

The stranger's terrible dark eye swept from face to face.

Each man breathed more freely when he had passed him.

Presently he stopped.

His gaze was fixed upon a low-bred ruffian, whose face went ashy pale, and his lips turned a purple hue.

Every eye was turned upon what each knew to be a doomed man.

"That is the scoundrel—Bull-dog Jim," said the stranger, never once removing his terrible gaze.

And the man's terror became awful to behold when his name was pronounced.

"His offence?" demanded Burkett, who did not quite like the terrible and mysterious power that the stranger wielded over himself and companions, although he was bound to recognise it.

"For garroting, stabbing, and robbing Captain Black, known as the Flash Captain," said the stranger, turning to Bull-dog Jim. "He had in his pocket the sum of nearly three hundred pounds, won at cards. You knew it, and wanting to possess yourself of the money, followed him, and, in garroting him, he struggled, and saw your face. You knew the penalty for attacking one of the gang, and, to prevent him from telling, you stabbed him twice and robbed him."

Every eye was turned upon the trembling wretch menacingly.

Burkett glared at him savagely, and his hand went instinctively to his bludgeon. In a tone, not at all inspiring to the unfortunate wretch, he queried—

"Can you deny it?"

"It was an accident," faltered the ruffian.

"Bull-dog Jim, your time has come," said the stranger, coolly.

The man did not move, but appealed mutely for mercy.

The Bosker immediately stamped his foot upon the floor.

The trap of the water cellar sprung open, displaying that dark, awful aperture, down which Grant so nearly lost his life.

Then came the climax to a fearful tragedy.

Without a pang of remorse Bull-dog Jim was dragged to the edge of the deep and tomb-like abyss.

His terror became awful.

With wild despair he clung to the neck of one of his executioners.

"Let go your hold!" said the man.

"I won't! You sha'n't murder me!" shrieked the wretch.

Not another word was spoken, but with irresistible power Bull-dog Jim was thrust down and the trap closed over him.

The stranger, who was the ruling spirit of the gang, whispered a few words to the Bosker, and then departed in the same silent manner as he had entered.

The men began to breathe more freely after he had left.

Each looked into the other's face, as though to assure themselves that they were safe.

Burkett's appearance was forbidding in the extreme.

His face was pale and wan, but his eyes were still bright and deadly as he glanced round with an unearthly stare.

Suddenly Burkett rose to his feet and left the room.

'I am going to get a breath of fresh air," he said. "I feel as faint as a woman at the sight of blood."

Leaving the house by the back way he walked to the waterside.

Two ragged boys were playing on a ruined landing-stage, while another, who was standing apart and watching them moodily, shrank back at the Bosker's approach.

"Come here, Tike," said Burkett, as he recognised the boy.

"What do you want me for?" queried the boy, sulkily.

"Come here quickly," growled the Bosker, "or I'll pitch you into the river. What are you skulking about here for?"

"I am afraid to go in there," Tike faltered, as he pointed to the house. "The 'tecs are swarming as thick as bees. Grant is abroad again, and looking for—"

"Me, of course," the Bosker interrupted. "Well, what about the boy Gilbert—where is he?"

"Captain Jack had him in tow when I last heard of him," Tike replied; "and I s'pose he is back with Whitechapel Dick by this time."

The Bosker's brow grew dark, and he showered a volley of imprecations on the devoted head of the cheap-jack.

"Very well," he said, after a pause. "The caravan must be watched. I'll see to that. Now go to Nathan's, for there is no safer place for you. If Grant and his followers make a raid, we shall be ready for them."

## CHAPTER XXVIII.

### THE DEED OF A VILLAIN.

GILBERT'S adventure with the Bosker and the Gorger so filled the lad with terror that he could scarcely realise that he was rescued; but Alick reassured him in a few words.

"You must go back to Whitechapel Dick without delay," Alick said. "It is more than possible that the Bosker will escape again, for he is bold enough for anything. Oh! Gilbert, you did wrong to come here."

"But you sent for me," Gilbert said. "Here is your own writing to prove it."

Alick whistled as he took the paper in his hand.

"This is not my writing," he said. "It was given to you as a decoy, so that you might fall into the Bosker's clutches. Come along, the air is full of danger for you."

When Gilbert reached the caravan he found Whitechapel Dick and Minnie nearly distracted, and their joy at seeing him safe was so great that they hovered round him and hugged him fondly.

"My boy," said Dick, shaking his head gravely, "you must pay no more attention to notes given to you in the street. But all's well that ends well, and I will not let you out of my sight again until I see you safe in the hands of your schoolmaster."

Poor Gilbert was so fatigued and overcome that he was glad to go to bed, and Minnie and Whitechapel Dick could hear him murmuring in his sleep.

Two days passed away, and on the night previous to Gilbert's departure Whitechapel Dick sat thinking in the caravan.

It was late, and the cheap-jack was drowsy, but he could not go to bed.

His mind was filled with an evil foreboding that something would happen before the morning, but at last his head drooped forward, and in another minute he was sound asleep.

Suddenly he awoke with a start.

He had been dreaming that the Bosker had forced his way into the caravan, and captured Gilbert in spite of all opposition.

Whitechapel Dick smiled as he glanced round, and saw that everything was safe, but he could not resist the temptation of peeping at Gilbert.

The boy was sound asleep, and lay with his head pillowed on his arm.

"That's all right," Dick said, as he returned to his chair. "Dawn is coming, and my vigil will soon be at an end."

He glanced at his watch and saw that it was four o'clock.

Taking up a book Dick tried to read, but the swam before his aching gaze.

He was terribly tired, but having fully made up his mind not to go to sleep again until daylight, he opened the caravan door softly and stepped into the road.

He had scarcely done so than the dark shadow of a man followed his own.

A slight sound caused him to turn, and as he did so a bludgeon was brought down upon his head, and without a groan or cry he fell senseless to the ground.

The deed was done by the experienced hand of the Bosker, and a smile of satisfaction stole over his brutal features as he regarded the prostrate form of his victim.

Presently the Bosker was joined by Michael the gipsy.

"You promised me that no violence should be done," the gipsy said, sternly. "Is this the way you keep your word?"

"Bah! That tap will not hurt him," the Bosker replied, contemptuously. "He will come round in an hour or two. Now for the boy. Have you got the stuff ready?"

"Yes," Michael replied, producing a handkerchief which emitted a pungent aroma; "but, mind, the lad is to be in my charge."

"Just as you like," the Bosker growled, "only be quick."

"You remember our agreement?" said Michael, sternly.

"A bargain is a bargain all the world over," replied the Bosker; "but I should like to settle with the young whelp."

"I daresay you would," Michael returned; "but I intend to have my own way in this affair. Attempt to harm one hair of the boy's head and your life shall answer for it."

"Why do you stand chattering there when there is so much to be done?" the Bosker said, savagely. "Do your work quickly, or we shall have the policeman round on his beat."

The gipsy stole into the caravan, and, approaching Gilbert, pressed the handkerchief softly on his face.

The boy turned slightly, moaned, moved his hands feebly, and then lay as still as if death had overtaken him.

Then Michael wrapped the bedclothes round the boy's unconscious form and carried him outside the caravan.

*"Come here, Tike," said the Bosker, "come here quietly, or I'll pitch you into the river."*

The Bosker's eyes glistened as he put his fingers into his mouth and whistled.

A cart, apparently filled with straw, rattled up, and in another minute Gilbert and his captors were leaving London behind. It was about this time that David Eastlake, anxious to find out how the Bosker and Michael were progressing with the work they had in hand, came up to London.

He paid a visit to the Pig and Porridge Pot, but gaining no information there, stole about the banks of the river in the hope of meeting either of them accidentally.

It was not, however, the Bosker or Michael that Eastlake met, but the Poor Boys of London, with Alick at their head.

Like a swarm of bees they swooped down upon him.

A sudden blow sent him reeling to the earth, and when he recovered consciousness he was a prisoner in the haunt under the Thames.

"I am glad to see you so much better, sir," said Alick.

Eastlake started, for he recognised the boy's voice, and a slight qualm of fear went through him.

He had expected to see a huge, burly vagabond the ruler of that wild crew, and one who would demand money of him and then let him go.

"Thank you—yes, I am better; and I have no doubt that I owe my recovery to your kind attention."

This was said with a quiet sneer.

Alick noticed it and bowed, not trusting himself to answer.

"Why am I kept here?" Eastlake demanded. "How dare you keep me — one of England's squirearchy—against my inclination?"

"I keep you here, sir, simply because you are not fit to be entrusted outside," Alick replied; "and I also have another reason."

"Very considerate. And pray what is the other reason—to extort money, I suppose, which—"

"No," Alick interrupted, a flush rising to his cheek and his eyes flashing indignantly at the cynical, mocking way in which Eastlake addressed him. "I do not want your money. I wish to know what has become of my sister—and, by Heavens! you shall tell me. Mark me, if any harm has befallen her you shall remain here much longer than you probably expect!"

Eastlake started—shamed at first by the boy's real chivalrous feeling; but when he found he was recognised he went a shade paler.

He knew the lad he had to deal with, and had he been alone he would have rid himself of his young antagonist quickly.

He could not, however, do so as it was, and surmised that the only thing left for him to do was to present a bold appearance to the enemy.

"You dare not!" he said. "I would have you punished for detaining me here against my inclination, and this den should be pulled down over your heads."

Alick laughed.

"I know you better, David Eastlake; you would not dare—"

"Dare?"

"Aye, that is the word. Do you suppose I would have run the risk of detaining you without knowing the character of my visitor?"

Eastlake bit his lips till the blood started.

The unpleasantness of the situation he was placed in began to dawn upon him, for apparently he had no chance of escape.

Every now and then he had made a movement towards his youthful interrogator as if to strike him, but he was warned by the other boys, who watched him closely, not to attempt anything of the kind, or it would not be well for him.

"And," continued Alick, "if you escaped and proceeded against me I should tell why I have kept you here. I would point you out as the man who hired a cut-throat to slay an innocent boy—the man who goes about like a wolf in sheep's clothing to decoy young girls from their homes. Where is my sister?"

The subtle, plotting villain turned a shade paler still, and his lips wore a deadly hue.

Alick watched his increasing fear, and rejoiced at it.

"I don't know."

This was the truth, of which the reader is already aware.

"Liar!" shouted Alick. "You do know."

"Beware!" hissed the other, a dangerous-looking gleam shooting from his eyes.

"I do not fear you," Alick cried. "You took her away, and you shall restore her to me. Tell me where she is, before I spring at your throat."

Eastlake leaped to his feet, with all his passions fully aroused.

He faced Alick, and, grinding his teeth, appeared about to rush upon him.

"Insolent brat!" he yelled. "Dare say another word, and, by Heaven, in spite of your companions, I will tear your tongue from your throat!"

"I defy you—braggart!" Alick cried. "I am not afraid of you. Tell me, where is my sister? You, David Eastlake, are a black-hearted villain and liar."

"Calm yourself, my lad, and listen to me," Eastlake said, temporising. "I assure you, on the word of a—"

"Libertine and rogue," broke in Alick.

"That is as you please," Eastlake said. "But I tell you I have not seen your sister."

"You did see her."

"Wait a moment. She went with me into the country of her own free will."

Alick was about to interrupt, but he thought, if he wished to find out the truth, he had better keep quiet.

"She left my country residence," Eastlake continued, "and went away I know not whither."

Alick regarded Eastlake for some few minutes in silence, wondering whether he had spoken the truth.

The boy's heart sank within him when he saw how useless it was to try and make him confess. It was impossible to find his sister if Eastlake would or could not give him a clue.

"Now I can quit this place, I presume—I am at liberty to go?" Eastlake said, as he threw a purse at Alick's feet.

Alick spurned it from him.

"We don't want blood-money here," he replied.

At that moment a boy entered the haunt whose face wore a look of great importance.

He stepped up to Alick and whispered a few words in his ear, and the next instant all was bustle and confusion.

Eastlake looked on in surprise, for the boys were attiring themselves in a number of different costumes, and all save two left the haunt.

For two whole days David Eastlake was kept a prisoner by the Poor Boys of London, who watched him as closely as a cat watches a mouse.

Alick questioned and cross-questioned him with regard to his sister, but Eastlake stuck to one line of reply, vowing that the girl had left his house, as she had entered it, of her own free will, and that he was ignorant of her whereabouts.

At last Alick determined to set him at liberty.

"Mark me, David Eastlake," the lad said, "if you have deceived me you shall suffer for it. You shall now leave this place, but if I find that you have harmed one hair of my sister's head you shall return to it, never to depart."

Eastlake was then blindfolded and escorted far away from the haunt.

Then with a whoop and a yell the boys left him, and Eastlake, tearing off the bandage, found himself in a dismal labyrinth of streets.

"Curse them!" he muttered; "they shall pay dearly for keeping me prisoner. Burkett must have returned to the den by this time."

He enquired his way to the Pig and Porridge Pot, and was informed by the landlord that the Bosker had just returned from a journey.

"That is well," Eastlake said. "Take me to him at once. I desire to see him on particular business."

The Bosker scowled as Eastlake entered a room in which the ruffian was sitting.

"Well?" said Eastlake.

"It is well," Burkett growled. "Michael has the boy safe with his tribe."

"Then all we have to do is to come to terms," Eastlake returned.

"That is easily settled—you know what I want."

"Money, of course. But don't be exorbitant."

"Exorbitant!" the Bosker repeated. "Think what risks I have run. Give me a thousand pounds and I will quit the country."

"A thousand pounds!" Eastlake cried. "It is a great deal too much."

"Why do you think so?" replied the Bosker. "I do not ask a tenth of what you gain by the transaction, therefore I am not so very greedy."

Eastlake's cheeks glowed with rage, and the light in his fierce, dark eyes boded no good to the daring speaker.

"I'll remove this low-bred hound from my path when he has accomplished all I require of him—but I have not done with him yet," mused Eastlake.

The Bosker seemed to read the other's thoughts, and a quiet smile passed over his hard features.

Eastlake saw it, and he instinctively felt that Burkett mocked and defied him.

"Have you that pocket-book from Grant yet?"

"No, but I shall be sure to settle with Grant, even if it is only for the satisfaction of taking his life," the Bosker replied.

"He is an enemy of yours, then?"

"Of course he is, and your enemy too," Burkett said. "Why ask me such a foolish question?"

"Well, we have a slight dislike for each other,"

Eastlake returned, "but that is not the question. Would you do as you have just said if I put Grant in your power?"

Burkett leaped to his feet and gave utterance to an awful oath.

"Yes, I would. Is he here?"

"No."

The reply seemed to disappoint the Bosker, for he gave his hat, which lay at his feet, a vicious kick, and sent it flying across the room.

Eastlake smiled, for he had gained a point, and now knew how to play his cards.

"I will have them both removed from my path," he mused again.

Burkett's passion was too great to notice either the exultant look or the smile of his employer.

"I have reason to believe that he has been putting people on my track," Eastlake said, after a pause, "and therefore he will be best out of the way."

"He knows enough to hang us both," Burkett said. "Only let me get within arm's reach of him once again, and I will silence him for ever."

"Be true to your threat for your own sake," Eastlake replied, "for my own part I can snap my fingers at him."

Burkett glared at him savagely.

"Stuff," he said. "Why do you pretend to defy everyone? I tell you, and you know it is true that Grant could hang us both, and he'll do it unless he is stopped. Mark you, David Eastlake, you will not be the first rich man he has lodged in the Old Bailey."

Eastlake shuddered, for in his heart he feared Richard Grant more than any one person on earth; but, not liking Burkett to know that such was the case, he made an attempt to laugh, and retorted—

"You, at all events, appear to be terrorised by this detective?"

"I fear no one," the Bosker growled. "You thought I feared you once, but that was only a little conceit on your part. This Richard Grant appears to be possessed of supernatural powers. We have met, and have fought hand to hand, and yet he has escaped. I had him by himself in Nathan's kitchen; he is the only man that ever left that place alive—yet he did, though he was put in the same place as the others."

"A miraculous escape, undoubtedly," Eastlake suggested. "Now, if I mistake not, I saw him hanging about here as I entered. Here is a chance to show your courage. The night is dark and silent. Have you the pluck to go out and face him?"

"Yes," the Bosker replied, clutching his bludgeon. "I'll go at once, and woe to him if he bars my path."

"See me at my town house to-morrow night at eight," Eastlake said. "Good luck to your expedition. We will talk about the money when you return. Burkett!"

"Well?" the Bosker said, as he turned in the doorway.

"Don't forget to bring the pocket-book with you."

Burkett went forth, but no signs of the detective could he see, and he walked on until he entered a part where the streets were better lighted.

As the Bosker turned a corner leading to a busy thoroughfare a dark form stood in his path.

Burkett looked up as he felt himself gripped tightly by the collar.

His eyes fairly blazed, and he ground his teeth in suppressed fury, as he yelled out the detective's name.

"Aye, we meet again, James Burkett—come—you are my prisoner," Richard Grant said.

Burkett was so taken aback by the sudden appearance of the detective that he stood dumbfounded.

Grant held him firmly by the throat.

"Burkett," he said, "it is useless for you to struggle. I told you I would have you some time or the other. Come quietly ; if you move I shall strangle you. I want you very particularly."

The only reply the Bosker made was to glare at him savagely and to feel in his pocket for a knife.

To his mortification he discovered that he had left it at home, and Grant had very considerately taken care of the bludgeon, which was a dangerous weapon in the hands of the infuriated ruffian.

A strange feeling crept over Burkett as he gazed upon the calm handsome face of the powerful detective, who was the only man he had ever been pitted against who matched the ruffian in strength.

When Grant deliberately placed his hand in his pocket and drew forth a pair of shining handcuffs, Burkett gave utterance to one savage cry and attempted, with all his tremendous power, to break away from his captor.

But so quick were the movements of the detective that the burglar had only time to thrust his hand out towards his adversary's throat before he felt something cold glide round his wrist and close with an unpleasant snap.

The sound of the handcuff as it fastened round his wrist seemed to terrify the Bosker.

His blood was on fire, and he appeared to have supernatural strength given him as he fought to free himself.

So fierce was the onslaught that Grant found it an utter impossibility to secure the other hand.

The lowest instincts of the Bosker were fully aroused, and he began to plunge and kick like a madman.

"Brutal hound !" Grant muttered, "I wished to take you quietly, though you have several times attempted my life. But now you shall come, if I have to strangle you !"

"You sha'n't take me," hissed Burkett, with an awful execration.

"We shall see."

"I tell you, Grant," roared the Bosker more like a wild beast than a human being, "you never shall secure me alive—one shall conquer—you or I !"

Not another word was said.

Each knew that it would be a hard and terrible struggle, and they prepared themselves for it.

They grappled each other by the throat, and swayed to and fro, every few moments coming in violent contact with the wall.

The scuffling noise they made soon brought a wondering throng around.

The crowd thickened every moment, yet none interfered.

"Hullo ! what's up?" exclaimed a member of the blue guernsey and black corduroy fraternity to another rough.

"A slogging match, I s'pose," answered the other with an oath.

"Why doesn't somebody part 'em," suggested a little weak man in spectacles.

"Why don't yer go and try," said the first speaker ; "a tap on the beak would make a nice mess of your barnacles."

This elicited a general laugh, and the little man in specs, being very nervous, toddled off to his better half, whom he knew would take care of him, which was more than he could do himself.

Soon they were both on the ground, and then nothing but the heavy breathing of the detective and the stifled oaths of Burkett were heard, as they rolled to and fro in the fierce struggle for mastery.

Each time the Bosker tried to rise Grant forced him down again, and when the detective attempted to get up the burglar clung to him and by his heavy weight kept him down.

People began to get alarmed, for it certainly appeared as if the men intended to kill each other.

"It's a shame ; why don't somebody separate them, and let them fight fair ; they'll choke each other," said one of the crowd.

"'Tain't a fair fight," said another.

"No, make 'em get up," said a third person.

"Where's the police? What a shame it is to be sure—there's never any about when they are wanted," screamed an elderly dame.

At this moment two of the most courageous stepped forward with the intention of parting the combatants.

They, however, were saved the trouble of doing such a kindness, for Grant rose, having at length got the better of Burkett, and placing one knee upon the burglar's breast, said—

"My men, one of you be kind enough to fasten the handcuff upon this desperate burglar and murderer."

The people hung back, as is usually the case when the police ask for assistance.

"I am Richard Grant, the detective," he said, to assure the people he was justified in what he was doing.

Many knew that name, and half-a-dozen sprang forward to assist him. Wonderful to relate, a policeman had also found his way to the spot by this time, and he was soon at the side of the detective.

But as he touched the handcuff a fierce growl was heard, and a huge white animal bounded through the crowd. It leaped at the throat of Richard Grant, taking him to the ground, and causing the astonished constable to roll on his back in alarm.

It was Burkett's white bull-dog, which had awakened from a doze under a bench at the Pig and Porridge Pot and followed its master's scent.

The Bosker recognised the dog instantly, and uttering a gladdened cry he sprang to his feet and glared round him savagely.

His first impulse was to turn and use his heavy

hob-nailed boots on Grant's prostrate form, but he saw the folly of that.

The policeman had scrambled to his feet, and the people were closing round him.

So he gave vent to a few of his favourite oaths, and, calling his dog, he dashed in among the crowd.

At first the people showed some slight opposition to his departure, but when the faithful animal saw his master in danger he relinquished his attack upon the detective, and with his long fangs glistening like ivory, and gnashing in a most suggestive manner, came forward.

The lookers-on fell back, and made quite a path, through which the burglar and his faithful animal went, and they were soon out of sight.

Luckily Burkett had not his bludgeon, or there would have been a few broken skulls and aching knuckles.

Burkett had not gone far when he came face to face with the girl who had decoyed little Flo from Jacob Primrose's home.

He gave an exclamation of surprise.

"Rose!" he said.

"It's me, Jem; but there is a crowd coming after you. What is the cause of this disturbance? Hi!" she called, and waved her hand to a passing cab, into which they got, and told the cabby to drive with all possible speed.

"All right, mum," said the model Jehu, giving his horse a flick under the ear with his whip, and galloping off, just as a number of men came running round the corner in search of the desperate ruffian who had escaped from the detective. Like Richard Grant, they had to return baffled and disappointed.

---

## CHAPTER XXIX.

### A MESSAGE FOR WHITECHAPEL DICK.

TIME passed away, and we find Whitechapel Dick still pining for Gilbert, of whom nothing had been heard.

The cheap-jack soon recovered from the blow he had received from the Bosker's bludgeon, and at once set off on his track, but his efforts were fruitless.

He followed every clue, offered rewards, sought the assistance of the Poor Boys of London, but all in vain.

Gilbert had disappeared, and Whitechapel Dick despaired of ever seeing him again.

Worried and sick at heart, he gave up his business, for he had plenty of money, and sought peace of mind in retirement; but he failed to find it, and roved about the country disconsolate and unhappy.

Minnie knew the history of this strange man.

A Romany by birth, Whitechapel Dick, as he called himself, married a faithless woman. He left his tribe, seeking to forget his sorrow in a busy life, and kept the secret of his aching heart to himself.

Once more he returned to London, wandering about familiar places in his caravan, clinging to the forlorn hope that he might meet the boy whom he loved so well—the face that would have been so welcome to him.

One day a bronzed-faced man, no other than Michael the gipsy, brought him a letter, telling Whitechapel Dick that if he would follow the bearer of the missive to his tribe who were encamped at a place near Rome, he would hear startling news.

Michael, of course, forbore to tell Dick of the visit he had paid to the caravan on a memorable night, and after some conversation Whitechapel Dick determined to make the journey.

During the voyage, as he and Michael were relating their different experiences to each other, the latter observed—

"I have a deal to tell you when we reach our destination, independent of what you will hear from others."

"Concerning what?" demanded Dick, elevating his eyebrows.

"Some very strange business I did in London," Michael replied, passing his hand before his face to hide his confusion.

Whitechapel Dick looked at him interrogatively.

"I will tell you all when we land," said Michael, in a tone that showed a great disinclination to say much at present.

The following evening they reached their landing place, but for private reasons Michael would not go ashore until it was quite dark.

When the pall of night had thrown its sombre shadow over the earth they disembarked, and the journey overland began.

They travelled by the light of the stars all night, and by the break of morn they had gone many leagues through the splendid country.

Up hills, down slopes, amid trees and foliage, they continued until the heat of the midday sun compelled them to rest, weary and exhausted.

They had a good meal, and then lay down to rest until sunset.

As the glorious orb of day slowly sank behind the picturesque hills far, far away, and the grey light of eventide cast its shadows upon the earth, the travellers awoke much refreshed, and with anxious hearts they again set out, hoping soon to reach the camp.

Darkness came once more as they were slowly making their way through a difficult bit of country.

An army might have laid in ambush there without being seen.

As the travellers reached a gigantic tree, growing on the summit of a wooded slope, a dark figure arose from the ground, like some phantom, and confronted Michael.

He stood immovable, and appeared more like a piece of the tree than a human being.

The sound of a hammer being drawn back upon a flint lock brought the two to a halt.

"Who comes there?" asked the dusky figure.

"Friends," said Michael.

"Give the pass-word."

"Leopard."

"All's well!—pass on." And the figure moved aside.

"Is it you, Jim?" asked Michael.

"Yes."

"How have you been going on?"

"Very comfortably."

" No disturbance ?"

" None whatever, sir. Stay, I had better give the signal you have arrived."

With that the gipsy sentinel vanished. Presently was heard the sound of people and bushes stirring, and soon the blaze of a number of lighted torches lit up the swarthy features of a band of brawny men, who came to meet Michael, and to inform him that he had been elected a Romany chief.

A faint smile of pleasure illuminated the handsome face of Michael, who felt proud of the honour done him, though he had been absent for some time.

Loud were the exclamations of joy from the faithful fellows at the appearance of their chief.

Little or no attention was paid to Whitechapel Dick.

He excited some little curiosity, but the gipsies, perceiving the respectful way their young chief and companion treated him, kept a respectful distance from him.

They now approached the tents, before several of which burnt bright and cheerful fires, the glow of which displayed groups of male and female gipsies, who rose and greeted Michael and Dick solemnly.

The most conspicuous forms among them were the old crone Martel, leaning upon the delicate arm of Mina, whose lovely eyes glowed with an unwonted lustre at the fine form of her betrothed.

" Why, Mina, you have become quite a woman since we last met," said Michael. " I left you a sweet, wayward little gipsy girl, and now I behold a lovely woman. I know you are glad to see me, darling."

" Ah ! Michael, that I am, for the days have been long and weary without you," Mina replied.

Morn broke calm and beautiful as the first rays of the morning sun tinted the tops of the gigantic trees with its golden lustre.

Some of the gipsies were already astir, while others, who were luxuriating in an hour's extra rest, rolled over in their blankets and snored themselves into a sound sleep.

Among those who were astir were Michael and his Mina, the former walking to and fro in deep thought, and the latter busy in preparing breakfast for a portion of the tribe.

It is hardly necessary to say that the old crone, Martel, was seated upon a stool, indulging in a morning pipe, and muttering all manner of incomprehensible things under her breath.

Dick had not yet made his appearance, but soon the noise and babble of the camp became so loud that he found it impossible to remain any longer upon his comfortable couch of dried leaves.

Some of the men were singing snatches of songs, others were talking and shouting, while a noisy group were just returning from a foraging excursion.

Michael, who had been holding a deep consultation with old Martel, now approached Whitechapel Dick.

" Follow me," he said.

Dick rose and walked with Michael to the door of a tent, far apart from the rest, at which a girl and a boy were sitting.

The boy stared at Dick for a moment, and then uttered a cry of delight and ran into his arms.

" I am Gilbert," he almost shrieked. " Oh ! Dick, dear Dick, don't you know me ?"

" Great Heaven ! how came you here ?" Dick said, as soon as he could speak. " Am I dreaming —am I mad ?"

" Michael brought me here," the boy said, still clinging to his old protector.

" Michael brought you here !" Dick cried, starting. " Do I hear aright ?"

" Aye !" croaked Martel, as she hobbled up, " and Michael shall tell you who hired him to abduct the boy."

" David Eastlake," Michael quietly observed.

" David Eastlake !" echoed Whitechapel Dick, in surprise. " Impossible !"

" Too true," Michael said ; " but do not misjudge me—I dared not refuse."

" Dared not ?" repeated Whitechapel Dick, in some astonishment.

" Do you remember the circumstance that put my life in the power of that villain ?" replied the other, slowly.

His interrogator turned slightly pale.

" Aye, I do, though I had forgotten it."

" When he threatened to use his knowledge unless I did what he required I swore to aid him. He then told me the names of the children he wanted brought here. Martel has a wonderful memory, and she told me something concerning these children. I instantly resolved to abduct them—not to destroy, but to save—and bring them up. Ask the boy how he has been treated."

" Oh ! Dick," said Gilbert, " I should have been happy but for thinking of you. Your presence was the only thing I craved for."

" They have been treated in a manner becoming their station and birth," replied Michael, significantly " Martel will tell you all."

" But who is this fairy ?" asked Dick.

" My name's Flo, sir," the girl replied, in a timid voice.

Dick caressed her fondly, and looked at Martel interrogatively, and she motioned him to come near her.

For some time did they carry on a whispered conversation, and if Dick had been surprised before it was nothing to his astonishment as Martel proceeded.

" Wonderful are the ways of Providence," Dick said, as the crone finished speaking. " Here are two children thrown into each other's arms, living in childish innocence, little thinking they are brother and sister. Is it possible ?"

With that ejaculation he went to the children and caught little Flo in his arms.

Gilbert and Flo had very much improved since their last appearance before our readers.

They were showily but prettily dressed, and were immense favourites with the whole tribe.

Never had the gipsies such a jolly day as upon this occasion, and the time seemed to fly.

At length night came, spreading its dark mantle over the encampment.

The tents were still untenanted, for the tribe

were thoroughly enjoying a steaming hot supper. Jests were bandied from mouth to mouth, and boisterous laughter and singing made it a scene of wild mirth.

"I don't want to stop your fun, my boys, but we ought to have the sentries at their various posts," said a gipsy.

"What for?" shouted a chorus of voices.

"Because there is a band of brigands lurking about the neighbourhood."

This elicited a loud shout of laughter from the reckless fellows; but their mirth changed to consternation when a succession of ringing reports came from the wood beyond the encampment.

"To your arms!" shouted Michael.

He then ordered the women under cover, and thrusting a brace of revolvers in his belt and buckling on a sword, he stationed himself at the head of the men.

At that instant a man came running into the encampment.

"What is the matter?" demanded Michael.

"The brigands are upon us, chief," he shouted.

A savage cry escaped Michael's lips, and it was echoed by those who stood near him.

Their gipsy blood was aroused, and not one of them would rest until the intruders had paid dearly for their daring.

The band of brigands far outnumbered their opponents, but the gipsies had a skilful leader.

He ordered his men to advance slowly, and the order was instantly obeyed.

"Fire!" he shouted.

A deafening report followed.

Loud shrieks of agony told how deadly had been the effect upon their foes, who now came rushing upon the gipsy band.

The brigands discharged their pieces in a most irregular manner, but before they could see the effect of their fire another destructive volley was poured into them.

They were panic stricken after the second volley, and had not their leader urged them on they would have fled, but his stentorian voice steadied them, and a hand-to-hand conflict took place.

The cries of the dying and the wounded were dreadful to hear.

The women and children were flying in all directions, tents had been knocked down and destroyed, and one of the caravans had been smashed in the fearful conflict; but the battle soon came to an end, and eventually the brigands turned and took to their heels, having had very much the worst of the encounter.

## CHAPTER XXX.

DOUBLE TREACHERY—ATTEMPT TO ASSASSINATE RICHARD GRANT IN THE RED CHAMBER.

THOUGH Burkett had so recently escaped from his dreaded enemy he did not hesitate to keep his appointment with David Eastlake.

He bid an affectionate farewell to Rose, who felt a strange misgiving at her heart as the burglar strode away and was lost to view.

The Bosker, deep in thought, made his way to the house of his employer. He was thinking of the probable chances of his coming in contact with the brave detective again, and wondering whether he should leave the crime-stained abode of his base patron without something happening out of the common.

In an unpleasant mood Burkett arrived at the fashionable house, the ponderous door of which was opened by a bullet-headed groom.

He gave a hideous grin, and said, "Mr. Eastlake is engaged, sir—you can't see him."

"I'll wait till I can, then," said the Bosker, savagely.

"You can't wait, sir—better call again," replied the servant, who evidently intended shutting the door had not Burkett given him a slight tap between the eyes with his fist, which caused a number of lamps to dance about before the astonished groom, who thought his bullet-head had been smashed.

By the time he had finished rubbing the injured part, and the lamps had discontinued dancing, he discovered that the Bosker had vanished.

The man's face wore a look of consternation, and, closing the door, he sneaked to the reception-room and poked his head in, which he quickly withdrew upon catching sight of the Bosker.

In his haste to withdraw his head the groom brought it with great force against the edge of the door.

He gave a yell of pain and clapped both hands to a rapidly-growing lump.

David Eastlake being attracted by the noise now made his appearance upon the scene.

When he discovered the cause he said something considerably more expressive than polite, and, after aiming a kick at the unlucky groom, entered the room in which the Bosker sat.

"You here?" Eastlake said.

"Seems like it," replied the other, with his usual mocking smile. "You told me to come, didn't you?"

Eastlake frowned, but vouchsafed no reply.

Their meeting was anything but a friendly one, for they mistrusted each other, and Burkett had an involuntary feeling that all was not well.

"Follow me, Burkett," Eastlake said, "we will go where prying eyes cannot see and listening ears cannot hear."

The Bosker rose from his chair, and motioned to his employer to lead the way.

Eastlake conducted him up a private staircase, and after threading a suite of apartments the polished villain paused before a massive door, which he opened, and ushered his companion into a room which was large and strangely furnished.

Burkett entered without the slightest hesitation.

Eastlake followed, and the door closed with an unpleasant snap.

The villains seated themselves, then they glanced at each other for some time in perfect silence.

Eastlake spoke first.

"James Burkett," he said, speaking slowly, "you have a small packet of papers in your possession belonging to me."

"I have not," the Bosker replied, shrugging his huge shoulders.

"Dated, and with a crest upon the outside," David Eastlake continued. "You stole them exactly eighteen months since, from an ebony box in the black cabinet."

The Bosker looked at his employer in blank amazement.

An exultant smile played about the lips of Eastlake as he watched the other's changing countenance.

"Where are they?" Eastlake demanded. "I must have them to-night—now."

Burkett gave a forced laugh as he said—

"What the deuce are you driving at?"

"Bah! Burkett," retorted Eastlake. "Why do you attempt this style of thing with me; you will not find it a paying game?"

"I don't understand."

"Shall I explain?"

"If it will afford you any pleasure."

"It might refresh your memory if it does not afford me pleasure."

Burkett bit his lip and scowled most demoniacally.

"David Eastlake, you have asked me the same question once before," said the Bosker. "Do you remember the answer? I tell you that I have not the papers, but I know where they are."

"Ah!" exclaimed Eastlake.

"Yes, I know where to put my hand on them; but not another soul upon earth could find them," said the Bosker.

Eastlake had to turn his head away to hide the look of emotion that came over his face at the Bosker's information.

"Fool! he has signed his own death-warrant. I can rid myself of him now in safety," muttered Eastlake.

"I hear the bell ringing; it must be Grant. He called on me this morning, and promised to be here to night. I will bring him upstairs."

"Here?"

"Yes."

"Then, where am I to hide, so that I may pounce on him when his back is turned towards me."

Eastlake strode across the room, and, drawing the heavy tapestry aside, he opened a secret door.

"This will conceal you safely—you will not lack courage?"

"Bah! Why do you ask? You know I can kill him, and you too, for that matter, without much hesitation," the Bosker growled.

"Cheerful, that," replied Eastlake, with a sorry attempt at a laugh.

The Bosker, not suspecting any treachery, entered the closet.

He did not see the look which came into Eastlake's face, or he would have hesitated ere he trusted himself in the secret closet.

"When I tap three times come out," Eastlake said.

Burkett evinced some surprise when he saw another door about three yards in front of him, but, thinking it an old portion of the house, and that the door was not used, he walked through the opening and found himself in a very peculiar chamber.

He had only time to cast his eyes around, when,

with a loud bang, the door closed, and he was in total darkness.

"What could be the meaning of this?" he thought.

He tried the door and found it immovable.

Instead of being an old one, as he had anticipated, he discovered that it was of tremendous thickness, iron-bound, and thickly padded.

A loud oath escaped the Bosker's lips, for he had been ensnared, and outwitted when he least expected it, and this place might be his tomb.

His fury knew no bounds.

He gnashed his teeth and cursed in an awful manner, but presently he stopped raving, and an awful chill crept over him.

He heard strange sounds, that grated horribly upon his ears. The suspense became awful.

A clammy sweat came upon his brow, and he could not shake off the idea that some dreadful tragedy was about to be enacted.

Then he heard a noise close to his feet. Though he did not know it he was standing in the middle of a horrible torture chamber.

He remembered he had some matches with him, so he struck one and glanced round the apartment.

As he did so his face turned deadly pale, and uttering a cry he dropped the match and was again in darkness.

But in that momentary glance he had seen enough to increase his fears.

He was in a circular chamber of most peculiar construction; but it was not the shape of the room that had caused him to utter a cry of surprise.

The noise he had heard at his feet was caused by the removal of a round iron disc, leaving a dark yawning abyss, upon the very edge of which he had been standing.

One step forward would have precipitated him below and smashed him to pieces.

The Bosker lighted another match, and having made a more lengthened inspection of his prison, he became calmer.

His courage returned, and he tapped the wall of the chamber with his fingers.

He uttered an exclamation of surprise when he discovered that it was made of iron.

Now a look of horror came upon his ghastly face, for the chamber had become considerably smaller since he had been in it.

"I am lost—I am lost," he yelled, in an awful tone of voice. "Curse him! Oh, what would I give to have him here one minute."

The Bosker tried every means in his power to open the massive door, but without success.

Wildly he dashed against it. He kicked, he hammered with his bludgeon, but with the same result.

At last he paused to take breath, and listened painfully.

A sound of some terrible machinery, working slowly, caused him to shriek, and a new horror came upon him.

The air was getting quite warm.

"Furies, what can this mean?" he muttered, hoarsely.

He was unable to move, the perspiration poured from him, his hands worked nervously, and his limbs lost their strength.

The slow grinding of the machinery continued, and each moment the place became hotter.

Presently his attention was directed to a bright red line directly opposite him, and he fixed his eyes upon it in speechless horror.

It became brighter and larger, and as the heat was becoming excessive the Bosker took a step back.

His hand was behind him, and it came in contact with the side of the terrible chamber.

He uttered an awful scream and leapt away, for the iron was burning hot.

Could any one have seen Burkett's face at that moment it would have been awful to behold.

His eyes were fixed involuntarily on the bright red mark, and he would have uttered another scream, but horror held him speechless.

The agonised face of the Bosker would have softened a heart of stone as he watched that dreadful glowing spot increase.

The place was like an oven, and the suffering prisoner could plainly see around him now, but it only intensified his agonising torture—if that were possible—for the chamber was not one half the size it was when he had first entered.

The Bosker's face and hands were blistered with the heat, and his eyes were burning and starting from their sockets.

His tongue, parched and blistered, was lolling out of his scorched and cracking lips, and yet the shocking torture continued.

The heat became still more oppressive, and the dimensions of his awful prison chamber became less.

Slowly, but surely, it contracted, each turn of the fiendish machine bringing the circle smaller, and driving the tortured occupant to the brink of the deep chasm.

The terrible winding-sheet of iron drove the Bosker to the very edge of the abyss.

It came so close that he screamed in agony.

"Help! Help!" he cried. "Cruel torturing fiend! Oh! if I were only spared to punish you for this. Curses on you, David Eastlake; you triumph now, but it shall not be for long. A day will come when you will suffer ten times what I have! Judgment will overtake you, and then you will endure all the tortures of perdition! Aye, tenfold—curse you! You have conquered—now I go. Oh, help—oh, help! This is horrible—horrible! Oh, this fiendish work! I shall go mad—mad! Death—aye, death is sweet to this dreadful torture! I go—my last dying curse is for that demoniac fiend. Curse him—curse him!"

He raised his voice to a terrible pitch, and as he uttered the last words the hot iron touched him, and with a wild, unearthly shriek, a deep sob of pent-up agony, he threw his arms up, and disappeared swiftly down the fearful chasm.

Down, down, he went, cleaving the fearful darkness, and a thousand fiends seemed to be shouting in his ears, mocking his death cry.

They clutched him with their deathly hands—

they laughed in derision as they bore him from that terrible chamber into the bottomless pit.

David Eastlake must certainly have been what he had more than once boasted—a man without a soul—to have consigned the Bosker to such a horrid death.

But the black-hearted villain had not finished his night's work yet; there remained Richard Grant to remove from his path.

Eastlake would have done honour to Satan, for he was a fiend in human shape

Not a second thought did he bestow upon the suffering burglar, but hiding his demoniac nature behind an oily smile and easy manner, he descended the stairs to receive his second visitor, Richard Grant, the detective.

He made a graceful bow to the detective, who returned his salute with a cool nod and strode into the hall.

"You had better arrange this business in my private room, as the servants are ever prying into one's affairs," Eastlake said.

Grant readily acquiesced.

The polished villain then led h m into the same aparment in which he had held the interview with Burkett.

Grant glanced curiously around, and then gazed at David Eastlake, who slightly quailed under the stern glance of the other.

Grant opened the conversation by saying—

"You are aware of the object of my visit?"

"Partially."

"Well, have you any terms to propose?"

"I scarcely know sufficient of your business yet, therefore I have not thought anything about the terms."

This was a bold lie—the detective knew it, and his lip curled scornfully.

"Bah! David Eastlake, why do you try to deceive me," he said. "We are too old friends for that. Come, speak candidly—no hypocrisy. I am determined that justice shall be done, as I told you this morning. I shall name the terms. Refuse, and I'll put you in Newgate."

"Well?"

"I am very glad you think it well—I don't. But I have come to warn you—'tis for your good. I have a pocket-book of yours."

"You have?"

"And I intend to keep it," laughed Grant.

"Perhaps," replied the other, with a dark scowl.

"Bosh!" said Richard Grant, sneeringly. "Don't presume to threaten me. You know I could hang you if I chose."

"You are very bold for one in another person's house," Eastlake observed, significantly.

"Ha, ha! I might be in the lion's den, but then I should not fear the lion," Grant replied.

"You might rouse him."

"Bah! I could crush him as easy as I could a puppy, and leave him a mangled corpse in his cage," laughed Grant, tauntingly.

Eastlake's eyes shone evilly, and the detective saw it, but only smiled in scorn.

He knew he had roused Eastlake's black, evil

passions, but he was thoroughly prepared to take the consequences.

"Why snarl at each other like schoolboys? You have come upon business. Name your terms," said Eastlake.

"Nothing will give me greater pleasure. They are simply these," Grant replied, speaking slow and seriously. "I am acquainted with many things you dream not of. I have already told you I could hang you, and perhaps I shall do it yet."

David Eastlake's brow grew darker, but the detective continued in the same determined voice—

"The estates you have usurped were gained by the shedding of more than one person's blood; but with all your fiendish plots and crimes you did not remove the right party. All I wish you to do is to give into my hands all the title deeds, both legal and forged, and then for your own safety you had better go abroad. I will see that the rightful heir enjoys his own again. Refuse my terms and I will hurl you from your high pinnacle down to the lowest depths of degradation, and your shame and humiliation shall be ten times more stinging than your poverty, with nothing but the gallows staring you in the face."

He ceased speaking, to note the effect of his words, and the expression of Eastlake's face warned him to be on his guard.

"Never!" Eastlake hissed. "I will not give up the deeds. I defy you. There is no heir."

"Where is the boy Gilbert?" Grant demanded, quietly.

Eastlake nearly leaped from his chair.

"Perdition!" he muttered. "But, if living, he is not of an age to come into the property."

"You forget the rightful owner is not dead."

"Liar! he—"

"Speak a little more respectfully, Mr. Eastlake, or we may fall out," said Grant, interrupting him.

"Richard Grant, I am not to be frightened," Eastlake replied. "Think you I would now give up that which has already cost me so much? Do your worst—I defy you. And, in spite of all, I will keep possession. Let anyone take it from me who can. You have heard. I scorn your threats."

Grant listened quietly; it was nothing more than he expected.

"You are a bold villain," he said.

"I am desperate," replied Eastlake, with a savage laugh.

"Eastlake, you have done wrong to defy me. I know more than you think," Grant said. "In less than a month I will bring the rightful heir, and establish his legal right without the aid of yourself. I have given you a chance—it is the last. The alternative is the gallows."

"Beware, Richard Grant!" hissed the villain.

The detective laughed scornfully and whispered something in the other's ear.

The effect was most startling. Eastlake's eyes sparkled with a sardonic glitter.

"You know too much, Richard Grant," he cried.

"I give you three minutes to decide," the detective replied.

"Grant, this has been your seeking, not mine. You have me at your mercy," David Eastlake said.

"The power you hold over me you intend to use. There is not room for the two of us. Restore that pocket-book, with its contents untouched, or you never leave this place alive. You have bearded the tiger in its lair. Beware of its fangs."

Grant smiled cooly and did not move an inch, but replied, in a bantering voice—

"My precious, spiteful-looking tiger, I neither fear you nor your fangs, for, if I chose, I could crush the life from your black heart. Besides," he continued "you do not suppose I was fool enough to come here without making special arrangements. If I do not leave this place in ten minutes' time it will be entered and searched."

This was true, for the detective had secured the services of Captain Jack and two of his boys, who had instructions to sound an alarm should his absence be prolonged.

Eastlake muttered a deep curse, but he did not alter his intention, for he had gone too far to retreat.

His accomplice was dead by this time he knew, and the only man he really feared now stood before him, with the documents in his possession that endangered his life.

And, again, what was one more life to him?

Now that he had begun, he must go on to the end, so, when the detective rose to depart, Eastlake pretended to accidentally kick the chair over.

But in reality it was a signal for his ruffian groom to be at hand.

"As we cannot come to terms, David Eastlake, I shall wish you a very good morning," Grant said. "When next you hear from me be prepared for the worst. Adieu!"

Grant strode towards the door, but Eastlake confronted him and said in a hoarse whisper—

"Richard Grant, you will not leave this place alive unless you comply with my demands."

"Out of my path. I comply with no demands," cried the detective, contemptuously.

David Eastlake took from a desk a long gleaming dagger, and Grant saw his position was a dangerous one.

He took one step back as he was menaced with the shining blade, and placing a whistle to his mouth he blew a shrill note.

Eastlake gave a half-savage, half-mocking laugh.

"Ha—ha! Blow again, Richard Grant. Think you I was fool enough to receive you in a part of the house where we might be heard?" he said, tauntingly.

Grant made no reply.

He saw he had been trapped. Setting his teeth hard, and placing his hand in his pocket, he drew forth a six-barrelled revolver.

As his assailant was about to make a spring forward he presented the shining barrel in a straight line with his head.

David Eastlake stopped and gazed savagely upon the brave detective, whose determined look told the villain that he might expect no mercy.

Grant was thoroughly on his mettle.

He pulled the trigger, but what was his surprise when nothing but a click was heard.

One of the percussion caps had fallen off, and

almost before he had time to draw back the trigger David Eastlake was upon him.

It was with great difficulty that Richard Grant prevented the murderous blade from entering his heart.

A terrible struggle ensued.

The detective could not get a fair chance of using his pistol, nor could Eastlake use his dagger.

Grant, by superior strength, soon got his right hand free, and pointing the shining tube of the pistol at his foe's breast he fired.

This time the bullet took effect, but not as he had expected.

They had been swaying about in such a manner that it was impossible to aim with any exactness, and the bullet went a little wide of its mark, taking a piece out of Eastlake's neck.

Eastlake uttered a howl of rage and maddened pain, and fought with greater fury ; but he was nothing in the hands of his powerful adversary.

He had already received two blows upon the head—a third was impending.

The last would undoubtedly have been the *coup de grace* had not a most unexpected occurrence taken place.

The bullet-headed groom, with a diabolical look upon his face, entered the apartment.

He had a murderous-looking life preserver in his hand, with which he commenced to attack Grant, who, finding himself assailed by another, disengaged himself from his almost exhausted antagonist, and placed his back against the wall.

"Murderous wretches, you shall suffer for this !" he cried.

The brutal groom laughed, and took a step forward.

Grant fired at him, and the bullet struck the groom's left wrist sideways, cutting right through the bone, and nearly severing his hand from his wrist.

The awful shriek he gave echoed through the house, and he jumped about like a maniac his agony was so great.

His villainous master stood looking on in speechless horror.

Presently a wild, savage, half-mad light shone in the hireling's eye, and before either knew his intention he clutched the dagger from Eastlake's hand and with a bound leapt at the throat of Grant.

The detective gave a cry of pain.

So unexpected had been the onslaught that the long blade entered his shoulder before he could raise his arm to defend himself.

With a great effort Grant recovered himself, and, clutching his revolver by the muzzle, he rained a torrent of blows upon the ruffian's head.

Whether the fellow's skull was extra thick, or he was too maddened to heed the blows, it is impossible to say, but they did not seem to have much effect upon him.

It became a fearful struggle now.

Eastlake was spellbound, gazing upon the fearful scene, and his blood curdled in his veins.

Presently he shook off the lethargy that held him.

He was smarting terribly from his own wounds, but he saw that unless he went to his servant's aid Grant would be the victor.

A sudden gleam of joy shot from Eastlake's eyes, and, raising the curtains exactly facing those that hid the door through which the unfortunate Burkett had passed, the villain unfastened another door.

"Through here—thrust him through—put him in the red chamber !" cried Eastlake, excitedly.

His servitor made no reply, but fought madly.

The detective's arm was lacerated from dagger thrusts, and he had all his work cut out to prevent the weapon entering his heart.

Now Eastlake came upon him.

He was getting rather faint, and found himself utterly unable to contend against both of them, and by degrees they forced him into the red chamber.

Eastlake then called to his servant to come away, but he only laughed wildly and clung tighter to Grant.

"Strike him—strike deep !" cried Eastlake.

At that moment Grant gave a cry as he staggered back—"Fiend ! you have done for me at last."

A wild laugh answered him as he slowly staggered against the wall, and the groom rushed upon him to deal still another blow.

Grant gave up all hope, feeling that he was lost indeed.

The blood-begrimed disfigured groom presented an awful spectacle.

He looked a perfect demon.

The gallant detective felt himself fainting—dying, in fact—and yet the murderous knife was descending.

Down—down it came, cleaving through the air.

Grant threw all his energies into one last act, and when the knife was within an inch of his breast he struck the maniac a terrible blow upon the centre of his forehead with the butt-end of his pistol.

The laugh died from the groom's lips—he leapt high in the air, and, making one more attempt to reach his foe, sank to the floor in a fit. Grant fell almost beside him, apparently lifeless.

Eastlake could not check a cry of horror, but even then a subtle idea crossed his brain.

Should he shut the door upon them and leave them both to die ?

At that moment there was a loud knocking at the street-door, followed by a shuffling of feet, and then a voice inquired for "Richard Grant, the Detective !"

---

## CHAPTER XXXI.

### CAPTAIN JACK LEARNS STRANGE THINGS AND DARK DOINGS.

CAPTAIN JACK, in accordance with orders he had received from Grant, was on the watch near Eastlake's house.

He was accompanied by Chimbley Joe and little Dan.

The trio kept a vigilant look-out upon the house. They were to wait for a signal from within, which Captain Jack would answer.

They waited and listened for a long time, but

no signal was heard, and Jack began to get anxious.

"It only wants twenty minutes to ten," he said.

At that moment he was joined by two other boys, and Jack felt a little more easy at this addition.

A misgiving that all was not well stole over his heart, but he decided to wait, for he thought that Grant might be arranging some important business matters.

At last Jack called his companions round him.

"Don't you think it's time we inquired for him?" he said.

"Yes," replied Joe.

"I haven't heard the signal," vociferated Dan.

"No, but it's past the time."

"But it's agin orders," said little Dan.

"I'll chance that," said Jack, with determination.

He gave a shrill whistle, and the sound had scarcely died away when a tall individual strode in among the little group, and, placing his heavy hand upon Captain Jack's shoulder, he whispered something in his ear.

Jack then held a brief conversation with him in the same low tone of voice.

"We will see," said the stranger, speaking in a loud and determined voice.

He then walked to the door of Eastlake's residence, and giving a sonorous knock at the massive door, waited impatiently for it to be opened.

They did not have to wait long.

A manservant came up in a hurry, and enquired their business.

"Richard Grant is here with your master—I wish to see him."

The man stared at the tall stranger in great astonishment.

"There must be some mistake, sir," he said.

"There is no mistake," the stranger replied. "Go and bid him or your master to come here immediately."

"Indeed, sir, he left with master more than half an hour ago."

The stranger glanced at Captain Jack sternly, and the leader of the Poor Boys of London gave a sign.

The stranger repeated his question, but to no purpose.

He could see the servant was not playing a part, for the man's surprise was genuine.

They were baffled, and left the house, but were not thrown off their guard.

A long consultation was held between Captain Jack and the stranger, but they could come to no conclusion that night.

"See me to-morrow—twelve o'clock," said the man.

"I will sir."

"Good," and with that he strode away, leaving Captain Jack to return to the boys, which he did, very much chagrined at being outwitted.

There was a mystery hanging over the affair, and he intended to solve it, but how was he to begin?

An occurrence the next morning threw a chance in his way, and then Captain Jack determined on what course to pursue.

We will follow him in his daring undertaking.

Captain Jack was perusing one of the morning papers in the haunt of the Poor Boys of London.

He glanced down the columns filled with advertisements, and presently his eye lighted on one that caused him a little surprise.

He read and re-read it, to be thoroughly certain he was right.

Throwing the paper down, he dashed to the part of the haunt he called his own room, and commenced the operation of dressing himself in a suit of good clothes, purchased with his share of the money given by Whitechapel Dick.

Never had he been so particular as he was on this occasion, and when at last he had completed his toilet to his own satisfaction, he sallied forth to keep his appointment with the dark stranger.

"Well, my boy, have you thought of anything that might aid us?" he said.

"Yes, sir," replied Jack, with an air of self satisfaction.

"Explain, as briefly as possible."

"Well, sir, I saw an advertisement in the paper for a 'tiger,' and to my astonishment it said apply to the head footman at Mr. Eastlake's residence."

The man started, and an expression of pleasure illuminated his face.

"Well," he said, after a pause.

"Well, sir, I thought that if there was a chance of my getting the place, I might—"

"Oh, yes, I see—I see," interrupted his interlocutor.

There was a short pause.

"But have you courage enough to enter that house and solve its dark mysteries!"

"Yes, sir, or die in the undertaking," replied Jack.

"You are a brave lad. But are you sure there has been treachery?"

"Quite, sir. I can swear Richard Grant never left that house last night, and I will find him alive or dead before the week has gone."

"Well, start now, and let me know whether you succeed or not."

"Yes, sir; but there is something wanting, and that is my character," said Captain Jack.

"Your character?" reiterated the other.

"Yes, sir, they will not take me without one; I am going to pretend I have been brought up in a stable all my life."

"Ah! now I understand. You require a character from your last employer?"

"Exactly, sir."

"Well, then, I'll be that individual. You have been my tiger, but have left my service about a fortnight," replied the detective (for such he was), as he took a pen and paper, upon which he wrote the required credentials. "There, that will do, I think," he added, handing the written sheet to Jack.

"Thank you sir, that will do."

"When shall I hear how you have succeeded?"

*The boy rushed to the rescue, and was only just in time.*

"Well, sir, if I succeed perhaps I shall not have an opportunity of coming to you; but if I should fail I will endeavour to return almost immediately."

"That will do, my boy. Stay—take this with you, it may be useful."

While the detective was finishing the latter part of his speech he took from a case a beautiful small five-chambered revolver and handed it to Captain Jack.

"Oh, thank you, sir," said the young captain, in raptures at the splendid present, for the weapon was indeed a lovely piece of workmanship.

The leader of the Poor Boys of London then departed and hastened to the house of David Eastlake.

"Can I see the head footman, please?" he asked, when his summons at the door had been answered by the same individual that had spoken to them on the night previous, but of course he did not recognise Jack in his new attire.

"Step this way," he said.

Just as Jack had seated himself in the hall Eastlake came out of the dining-room and stopped the servant as he was about to descend the kitchen stairs.

"Charles," he said.

"Yes, sir?"

"Order my carriage."

"Yes, sir."

"What does that boy want?"

"Come to see the head footman, sir."

"I will speak to him myself," Eastlake said.

Captain Jack had great difficulty in keeping himself calm when he found the penetrating eyes of Eastlake upon him.

His face seemed to smart and burn, and he set his teeth hard.

He longed to spring at the handsome villain's throat and demand what had become of Richard Grant.

"If you please, sir," he said, "I saw an advertisement this morning for—"

Eastlake interrupted him, and fixing his piercing gaze upon the lad, said—

"Oh, step in here."

Jack felt slightly uncomfortable at this—he fancied that Eastlake had recognised him.

His uneasiness increased when he entered the dining-room, for again those terrible dark eyes were bent upon him, as though they would read him through and through.

He dared not look up—he could not.

Eastlake did not recognise Captain Jack, but he had an idea he had seen him before.

He questioned our young friend, who, of course, had a nice little tale all ready manufactured.

Jack's story and his excellent character, coupled with his intelligence and well-behaved manner, deceived the villain, who took almost a fancy to him, and engaged the lad at once.

Jack could not conceal his joy.

"When am I to come, sir?"

"Immediately."

"Yes, sir," replied Jack, more delighted still.

His new master then wrote a note.

"You cannot go out with me like that," he said, eyeing Jack up and down. "Take this note to the tailor's; then get your luggage, and return to-night —the head footman will attend to you."

Jack saluted; he then took the note and started off to the tailor's.

Having executed his commission he went to the detective and informed him of his success.

Early the same evening Captain Jack returned to his situation with an old carpet bag, which was a long way from full.

Jack soon found out, by sundry little dainties that were being prepared, that there was a sick person in the house, and presently the lad was selected to attend upon him.

He was sent to the invalid's room with some refreshments, which, however, were wasted, as the patient was delirious.

Jack felt a cold thrill of horror creep over him as he gazed upon the sufferer.

His face had apparently been beaten about in a most frightful manner, and his head was covered with surgical bandages; but even these were as naught to what Jack was destined to see a little later on.

The young man tossed about in a most restless manner, and every now and then raving most frantically.

At length he drew his left arm from under the bed-clothes, and Jack's eyes became riveted upon the sufferer's arm.

There was something terribly suggestive of a dark and awful deed in the fact that the hand had been severed from the wrist!

Our readers can easily imagine who this unfortunate individual was.

It was the villainous groom of Eastlake's, who had lost his hand in that dreadful combat with Grant.

It may be necessary to explain how he had been saved.

When last we saw him he was lying by the side of the detective in the mysterious closet.

The villainous Eastlake would have shut him in the red closet and left him to die there without compunction, but on second thoughts he remembered that his services were still required.

He therefore carried him to his room, summoned the servants, sent for a doctor, and gave it out that the young fellow had met with an accident.

Captain Jack had not been in the room many minutes before the strange ravings of the invalid attracted his attention, and caused him no small amount of surprise.

A determined look came over the lad's face, and he vainly tried to still the pulsations of his heart as he bent over the man and caught every murmured syllable.

What to anyone else would have been a mystery was perfectly intelligible to Jack.

Fortune had indeed favoured him.

Long did he listen to the delirious ravings of the patient, and it was not until he thought he might excite suspicion that he left the room.

He had learnt enough and to spare to clear up the late mystery.

"Strange," he thought. "So this man has lost his hand in a conflict with Grant. Murderous wretches! But they shall be dragged to justice yet. Now may fortune favour me. First I must discover this chamber of dark deeds and hidden crimes the wounded man has been raving about."

He had resolved to search for the body of the

gallant detective that very night ; but he had need to be careful, for he knew that he had a black-hearted villain to deal with, and one that would not hesitate to murder him, should he be discovered.

Jack quite recognised the seriousness of his perilous situation.

Nothing but the deepest cunning and extreme finesse would take him through his hazardous task.

Night came—dark, damp, and dreary.

It was a night fitted for evil deeds of every kind.

The rain pattered down upon the pavement, and the wind sighed and moaned round the street corners.

Not a soul was to be seen anywhere.

The stillness that reigned through the house of David Eastlake was only broken by the occasional rumbling of some belated vehicle outside.

The whole household were locked in slumber.

Even Eastlake, with his terrible burden of sin, was asleep.

But we are wrong when we say that the whole household are locked in slumber, for Captain Jack, when the night was far advanced, stole from his sleeping apartment.

Silently he groped his way about the house.

In his left hand there was a dark lantern, while his right tightly clutched a revolver.

At last he found the secret staircase and a sigh of relief escaped his lips.

Presently he came to a door—the entrance to the red closet ; it was locked, but the key had been only half turned, and Jack, after a little time, contrived to open it.

As he did so he heard a hollow groan.

---

## CHAPTER XXXII.

### HOW THINGS ARE BROUGHT TO LIGHT.

WE will now return to Richard Grant, so that the reader may better understand and realise the startling incidents we are about to relate.

He had fainted from excitement, and lay powerless beside his would-be assassin.

Eastlake was still undecided how to act when the tumult at the street door startled him.

He immediately closed the approaches to his secret apartment, and remained waiting in a room next to them.

The servant who answered the detective and Captain Jack when they enquired for Richard Grant had been previously instructed by the villainous groom to say that he had gone out with his master.

When they had departed David Eastlake stole back to the fatal apartment.

He trembled as though he had been stricken with the palsy, and after removing the groom he was so terrified that he even forgot to search the person of the detective for the much coveted pocket-book.

Eastlake fully believed his enemy was at last dead ; but he was mistaken.

Eastlake—the cruel, pitiless, crafty Eastlake—did not imagine that the saving of the life of his ruffianly groom and advertising for a tiger would be the means of his destruction.

But let us say a word or two about Burkett.

We left him falling down that fearful chasm, at the bottom of which he landed with a crash.

Hours flew by and yet there were no signs of returning consciousness.

To all appearance Burkett was certainly dead, but consciousness at last slowly returned.

He groped about him as well as he could.

He suffered much pain, and was very weak and exhausted, as his position slowly began to dawn upon him.

Many long, weary hours passed, and no help came to him. Like Leary Jock, he had been left to a horrible fate—death—by starvation and thirst.

He was in a dreamy kind of trance, wishing for what he had tried to avoid only a few short hours before—death.

While he lay in this state he fancied he heard a strange noise.

Then came a loud click, as though a bolt had been drawn back.

This was followed by the opening of a door.

Anon a few faint streaks of light seemed to flitter across his face, and then in another instant, kneeling by his side, was Captain Jack, trying all he knew to restore the Bosker.

"Good Heaven !" the boy cried. ' how came you here, James Burkett ?"

Burkett made no reply, but a savage expression passed over his features.

"Have you been here long ?" Jack enquired.

"I know not—it seems ages to me. But who are you ?"

"I will tell you by-and-bye ; at present you must not talk," said Jack. "I will fetch some water at once. I am sure you must need it."

The Bosker glanced at him gratefully.

Jack then departed, with strict injunctions that Burkett was to remain perfectly still and quiet until he returned, which he did in a very short time.

He brought both drink and eatables from the kitchen, the latter of which the Bosker partook of very sparingly.

Captain Jack then began to question him.

"How came you here ?" he said.

Burkett regarded him for a few minutes in silence, and then said, without answering the good lad's question—

"Have I not seen you before ?"

"You have, James Burkett—as an enemy. But animosity should not prevent me from performing an act of kindness to one so much distressed."

Burkett looked at Jack admiringly.

Villain as he was, he still had some gratitude left.

Burkett then related how he had been trapped, and finished by swearing to have his revenge upon David Eastlake.

"Burkett, in return for saving your life will you promise me one thing ?"

"What may that be, lad ?"

"Help me to discover what the villain has done with Richard Grant."

Burkett considered for a few moments.

"My boy," he said, "you have saved my life, and you will find that even the savage Bosker, the lawless criminal, can be grateful. Though Grant is my deadly enemy I will find his body, dead or alive ; and what is more, I promise you that if he should be dead I will bring this gentleman villain —David Eastlake—to the gallows ! Curse him, his race is almost run, and I'll help to finish it !"

" I am glad I have saved you, Burkett ; nor do I think you quite so bad as the world says you are !"

" Thank you, my lad, for that," the Bosker returned. " Is anyone as bad as he is represented ? And if I am, who has driven me to it ? Did I seek this life myself ? No ! But once get into the clutches of the police and it is all over with you. Once you are condemned, though they afterwards discover you are innocent, the bloodhounds will still follow you the same. Go and seek employment, and while you are speaking to the tradesman a policeman will interfere and denounce you as a felon just come from prison."

" Can you move yet ?" Jack demanded.

" I can just crawl and that is all," the Bosker moaned.

" Stay, then," said Jack. " I will leave you some water and food, with a light, and in the meantime I will search for Grant. We must be careful or we may be discovered, and then all will be lost."

After showing Burkett how to open the door through which he had come, Captain Jack left him and renewed his search for the gallant detective.

Night was on the wane and the morn of a new day was quickly approaching.

In a few short hours the people of the vast city would be astir, yet that brave boy, Captain Jack, was still exploring the secret apartments.

He would not give in until his task was performed, or he was compelled to do so by the rising of the domestics.

None can tell what the boy suffered through his non-success.

He had systematically searched through nearly every part of the house, and being very tired, at length mechanically took a seat.

It was almost opposite the door of the red closet.

" Merciful Heaven ! what has the heartless wretch done with him ? Oh ! this delay. What may Grant be enduring all this time ! Heaven help me in my task," murmured Jack, thoroughly overcome.

After a slight pause he continued—

" Ah ! I have it. If I should fail I will descend the stairs, go to the room of the villain, drag him from his bed, and demand from him Richard Grant, dead or alive. Let him do his worst—I am prepared !" and Captain Jack tightened his grasp upon the butt of his revolver.

He was in the act of rising from his seat when a deep moaning sound came plainly to his ears.

Leaping to his feet he clutched the lantern in one hand and his pistol in the other.

His face was flushed and excited and his breath came short.

The noise evidently proceeded from exactly behind where he had been sitting.

Pulling the thick curtains aside that hid the door of the red closet from view, he attempted to open it.

But his efforts were in vain.

He was in the act of stepping back, that he might throw himself against it, when his foot touched a spring about three inches from the bottom of the door, which immediately flew open with tremendous force, and struck against Jack so violently that he was felled to the floor ; but in a moment he recovered his feet, and, taking his lantern, began to reconnoitre.

In a few minutes he found himself in the closet in which Grant was confined.

Another moan caused Captain Jack to direct the light of the lamp downwards, and he gave a cry of rage and sorrow as the rays of the lantern fell full upon the pale, blood-stained features of the bold detective.

Captain Jack dropped upon his knees by the side of the inanimate form and wept like a child

His tears fell fast upon Grant's upturned face, bathing his temples, and washing the blood from his brow.

Grant moved and a heavy sigh came from his lips. He seemed conscious that someone was near him.

With a great effort he unclosed his eyes, and fixed them upon his young deliverer in a dreamy kind of stare, but they closed almost immediately, as though the effort to keep them open was painful.

Captain Jack commenced to restore him by the same method he had so successfully applied to the Bosker.

His efforts were soon rewarded with success.

Jack dried his eyes as well as he could, and then called upon the detective by name—

" Mr. Grant, open your eyes, sir. Speak—please —speak. It's me—Captain Jack. I'm here," he said, excitedly.

Again the detective opened his eyes and gazed upon our young friend, this time appearing to comprehend what was being said to him.

" Take this, sir. Drink—it will revive you," said Jack, putting some water to the detective's lips.

Grant clutched the vessel eagerly and took a deep draught.

Its effect was almost magical.

He drew a long breath and raised himself up.

As he glanced around the place a light shone in his eyes as they alighted upon Jack.

" Is it possible ? How came you here ?" he said, faintly.

" Hush, sir—do not speak yet. I will tell you all presently. Take some nourishment first."

In less than a quarter of an hour the detective was able to converse.

Jack then briefly explained how he came there, and where he had found the Bosker.

Nothing could exceed the detective's surprise at the strange but brief story.

" And now what is to be done ?" he asked.

" Well, sir, you are not strong enough to leave here yet."

" I fear not, Jack, my boy."

" Then I will dress your wounds and bring some food and drink ; but I fear you must remain here for a day or so; but unless we are very cautious we shall be discovered. It is now nearly daylight, sir. I will soon bring all the necessaries, and then you must remain quiet until to-morrow night, when I hope you will be able to depart."

"Ay! my boy, and then let the villainous usurper beware, for, by Heaven! I swear before a month has passed to bring him to the gallows," said Grant, with terrible determination.

After a brief conversation Captain Jack examined the nature of the fastening of the door.

He then departed to the kitchen, from whence he quickly returned with the necessaries for the gallant detective.

By the time he had finished dressing the wounds of Richard Grant it was broad daylight, and Captain Jack's position was becoming an extremely dangerous one.

It was already time for the servants to be astir and about their duties, so after exchanging a few words with Grant, he retired to his bed to snatch an hour's rest.

And this lad, a boy in years, was to be the means of bringing the dark-souled villain, David Eastlake, to justice.

Captain Jack did not rest long, for the awful events of the past night haunted him.

How his youthful heart beat with joy when the thought flashed through his brain that he had saved more than one human life, and it was indeed enough to fill even the heart of a man with emotions of pride.

He had ever been a favourite with the detective, and respected and esteemed by his companions, and now—now what would they think?

And even the daring outlaws at old Nathan's would applaud and admire him, because he had rescued their greatest favourite—their bravest companion—their lieutenant, in fact—yes, he had saved the life of James Burkett the burglar.

All that day he was as merry as possible, and went cheerfully about his duties.

His clothes had not yet come home, so he was prevented from going out with his master, who he only saw once or twice.

Jack had been hoping he would go out, but, greatly to his annoyance, Eastlake remained in the house the whole of the day.

Evening came at last.

And now Jack began to get anxious. He wanted to visit his patients in the secret chamber. A little after nine o'clock Eastlake went out.

The young captain at once smuggled a few good things from the larder to his own room, and, making the excuse that he was going to write some letters, he left the servants in the kitchen. After assuring himself that no one was watching him, he ascended the private staircase, and made his way to the mysterious portion of the building.

He paid his first visit to Grant, whom he found much improved, and he then proposed that he should see the Bosker and acquaint him with the nature of their arrangements, which Grant readily acceded to.

Captain Jack had not thought of Eastlake returning. He was under the impression that his master would not come back for several hours.

What was his surprise, then, as he led Burket in from the secret chamber into the large apartment, to hear a loud knock at the door, and a few minutes after the hasty strides of Eastlake as he ascended the stairs.

A chill crept over Jack, and he felt as though he should drop, while Burkett's dark eyes fairly blazed.

"Hide yourself, and leave all to me," he said.

"Good Heaven! what are you going to do?" asked Jack.

"Fear not for me. Conceal yourself," replied Burkett, in a hollow whisper.

Jack was both frightened and puzzled, and he had no idea what the Bosker intended to do.

But there was no time to be lost, for the libertine was only a few strides from the room.

Burkett's face wore a terrible expression as he clutched Captain Jack by the arm and led him across the room.

He thrust him behind the heavy curtains and then leapt back to the door leading to his torture chamber.

At that moment Eastlake walked into the apartment through the principal entrance and looked cautiously around.

The moon threw its pale, silvery light through a small window, faintly lighting up the apartment.

Eastlake was pale, and he trembled from head to foot as he strode in.

The fearful scenes in which he had been principal actor rose vividly before him now.

He had not intended to enter the horrible place again, but he had been too much unnerved at the time to search the body of Grant for the pocket-book.

He had come to do so now, and once the pocket-book was in his possession he would close that part of the house altogether.

Hush!

What was that?

The gentlemanly ruffian paused and cast a half-frightened look around.

"Fool! am I getting so childish that I cannot bear to hear my own footfall?" he muttered. "No, in spite of Satan himself I will have that book. Have I dared so much to lose it now? No, no, I say again, in spite of— Hah! what was that?"

A strange, hollow laugh greeted his ears, and at that moment a black cloud passed over the face of the hitherto brilliant moon.

Eastlake's heart seemed to cease beating.

He placed his hand to his brow and peered through the gloom, then a cry of terror escaped him, and he drew back shuddering.

But he could not remove his gaze from an awful object standing before him.

It seemed to fascinate David Eastlake.

His tongue clove to the roof of his mouth and his eyes almost started from their sockets as he gazed upon the pale, haggard countenance and weird form of the Bosker, standing between the heavy curtains that partially concealed the door of his torture chamber from view.

Eastlake felt all the awful fear of a guilty wretch who stands before the phantom of his murdered victim.

He would have screamed, but his tongue refused its office.

What moments of dreadful agony were those in which he stood crouching before the supposed apparition of Burkett.

Now his horror increased.

Slowly was the right hand of the supposed spectre raised until it was in a line with the villain's face, the forefinger pointing ominously at the stricken wretch.

Then the Bosker took one step forward, and Eastlake recoiled.

Never once moving his finger—on, on he came, the eyes glaring upon the fear-stricken wretch with a supernatural lustre.

All this time Eastlake receded slowly backwards until he stood upon the threshold of the door.

Then the Bosker stopped.

His colourless lips moved, his teeth gleamed like the fangs of a tiger, he seemed about to speak—slowly his arm dropped to his side, and that unearthly laugh was heard again.

"Eastlake, your time has come," he said, in a sepulchral tone of voice. "Your triumph has been short. I have come for revenge—aye, revenge. You shall bear me company to perdition—ha! ha! —down—down."

Another hollow laugh.

Then the Bosker seemed to rise slowly inch by inch—his face wore a demoniac expression, and both his arms were raised, as though he intended grappling Eastlake by the throat.

Nature could stand no more—the spell was broken.

All the sinews and muscles in Eastlake's body relaxed.

One piercing cry escaped him and he turned and fled down the stairs.

Again that awful laugh sounded upon his ears.

Oh, mercy! the phantom was following him. Another heart-rending cry, and then he flung his arms in the air and fell to the floor in a fit.

"So much for superstition," muttered Burkett, as with a grim smile he re-entered the apartment.

Captain Jack immediately came from his place of concealment.

"What have you done?" he asked.

"Nothing—I have merely frightened him into a fit," replied Burkett, with a smile.

"A just punishment," replied Jack; "and now to leave this house of crime. But—good Heavens! Burkett, you are ill?"

Burkett smiled faintly and shook his head.

He had not yet recovered, nor would he do so for some time to come.

Captain Jack was afraid lest he should not be able to get him from the house.

"Are you too bad to escape now?"

"No, boy—fear not. Get me out of this cursed place and then let Eastlake look to it," replied Burkett, a sudden fire lighting up his haggard face, and his lion chest expanding at the idea of again being free.

Jack then took Burkett to Grant, who was waiting for his young preserver.

A pang shot through the generous heart of the detective as he looked upon the Bosker's face, so terribly marked with suffering, and Burkett was no less sorry to see the dreadful alteration in the gallant Richard Grant.

Their feelings of enmity seemed to have vanished, for each had suffered, and both had been saved by little short of a miracle.

These two men, thrown thus together, forgot all their past animosity, and instinctively they held out their hands, Englishmen like, and swore to punish the doer of all this evil.

"Rather a novelty this—a detective shaking hands with a burglar," said Burkett, with a smile.

"James Burkett," said Grant, earnestly, "we meet here as men who have passed through much. Each of us has suffered from the same hand and the same treachery. Providence has decreed that we should escape, and he has chosen his agent in this brave young lad, Captain Jack. Freedom is before us, and we will punish the vile assassin who owns this house of crime."

Burkett grasped his hand and looked at the detective admiringly.

"Noble, generous fellow!" he muttered, as Grant followed Jack from the closet and entered the principal apartment.

Silently the trio descended the private staircase and made their way to the hall door.

They were unobserved, as the servants were crowding, a panic-stricken group, around Eastlake, who was still writhing in the paroxysms of an epileptic fit.

For a few minutes Grant and Burkett stood in the street inhaling the fresh air.

What a joyous sensation ran through their frames as the night cooled their fevered temples.

Captain Jack blew a shrill blast between his fingers twice, in quick succession.

The next instant there was a patter of feet, and they were surrounded by the Poor Boys of London. Then a cab rattled up to the door.

In less than a minute Grant was thrust inside with Burkett, and the cab rattled over the stones with the two men who had been enemies through life up till now.

---

## CHAPTER XXXIII.

### A SCENE IN THE DEN.

ON the night when the incidents related in the preceding chapter occurred there was an unusual number of the gang at Nathan Claws'.

They sat round the large tables, smoking and drinking, and relating anecdotes to each other.

Presently the door was opened and a newcomer shuffled into the kitchen.

Some of the thieves looked up and instantly recognised the individual.

His short hair and cleanly-shaven face spoke of a recent visit to prison—in fact he had but that morning come out.

Our readers have been introduced to the party before, who was no other than the Spitalfields Boozer.

"What cheer, Boozer, old pal?" shouted a chorus of voices.

"Done your stretch at last, old pal?" said one, with a laugh.

"Yes, and I ain't sorry neither. I is wery nigh a-croaking. It takes the pluck out of a feller," replied Boozer, with a shudder.

"Well, you don't look wery fat on it, old son. Take a swig," said his interlocutor.

The proffered "swig" was readily accepted by Spitals, who expressed his gratification by a nod of the head and then emptying the pot, which he returned to his generous friend, who looked into the vessel with a serio-comic kind of face, remarking—

"Rather dry, warn't you, Spitals, old boy?"

To which query Spitals answered—

"Wery! So would you be arter my spell, and feeding on toke and skilly."

His companions shrugged their shoulders in evident disgust.

At that moment Joe Lewis, the Burker, came up to the Boozer.

"Why, Joe, you look down in the mouth," said Spitals. "Got a plant on?"

"No," answered Lewis, somewhat abstractedly, and compressing his lips. "Have you seen anything of the Bosker?" he continued.

"Of course I ain't. I only came from my spell this 'ere evening," said the Boozer.

The Burker hardly stopped to hear the conclusion of the other's speech, but with a dark scowl moved away to another part of the kitchen.

The thieves' kitchen was being slowly deserted, as it always was at the latter part of the evening.

A few minutes after the above conversation the Burker left Nathan's and strolled leisurely towards the west.

He had evidently some dark intent from his moody manner, and in his pocket was that dreadful instrument, the sling-shot.

It was getting late, the shops were closed, and the streets were being slowly deserted, save by the pleasure-seekers, a few gamblers and sharpers, and men who always turn night into day.

Lewis soon quickened his pace and made his way to the vicinity of Leicester-square, and, after threading a number of intricate thoroughfares, he at last stopped in front of a large plain building.

Every blind was drawn down to prevent people seeing within, but the occupiers could not conceal the bright glow of the costly chandeliers.

Very unlike the exterior was the interior of that building.

It was a place of luxury and splendour, in fact, it was the most fashionable gaming-house in London.

The Burker glanced up at the windows for a few moments. Then he hid himself in the dark recess of an adjacent doorway.

The mighty clock at Westminster had long since struck the midnight hour, still the Burker remained in his hidden position, ever and anon peering up at the windows.

He evidently began to tire, for he was becoming terribly restless.

The Burker was about to come forth from his hiding-place when the door of the gaming-house opened, and a fashionably-dressed personage emerged and passed down the street with an unsteady gait.

The Burker drew back and eagerly watched him until he had got some thirty yards in advance, then, pulling his cap over his face, he followed.

The gentleman, innocent of the ruffian being on his track, threaded his way through St. Giles's and the Seven Dials.

This was certainly a peculiar neighbourhood for so fashionable a man to traverse at so late an hour of the night.

The instant he had entered Seven Dials the Burker quickened his pace, and he was now only a few yards behind him. Soon his actions became peculiarly suspicious.

He went into the road, that his footsteps might not make noise enough to startle the person who was walking on before him, and he constantly cast his eyes around, as though to take note of various dark turnings.

They had now arrived in one of the worst parts of that disreputable neighbourhood.

The gentleman still proceeded on his way, either unconscious of anyone's presence or indifferent about it.

Lewis now crept close behind the man he was following.

He bent forward, and, with one long stride, was upon the gambler's heels, who instinctively turned round to see whom it was.

As he did so Lewis leapt upon him. He placed his powerful arms like a vice round the man's throat, and hugged him like a bear.

His victim could only utter one slight cry before his assailant "put the screw on" with such force as to completely stifle him.

A convulsive shiver passed through his frame, and he lay a dead weight in the ruffian's brawny arms.

Then the garroter released his embrace and his victim fell a huddled-up form at his feet.

"Ah! I think I've done for you at last," said the ruffian, in a hoarse whisper. "That was well carried out, Major Carleton."

At that moment Big Ben struck one.

It was indeed that fashionable *roué*, Major Carleton, who so brutally murdered Captain Hamilton, and whom Leary Jock had watched.

Lewis was in the act of searching his purse for plunder when a light flashed behind and caused him to start up.

He turned deadly pale as his eyes fell upon a tall, graceful young man, who stood watching him.

"A nice night's work this, Joe Lewis," he said. "You have done that which you have been warned against. I thought I should catch you at last. Well, well, it is your own fault."

The stranger ceased speaking, and Lewis stood cowering before him.

At length he found courage to reply.

"Devil!" he gasped, "what are you that you haunt me thus?"

A scornful laugh was the only answer of the young stranger.

Lewis clutched the sling-shot nervously, but he

seemed too much afraid to use it, and his terror increased when the stranger spoke again.

"Lewis, you have done enough already," he said, pointing to the inanimate form of Carlton; "do not make it worse by being rash. Keep that murderous instrument in your pocket."

Lewis glared at him savagely, and some of his brute hardihood returned.

"Look here, you fiend!" he said, "I've had enough of you. Who are you to threaten me? I've done this little job, and mean to finish it, so look out and don't stand in my way."

"Ah! would you dare?" said the young stranger, his eyes flashing. "Hound, you shall suffer for this!"

Our readers, no doubt, have recognised the young stranger as the person who entered Nathan's and is known as the Young Chief.

Lewis had gone too far to retreat, and he knew it, so he drew his favourite weapon, and took a step forward.

His foe appeared as active as a young tiger, for he sprang upon Lewis before he could use his weapon and hurled him to the ground.

The young chief raised an alarm, and the next instant the Burker found himself in the clutches of two policemen.

He cursed and swore like a madman, and so violent did he become that the police had to spring their rattles and procure assistance. Even then there was a desperate struggle before he was secured, and two of the officers suffered rather severely.

"You see what the scoundrel has done?" said the chief to a sergeant, pointing to the still insensible form of the major.

"Yes, sir. Shall I take the gentleman to the hospital, while you sign the charge sheet?"

"No. I know this unfortunate man. Fetch me a cab, and I will carry him home. You can simply charge your prisoner with garroting a gentleman. Call upon me in the morning to see if he lives."

"Yes, sir."

The sergeant sent one of the constables to procure a four-wheeler, and ordered the others to proceed with their prisoner, who was handcuffed and scowling most viciously at his captors.

It was some time before the functionary returned with the cab, he having had some trouble to procure one.

The senseless form of Carleton was placed within, and the young chief, giving Jehu the direction, seated himself opposite the Burker's victim.

The cab soon drove up to the house where Leary Jock had first been employed by the young and terrible chief.

A surgeon was sent for, and in a few hours the major had recovered slightly.

Since the first sign of his returning consciousness the much dreaded chief kept himself out of sight.

The reasons he had for doing so the reader will shortly see.

Early the following morning Carleton rose and rang the bell, which was answered by a strange man.

"What is it, sir?" he asked, when he stood before the pale, haggard major.

"I wish you to explain the cause of my being here, for I cannot recollect anything myself."

"Well, sir, I believe you were garroted by some ruffian last night. My master arrived upon the spot in time to prevent you from being robbed, had the villain taken into custody, and brought you here to recover."

"And this kind gentleman, your master—tell me his name, that I may know whom to thank."

"He is at your service, sir, and will wait upon you himself, and answer any questions you wish to put to him."

With that the man closed the door and withdrew.

In spite of himself a strange feeling crept over Carleton when the servant had gone, for he did not like the fellow's manner.

He glanced round the apartment, but there was nothing there to excite his suspicions, although troubled thoughts flashed across his mind.

As he gazed at the pictures on the walls of the strange room the terrible scene of that night when he pitilessly shot the poor young captain seemed to haunt him. He tried to forget it but in vain.

Presently he heard the street door open, and immediately after there sounded a heavy tread in the passage.

He knew not why, but at the sound of that footstep his heart seemed to sink within him.

Ah! he little knew how near retribution was at hand for the base murder of the young officer.

For a few moments we will leave him, and introduce our readers to the occupants of a room just beneath him.

Sitting at a table strewed with books, papers, and documents of all kinds, was the young chief who seemed to hold such power over lawless men.

Opposite him was a man whose figure was tall and commanding, his well-knit frame denoting immense power.

Anyone at all used to study human nature would immediately have stamped him as a man of great strength and nerve and iron will.

He was a detective—a brave, clever fellow, too, known as Jasper Lea, and his was the heavy footfall the guilty Carleton had heard.

Jasper Lea now sat waiting for the young chief to speak, and he did not have to wait long.

"Did my message arrive in time, Lea?"

"Yes, sir," said Lea, who was a man of very few words.

"You have two men with you," said the chief, in his calm, clear voice.

"Waiting outside."

"Good. Now I will open the business."

The detective nodded, to imply that he was paying attention.

"Some time ago a Captain Hamilton was missed —he suddenly disappeared."

"He did," replied Lea.

"No one knew whither he had gone. A description of him was circulated, and you, with four other men, were instructed to find out his whereabouts. By the evidence you obtained you learnt that the last person he was seen with was Major Carleton. Was it not so?"

"Quite correct, sir."

"I took the affair in hand, and said I would find him, dead or alive."

"You did."

"I have done it—he was murdered."

"Ah !" exclaimed the detective, starting up. "By whom ?"

"His friend, Major Carleton."

"By Heaven, I thought as much."

"I have the murderer near at hand prostrate in the room above us."

"Thank goodness for that," said Jasper Lea. "But, sir, your knowledge is wonderful. The mysterious way in which you rout out things is indeed a miracle."

The young chief smiled.

"You, of course, now know why I wanted you— to give the murderer into your keeping."

"But as regards your proof—"

"I have every proof of his guilt."

"And that—"

"Is the murdered man's body."

"Enough. I will bring in my men and secure the villain."

As the detective finished speaking he opened the door and gave a low whistle.

Instantly two officers in plain clothes stepped up to him.

Motioning them to be silent, Lea ushered them into the presence of the young chief.

"I had better go to the room alone at first," he said to the chief.

"Certainly."

The detective mounted the stairs, and beckoned his men to follow quietly.

He then placed them upon the landing, and entered the apartment occupied by Major Carleton, who looked up in surprise at the intruder.

A slight exclamation broke from his lips, and he leapt to his feet.

"You are Major Carleton, I presume," asked Lea, as the other stood pale and trembling before him.

"I—I—am," faltered the murderer. "Have I the honour of speaking to my preserver, and the master of this house ?" he continued.

"Well, not exactly," Lea replied. "I am sorry to say my business is of a rather disagreeable nature, and I hope you will be able to answer my questions in a manner that will clear you of a terrible suspicion."

Carleton clutched at a chair for support, and glared at his questioner in a terrified manner, as he stammered—

"Sir, I—d—do not understand you !"

Lea watched him closely, to see what effect his next words would have upon him.

"I am Detective Jasper Lea."

"Well, sir ?" said Carleton, vainly striving to smile.

"Do you not know him ?" said the young chief, entering the apartment.

"No," replied the detective.

The major's heart gave a throb of joy, for he fancied he had seen the detective before ; but at the next words spoken by Lea he almost fell to the floor.

"No, I do not know Major Carleton ; but I know Captain Gerald Leigh."

"I am lost !" muttered Carleton *alias* Leigh, and it was with the greatest difficulty he could support himself.

"What mean you, sir ? This is some base plot ; who dare accuse me of aught unbefitting the conduct of a gentleman ?" he demanded, aloud.

"I do," said the young chief. "I give you in charge for having committed a horrible murder.

"To make my story short, a Captain Hamilton has lately disappeared ; you were the last person he was seen with, and circumstances cause the dark finger of suspicion to point at you."

"At me—impossible!" Carleton stammered. "Sir, this is absurd !"

"Nevertheless, you must come with me," said Jasper Lea, "until you can clear yourself of the charge."

Carleton felt his time had come, and he gasped for breath.

The detective noticed it, and with more consideration than could be expected, he kindly ordered the two constables to support him, which they did by clutching him by the collar, handcuffing him and dragging him down the stairs and into the street, where a cab was waiting.

Lea then whispered some words to the two officers, and seated himself by the side of Major Carleton, with the young chief opposite.

These somewhat strange proceedings puzzled the prisoner, but when he heard the officers tell the cabman to drive to Drury-lane, a very unpleasant train of thought ran through his brain.

When the cab stopped before the door of the house in which he had murdered and hidden the body of young Captain Hamilton, his teeth chattered, and his knees did a little knocking together upon their own account.

Major Carleton (we shall continue to use his assumed name) was no coward, but the unexpected incidents that had occurred had quite unnerved him. Though he had prepared himself for the worst, he did not imagine the appalling sight that would shortly meet his view.

They entered the house and ascended the stairs to the room in which the tragic scene had taken place betwen the major and his young victim.

To the major's surprise, in the room awaiting their coming were the two officers, and a stranger of a rather remarkable appearance.

This individual was no less a personage than Leary Jock.

"Captain Leigh," said the young chief, "this is a man who but a few days ago I rescued from a horrible death in the house of a villain as base as yourself. You have led a wild, reckless life, not even pausing at the blackest crimes to ensure your safety. Still, for all that, I would save you an unpleasant scene if you will confess your crime and tell us where you have hidden the body."

"I deny the charge !"

"Very well ; I have an eye-witness of the affair," replied the young chief.

"It's a base lie !" gasped the major.

"We have given you every chance," was the

reply ; " but, to show that we are justified in apprehending you—behold !"

The words had scarcely left the young chief's lips when Leary Jock, who was but the skeleton of his former self, walked across the room, and, opening the door of the secret closet, displayed to the horror-stricken gaze of Carleton the now decaying corpse of Captain Hamilton.

----

## CHAPTER XXXIV.

RECOVERY OF EASTLAKE — HIS HORROR AND SURPRISE AT THE DISAPPEARANCE OF RICHARD GRANT.

FOR many long hours Eastlake lay in a dangerous state. After the first effects of the fit had passed he became delirious and raved like a maniac, uttering sayings that sent the gaping menials to the servant's hall, wondering and speculating upon the strange words he had dropped.

There was a deal of confidential talk that slightly alarmed the female portion of the domestics, who, to use their own phraseology, " to keep their spirits from sinking," had recourse to a few drams of a very ardent spirit of a colourless kind, and for which one of the under servants was sent to an adjacent tavern—we are sorry to say rather more often than was necessary.

The result of these many journeys to the tavern ended in their all getting very communicative, and all talking at once, until they became personal in their conversation.

Things were brought to a climax by the fat cook wielding the kitchen poker in a wrathful manner upon the spotless stockings of the flunkey.

This was an insult that he could not stand, and one that he most readily resented by making a drive at the cook with the warming-pan ; but missing her ladyship, he struck the kitchen-maid upon the elbow, causing that amiable person such pain that her eyes watered.

Of course, she could not let an insult pass without retaliating.

An open packet of black lead lay upon the dresser.

This she clutched, and with a vigorous aim hurled it in the face of the unfortunate Jeames, who dropped the warming-pan (upon someone's head), placed his hands over his face, and did quite an original, though graceless dance, for the powder had gone into his eyes.

And now ensued a most discordant scene, and the flunkey's yells of rage and pain sounded above the rest of the noise, bringing the butler down to the kitchen.

In spite of his rage, he could scarcely refrain from laughing at the grotesque figure the footman presented.

But in a loud tone he threatened to discharge them all, which was the means of bringing the greater part of them to their senses, and greatly frightened the footman, who kicked his foot against a chair and fell head foremost under the kitchen range.

It was late in the day before Eastlake recovered consciousness.

The attack had greatly weakened him, and he had to keep his bed in consequence, especially as the physician respectfully informed him that unless he was very quiet it would bring on a fever.

When he had recovered sufficiently to hold a conversation, he summoned his butler, and questioned him as to what he had said during the time he had been delirious.

The butler cast his eyes down to hide a cunning leer, and replied that nobody could understand the wandering words he had uttered.

Had the dark-souled, plotting villain observed the look upon the man's face as he left the room, it is not unlikely Eastlake would have seen enough to have placed him on his guard.

And now the unpleasant occurrence of the previous night came vividly upon him, and caused a number of vague fears to crowd upon his guilty conscience.

At one moment he tried to persuade himself he had been deceived, for it seemed impossible that Burkett could escape from such a death as he had allotted to him, and in his calmer moments he scouted all superstitious ideas.

Through the skill of his surgeon he was enabled to leave his couch the following day.

But many strange suspicions had come upon him —suspicions that he could not dispel.

They seemed to haunt him ; but what caused him the most uneasiness was that, providing his surmises should be correct, he would not be safe another day.

We have before stated that Eastlake was a desperate man, and finding himself in such a dangerous position aroused all his daring passions into action.

He had resolved that night to again enter the private wing of the house, and ascertain, if he could, how matters stood.

At the same time he intended to obtain the pocket-book from Grant's person.

Night came, and desiring to know the worst, Eastlake started on his mission.

Silently he opened the door of the iron chamber and glared round.

A shudder passed through his frame when he gazed upon the yawning chasm in the centre of the floor.

With all his hardihood he could not summon courage enough to walk to the edge and glance down that horrible hole.

" No—no ; impossible. He could not have survived it," he muttered, hoarsely, as he turned away and closed the door.

It was some moments before he could gather strength to cross the centre room, and look into the red closet.

" I must, at all hazards," he muttered between his teeth, as his desperate position came fully upon him.

Clutching the light in his hand, he entered the closet in which Grant had been left for dead.

Reeling against the wall, he clasped his hands to his heated brow and exclaimed—

" Gone—gone !"

Not an instant did he stay after having made

the terrible discovery, but, gnashing his teeth with mingled rage and fear, he dashed wildly down the staircase and shut himself in his library.

Here he cursed and swore dreadfully, and raved like a maniac, but presently he became quiet and seemed to be meditating.

Something like a smile of fiendish satisfaction came over his pallid, haggard face.

He strode quickly across the room and pulled furiously at the bell.

A footman answered the summons, bowing and cringing.

"Send the boy I engaged to me," said the master.

"The lad, sir, that was to be tiger?"

"Yes."

"Most extraordinary thing, sir, but—"

"Well, but what?"

"I have searched everywhere for him, but I have not seen him since the night you were—were taken ill."

Eastlake clutched at the table for support.

"And what do you think has become of him?"

"Why, sir, he has gone—run away."

"Gone!" reiterated Eastlake, as he sank back in his chair.

"Go—leave me," he said, fiercely.

The footman retired, rather surprised, and Eastlake muttered—

"Fiends, I see it all now. Curse him! I have been juggled; but let them look to it! Curse my fate!" and giving vent to some fearful execrations, he snatched his hat up and rushed from the house.

We must now say a few words with regard to the Bosker.

His injuries had taken a serious turn and the day following their escape saw him on a bed of sickness, but at the expiration of a fortnight he was able to get about again.

The first day Burkett was up he was honoured with a visit from Grant.

"I am glad to see you up, Burkett," said the detective.

"Ay! it was wormwood to my soul," replied the Bosker, "to lie a-bed there, helpless. But I am pleased to see that you, at least, have not been laid up."

"No—I am happy to say that had it not been for my arm I should ere now have paid my respects to the scoundrel."

"Eastlake will die sooner than he expects," said the Bosker, with one of his oaths.

"Do not be rash, Burkett," said Grant.

"I do not wish to be so. But what are your intentions?" he asked.

"To drag him forth—a beggar and an assassin—with, as I told him, nothing but the gallows staring him in the face," said Grant.

Burkett grated his teeth, and replied—

"Aye! and I will have a hand in it, too, curse him."

"Yes, but do not be hasty—there is much to be done yet," said the detective.

"Will my services be required?" asked Burkett, somewhat eagerly.

"Yes, there is work cut out for each of us if what I have heard is true. But no matter, let us get our strength up a little—then let him look to it."

The Bosker gave one of his cruel smiles—he was contemplating the coming meeting between himself and Eastlake.

"And now I must bid you farewell for the present," said the detective, rising to depart.

On the third day subsequent to that on which Grant had visited Burkett he had recovered sufficiently to get out.

The last terrible incident in the Bosker's career had very much changed him.

It brought reflection—serious reflection, in which his past life rose up vividly before him. He saw himself in the darkest possible colours.

He knew there was an altogether hopeless chance of redemption in this world for his lawless life, and he felt that to atone for the past entirely was quite impossible.

The instant he found himself strong enough to see a little life he sallied forth, with no fixed destination.

As he wandered along a figure darkened his path.

Burkett had come face to face with David Eastlake.

Eastlake reeled and nearly fell at what he thought was the sudden apparition of the murdered Bosker.

Burkett scowled grimly at the other's terror.

"Can the grave give up its dead?" gasped the guilty wretch.

The sound of his voice seemed to arouse a latent devil in Burkett's breast.

His eyes glistened with a deadly light as his hand instinctively went to the bludgeon in his pocket.

But he checked with a great effort the impulse to brain his foe where he stood.

Remembering Grant's request that he would not harm the scoundrel yet, he quickly put the bludgeon back.

"Ah! David Eastlake," he said, "you did not expect to see me, but we meet again, and I'll make you suffer tenfold what I suffered at your hands. Beware, David Eastlake—the hour of retribution is at hand."

He hissed the last few words in the other's ear, and passed by the terror-stricken villain with a taunting laugh, lest his passion should urge him on to a deed he would repent of.

While Burkett had been speaking his victim stood with trembling limbs and blanched cheeks.

It was not until his footsteps had died away in the distance that Eastlake shook off the lethargy that had held him spellbound.

He dashed home at a rapid pace, cursing bitterly as he went.

He shut himself in his room, and gave way to a paroxysm of passion and despair, for at last he felt that his guilty career was drawing to an end.

Ah!—what was to be the end?

He shrank at the awful thought, and, covering his face in his hands, he groaned aloud.

## CHAPTER XXXV.

### BURKETT VISITS THE THIEVES' KITCHEN—THE COMPACT.

WHEN Burkett left Eastlake he strode rapidly along. His thoughtful mood had passed away and given place to a feeling of fierce and revengeful passions.

Instinctively he pursued his way in the direction of Nathan Claws'.

He found himself at the door of the Jew's shop long before he had become cool.

Nathan sprang up in surprise, and greeted the burglar with a mixture of pleasure and fear.

"Ish tat you, Mr. Burkett?" he cried. "Where ash you peen? How very thin you ish looking. Vot is te matter—monish? We ish glad to see you—phery," he continued, rubbing his bony hands together.

Burkett addressed one or two words to him and with a dark scowl entered the kitchen.

A discordant din greeted the Bosker's ears as he opened the door, which increased to a loud shout from nearly every mouth in the place when they beheld who the newcomer was.

The kitchen was crowded with the lawless gang, and some moments elapsed before Burkett could quiet them.

In fact it was impossible until they had drank his health in a very noisy manner.

In spite of himself some of his old devil-may-care recklessness returned in this noisy scene of wild, lawless pleasure. Resuming his stern, almost sullen air, he amused the company by relating to them the horrible torture he had gone through, and how he was saved by Captain Jack, but carefully omitted everything concerning Grant.

At this moment a powerful-built fellow came in in a hurry.

"The Burker's lagged, mates," he exclaimed.

"What was the plant?" asked a chorus of voices.

"For putting the hug on one of the West-end toffs."

The hardened ruffians looked grave, for they well knew the penalty of garroting, and there were several charges against the Burker, who for some time had been hunted by the police.

The most dreadful curses were heaped upon the heads of the police, and the one who had brought the unwelcome tidings enraged them yet more by speaking of the term he was likely to get.

"It'll be a twenty year stretch, or p'raps for life, besides having a touch of the cat," he said.

Shortly after this startling intelligence had been brought to the den Burkett departed, and early the following morning he was surprised by a visit from Richard Grant.

"Good morning, sir," said Burkett, who was indulging in a morning pipe.

"Glad to see you recovered, Burkett," replied the detective.

The Bosker then mentioned his meeting with Eastlake, and Grant smiled grimly at the account.

"I have a deal to do to-day," he said, after a pause, in which there had been slight embarrassment.

"Something up!"

"Oh, no. I don't intend to undertake anything until I have cleared up the affair with Eastlake. I am going to see a fellow named Bartlett, who once took a child—a stranger—into his care."

"The child—"

"Well, of course I don't yet know who she is, though I doubt not I shall discover."

Another pause followed, and Grant evidently had something unpleasant to say.

"Mr. Burkett, the fact is I—"

The Bosker looked up in surprise and said—

"Look here, if you have anything particular to say, why let us have something to wet our whistles with, eh?"

Grant being nothing loth a couple of bottles of very good wine were placed upon the table.

The detective having commenced found it easier to continue, which he did as follows—

"Well, what I was going to say was that, as you of course know, our positions are at present strange, and it will depend upon you how we agree in the future."

Burkett's surprise increased.

For a moment he felt uncomfortable, but did not interrupt, so Grant continued—

"It will be as well for us to understand each other, and to do so I must mention a few circumstances that may be slightly unpleasant to you."

"Proceed," said the Bosker.

"You see, if our friendship becomes known it would place me in rather an awkward position with the law. I need not say that any private matters that may be between us ought not to interfere with my professional duties."

"I understand."

"I, as you are aware, was particularly put upon your track, which makes the situation still more embarrassing. Are you willing to make a compact with me?"

"Anything in fairness, Richard Grant."

"Have you any love for your past mode of life?"

"None."

"Are you willing to relinquish it and alter your future career?"

"If there is a chance—yes."

"Well, what I have to say is simply this—if ever you were charged I should be the chief witness against you."

"Thank you!" replied Burkett, laughing.

"By keeping quiet and deserting your companions you will be free. Consent to what I ask and we shall be friends."

"What do you require?"

"You to swear that you will aid me in bringing Eastlake to justice, and to use what knowledge you have in reinstating the rightful heir in his defrauded rights."

Burkett rose—his eyes flashed fire.

"Richard Grant, is that all you want?"

"It is."

"Here, then, is my hand. I have already sworn, but I will repeat the oath, to have fearful revenge upon Eastlake," the Bosker said. "I know enough, in the absence of any legal proofs, to crush him and bring together the wronged—aye, deeply wronged—children."

# POOR BOYS OF LONDON

## OR, DRIVEN TO CRIME.

No. 12.] **A LIFE STORY FOR THE PEOPLE.** [ONE PENNY.

*The villain uttered a horrible cry as he fell through the trap.*

Grant gave a smile of delight, and, taking Burkett's hand, said—

"Good! I am indeed glad you have given me hope of your yet becoming a better man."

Burkett cast down his eyes, and his lips twitched nervously with some inward emotion.

"I know there is good stuff in you, and you may turn it to a better purpose than you have done."

Burkett made no reply, but Grant thought he felt the pressure of his hand increase.

"Come !—this is a compact—promise me," said the detective.

"I do—I do !" replied the Bosker.

"And now, for the present, farewell !" said the detective.

A few minutes later Richard Grant left the Bosker's residence with a suspicious twinkle in his eye, and there was very little of the sparkling hock remaining in the second bottle.

While Grant pursued his way to Jacob Primrose's house, where Philip Bartlett was staying, Burkett sat in deep thought.

Philip Bartlett, who had been so strangely entrusted with the guardianship of little Flo, still remained in the force.

The mysterious disappearance of Flo caused him deep pain—such mental suffering as would render him in appearance an old man in a very few years.

Mr. and Mrs. Primrose, too, were very unhappy at the loss.

Philip had lately been on night duty, and on the day in question he sat in the snug little parlour brooding deeply over the loss of the pretty child he had so strangely taken under his care.

His face wore a look of deep melancholy, and he sighed as he rested his face on his hands and gave way to silent despair.

He had, of course, made enquiries everywhere concerning the child, and, in fact, had done all he possibly could to aid in her recovery.

It was through his efforts to trace the girl that Richard Grant first gleaned the circumstances of the case.

We have hitherto omitted a piece of particular information connected with this portion of the story.

Richard Grant, through some mysterious means, had found out exactly where Whitechapel Dick was, and also that the children were in the same place.

He had not learnt this until lately, and as it was valuable knowledge it was received gladly by him when it did come.

As Bartlett looked up, he saw the tall, commanding figure of Richard Grant.

"Am I speaking to Mr. Philip Bartlett ?" said the detective.

"You are, sir."

"I should like a private interview with you for a short time—my visit is a strange one."

"Concerning what, sir ?"

"Yourself and the child Flo."

Bartlett's heart almost leapt to his throat with joy.

"Sir, I am at your service—proceed."

"In the first instance," said the detective, "it is very necessary I should know her history, as it is most important, for the child's future depends upon what proofs of her brith and parentage you can furnish me with."

"Thank Heaven !" ejaculated Bartlett, springing up in great excitement, "then she is safe ?"

"Well, yes ; no harm has befallen her."

"Sir, this is indeed joy to me."

"My dear friend," the detective replied, "I can really feel for you, as I well understand the position you are in. Now kindly acquaint me with every incident you know of the child's life."

"Firstly, sir, I must know who I have the honour of addressing ?" Philip Bartlett said, cautiously.

"Richard Grant the detective."

"Ah ! my brave sir, I am delighted to make your acquaintance."

He then carefully and distinctly narrated how he came into possession of the child.

Grant listened quietly and patiently, without making the slightest comment.

The detective then informed Bartlett what he knew, and what were his suspicions and his intentions.

Bartlett then inquired most anxiously after the child.

"She was stolen," Grant said, "and was sent away many miles from England, but she fell into the hands of friends instead of enemies, who will bring her back when I want her."

The joy of Philip Bartlett baffles description.

His eyes filled with tears of gratitude, and for months he had not felt so happy.

The detective then took his leave, and Bartlett ran to Mrs. Primrose with the intelligence.

Richard Grant went out with a peculiar smile upon his face—it was such a smile as a man would wear when he is thoroughly satisfied with himself—for Grant intended to fulfil another mission that day, and arrest David Eastlake !

In silence he made his way to the villain's residence, near which some of the detective's satellites were stationed.

Grant did not notice that all the shutters were closed, with the exception of those at the kitchen window, or his suspicions might have been aroused.

The door was opened by a servant in answer to the detective's knock.

"I desire to see Mr. Eastlake without delay," he said.

"He went away this morning, sir."

The detective uttered an ejaculation expressing his disappointment.

"Where is he gone ?"

"Ah ! now you ask more than I know, sir. He kept that a secret."

Richard Grant found all questioning useless—the only information he could get was Eastlake had left for some distant part.

He had engaged an old married couple to take care of the house until it was let or sold, the agent being a certain Mr. Skimp.

To the offices of this said Mr. Skimp Grant hastened as fast as a hansom cab could take him.

He found that individual in a dirty old office, the two most prominent things being discoloured paper and red tape, among which Mr. Skimp felt quite in his glory.

The instant Grant set eyes upon the man he took a dislike to him, and the worthy lawyer felt slightly uneasy under the searching glance of his visitor.

Having passed the customary compliments, Grant questioned him.

"You have the management of Mr. Eastlake's business in town?"

"Yes, sir."

"Just so—and therefore are perfectly aware of the destination of Mr. Eastlake."

"I-i-indeed, sir!"

"Mr. Skimp," said the detective, "it is useless for you to attempt to deceive me; nor shall I waste words. I will be plain with you—I am certain you know where he has gone or is going. Give me the information I require, or beware of the consequences of shielding a usurper and a murderer."

Mr. Skimp began to tremble.

The profession of the gentleman before him began slowly to dawn upon him.

"I assure you I am ignorant of it, indeed—"

"Thank you, that will do," Grant interposed. "You refuse to tell. The next time we meet you will have cause to regret this and to remember Richard Grant the detective."

While his well-known and dreaded name was ringing in the ears of the astonished and terrified lawyer, Grant strode out, and, entering a hansom cab, ordered the driver to gallop to the nearest railway station.

In less than an hour after Grant had visited the lawyer there were detectives at nearly every railway terminus, and the telegraph wires were working in nearly all parts of England to stop a person answering to the description of David Eastlake.

Dearly would the villain repent his attempt upon the life of Richard Grant, for the detective had taken his measures surely and swiftly.

A printed description of the miscreant was soon sent out, and a request for his arrest forwarded to all the shipping places in England.

The same night Burkett was surprised by a messenger leaving a small packet with him.

It was from Grant.

A note informed him what had taken place. At the bottom there was a paragraph that caused him some little excitement.

It ran as follows—

"You are better acquainted with Eastlake than anyone. Having such strong reasons for remembering him, I think any disguise he may have assumed would fail to deceive you. Feeling so assured of the utter impossibility of his concealing himself from you if you once set eyes on him, I have to request that you at once commence a search for him, and do not discontinue it until he is apprehended. You had better proceed according to the secret information just received.
"R. G."

Then followed directions as to the course he was to pursue.

Burkett's eyes glistened, and he smiled when he had finished reading the note.

"Here's a go!" he muttered. "Aye! aye! I'll hunt him to the end of the earth. Ha—ha! Eastlake, you made a bad day's work of it by your cold-blooded treachery. Look to it. The Bosker is on your track."

His fierce mutterings ceased and he continued in a calm tone—

"Strange, the wonderful knowledge of the detective. By Jove! he is a splendid fellow. His prompt action, too. He's like an Indian on the war-trail. Started already, has he? Ah! I will follow him at once. 'Tis quick work. So much the better, it will be all the more exciting."

But for once the Bosker made a mistake. He followed the wrong scent, and the capture of David Eastlake was left to Richard Grant.

---

## CHAPTER XXXVI.

### THE CAPTURE OF DAVID EASTLAKE.

IT was yet early morning, and the mists still hung over gigantic, bustling Liverpool, but David Eastlake had risen some hours ago, and was pacing the coffee-room of a small hotel.

Before noon he hoped to be on his way to America, but Eastlake had reason to remember the truth of the old adage that "there is many a slip between the cup and the lip."

A waiter entered the room.

"A gentleman wishes to see you, sir," he said.

"To see me?" gasped Eastlake. "Tell—tell him that I cannot receive visitors."

"I am here, David Eastlake," said a loud, clear voice behind the waiter, who was pushed aside, and a tall stranger entered.

Eastlake gasped for breath and sank back into a chair.

The stranger motioned for the waiter to retire, and as the door closed he fixed his piercing glance upon the shrinking villain.

"David Eastlake," he began, "having gone thus far without a formal introduction, I may as well proceed—"

"Stay!" cried Eastlake, hoarsely, recovering himself with a great effort. "Who and what are you to dare intrude upon me at such a time as this?"

"Look, merciless villain! Behold your mortal foe, Richard Grant, the detective!"

As he gave utterance to these words he removed a false beard, and revealed the quiet, handsome features of the bold detective.

The villainous Eastlake became utterly powerless, and he felt that his career was at an end.

"I know that I am lost," he said, after a pause. "A few words from your lips would be sufficient to hang me, so what chance have I? All the influence in the world could not save me if one third of those I have wronged were to appear against me. Grant, my life has been one of desperate crime and villainy. I have outraged the law and my fellow men. Fortune has deserted me at last, and I am in the hands of the man to whom I showed no mercy, therefore I expect none from him. I give myself entirely up to fate. Come what may I am prepared."

"Such is your resolution?" the detective returned.

Eastlake bowed.

"Still there might be a slight chance for you."

"Yes, a deal of chance when once I am enmeshed in the toils of the law—"

"You will get justice."

"Bah! what does justice signify? I shall be

... and either hanged or imprisoned for life."

"But supposing you do not go to prison !"

Eastlake started, and for a moment his face lighted up with a ray of hope, which, however, quickly passed away.

"Why do you mock me ?" he said.

"I do not mock you. I am sincere, David Eastlake. Richard Grant never tortures even his bitterest foes."

"Then what do you mean ?" demanded Eastlake.

"What I before said—and it all depends upon yourself. I pity you from my heart, and freely forgive your attempt upon my life ; but still, I have a sacred duty to perform, and it must be done."

Eastlake motioned him to proceed.

"I will do all that lies in my power for you, upon certain conditions," the detective said.

"Something impossible ?" queried Eastlake, with a ghastly smile.

"Not so, something very simple."

"Name it," he said.

"Before doing so I will tell you what you will gain by acceding to my terms. I shall take you back to your home instead of prison."

Eastlake sprang up greatly agitated.

"Will you, can you do this ?" he exclaimed, making a step forward, as though he would have grasped the hand of the man he had wronged.

"I can and will," replied Grant, sorrowfully, for in his heart he felt for the sinful wretch who was lost, both body and soul, "but only on certain conditions."

"Name them. Anything in the world—"

"Be not rash, David Eastlake, but listen to me."

Grant took a note-book from his pocket, and seated himself near his prisoner, whom he looked full in the face with a steady gaze.

"David Eastlake," he began, "I will be plain and candid with you. Listen quietly to what I have to say."

"I am all attention."

"I can give you no hope of entire escape—you must feel all hope is past."

Eastlake's ashy lips quivered as he inclined his head.

"But still you have a horror of dying an ignominious death upon the scaffold ?"

Eastlake shuddered, but did not reply.

"This can be prevented. I can save you shame and misery, but I cannot save your life."

Eastlake looked at the detective with a vacant stare and then he strode up and down the room.

"Richard Grant," he said at length, "I begin to understand your meaning. I thank you. Please to proceed. If death must come, let it come quickly. I could meet it in any other shape, but not—not—upon the scaffold. Give me your advice, Richard Grant, and I shall look upon you as a friend—a generous friend."

His agitation was dreadful.

"Sit down," said Grant, "and listen quietly to me."

Eastlake obeyed.

Grant began speaking in a low voice.

"This is my plan. When we arrive in London I will have you conducted to the house from which you departed. You, as my prisoner, will be entirely under my care. Thus I can keep your enemies away. I need not say that I will have all the necessary business arranged. I will give out that you are too ill to be removed."

"I understand," replied Eastlake, eagerly.

"In consequence of your supposed dangerous state I will bring a lawyer with me. You must be confronted by Lord Herling, your brother, who has been living under the name of Philip Bartlett—the man who was accused of forgery when the crime was yours. Great Heaven ! what have you done ? Even his innocent little children, when their mother died broken hearted, became the objects of your vengeance. They were stolen by you when the girl was but a few months old and the boy was just over a year. You see I know all. The boy was sent to Norwich," the detective continued, "and the girl was placed in charge of a woman known as Mrs. Lake, whom you deserted, and allowed to perish in a casual ward. Shall I go on ?"

"No," Eastlake replied, hoarsely. "What shall I do ? Is my brother really alive ?"

"Yes, and you must produce the papers and title deeds that prove the birth of the children and the right of Lord Herling to the estates you usurped," Grant replied. "Everything legally secured to him and his, you must, of course, make your confession. Believe me, David Eastlake, I would, if I dared, let it end there, so that you might depart to some foreign clime ; but the English law never overlooks murder. There are three men besides myself with warrants to arrest you as a murderer. Therefore you cannot escape, and there is only one refuge from your despair."

"And that is—"

"Death by your own hands."

"Horrible—horrible," murmured the guilty man.

"Is it more horrible than dying upon a scaffold, surrounded by a gaping, jeering crowd of brutal wretches, who would make sport of your death struggle ?"

Eastlake's blood seemed to turn to ice.

"I dare not think of it," he murmured.

"Still, while there is life there is hope, and there is no knowing what may yet be done," said Grant. "I promise you my aid upon the condition that you make all the recompense in your power to those innocent beings who have suffered through you, and that you remove any obstacle that may prevent the rightful heir from getting his own."

Eastlake raised his eyes to the handsome face of the detective.

"Richard Grant, I solemnly swear to you I will do all you have asked."

"I have no more to say, David Eastlake. I will trust you," said Grant, as Eastlake, muttering some unintelligible words, sank back into his chair.

## CHAPTER XXXVII.

### THE BREAKING UP OF THE THIEVES GANG.

TOWARDS the close of the day, as the thick murky evening fogs were sweeping over London and shrouding the Thames in its misty clouds, a member of the shoeblack brigade took his station at the foot of Waterloo-bridge.

It was our young friend, Captain Jack, who had taken up his stand upon the very spot where he was first introduced to our readers, and for a similar purpose.

There had been several daring burglaries committed, and in one case murder was added to robbery.

The Boozer and several other desperate characters were suspected. The Gorger was also trembling for his safety. In the hopes of getting money he had attacked a poor old cobbler and nearly throttled him, but Jack appeared in the nick of time, and dealt the everlastingly hungry one such a blow on the head with a wooden instrument that he rushed howling from the place.

But so effectually were the ruffians concealed by the villainous old Jew thief, Nathan Claws, that all attempts made by the police to capture any of the daring band were entirely unsuccessful.

The detectives, having hitherto failed, were afraid that unless some special effort was made the criminals would escape altogether.

Having come to this conclusion, there was no time lost in setting to work all their agencies, and the Poor Boys of London were the first who volunteered to ferret out the men who were wanted.

This explains the cause of Captain Jack being at his favourite spot at such an hour of the day.

As usual, he knelt behind his box with the greatest *sang-froid*, calling out at intervals—

"Clean your boots, sir !"

And then he would commence tattooing upon his box with two brushes.

But, in reality, he paid no attention to his customers or his drumming.

Not a person passed him, whether on the same side of the street or on the opposite, but what he took a quick survey of.

Once a seedy-looking swell came towards Jack, stroking his moustache, evidently with the intention of having a "shine."

Instead of Jack showing that eagerness for a job shoeblacks usually do, he coolly put his brushes in their place, and turned his head another way, at the same time giving a loud whistle.

The seedy-looking individual was in the act of placing his foot upon Jack's box when a little fellow ran up with a boot - cleaning apparatus slung over his shoulder.

Down went his box with a bang as he shouted—

"Shine 'em, sir ?—yes, sir. This box, sir—yes, sir—please, sir !"

All this was done so quickly that the customer hardly knew what to make of it, but liking the activity of the little fellow he decided to employ him.

The shoeblack did not take many minutes to discharge his customer, with such a polish upon his boots as he had rarely seen.

He had not gone out of sight before the two boys indulged in a number of grimaces.

"You were only just in time there, Curly," laughed Jack.

"No," replied Curly, doing a shine.

"You must keep closer, because I don't want any jobs myself."

"All right, captain."

"And keep a sharp look out, too."

"Make no error, captain ; I've got my eyes open," Curly replied, as he walked a short distance away.

Captain Jack was hardly alone before a well-known voice attracted his attention.

"Ain't you cold, old boy ?"

Captain Jack looked up and beheld the good-humoured face of Chimbley Joe, who was accompanied by little Dan.

"Haven't you come away before your time ?" said the young shoeblack.

"No, captain," replied Joe, in a low voice, going closer to him.

"You have left the others to take their turn upon the watch ?"

"Yes."

"Seen anything ?"

"I should say so," Chimbley Joe replied. "It'll be a scrimmage. Nearly all the gang are in the den."

At that moment a gentleman came up and placed his handsomely booted foot upon the block made for it.

By some almost imperceptible motion of the hand Captain Jack started his companions.

He then commenced polishing the stranger's boots, which were quite clean enough already.

"Jack," said the stranger, in a low tone.

"Yes, sir," replied Jack, without looking up. "I'm listening."

"You recognise me, then ?"

"I think it would be impossible for Richard Grant to so disguise himself that I could not recognise him."

"Hush! Don't speak my name too loud," said Grant.

"No fear, sir."

"What are you here for ?"

"Haven't you heard, sir ?"

"No."

"Then you haven't been back long, sir."

"I only arrived in London this morning."

"Have you got him, sir ?"

"Yes, my boy, at last."

"It is time, sir, he was stopped."

"Yes, but you have not answered my question yet."

"I beg your pardon, sir. They intend destroying the gang at Nathan Claws'."

"Keep the boys well on the alert, and be yourself at the Jew's by nine to-night," said Grant, throwing Jack a silver coin.

"Yes, sir—thank you, sir," he answered, touching his cap.

Grant soon vanished out of sight, and Chimbley Joe and two or three of his companions returned.

Captain Jack, after satisfying their curiosity, slung his box across his shoulders and walked away, calling upon the others to follow him.

Situated some fifty yards from Nathan Claws', at the corner of a street, not highly to be recommended for its ... ...cratic appearance, was a gin palace.

It was well known by the inhabitants of that particular neighbourhood, but was by no means a favourite resort, as the landlord, for his own sake, had several times given criminals up to the law.

It was to this house that Captain Jack bent his steps.

Leaving his companions outside to await his coming, he entered the tap-room, which was occupied by a number of men, dressed in the style of workmen.

Glancing carefully around, Jack scrutinised each face, until he came to that of the tallest labourer.

Captain Jack approached this individual, and held a whispered consultation with him.

Then Jack stood by the huge tap-room fire until he was beckoned to by the before-mentioned labourer, who had just finished a short discussion with his associates.

Whatever the instructions were he gave Jack, none of the other men heard them, but Captain Jack commenced to transform himself from a very intelligent shoeblack to a low-looking little blackguard.

"Shall I do?" he asked, with a laugh.

Jack then returned to his companions, who were surprised at the change in Captain Jack's appearance.

Jack exchanged a few words with Alick, Chimbley Joe, and the others, and then proceeded to shuffle along in a manner peculiar to the lowest class of young thieves.

He soon arrived at the marine store shop, which he entered, and found the villainous old Jew thief in his little parlour.

"Vell, my poy, vot ish it you vant?" said the old Jew, coming forward.

Jack replied by a series of extraordinary grimaces and gesticulations.

"Eh, vot, you vant—monish?"

"Are you all by yourself?" Jack demanded, looking as though he had something very mysterious to commuicate.

"Yesh, I ish alone, my poy," Nathan Claws replied.

"Is Tike in the kitchen? He promised to mention me to you, Mr. Nathan."

"Yesh, he did say something about a clever little boy—is it you?"

"Yes, sir," replied Jack; "but I have come for somethin' more pertickler nor that."

"Vell, shpeak, my poy."

"It's this," replied Jack, in a whisper. "I was a-going out on a plant to-day. Tike promised to help me. I followed two boys who was talking, and they keeps mentioning your name, so I thinks I'll listen. I did."

"Yesh, and vot did you hear?"

"That they had heard some detectives was coming down to your place to-morrow night to search for some swag," Jack replied. "The boys were laughing, saying what a lark it would be, 'cos they intended to take you. So I thought I'd come and warn you, and as I comes past that pub at the corner one of your gang asks me to tell

you to go to the tap room, the private one, 'cos he had got summit to tell yer that 'ud save yer from the police."

"But why dosen't he come here?"

"'Cos he's got some flimsies, and a hemerald he wants you to take off on him, and there is peelers on the watch to nab him."

"Mosesh! But—but I can't leave the shop."

"He said if you don't go he'll chuck 'em all away, 'cos he can't stop there much longer," Jack replied.

"Mosesh! Some flimsies, and von emerald. Mosesh! vot a pity. But tere, I must not go, 'cos I has to give the signal in case anyting shood happen, but to lose all those fine things is a pity."

In such manner the fence continued to mutter, until his love for gain caused him to decide upon going to relieve the man of the valuables.

Captain Jack could scarcely conceal his delight as he watched the avaricious Jew retire to his miserable parlour, where, after addressing a few words to a stout Jewess, he put his hat on, and followed Jack to the tavern.

Captain Jack kept a few paces ahead, and soon entered the bar.

He exchanged a number of significant nods with the landlord, who returned a very knowing wink, and just managed to pull a serious face as Nathan Claws entered.

He looked cautiously round.

"All right," said the tavern-keeper, accompanying his words by sundry nods and winks, and jerking his thumb over his right shoulder.

Nathan also indulged in some dumb motions, which consisted of elevating his shaggy eyebrows, twitching his mouth, and pointing to a door on the right.

The cunning Hebrew, little thinking he was being nicely entrapped, gave a hideous grin, and proceeded to the apartment, in which he expected to find the man with the swag.

He approached the door and gave it a push, but it did not open, as it was held by a secret fastening. No one could gain admittance until the landlord pulled a bell-handle which was attached to a wire communicating from the bar to the room.

Nathan had only just removed his hand from the door when the click of the fastening being drawn from its socket sounded ominously.

The Jew stepped into the room, and then he started back with an exclamation.

"Aha! betrayed!" he muttered, as he glanced round in great alarm.

The room was empty, and he would have instantly retreated, but the door closed with a more unpleasant click than the first.

What could be the meaning of this?

A cold, clammy sweat oozed out of the old scoundrel's parchment-like forehead, and he trembled in every limb.

He too well knew what would be the consequence should he be captured now.

His place would be entered, and everyone taken so unawares that all would be disclosed.

Little did he think that his thoughts were prophesying what would occur.

He did not have much time to think.

The sound of a heavy footfall caused him to start and stand, pale and trembling, in the middle of the room.

Again the door was opened by invisible means.

Nathan Claws cowered in terror as three tall, powerful men entered the room.

There was no necessity for them to speak to confirm his terrible suspicions, for he saw by the first glance at those stern, rigid faces that his fate was sealed, and he knew he was in the hands of a set of determined detectives.

His knees gave way from under him as the leader of the officers spoke.

"Nathan Claws," he said, "you are at last in my power. Be careful how you answer, or it may go hard with you."

"Mercy! I ish only a poor marine shtore dealer; I has tone noting."

"Silence!" said the detective, sternly, as his two companions took the terrified wretch in their powerful grasp and held him firmly.

"Listen, old hucksterer," continued the detective; "I have long sworn to arrest you for the attempt upon the life of Richard Grant."

The Jew shivered as though he had suddenly caught cold.

"I have waited long and patiently," the detective resumed, "and the time has now come. I intend this night to destroy the gang that your villainous contrivances have so long kept from the law."

Nathan could not speak, and he stared in a vacant, stupefied manner at his captors, but no word left his parched lips.

"In the first place," the detective went on, "give me the password for to-night, and surrender up all your keys."

"They—are—not—here," stammered the Jew.

"Don't lie, old man, or attempt to thwart me, or you will suffer in proportion."

Nathan groaned aloud, and cursed Captain Jack for leading him into the snare.

"Come, I shall not ask again," said the detective, quietly, but the Jew saw by the look in his eye that it would be a dangerous game to play with him.

He complied with the detective's request, and was then left in charge of two men, while the officer, followed by eight or nine policemen, surrounded all the entrances to the thieves' den, and, meeting with no opposition, reached the kitchen.

Around the table were seated nearly the whole gang, who sprang to their feet at the unexpected entrance of the stranger.

A savage murmur came from their throats as they beheld a body of men standing behind the detective, who led the way.

"My men, listen to me," he said, stepping fearlessly into their midst. "'Tis useless your attempting resistance. I have captured Nathan Claws, and every exit from this place is guarded by a body of police. I warn those who resist that they will suffer dearly."

A momentary silence followed this speech, and then came the noise and confusion of a panic.

Some seemed inclined to give in passively, but others dashed away in all directions.

This the detective only smiled at, for he knew they were running into the arms of his men.

The most daring remained motionless, exchanging murderous and significant glances.

The crisis was decided by a sullen-looking ruffian, who, leaping upon a table, addressed his associates.

"Mates," he said, "are you going to give in without a struggle? I say no—if we go to Newgate we'll go there for something; we'll have, at least, a few smashed skulls. Down with the crushers!"

The detective sounded a call on a whistle, and in rushed such a number of police that the thieves gave up all hope of resisting successfully.

In less than ten minutes all were captured and handcuffed, and thus was broken up one of the greatest and most desperate gangs of thieves that had ever banded themselves against society.

After the detectives and their prisoners had departed, Captain Jack lingered in the place in which so many crimes had been committed.

Taking a lamp from a table, and setting it down on the floor, he gazed curiously at a trap-door.

"This was the place down which Grant was thrust and left to die," the boy said, as he raised the trap. "Oh! horrible—horrible!"

A slight sound caused him to start, and, turning suddenly, he saw a man gliding towards him.

This was one of the gang who had avoided the notice of the detectives by creeping into a small cupboard, artfully concealed by a sliding panel.

"So," said the ruffian, who went by the name of the Kangaroo, "you thought all of us were taken— but one is left. Boy, you shall never live to enjoy your triumph. Down you shall go to make food for rats."

Tiger-like he sprang upon Jack, but the brave boy, anticipating the movement, stepped adroitly on one side, and the Kangaroo, uttering a horrible cry, fell through the trap. Jack, pale and trembling, rushed from the den of infamy with the yells of the doomed man ringing in his ears.

Yes, the last of Nathan Claws' gang was doomed to die in the very place where so many hapless victims had perished miserably.

The fall broke his leg, and he lay screaming for help where no help could come. The water rose swiftly, and bore him away a corpse, to be tossed hither and thither—a hideous, ghastly toy for the fast-flowing tide of the river to sport with.

. . . . . .

The news soon spread all over London that the gang of thieves had been broken up, and it became a universal topic of conversation for at least a week.

The public excitement increased as the time for the trial of the ruffians arrived.

The villainous Jew fence, whose crimes had been literally frightful, was sentenced to remain for the rest of his wretched life in penal servitude; and his accomplices received adequate sentences, save the Gorger, whose tears and whining stood him in such stead that he escaped with two years' hard labour.

Joe Lewis *alias* the Burker stood his trial and received sentence upon the same eventful day.

Having been convicted so many times, it went

hard with him, especially as he had been brought up for garroting on more than one occasion.

His associates were taught a lesson when they heard that in addition to the term of his sentence he was to be flogged, and the Burker clung frantically to the dock, murmuring out a prayer and begging the judge to be merciful; but two warders settled the question by dragging him away, and the scoundrel was thrust into a cell to await his just punishment.

We must not omit to mention that the boy thief Tike was captured, but on account of his age he was only sentenced to twelve months' hard labour.

Alick, Captain Jack, Chimbley Joe, and one or two other friends were at the Old Bailey.

Alick sighed as he saw Tike removed, and he motioned for his companions to depart.

"What a pity it is to see a boy of Tike's age so hardened," he said, as he strode out accompanied by Captain Jack and the others.

"It is indeed," replied Jack, "and I am delighted to think Chimbley and the others had cut the little thief's acquaintance."

"Thanks to you, Alick," said Chimbley.

"How?" asked Alick, thoughtfully.

"Because I am certain that had it not been for your companionship, and the strange control you had over the boys, Tike would have made them as bad as himself," interposed Captain Jack.

"Then I ought to feel proud of having done so much good," said Alick, smiling.

We must now take leave of the lads for the present, and return to the mansion of David Eastlake.

The ever bold and fearless man of fashion had been saved from adopting the terrible alternative suggested by Richard Grant, for he had been stricken by a terrible disease, that left him each day more wan and feeble.

His frame had wasted away until he seemed a mere skeleton covered with skin; his eyes were sunken, and had lost their defiant look and brilliant lustre.

His face was pinched, his voice was feeble, and his words were almost inarticulate.

Such is the picture our readers will imagine they see lying on a luxurious bed, and this poor suffering wretch was the once handsome, dashing David Eastlake.

His most bitter enemy would have pitied him from the bottom of his heart, for nothing on earth could save the miserable wretch.

Every attention was paid him, the most skilful doctors were in constant attendance, but all to no avail.

Each day he sunk faster and faster.

He was being dragged down by something more terrible than bodily illness.

The fearful racking of his guilty conscience was killing him—it was mental, not bodily suffering that was sending him so swiftly to the grave.

He was now awaiting the final ordeal.

The lawyers in whose hands Philip Bartlett's, or rather Lord Herling's, affairs were entrusted were momentarily expected.

Richard Grant and Burkett, now a much changed man, were to witness the scene so soon to take place.

"Why do they not come?" murmured the sick man.

The sound of carriage wheels, followed by a soft knock at the door below, caused the sufferer to start.

A moment after Richard Grant stood in the sick chamber.

His noble heart was touched as he gazed upon the once brilliant man of fashion, and extending his hand he took the shrunken, feverish palm of David Eastlake in his own.

"Are you better, Mr. Eastlake?" he asked.

The patient shook his head and a faint smile played about his lips.

"No, Richard Grant—I have not two hours to live. I wish they were here."

He sank back upon his pillow exhausted.

"Can you go through the exertion now?" asked Grant, kindly.

"Yes, yes; for Heaven's sake lose no time."

Grant rang the bell, and a nurse entered.

The detective then left and proceeded to an outer chamber, which seemed crowded with people, who were carrying on a conversation with bated breath.

Motioning to three individuals to follow him, Grant returned to the dying man's chamber.

Eastlake was in a sitting posture, propped up with pillows—he made a faint gesture of acknowledgment as the three men entered.

They were James Burkett and the lawyers.

Papers and title-deeds were instantly produced and read over by the lawyers.

Some were laid aside—the legal ones were spread upon the table.

Grant approached the bedside and addressed Eastlake in a low voice.

"David Eastlake, have you written your confession—it is essential?"

"It is here," replied Eastlake, taking from beneath his pillow a sealed packet and placing it in the hands of Grant. "Now let me see those I have wronged. You have not deceived me, Grant—he is living?"

"Behold!" said Grant, striding across the apartment and throwing open a door.

A tall, handsome form entered and stood in the centre of the room.

Eastlake started up with a cry.

"Yes—yes—'tis he, thank Heaven!" cried Eastlake, but the exertion proved too much for him and he sank back exhausted.

Burkett looked up on the entrance of the stranger.

He had a dim idea he had seen him before, and Burkett was right, for it was none other than Philip Bartlett.

A dead silence reigned as he walked up to Eastlake and took his hand.

"Brother," he said, "in such a moment as this it is well to forget and forgive everything. For your sake I parted with name, title, fortune—I would rather have starved than seen one of my own flesh and blood standing in a felon's dock. I went away, lost to everybody, save to my poor wife, who was willing to suffer patiently rather than see you disgraced. She died—"

"For the love of Heaven say no more," Eastlake interposed. "Let the rest come from my lips. Your wife died while you were in a foreign land, struggling bravely to support herself and her children, one then as yet unborn. It was I who caused the children to be stolen, yes, I—black-souled villain that I am—but, as sure as I am on the brink of eternity, I thought you had ceased to live. Where are they? I must see them ere I die. My bones will not rest in the grave if any harm has come to them."

"They are alive and well," Lord Herling replied, "and are in this very house, only just returned from a long journey with noble-hearted Whitechapel Dick."

"Thank Heaven for that," Eastlake said, faintly. "Brother, my wronged brother, my sight grows dim. Before my eyes close for ever on this world let me see the children."

He motioned to Burkett, who left the room and almost instantly returned with Whitechapel Dick, leading Gilbert and Flo by the hand.

Eastlake put out his arms and clapsed them round the children's necks.

Gilbert recoiled for a moment.

He remembered the attempt to murder him, but the deep look of anguish upon Eastlake's face moved the tender-hearted little fellow to tears.

"Do you forgive a wicked man like I have been?" asked Eastlake, hoarsely, straining the boy to his breast.

"Yes—yes," sobbed Gilbert.

Eastlake kissed his youthful brow, and then turned to Flo.

For a moment he glanced at her in a manner that would have softened the hardest heart.

"My niece—my own niece," he cried; "look, angel, upon your unhappy uncle."

Flo sobbed pitifully.

"Kiss your uncle, dear; he is going to be taken from you," said the dying man.

"Oh! no, no, no— they must not take you away," moaned the poor child, the tears streaming down her cheeks.

All in the room were moved to tears, for it was indeed a distressing scene.

Eastlake kissed the child passionately, and then fell back in a swoon.

The physician was immediately summoned, and after some slight trouble Eastlake was restored to consciousness. One feeble effort he made to rise, but appeared too far gone.

He called Lord Herling to him, begged again for forgiveness, and clung to his hand.

"Heaven bless you! and protect the children."

These were the last words Eastlake uttered.

His jaw fell, his eyes became fixed, and his spirit left the body.

An unbroken stillness reigned in the chamber of death, until Lord Herling, by a wave of the hand, dismissed those who were present, and he stood, with bowed head and eyes swimming with tears, alone with the dead.

. . . . . . .

A month after the scene just recorded, Lord Herling sat in a splendid drawing-room, amid luxury and elegance.

Stretching out his hand he rang a bell, and a moment after a young "tiger" entered.

The boy was a splendidly built little fellow, with a good-humoured face and a mischievous twinkle in his dark eye.

"Joseph," said his lordship.

"Yes, my lord," replied the boy.

"Tell my secretary I wish to see him."

Joe retired and entered the study.

"His lordship wants you, sir," said Joe.

"Joe!" said the young secretary. He was very young indeed for such a position, he could not have been more than eighteen.

"Yes, sir."

"I shall be very angry if you call me sir. Remember, when we are alone I am plain Alick always to you."

But Joseph — no other than our old friend, Chimbley Joe—could not see it.

Alick was doing remarkably well, young as he was, for Lord Herling had placed him under a tutor, and engaged him at a salary of a hundred a-year to fulfil the duties of secretary.

Gilbert and Flo had been sent to school, and were being educated suitable to their station in life. The house was always full of light and laughter when they returned home for the holidays.

---

## CHAPTER XXXVIII.

BETTER TIMES FOR THE POOR BOYS OF LONDON.

YEARS passed away, and with their passage came great changes.

The authorities woke up to the disgraceful state of the casual wards, and a clean sweep was made of all the filth, if not the degradation, of such places.

We have done, however, with such gloomy surroundings, and finish our story with other and brighter scenes.

One evening, as the bells of St. Martin's-in-the-Fields were ringing blithely, a handsome young fellow, whose arm was linked in that of a man who might have passed as his father, wended their way down the Strand, and, turning into Whitehall, passed under the archway of Scotland Yard.

The officers on duty saluted them respectfully, for they were no other than Richard Grant and Captain Jack, now an experienced and trusted detective.

He was known by those who feared him as the "Ferret," for nothing escaped his keen eyes, and in overcoming apparently insurmountable difficulties was as cunning and persistent as a bloodhound.

"I don't think that there is much more for us to do to-night but to report ourselves," Grant said.

"You forget our appointments," Jack said.

"No I do not," Grant replied. "Jack, you made that swell mobsman turn pale just now."

"Oh! he and I will be better acquainted by-and-by," Jack said, laughing. "He knew me well enough, and slunk away like a cur. If we had only *carte blanche* we would soon clear the streets of such scum."

"That is true," Grant returned; "but you must remember that we are only servants. Our superiors pull the strings and we have to dance. The public pester and abuse us for doing our duty, and raise a howl of indignation if we are not on the spot the moment when required."

"It would be a wonderful man who could please the public," Jack observed, shrugging his shoulders. "Let me think! we have two appointments."

"Yes," Grant replied. "I think we have allowed Garnett rope enough. He has had plenty of chances to mend his manners; but, as he persists in going on in the same old way, it is high time that we dropped down on him."

"I am ready," said Jack, glancing at his watch; "but Dan promised to be here at seven, and it is five minutes past, an unusual thing for him, for he is generally the impersonation of Greenwich time."

"And here I am, Jack," said Dan, whom our readers will remember as one of the Poor Boys of London; "and I'll bet you a box of cigars that your watch is five minutes fast. Listen! there go the chimes."

"I apologise most humbly," Jack replied. "Well, any news?"

"Not much; but I have seen something rather surprising."

"What is it?"

Dan threw his head back and laughed.

"It's a thing on two legs, with a lantern face and a hungry stomach," he said.

"Not Nicholas Slime, the Gorger, surely," cried Jack.

"Yes," Dan replied, "you've guessed it in once. Just turn your head to the right and you will see him with your own eyes."

Jack followed the direction indicated, and, surely enough, there stood the hungry one, a sorry and a pitiable spectacle.

He was leaning against a lamp-post, his hands were thrust deep down into the pockets of his ragged unspeakables, and every now and then he gazed ruefully at sundry toes protruding from patches of worn-out leather, which he was pleased to call his boots.

"Poor devil!" Jack said; "it is hard for even the meanest wretch to come down so low as that. I'll speak to him. Hi! Slime, come here."

The Gorger, digging his grimy knuckles into his eyes, shuffled forward, looking for all the world like a homeless dog.

"Where have you been?" Jack demanded.

"In again," Gorger whined, "and I wish I was in now, for coming out means the streets and starvation to me."

"Ah!" said Jack, drawing a long breath, "I thought you would not keep out of prison for any length of time."

"What am I to do?" said the Gorger, in an injured tone of voice. "Nobody will give me employment, for where's the man who'd believe me if I swore I'd be honest? Nobody is left," he added, tearfully, "to lend me sixpence. Burkett is gone abroad, and they say that he is doing well—that's a great deal more than I am."

"Yes," chimed in Richard Grant, "he is doing better than could be expected. I received a letter from him, posted at a station in Australia, and it appears that he is working hard on a sheep farm."

"If I had anything to do with sheep just now I think I should eat one of 'em alive," the Gorger observed. "I—I suppose that one of you gentlemen couldn't lend me sixpence."

"The same old characteristic," said Jack, smiling, as he spun half-a-crown into the air.

"Oh! thank 'ee, sir," the Gorger gasped, as he caught the coin. "I never expected it—never deserved it. The money will get me a decent bed and two square meals. Let me see, I'll have—"

"Never mind what you intend to have, but just listen to me," Jack said, interrupting him. "I think I know of somebody who will keep you out of mischief, and give you a few shillings a week into the bargain. Come here to-morrow at eleven and I will see what can be done for you. Now go."

Nicholas Slime looked as if he could have gone down on his knees and blessed his patron, but he wept copiously instead, and when he removed his hands from his eyes he found that the detectives had vanished, and that he was blubbering with nobody to observe him but a stalwart policeman, who was gazing at him as an object of natural curiosity.

"You'd better cut it," said the officer, not unkindly. "I'm on point duty, and I don't want to run the risk of being drowned in your tears."

"I'm a-going," the Gorger replied; "but if you knew what it was to be forty-eight hours in the street without food or a civil word the sight of a half-crown would make you weep. Ha, ha! won't I have a feed. Good-night."

   .      .      .      .

The Pig and Porridge Pot was almost deserted when Grant, Jack, and Dan stopped at the door.

There were only three customers lounging over the pewter-covered counter, and they were of the lowest class of humanity, as vile of feature as the rags that clung to them.

One was younger than the rest, and he was talking to Garnett in a strain of language more forcible than polite.

"Bosh!" said Garnett, following up the conversation. "If Grant and Co. had wanted anybody they would have come here long ago. Take care of yourself, Tike. You have done one spell, and are likely enough to do another."

"Who said I wasn't?" Tike growled. "When I think of them mealy-mouthed curs, Jack and Dan, being detectives, I could eat my fingers."

"Keep them for something more useful," Garnett returned, with a hoarse laugh. "I'll be bound that they have been to work to-day."

"No luck," the Tike replied. "The ladies don't wear nice open pockets in their jackets now, and even old gents are too fly to walk about with their coats open and watch-chains dangling. I'm blowed if I know what the world is coming to."

This seemed to tickle Garnett so much that he burst into a loud roar of laughter.

"Well," he said, wiping the tears of mirth from his eyes, "have what you like and I'll put it on the slate."

As he spoke he happened to glance at the door and his face fell.

"There isn't any wind to-night," he said, "and yet that door swung open. It can't be a pal outside or he would come straight in."

Tike looked uncomfortable, but, feigning to be at ease, he put his hands in his pockets and whistled.

"I wish one of you would go to the door and see who is sneaking about," said Garnett.

Not one of the three moved, but they glanced furtively at each other, and then behind the bar, at a door that led to the upper part of the house.

"You are a nice set of cowards," Garnett said, contemptuously. "I suppose I must go and see for myself."

Without troubling to lift the flap he leaped over the counter and went to the door.

Scarcely was his hand upon it than another clutched his collar and he was dragged out into the street.

The capture was so suddenly made that the Tike and his companions stood as if their feet had been rooted to the floor; but, as the truth of what had happened flashed into their brains, they made preparations to reach the inner door.

"Stay where you are!" cried Richard Grant, as he strode into the bar. "My lads, it seems that we have killed several birds with one stone. Tike, hold out your hands!"

The thief shrank back and turned pale as the bright handcuffs gleamed before his eyes.

"I have done nothing," he said. "Why do you follow me about?"

"Because you follow other people about," Grant retorted. "You are a pest to society, and there is only one way to deal with you."

"It ain't worth making a fuss about," Tike replied, as he stretched out his hands. "I suppose I am booked for five years this time."

"At least," Grant replied, coolly. "As for you," he added, turning to the others, "you may go, and think yourselves lucky that I have something more to do than to trouble myself about your histories. Tike, your old friend Garnett is outside waiting to take a short walk with you."

Tike howled with rage when he saw Garnett in the hands of Jack and Dan.

"You're a pretty pair now that you've got rid of your rags and misery," he said. "You're so full of honesty that I wonder you don't bust."

"Such a calamity will never happen to you, at any rate," Jack replied. "If you had tried a little more honesty and less thieving you would be able to look me in the face."

"Only hear him," the Tike said, with a faint attempt at sarcasm. "Why didn't he turn parson? But I s'pose he thought that a rise from a blacking-box to a mean detective was good enough. Bah! take me away, I'm tired of being in such company."

One more scene and the curtain will fall upon the characters of our story and hide them from view.

As pretty a girl as ever England boasted of is talking to her lover, and who should he be but Alick.

"Flo," he was saying, "sometimes when I look at you I think I must be dreaming. It seems only yesterday that I was a poor ragged, homeless boy, without a creature in the whole world to point out the right way to gain a honest livelihood."

"But you were always good and true," Flo replied. "Father says so, and he knows. Oh! Alick, here is Jacob—good old Jacob Primrose and his wife. This is really delightful."

She ran to them, first hugging the cabman's wife and then Primrose, much to that individual's surprise and confusion.

Jacob positively blushed, and on being requested to seat himself in a velvet-covered chair shook his head.

"Bless you, miss," he said, "I should spile it—a good substantial wooden one is more in my line."

"You are the same good old Jacob," the girl said, as she enforced her request by pushing him playfully into the chair; "but you must call me Flo, as you did years ago. Why have you kept away from us so long?"

"Well, you see, miss, which I meant to say Flo," Jacob Primrose replied, running his fingers through his hair, which was invariably on end, "there's a slight difference between a cab-yard and a drawing-room, but me and the old woman plucked up courage to come at last, and ain't we glad to see you!"

"Yes, that we are!" cried Mrs. Primrose, clasping her hands. "Oh! my dear Flo, when I think of you here, with never so many beautiful things round you, my heart seems as big as my body."

"Why, as for beautiful things," said Jacob, "there's your father, Lord Herling—he goes and buys me a new rig out from cabs down to buckles, and I'm doing so well that I could shut the cab-yard gate to-morrow and walk off with five hundred pounds in my pocket. And how is Mister Gilbert?"

"Very well, I thank you," said a voice near the open door. "And were I not so I think the sight of your kindly faces would effect a cure."

Gilbert was followed into the room by his father and Whitechapel Dick, who was now "something in the City," meaning in his case sundry walks round to pass an hour with old chums and to revisit the scenes of his London experiences.

Alick's sister and Minnie were also present, both looking wondrously fresh and beautiful considering the many vicissitudes they had passed through.

Lord Herling and his children set the company so much at their ease that Mrs. Primrose told her husband afterwards that she never felt so "nice and genteel" in her life, to which Jacob replied—

"When you meets a gentleman you knows him by his ways. He never tells lies, not even to screen himself. And he never allows other people to do the work for which he has been paid. I've known a man to borrow money of some of his friends and then forget to pay 'em back, but, lor'-a-mercy, I shouldn't call he a gentleman, although the world generally don't take much notice of such scurvy tricks. Now, Lord Herling is what I call a real, live, honest English gentleman—not a made-up one like some of them there authors inwent and write about until they fancy they themselves are the real genuine article."

But now a most wonderful thing happened.

A servant entered, bearing a letter on a salver, which he presented to Lord Herling.

An expression of astonishment stole over his lordship's face as he read the note.

"Gilbert," he said, drawing his son aside, "who do you think this comes from ?"

"I have not the slightest idea, father."

"From James Burkett," Lord Herling replied. "This note tells me that he is waiting in the hall. He asks whether we will see him."

"I—I don't know what to say," Gilbert faltered. "I think I had better leave the matter in your own hands."

"Very well," his lordship replied, "then we will see the man. Show him up," he added, turning to the servant who still lingered in the doorway.

In less than a minute James Burkett was in the room, but he was not alone.

Richard Grant stood behind him, peering over his shoulder and marking the effect made by the ex-burglar's appearance on the assembly.

Burkett, dressed as a farmer, was changed in every respect.

The hard brutal lines had died out of his face, his eyes were soft and sad, and though his cheeks were bronzed it was easy to see that he had suffered mentally.

"Mr. Gilbert," he said. "I went away, hoping to find peace of mind in a new land, but it has been denied me. I could not rest until I asked your forgiveness. When we last met you were a boy, but now I see you a man full of health and hope, and the sight does my eyes good."

"We will not remember the past, Burkett," Gilbert replied, striding forward and taking his hand. "I'm glad you have come, and when I say that I forgive you the words come from my heart."

Burkett swept his hand across his eyes.

"Often and often," he said, "I have awoke in the dead of the night, startled from my sleep by the sound of your voice. Sometimes, when I thought of what I had done, I felt that I must go mad. I prospered—everything I touched turned to gold—but," he cried, striking his chest, "there was lead here—a weight that bore me down and crushed me."

The colour left his face and he reeled against Richard Grant.

"You are not well," Lord Herling said ; "pray be seated. The excitement of the meeting has proved too much for you."

"I have come from Australia but to start on a longer journey," Burkett replied, smiling sadly ; "it is better that it should be so. The life I led planted the germs of death in me, and I feel that the sands of my life are running out swiftly."

"Oh ! dear—oh ! dear," cried Mrs. Primrose. "It is dreadful to hear such a fine man talk like that. If it's a cold he's caught why doesn't he take something for it ?"

"Wife," Jacob whispered, "we ain't talkin' at home, so just mind what you are about."

"I'm sure I didn't mean any harm," the cabman's good lady said, wiping her eyes. "Our chemist round the corner would give him a bottle of something for eighteen pence which would make him sleep nicely of nights, and pull him round in no time."

"Lor' a mussy ! how you do chatter, old girl," Jacob gasped. "Do be quiet. Don't you see that you're upsettin' of everybody ?"

"I am sorry to hear you give so bad an account of yourself," Lord Herling said. "Have you had advice ?"

"Yes," Richard Grant replied, speaking for Burkett. "He has seen a physician this day, and been told to prepare for the worst."

"It does not surprise me," said James Burkett, after a slight pause, "and is no more than I could expect. I have seen what my heart has yearned for, and I am satisfied. I have been told that there is hope for even worse men than I beyond the grave."

"Yes, yes," Gilbert said, kindly ; "there can be no doubt about that. If you had had better training when you were young you would never have thought of doing such things."

"That is the truth," Burkett rejoined. "Dragged up in the gutter—hunted, kicked, cuffed, and half-starved—I grew up like thousands around me—vile, impure, and loathsome. It is easy to be respectable on five hundred a year, but try it on five pence, or less, a day. There was always plenty of preaching to be had for nothing, but when it came to a decent place to live in and wholesome food to eat, it was quite a different matter. I was twisted and warped into what I became, and who was to blame ?"

"Them as make laws to suit themselves," Jacob Primrose interposed, with the air of a philosopher. "You can't chip a brick of a rich man's house without runnin' the risk of imprisonment, but you may keep a poor man so down in body and soul that he turns from his better nature and becomes an out and out blackguard, without any fear. I'd like some o' the easy young gents who preach patience to the poor to try it themselves, and then there'd jolly soon be an alteration of things all round, or my name ain't Jacob Primrose, and I never set behind a 'ansom."

"Quite true," Richard Grant said ; "but what would you do to the thousands of men who neglect good chances and prefer idle and vicious lives to honest work ?"

"I'd give 'em the cat o' nine tails as often as required," Jacob Primrose replied.

We agree with the honest cabman, and if this story has pointed a moral it is that patience, perseverance, and pluck win in the long run—it is that honesty is the best policy, that the vile and the cruel meet with their deserts, and convert the blessing of life into a curse.

Fear not, but fight the battle of life stoutly. Remember the gloomy scenes depicted in this story as dark dreams, and while you look on the bright side of everything, buckle on the armour of courage, faith, and hope, as did Captain Jack and some of "The Poor Boys of London."

THE END.